Diamond Girl

Book #1 - G-Man Series

A Novel by Andrea Smith

Elizabeth –

Let Slate

rock your world!

Ara-Smith

Meatball Taster Publishing

Copyright 2013

ISBN: 978-0-578-12259-5 (Paperback)

ISBN-10: 0578122596 (E-Book)

Some of the content in this book is loosely based upon actual events which occurred in Indianapolis and Fort Wayne Indiana back in the summer of 2012. The characters, however, are fictional; any resemblance to actual persons or events, living or dead, is purely coincidental.

This book is intended for adult readers only.

Cover Design: Kim Black @ TOJ Publishing Services

Associate Editor: Janell Parque

Playlist

"*Diamond Girl*" by Seals & Crofts

"*Born To Be Wild*" by Steppenwolf

"Girls, Girls, Girls" by Motley Crue

"*Here I Go Again*" by Whitesnake

"*Feeling Good*" by Michael Bublé

"Pour Some Sugar on Me" by Def Leppard

"*Bad Girlfriend*" by Theory of a Dead Man

"Slow Dancing In a Burning Room" by John Mayer

"*Gimme Shelter*" by The Rolling Stones

I pulled the meatloaf out of the oven, slamming the oven door shut with my left thigh as my pot-holdered hands set the finished entrée on top of the counter. I glanced quickly at the clock on the stove. It was 6:45 p.m. I'd set the table with our good china and silverware. Meatloaf was Jack's favorite, along with cheesy potatoes. I'd made his favorite dessert as well: Boston Crème pie. I just needed to make a quick trip to the bathroom to check my hair and make-up.

This was the first dinner Jack and I were having together since Lindsey had left for college two days earlier. He'd promised he would be home on time after work. He'd been rolling in past 9:00 p.m. off and on over the past eighteen months. I'd finally told him enough was enough.

Jack explained that his promotion to the V.P. of marketing for the East coast region would require long hours. I got that. I had no clue that it would entail approximately months on end without sex, though. That part was getting to be a real drag.

Jack blamed his workload, jet lag and general exhaustion for his lack of sexual appetite. I knew there was more to it than that.

I studied myself in the bathroom mirror. I had to admit it. At thirty-five-years-old, I was officially a 'frumpy housewife.' I'd pulled my light brown hair up on top of my head with a clip. F-R-U-M-P-Y!

Thankfully, I'd put on a clean pair of jeans and a sweater. Jack was used to seeing me in sweats and a tee shirt. My jeans were noticeably tighter than when I wore them last. I was trying to remember exactly when that had been.

I reached into my cosmetic bag to get my compact out to dab a bit more blush onto my cheeks. I saw my fingers reflected in the vanity mirror. My God!

My nails were chewed down below the cuticle. Whatever had happened to the beautifully manicured nails that I had as a newlywed?

I knew the answer to that question before it had left my mind. The baby had followed the wedding ceremony, in short order. There were diapers, spit-up, formula, teething, cleaning, laundry, and trying to keep my head above water with Jack. He was a very persnickety man.

He liked order.

He liked perfection.

I didn't fit into either category.

I guessed the reason that Jack had been extremely patient with me over the years was because of the great relationship he had with my father.

When I had discovered that I was pregnant at sixteen, I'd been terrified of telling my folks. I was an only child, and I'd understood through my upbringing that there were certain expectations. Those expectations hadn't included my brief, sexual interlude with Jack Dennison.

Jack was two years older than me in high school. He was an all-around athlete. He played varsity football and was the star point guard for the Northwood High Raven's basketball team. I never thought he would have given me a second look. He was gorgeous and sexy, even in high school. There wasn't a girl at our school that hadn't drooled over him at some point in time.

The truth was he hadn't *really* given me a second look that night. It was more like we were at the same post-game party and he was drunk. He'd been extremely attentive to me at the party, and I was simply an infatuated sophomore girl on the cheer squad enamored with him like all of the others. I felt honored when he wanted to slip upstairs to be alone with me. We had talked and then started making out. I had no clue that the rest was going to happen.

I remember creeping back into my parents' home the next morning. I'd stayed the night with my best friend, Becky. My mother had been up putting the coffee on when she saw me quietly coming in at a little after 7:00 a.m.

"Samantha? Why are you home so early?" she had asked, eyeing my somewhat disheveled appearance. I was still in my cheerleading uniform.

"Oh, I couldn't sleep at Becky's, Mom. Kerry had the flu and was puking all night, so I had to get out of there, you know?"

"Now, Sam," she'd said, giving me the hairy eyeball, "Are you sure that Kerry had the flu, or were you girls drinking beer? I was a teenager once you know? And I know what went on back then."

"Mom, I *swear*, as far as I could tell, none of us girls drank any beer or alcohol of any kind."

"Well, alright then," she replied, shrugging. "Go get out of that uniform and into your PJ's. You need more sleep than what you probably got over at Becky's house. Don't wake Daddy."

"Okay, Mom," I had said, hugging her and giving her a kiss on the cheek. "I promise not to wake Daddy." I knew that she wouldn't wake Daddy, either. I was his princess and my mother wouldn't do anything to banish me from his kingdom.

I had collapsed into my own bed that morning, not realizing for an instant the implications of what had happened the previous night. The strange thing was that I couldn't recall wanting Jack to do the things that he'd done to me. I was positive that I'd heard myself telling him "no" beneath his lips that were crushing mine with passion and just plain old drunken horniness.

Afterwards, as I'd tried to sit up on the bed, my mascara streaming down my cheeks, searching for my ripped panties, I realized that I hadn't wanted what happened to happen at all. He was simply drunk and incoherent at the time. He seemed to be used to getting his way with girls, and I was sure that he generally met with no resistance.

I wasn't even sure that he had been aware of what happened. I mean I couldn't very well blame *him* for something that he'd done while under the influence. Afterwards, he had simply told me that I was a "great fuck" and then passed out next to me on the random bed where we'd done the dirty deed.

Six weeks later, I knew that something was terribly wrong.

So, I naturally did what any sixteen-year-old girl would've done when faced with such a dilemma: I confided to my best friend, Becky.

"Holy crap, Samantha, why didn't you tell me what happened that night? Aren't we supposed to be best friends?"

"Can you please be mad at me about that later, Bec? Right now, I'm freaking out. I needed to tell someone. I don't think Jack even remembers."

"Well, first of all, you need to make sure you're really pregnant. Let's stop by Whitaker's Drug Store after school and pick up one of those testing kits."

"I can't stop *there*," I had whined. "What if Mr. Whitaker is there? He knows my dad."

"Samantha," Becky had said in her matter-of-fact voice, "*Everyone* knows your dad, I mean there's no getting around *that*."

She was right. My father was the CEO of Banion Pharmaceuticals, one of the largest employers in town. His father, my grandfather, had founded the company fifty years prior. Like Becky, and most everyone else at our school, I'd been born and raised in Indianapolis, Indiana. My father sat on the board of trustees for two local banks and the Chamber of Commerce. He had recognition and power in the community.

"Okay," she had acquiesced, "I'll go get it and meet you at your house later."

'Later' had turned out to be the following morning before school. I'd called Becky telling her that my father had gotten home from work earlier than usual. He was taking Mom and me out for steaks at The Elite Cafe downtown. It was his favorite restaurant. He insisted on taking us there at least once a month. Mom was simply tickled that he'd gotten home early, for once.

I'd driven my car over to pick Becky up for school, as I'd done every morning since getting my driver's license.

I had held my pee, just as she had instructed me to do, in order to get the most accurate reading. I had covered my mouth to stifle my screams as the result came through loud and clear: knocked up.

My father is going to kill me.

My trip down memory lane was interrupted when I heard the sound of our garage door opening. Jack was home. I hurried to put the finishing touches on dinner.

I heard him talking as he came in through the garage to the family room. Our house had two stories with a loft from the second floor. Our master suite was the loft. The house was only two years old, and I hadn't finished decorating it yet. Jack had been on me about that, telling me I procrastinated far too much, and reminding me that most women would love to furnish and decorate such a gorgeous house with no worries about money or the confines of a budget.

I figured he was probably on his cell phone talking work on his way up until I realized the conversation was live. I heard a female voice laugh coyly at something he must've said.

Who the hell is with him?

"Sammie," he called out from the main hallway.

"I'm in the kitchen, Jack."

He entered the kitchen, setting his briefcase inside the door. A tall but petite, well-manicured woman was following behind him. She had perfect features, perfect make-up and she was dressed in a dark grey business suit that was tailored to accent her slim, yet shapely, figure. Her long, blonde hair flowed well past her shoulders. She had exquisite eyes. They were a mixture of greenish blue, almost a deep grey color to match her business suit.

"Sammie," he repeated, "I want you to meet Susan Reynard, my new administrative assistant at the office."

Oh, fucking great.

"It's Samantha," I replied, pasting what I hoped was a sincere-looking smile on my face as I held out my hand to clasp hers. "Very pleased to meet you, Susan."

She afforded me a smile, showing perfectly even, white teeth. Naturally, her nails were professionally manicured and matched the shade of lipstick she was wearing on her full, pouty lips.

"Samantha," she purred, "It's such a pleasure meeting you as well. Your husband told me what a beautiful home you have here and he sure wasn't exaggerating."

"Yes," he remarked, "if only I could motivate Sammie to finish furnishing it. Hey, perhaps Susan could help with some ideas on what the house needs to bring it all together. She's done an awesome job on my office."

"Oh, Mr. Dennison," she gushed, almost blushing, "I just narrowed the choices down. You made the ultimate selection. Your husband has great taste by the way."

"Now, Susan," Jack admonished with a smile, "There'll be none of this *Mr. Dennison* stuff. It's Jack."

"Yes, Jack," she replied obediently. "I keep forgetting."

I felt like a voyeur watching their interaction as I remained clueless as to why she was even here. I was hoping my husband was going to clue me in.

"Sammie," he said, as if sensing my curiosity, "I invited Susan to dinner. We have some work to finish up and I thought we might as well work here in my office. I'm sorry I didn't call you earlier, babe."

"Oh, it's no problem at all," I lied. "I'll just set another place."

"Can I help?" Susan asked.

"Everything's done," I replied. "All that's left is to take our places."

Dinner was strained. I felt like an intruder on both the small talk and office talk between Jack and Susan. She looked to be about in her mid-thirties, if that. She certainly hung on Jack's every word. I tuned them out, resuming my jog down memory lane.

I thought back to the ugly scene that had taken placed when I'd informed my parents that I was pregnant.

"I didn't even know you were *dating* anyone," my father had blurted out in pure confusion. "Why haven't we met the boy?"

My mother had been less vocal, simply wringing her hands, like she always did when my father was upset or displeased about something. She constantly ran interference when I had occasion to disappoint him.

I hadn't been sure how to explain what had happened without fear of my father hunting Jack down and killing him in cold blood. I merely told them that we were both drunk one night and it just sort of happened. In other words, I mostly lied. I had been stone cold sober at the time.

I remember my father's face turning red. He'd been livid about my behavior.

"No daughter of mine is going to be regarded as some party tramp," he bellowed. "I want the name and address of this boy, and I want it now! He'll damn well make this right. I'll see to that."

"Now, Sidney," my mother had whined, "Keep calm, remember your blood pressure."

Six weeks later, Jack Dennison and I had been married in a small civil ceremony in a judge's chambers. The judge was one of my father's closest friends.

Jack had been able to graduate high school with his class.

My parents gave us a seven-day cruise for our honeymoon. They purchased a two-bedroom condo for us as a wedding gift, and Jack was given an entry level position in the office of my father's company. My father had fixed the situation for us. He had a knack of doing just that. Unfortunately, no amount of my father's power or influence could force Jack to love me.

"Sammie? Hello?"

"Oh, I'm sorry," I said, shaking the memories of our shotgun wedding out of my mind for now. "What did you say, Jack?"

"I wondered if you made dessert."

"Of course, Boston crème pie," I replied, getting up to clear the dinner plates.

"Oh, none for me thanks," Susan said. "I ate too much as it was. I'll have to work out twice as long tomorrow morning."

I watched as Jack openly admired his assistant's physique.

"Speaking of which," he said, "Susan belongs to a great fitness club just a couple miles north of here, Sammie. Perhaps you two could meet mornings and work out together?"

That was Jack's not-so-subtle way of reminding me that I needed to get into shape. He worked out faithfully each day. Sometimes in the morning before work he stopped at his men's club and sometimes after work. His physique was perfect.

"Maybe I will," I replied. It was my standard reply to his nagging. If it shut him up for a day or two, then it worked.

After dessert, they both took mugs of coffee and went to Jack's office, which was on the second floor. I cleaned up the kitchen, thankful that I didn't have to continue to make small talk and observe Jack's beautiful and shapely assistant. Maybe it was time I did focus on myself. Our daughter Lindsey had encouraged me before she left for Cornell to do just that.

"Mom, you never do anything just for you," she'd stated. "It pisses me off, too."

"Why would it piss you off?"

"Because Daddy indulges himself and you never do anything just for you."

I'd argued that her father loved working out, buying new clothes for himself, and preening about. I just wasn't sure I would get that much enjoyment or satisfaction from it.

"At least you should try," she argued. "You need a hobby of some sort, besides looking after me and Daddy, especially now that I'm going away. I worry about you, Mom."

"I'll be fine, Lindsey. I swear that I'll find something outside of the home to do once you're gone, okay?"

"Promise?"

"Yes, Lindsey," I'd replied, laughing. "You do realize that you're a nag, right?"

I wiped the countertop off, thinking about my beautiful daughter. I missed her terribly. I knew that I would. We were close, very close. She'd made everything over the years worth it. Jack loved her - that was abundantly clear. Maybe that was all I could have hoped for under the circumstances.

I'd wanted more children, but Jack wouldn't budge on that topic. He'd gotten a vasectomy when Lindsey was seven years old, due to my pressuring him for another. He came home one day and said I could put my diaphragm away (not that it had gotten much use anyway). He'd taken care of the problem, stating that one child was enough.

Jack had come from a family of four children. They'd struggled financially. He'd been the oldest and when his father had taken off when he was just twelve years old, he'd borne a lot of the responsibility while his mother worked two jobs. She'd finally remarried when Jack was sixteen, but by then, he'd had his fill of caring for his younger siblings. He hadn't gotten on with his stepfather either. Even now, he had very little to do with his family.

The phone rang. I picked it up in the kitchen.

"Busy?"

"Hi Bec, just finished up the dinner dishes. What's up?"

"Not much. George is in Chicago on business for a couple of days. I wondered if you wanted to hang out tomorrow. I figured you might be having Lindsey withdrawals."

My friend knew me too well.

"That sounds great. I've been thinking I'm in dire need of having a spa afternoon. What do you think?"

"Let's do it," she said. "Meet me at Cappelli's at noon. We'll do lunch first."

I was showered, wearing my sexiest nightgown and reading a book on my iPad when Jack came to bed. He was fresh from the shower, his brown locks still damp.

"Tired?" I asked.

"I'm beat," he said, pulling the covers up and fluffing his pillow. "The light doesn't bother me, though. Go ahead and read."

I closed my iPad and set it on the nightstand. I switched the lamp off next to it and rolled over, scooting close to Jack.

I lowered my lips to his, kissing them gently. He wrapped his hand around my neck and pulled me closer, his tongue briefly tracing my lips.

"Good-night, Sammie."

"Jack, I kind of thought maybe we would make love tonight. It's been a while."

"Samantha," he sighed, a bit of impatience in his tone, "I told you how beat I am tonight. Rain check?"

"Sure," I said, rolling away from him. "Love you."

"Love you."

I lay in the darkness, a single tear escaped and rolled down my cheek. Within minutes, I heard Jack's even breathing signaling that he was sleeping.

What the hell was wrong with me? Becky said I was still gorgeous. That presumed I'd been gorgeous as a teen or as a twenty-something. I figured best friends were obligated to say things like that. Jack had never said that to me, though. I wanted Jack to think I was beautiful, or ravishing, or goddamn sexy.

My thoughts went back to the honeymoon cruise my parents had given us. Jack had been attentive then. He'd romanced me, charmed me, and we had sex every day of the cruise, sometimes even twice. The sex wasn't what I'd expected. Jack avoided kissing during sex. He had a tendency to be a bit rough. I attributed it to the fact that Jack had been pressured into marrying me. Still, I loved him, for whatever reason.

Once we returned from our honeymoon, I'd busied myself decorating our new condo, buying baby furniture, and outfitting the nursery.

Jack's family hadn't bothered to acknowledge our marriage or the impending birth of our daughter. They did, however, periodically hit us up for money.

My father had started Jack out at a generous salary. Money had never been an issue for us, though I suspected this was all new for him. He loved having money and sometimes flaunted it a bit when he got together with his buddies while they were home on summer breaks from college.

Jack's mother and step-father had come to the hospital to see Lindsey shortly after her birth. Jack's mother, Louise, had commented that Lindsey was probably set for life. It was a strange comment. I'd looked over at Jack to see his reaction to her comment. He'd remained impassive to it. The truth was, I think he somehow enjoyed the fact that we were financially comfortable in life and that the rest of his family continued to struggle. I knew deep inside that was the only reason he'd allowed my father to force our marriage. Jack was set for life, too.

I turned over on my side, clutching my pillow beneath me. Why had I settled, though? Perhaps contentment was all that mattered to me. I'd busied myself with Lindsey and her activities, and Jack had participated as well. He'd coached her softball team and never missed her soccer games, school concerts or plays. He'd taught her how to drive, and was extremely protective of her when she'd started dating. He was the one who had insisted on taking her to Cornell for freshman orientation. I knew that he loved Lindsey. I just couldn't figure out why he'd never come to love me.

I finally drifted off to sleep with the feeling of loneliness and uncertainty gnawing within me.

Chapter 2

Becky and I spent a lovely afternoon at the spa. We were massaged, given facials, waxed, manicured, and pedicured. We were now sitting in the sauna, white towels wrapped turban-style around our hair, another wrapped around our torsos.

"Now, this is just what the doctor ordered, right Sam?"

"Yeah. It does feel great."

"Come on, talk to me, Samantha."

I knew that Becky wouldn't let up until I shared whatever I was feeling with her. She knew me too well.

"It's just that, with Lindsey gone, I have nothing, Becky. I need something of my own. I even promised Lindsey I would find it."

"Okay, I get it. Lindsey is right, you know? I just can't figure out why you had to hear it from your daughter. How many times have I told you the same thing?"

I got up from the bench and dipped the wooden ladle into the bucket of water, pouring it over the hot stones. I took my place back on the bench, pulling my knees up and resting my chin on them.

"I don't know. I guess it was easier not to think about myself as long as I had Lindsey to take care of and to occupy my time with her activities."

"That's kind of a lot of bullshit, you know?"

I looked over at her quickly. Where was this coming from?

"You haven't had to take care of Lindsey for quite some time, Sam. She just didn't suddenly go from diapers to college in a day. You chose to fill your time over the past eighteen years by caring for her as an infant, then as an adolescent, but face it, once she hit her teen years, it was more of you and her buddying around together."

"I'm not sure if I understand what you're saying."

"What I'm saying is that, once Lindsey reached the point where she was independent, you know, dating, going to dances and parties, you kind of lived your life vicariously through her. I mean, come on; think about it."

I contemplated what she had said silently. She continued on a roll.

"All of the photos you took, the scrapbooks you made, the video journals you created to document the sports she played, the hobbies she had. What about you always being one of the chaperones on the class trips she took throughout high school?"

"What about it?" I asked, now getting a bit defensive.

"All I'm saying is that I can see why you're suddenly out of sorts with what to do next. You can't plan your life around Lindsey's anymore. You need to find a life of your own."

"What do you *suggest*? It's different with you. You still have your two kids at home."

"Yes, but I still have my own life, too."

I thought about it, and it was true. Everything that Becky was saying was true. I'd centered my life on Lindsey's. I'd not developed any interests or hobbies of my own. My only social activities, outside of volunteering at Lindsey's high school, were occasionally hanging out with Becky, or Jack and I having dinner with my parents. My father was retired now. He and my mother traveled quite a bit, so even seeing them socially was rare these days.

"You're right. I need to focus on myself. Jack has been nagging me to finish decorating the house. I guess I could throw myself into that."

Becky rolled her eyes and sat up from her reclining position.

"That's not what I'm talking about. I'm talking about something for you, Sam. You aren't into decorating. Let Jack decorate, if it's so damn important to him."

She shook her head as if she was becoming impatient with my cluelessness.

"I don't know what you want me to say? I agree with you, okay?"

"You're not getting it, Sam. Your daughter is off to college, so what? You're going to try and build some kind of life around that mannequin husband of yours?"

I was taken aback. Becky had never taken such a harsh attitude with me, ever! She had always stood by me through everything, as far back as high school. She was Lindsey's godmother, for Christ's sake. Why was she giving me shit? I didn't respond to what she said. I grabbed my thongs, putting them on my feet, and exited the sauna room, heading for the showers.

Once showered, I dressed and headed out to the front to pay the bill. Becky was just a couple of minutes behind me. I paid our spa bill, though Becky protested when I picked up her tab as well.

I was signing the credit card slip when I saw a stack of business cards on the counter in a holder that was labeled, "Take One." I did, not even sure what the card said, but I liked the artwork on it. It was a slender woman in a kick-boxing pose. I shoved it into my pocket and headed out the door.

"Samantha, please," Becky called after me. "Stop, I need to explain."

I stopped on the sidewalk outside to look at her.

"Look," she said, "all I'm saying is that you need to do something for you, Sam. Get a job, go back to school, or take an art class. Start living for yourself because you never have, and it hurts me to see that you have no identity of your own."

"Gee, thanks Becky, I think. Have you considered that my fate is to just be a *mannequin's* wife?" I hissed.

"I won't apologize for that, Sam. You know how I feel about Jack. I've never pretended otherwise."

She was being honest about that. Becky had little use for my husband. She considered him to be self-absorbed, demanding, and unable to bond or to be intimate with a woman.

I wasn't sure how qualified she was to make such a diagnosis, but I felt it was likely due to my intermittent complaints about him over the years. Perhaps it was my fault that Becky had developed the opinion she had of Jack. I never shared with her the good things about our life together.

"I know that you've never cared for him, but he is my husband and Lindsey's father."

"Just think about what I said, okay? I've got to run now. I'm late picking up Shawn from football practice. Call you tomorrow."

"Yeah, later," I said, suddenly absorbed in the business card that I'd picked up inside.

The name of the establishment was Foxy & Fierce Body Shaping Shop. It boasted several types of martial arts training, along with kick-boxing and yoga classes. Why the hell not?

I located Foxy's in a somewhat seedy neighborhood not far from campus. I decided that if everyone in there was Lindsey's age, I would turn around and leave. There was always the YWCA.

Once I stepped inside the doors, I was pleasantly surprised. The receptionist looked to be about the same age as my mother, but holy hell, was she ever fit.

"Hey, sweetie," she greeted me, "what can I do you for?" I noticed her nametag read "Vonda."

"Vonda," I said with more enthusiasm than I'd felt for quite some time, "I want a body just like yours."

Chapter 3

It had been nearly four weeks since I started my membership at Foxy's. I'd lost a total of twelve pounds, and dropped two sizes. My sweats were practically falling off of me. The part that I was most proud of, however, was the muscle tone that I'd developed, both in my lower and upper body.

The kick-boxing was awesome for building muscle tone in the legs. My other workouts included lifting with free weights for arms and shoulder toning, along with a Pilates class for my torso and abs. I'd been spending about four days a week at the gym. I hadn't told Jack any more than that. He'd mumbled an obligatory, "That's great, Sammie," not bothering to feign interest.

I'd just wrapped up my workout for the day and showered when Vonda came into the locker room looking for me.

"Glad I caught you, Sam," she said. "We need one more person to sign up for pole-dancing lessons. The instructor has a minimum registration number in order to meet what she charges. I figured you'd be perfect."

"Pole-dancing? Me?"

"Why not you? You're pretty damn limber and it's a hell of a way to build up your biceps and triceps that you're always whining about, sweetie."

"I know, but Vonda, come on. Don't you think I'm a little bit old for that type of --?"

"I think the word you're looking for is *exercise*, Sam. Good grief, it's not stripping. It's a great dance art form, and to answer your question, no. I'm on the roster. Do you think I'm too old?"

Vonda had me there. At fifty-six-years-old, there wasn't too much that Vonda couldn't do. Maybe it wasn't out of the question. After all, I'd taken three years of ballet under the tutelage of Madame LeBlanc when I was in grade school. She had told me I had natural grace. I had taken it to appease my mother, who insisted on lessons of some sort during my formative years.

"Okay Vonda, I'm in. When does it start?"

Vonda was tickled pink that we had enough members signed up to bring in who she claimed was the 'queen of pole-dancing.' The instructor's name was Ginger Cooper and she'd actually won a third place trophy in the Midwest Pole Dancing Competition the year before.

The lessons started the following week and were daily for the following three weeks. I had no clue that pole dancing was recognized globally as a competitive sport and art form. I'd always regarded it as being a second cousin to stripping. Boy, had I been misguided.

Ginger was extremely talented and driven. She expected no less from her students. She was brutal in her training and assessments.

After the third day of lessons, I told Vonda I was contemplating dropping out. I could barely move a muscle. It had certainly burst my "I'm in great shape" bubble. My God, I hadn't known the muscles that were now feeling a slow, burning pain even existed.

"No, you're not," Vonda stated, in her authoritative tone. "If I can hang with it, you sure as hell can, Sammie. Besides, you're doing great."

"How do you figure, Vonda? You heard Ginger today telling me to get the lead out of my gluteus maximus while she was instructing us on the snowflake or pretzel, or whatever the hell she called it."

"She's tough, I know, but really Sammie, you're doing great. Hey, I bet your husband would love a pole dance demo once you finish this class."

"Yeah, right," I said, getting clothes out of my locker. "He hasn't even noticed my new svelte body," I replied, rolling my eyes.

"What's his problem?"

"I guess he doesn't find me attractive anymore, maybe he never did," I replied with a shrug.

"Humph," Vonda said, shaking her head. "You're gorgeous. You do realize that, right? I hope to God you don't see yourself through his clueless eyes, Sammie."

"You're required to say stuff like that to paying members, right Vonda?"

"You're so full of shit, girlie," she replied, still shaking her head. "I hope to Christ you wake up and smell the coffee one of these days. That's all the pep talk you're getting from me today. I'll see your getting-tighter ass in here tomorrow for our lesson."

I started to say I wouldn't be coming, but then I thought about it. Maybe Vonda was right; maybe I did have potential. Maybe I would give Jack a demo when classes finished. Maybe he'd even want to touch me again.

I stopped by Becky's on my way home. I hadn't talked to her in the last couple of weeks. She knew I was totally wrapped up in my "exercise" classes as she called them. She was simply relieved that I was finally doing something just for me.

"Holy shit," she said, her eyes widening as she held the door open for me. "You've lost a ton of weight, Sam. You look fantastic!"

"Thanks," I said, rolling my eyes. I didn't do well with compliments. It was probably because I wasn't used to getting them.

"No, I mean it. Your damn body looks like a teenager's. What type of exercise class is it? Maybe I'll join you."

"It's kick-boxing and Pilates. I just added pole-dancing to it."

"Oh, God! There's no way I could hang with that, but Sam, it looks so freaking good on you! I bet Jack is drooling, right?"

"He thinks I look great," I lied.

"I bet the mannequin hasn't even noticed, has he?"

Becky knew me so well. She seemed to know Jack much better.

"You know, he's been pretty busy these days. He's been traveling for work quite a bit. We barely see one another."

"Uh huh," she replied. "He's such a fuckwad."

"Becky," I said, my tone cautioning her to just let it go, "how have things been with you?"

"Everything's good. Shawn's playing junior high football. Megan's doing well with her piano lessons. George still fucks me at least three times a week."

"Braggart," I said, with a smile. We both laughed, and the mood lightened.

I loved my best friend, but our worlds were different. That was just the way it was. She'd finished high school and college, married George, had two great kids: a boy and then a girl. She had done everything right. Her life was the American dream. It was the way that things were supposed to work out.

We made plans to meet the following day. I needed to shop for new clothes, she'd pointed out bluntly. She was right.

I was surprised that Jack was home by the time I got there. He'd been in Charlotte, North Carolina, for the past three days on business. Banion Pharmaceuticals had plans to open a large distribution center on the east coast.

Jack had been negotiating with members of the Chamber of Commerce both in Charlotte and in Charleston, South Carolina, for tax incentives. The two cities were competing with each other to be awarded the location where the facility would be built. It would employ up to five hundred people when completed.

He'd just finished up in the shower when I came into our bedroom. I made it a point to undress in front of him, hoping that he would notice and perhaps get the hint.

"How was your trip?" I asked, kicking off my shoes and lifting my sweatshirt up and over my head.

"Brutal," he replied, getting his nail clipper from the top of his dresser. "I have to fly to Charleston on Friday. Our meeting is early Monday morning, so I figured I would have the weekend to prepare my presentation."

I slipped my sweat pants off, and unhooked my sports bra, springing my breasts free. I'd always been rather proud of them. They were still full and perky. I sauntered by Jack who was now sitting on the bed, clipping his toenails. I got clean underwear from the drawer and sat down on the bed next to him.

He finally looked up at me, noticing that I was practically naked in front of him. His eyes narrowed infinitesimally, as he actually looked at me for the first time in weeks.

"Have you lost weight, Sammie?"

"It's nice of you to finally notice."

"Have you been feeling well?" he asked.

"I feel great. I've been working out, getting in shape. What do you think?"

"I think that you've probably lost all of the weight you need to lose. If you get much scrawnier, people will think that you're ill."

"Hey, "I said, moving closer to him on the bed. "How about I go with you to Charleston? We'll have a romantic weekend together. We haven't gone away together alone for as long as I can remember. This would be perfect."

"Babe," he said with a sigh, getting up off of the bed. "The whole point of me going down Friday and staying over the weekend is to prepare for Monday's meeting. I mean, you know how it is with me. I need that total concentration, no distractions when I'm preparing for a big presentation. How about a rain check?"

"Sure," I said. "I'll just list that in our rain check voucher. Maybe one day I'll be able to cash in on all of these IOUs."

Jack didn't even bother to respond.

Well, so much for that.

No mention of how my legs, arms, and abs had gotten into shape with ample muscle tone. No mention of how he missed our making love, since it had been months now. I guess that was too much to expect from my mannequin husband. Christ, I was sounding like Becky now. Maybe she was right. The bottom line was that I was getting sick to death of Jack's inattentiveness towards me. Maybe I needed to take the next step in getting a life of my own.

I sauntered into the bathroom and took a shower. I decided I would start looking for a part-time job as soon as possible. I needed more things of my own.

Chapter 4

It was the final day of our pole-dancing lessons, and Vonda and I were chatting in the locker room after showers.

"So, aren't you glad you finished the lessons?" she asked, towel drying her flaming red hair. "Ginger certainly gave you kudos today after your number. I was a bit jealous, Sam. Did you hire a choreographer to put that together?"

I knew Vonda was being funny. She loved to tease me about how well I was doing with the whole pole-dancing thing.

"Ha ha, Vonda," I replied, smiling. "You certainly didn't do too badly in Ginger's eyes, as I recall."

"Honey, she was just being nice to the old lady in the group. Plus, I'm the one who cuts the check for her hefty fee."

"Yeah, right. You know you have the body of a thirty-five year old," I chided.

"Aren't you thirty-five?"

"Yeah, so?"

"Well honey, I certainly don't have a body like yours, though I'll take the compliment. Thank you. Of course, you have to recognize your body has gone younger since you've been coming here."

"Gone younger?"

"Absolutely. You've got the bod of a twenty-something since you've started working out. Now, if we could just do something about your hair and make-up."

I rolled my eyes as I put a clean sweatshirt on over my head.

"Roll your eyes all you want. I mean it, though. Plus, you still wear clothes that cover all of your toned muscles and ligaments. What a shame." She was shaking her head and 'tsking' me.

I closed the door of my locker, fastening the lock into place.

"Hey Vonda, you wouldn't be in need of any part-time help here, would you?"

"You aren't seriously looking for a job are you? Come on Sam, I know you don't open up a lot about your personal life, but I wasn't born yesterday. I see the car you drive, the brands of the clothes and shoes you wear. I have a hard time believing you need money."

"It's not really about the money," I replied, tying the shoelaces on my Nike Air Max shoes. "I just want something of my own, I guess. A job working here would give me that, plus I'd be doing what I love to do."

Vonda was thoughtful for a moment.

"You know, Sam, I don't have anything at the moment. My tight-ass husband does the books for this place, and he keeps telling me to cut back as it is, but I might have something else for you. I just need to talk to my sister, Janine."

"Janine?"

"Yeah, Janine manages a gentleman's club over on West Washington Street. With your looks and dance skills, I'm sure she might be able to hook you up with some part-time hours."

"Uh . . . Vonda, I'm not thinking of stripping or giving lap dances. I was thinking more along the lines of personal trainer, maybe?"

"Well, good luck with that, sweetie. But before you slam the door on my suggestion, let me clarify it for you. This club has a variety of clientele. Granted, late night and early morning hours, the clientele wants to see a lot of skin and private dancing. I know that's not your gig, sweetie. I was thinking maybe she could hook you up with an early shift. That's when there's more interest from the after-five businessmen in viewing pole dancing with the classier chicks. That way, you will be doing what you love, right?"

"Well, I don't know. I mean I've never pictured myself as being a dancer at a gentleman's club. I mean, what do they wear?"

"Very little," she answered, honestly. "What are you worried about?"

"I don't think I'm the type, Vonda. It's just not me, you know?"

"What is *you*, Sam?"

I hesitated, trying to think about how I visualized myself. All I came up with was how other people visualized me.

I was visualized as a daughter, a wife, a mother, a best friend by those people in my life, but I had no clue as to how I viewed myself as a person. I'd never bothered to carve out an identity for myself.

"That's what I thought," Vonda replied with a smirk. "Look, before you shoot the idea down, visit Janine at the club. I'll give her a call and see if she can meet with you some afternoon next week. See you Monday?"

"I'll be here," I said, giving her a weak smile.

I convinced myself on my drive home that there would be no harm in at least meeting Janine and seeing what the club was like, but I sincerely doubted that pole dancing at a gentleman's club was the identity I truly wished to carve out for myself.

I spent the weekend cleaning the house. Jack was in Charlotte again, only this time he had mentioned the fact that Susan was accompanying him. They supposedly were meeting with the city government officials to wrap up the deal. The decision had been made to build the distribution center in Charlotte. Jack had said he'd be gone a week this time. They were meeting with surveyors and contractors.

I was fairly certain that Jack was fucking Susan. His increased obsession with his looks and wardrobe hadn't gone unnoticed by me. I was surprised at my own impassiveness about the situation. Perhaps having gained some self-confidence these past couple of months had given me some perspective on my marriage. Becky was right, Jack was a mannequin. Correction: Jack was a cheating mannequin.

I was putting some of the new clothes I'd purchased into our large, walk-in closet. I had to shove Jack's clothes over to make room. He had one whole side of the closet, and half of mine. Becky had pointed out how unacceptable it was that Jack had a much larger wardrobe than me.

On second thought, his clothes were all going to the other side. I wasn't going to have my new wardrobe getting wrinkled because they were all crowded together. I removed handfuls of hangers with Jack's shirts and sweaters on them and hung them on the bar on his side of the closet. There. His clothes could get smashed together now. My cell chimed from the bedroom. It was Lindsey.

"Hi, Mom," she greeted cheerily from the other end. "I've been worried about you."

"Me? Why?"

"You don't call me as often as you used to. I'm beginning to think you don't miss me anymore."

"Sweetie, you know better than that. I just know you're busy with college. I've been trying to find some hobbies of my own to fill the void."

"I'm so glad to hear you say that, Mom. What have you been doing?"

"I've been doing kick-boxing and Pilates."

"No, really Mom. I'm serious."

"So am I."

"Really? Well, that's fantastic. It just doesn't seem like you. So are you enjoying it?"

"I love it," I replied, honestly. "I had to buy all new clothes, though."

"You were due, Mom. I'm really happy that you're finally doing stuff for yourself. How does Daddy like it?"

"I'm not sure he's really noticed, Lindsey."

"I'm sure that he has. You know Daddy. He's just not one to make a big deal out of anything. Is he home?"

"No, sweetie, he's in Charlotte for a week or so. He finally tied up the deal with locating the new distribution facility for Banion. He's been pretty distracted."

"Well, see then," she replied, giving him the benefit of the doubt for his lack of attention to me. "I'm sure once that facility is up and running, Daddy will have more time to spend with you."

She didn't realize that the distraction wasn't the distribution facility. It was Susan.

"How are your classes going?" I asked, desperate to change the subject with her.

"For the most part fine. I mean there's the usual struggles with chemistry and trig, but no surprises there. I have an upperclassman tutoring me. He's totally hot so it's kind of distracting."

"Lindsey," I laughed, "Your dad and I aren't paying that kind of tuition for you to be distracted."

"No worries there. He's *totally* about the tutoring, trust me."

I breathed a silent sigh of relief. Lindsey had gone through a painful break-up the previous summer with her high school sweetheart, Lance. I'd done my best to soothe her pain, all the while really wanting to tell her that it was probably the best thing that could have happened. I'd seen a lot of Jack in Lance, and I wanted better for my daughter.

"Mom, I'm still planning to come home for Christmas, but I'm sticking around here for Thanksgiving. One of the girls in the dorm has invited me to her family's home in Connecticut. We're going to do a little skiing. Are you okay with that?"

"That's fine, Lindsey. I'm not even sure what we'll be doing. Your grandparents are still in Hawaii until after the first of the year. Things have sure changed in a year, I guess."

"You sound sad. If you want me to come home, I will."

"No sweetie, I'm fine. You stick with your plans, okay?"

"Okay, if you're sure."

"I am, sweetie."

Chapter 5

I was sitting at the bar at Jewels waiting for Janine to finish chewing out one of the employees in her office. Kevin, the bartender, had given me a glass of club soda to drink. He chatted with me for a few minutes. I picked up on a distinct Boston accent. He was a fairly friendly guy, telling me a little bit about the club and the clientele.

It was just after 11:30 a.m. The club officially opened in ninety minutes. I looked about, studying the layout. There were three separate horseshoe shaped stages with seating around each. Towards the back, there was a sunken seating area with round tables and cushioned seats. I figured those separate seating areas were for customers requesting private attention from a dancer.

The thought of doing lap dances or dancing privately for a customer didn't appeal to me whatsoever. Vonda had assured me that the club offered a variety of different types of dancers. She'd let Janine know that I was only interested in pole-dancing. The fact that I was here waiting to be interviewed by Janine meant that she must have been receptive to my conditions.

The door to Janine's office opened, and a teary-eyed, twenty-something girl came out. Her face was blotchy from crying. I felt sorry for her without even knowing why. She couldn't have been more than early twenties. I cringed at the thought of Lindsey ever having to make her living in a place like this.

What the hell? I was here fully prepared to do just that. What a contradiction. I rationalized that I wasn't here to really earn a living. I was here to find my identity. That made it more palatable in my mind.

I saw a woman who I presumed to be Janine poke her head out of the office and look over towards me.

"Are you Samantha?"

"Uh, yes. Janine?"

"You guessed it, sweetie. Come on in."

I made my way over to her office. She closed the door behind us and instructed me to take off my coat.

I'd worn a pair of my new, tight jeans with a clingy spandex top, and three-inch, heeled boots. This was done per Vonda's strict instructions.

"She has to see your body, sweetie,'" she explained. Vonda had also told me to wear a bikini underneath my clothes for my dancing demo. I'd been forced to order one online because it wasn't actually bikini season in Indianapolis. I'd paid more to have it shipped next-day than for the bikini itself. It was a simple black bikini, trimmed in gold. I thought it had a classy appeal to it.

"So, Red says you're looking for some part-time shifts, pole-dancing only. Let me take a look at you."

"Red?"

"Oh, sorry. That's what I call my sister, Vonda. I mean seriously that hair of hers is something else, right?"

I simply nodded.

She lifted my shirt up to look at my bare stomach. "Nice and flat tummy, no stretch marks. Those tits your own?"

"What? Oh, uh yeah. They're mine."

"Lower your jeans, babe. Red says you have a perky tush that's to die for."

I felt myself blush. I hadn't done that in ages because I hadn't had cause to do that in ages. I unfastened my jeans, kicking my boots off and lowered my jeans, stepping out of them.

"Now, turn around please."

I did as instructed, letting Janine peruse my bikini-clad body.

"Red's right. You've got the body for this place. Need to see what you can do on the pole, though. Follow me."

I followed Janine back out into the main room. She headed over to the jukebox, asking me what song I wanted for my dance.

"Is 'Pour Some Sugar on Me' by Def Leppard on there?"

"Honey, this is satellite music. We can get anything your little heart desires. Def Leppard it is."

'Boston Kevin' was still behind the bar, setting up glassware I noticed as I took the stage. He was totally inattentive to my dance demo, which made me more comfortable. It was probably old hat to him anyway.

The music started. This was the song I'd used for my dance at Foxy's. Ginger had given me a 9.5 out of a perfect 10 score. I now put everything out of my mind. I let the music take over. The length and width of the horseshoe stage allowed for lots of creativity, and there were three poles spaced apart on each stage.

I executed perfect form on my spins and climbs, twirling around and around on my triple snowflake. I ended the song with my upside-down twirl, hooking my outside leg around the pole, my arms outstretched, my back arched as I descended down the pole, my legs outstretched into straddle splits at the end, my head bowed down, my face buried behind my forearms that were now clutched in front of me.

"Not bad; not bad at all, girlie. Let's talk."

I followed Janine back into her office. I put my shirt and jeans back on while she gave me the lowdown on the club. There was an open slot left by the previous dancer, Diamond. Janine was willing to give me a shot at filling it.

All of the dancers had stage names. My name would be 'Diamond.' She cautioned me about giving personal information out to the other dancers or the clientele.

"This isn't a strip club and it's not a whore house. We provide entertainment to mostly male clients. Most of them are regulars, and some of them are wealthy. I don't know your particular situation, Samantha, but I have a feeling you're a babe in the woods, even at your ripe old age of thirty-five."

I started to say something, but Janine held her hand up to let her continue.

"I only know your age because Red told me. You look and dance like you're twenty-five. Trust me, if you looked your age, we wouldn't be having this conversation. That's not a jab, honey. Thirty-five is still young in my book, but in this business, it's a rarity to have anyone past thirty dancing. It's a shame because these young girls don't always have their shit together. That's where problems can and do occur. Diamond's gone because she made coke and Percocet her priority over everything else. My dancers need to stay clean. I know that isn't an issue for you. I can tell."

Someone tapped lightly on her door.

"What?" she hollered out.

'Boston Kevin' poked his head in the door to let Janine know that another candidate was waiting to be interviewed.

"Tell her to sit tight. I may not need to interview her, depending upon how things go here."

He nodded and shut the door.

"So, Sam, are you interested?"

"I might be," I said, surprising myself. "What will my shift be?"

"Tuesday, Thursday, and Friday from 6:00 p.m. until 10:30 p.m. That's considered our second shift. We stagger the dancers, so you'll dance about once every half hour. You're expected to socialize with the customers, up to a limit."

"What's the limit?"

"Don't worry. You'll be the first to know if any customers go beyond it. We have plenty of bouncers and servers that keep their eye out for any funny stuff. They report any behavioral issues directly to me or the assistant manager, Lenny. One of us is always here."

She pulled several forms out of her desk drawer and handed them to me.

"Here's a listing of proper attire and where to purchase it. You're required to have at least four different ensembles to wear and rotate them. The next sheet is our code of conduct which is strictly enforced. The third one is to be filled out and returned for setting you up on payroll. I'll need photo identification to copy for your personnel file."

This was all going so fast. I was in a fog, only half-hearing what Janine was saying. My God! What was Jack going to say when I told him?

Maybe I wouldn't tell him. Maybe this was something that would just be mine and no one else's.

"Now," Janine said, "you'll need to be fitted for a dancer's wig. Trust me, those suckers don't fall off...even when you're twirling upside down. You'll need to get here an hour before your first shift on your first day so that Margo can show you how you need to be made up. After that, you're responsible for doing your own make-up, unless you arrange in advance for Margo to do it. Don't forget, she works on total commission from the dancers. The club will provide you with your wig and make-up case. You're responsible for buying your own ensembles, per the listing I gave you. Make sure you get some coordinating palm gloves to go with your outfits or you'll have horrible blisters."

I continued to nod, as Janine continued to give me instructions.

"Lastly," she said, "you need to either get some tanning sessions or schedule a body spray tan session about once a week. Tanned bodies are sexier bodies. If you have an aversion to using a tanning bed, there are plenty of salons that do the spray tan thing."

I nodded again. That was going to be my choice. I'd never taken to using tanning beds.

"So, do you have any questions for me, Sam?"

"When do I start?"

Chapter 6

I sat in front of the lighted mirror in the dancer's dressing room right behind the stage. This was my third week working. It was a Friday, and the place had filled up fast. Margo came up behind me and twirled the chair around so that she could finish applying my false eyelashes. They had glitter in them.

After make-up, Margo would finish my hair. It was worth it to me to have her do this, and I'd been quick to line her up for my pre-shift appointments. She'd always done the former Diamond's hair and make-up.

Jack had returned from his nearly two-week trip to Charlotte unexpectedly this morning. We had spoken several times on the phone during his trip. It was mostly him calling to remind me to take something to the cleaners, and then again to remind me to pick it up. He'd talked to Lindsey because he knew about her going skiing over the Thanksgiving holiday, which was quickly approaching.

I'd concocted a last minute excuse for leaving at 4:30 to head to the club. I hadn't told Jack that I had a part-time job yet. I hadn't told anyone.

Luckily, I'd taken all of my dancing ensembles, including my six pairs of new spiked heels and boots to the club. We all had lockers there. My make-up case was in the back of my Mercedes, along with my wig case. I'd washed and conditioned the long, light brunette wig that I wore as 'Diamond.' It was cut beautifully in long layers. The front had long bangs, feathered around the face. It was quite stunning. I'd been surprised to find out that it was human hair. It had to have cost the club a pretty penny.

My own hair was a bit more of a blondish-brown. It fell almost to my shoulders. The hair in my wig fell way past my shoulders. I could wear it up in fancy hairstyles, with sexy tresses hanging down around my face to frame it in playful, wispy curls. Margo had styled it for me my first two nights dancing. She could work magic with everything having to do with hair, make-up and wardrobe. I loved her from the moment Janine introduced us.

Margo was in her mid-thirties, too. She'd shared with me that she had danced until about five years ago. Her husband had made her quit once they got married. She had laughed when she told me that they'd actually met due to him being a regular at the club.

"He used to leave me humungous tips," she said. "He always came in on just the nights I danced. He discouraged any other dudes from tipping me. He kind of staked his claim right off the bat, I guess you could say. It really kind of pissed me off at first, then when I saw how sweet and kind he was, I was in love. I guess I should be thankful he doesn't forbid me from doing the hair and make-up for the dancers."

Oh God, one of those...

I then mentally smacked myself for thinking like that. After all, I'd pretty much let Jack define me for all of these years.

"What does your husband do?" I asked, as she put the finishing touches on my hair with a generous sprinkling of glitter.

"He manages the Harley shop downtown. He's looking to buy into it because the current owner wants to spend more time at their vacation home in Denver during the summer. It's fine by me. We just have to see how we can swing the financial part of it. There you are, Diamond. You look perfect, once again."

She twirled the chair back around so that I could see the finished product. She did excellent work. I didn't recognize myself. Margo had, once again, successfully transformed me from plain old Samantha into the beautiful and mysterious 'Diamond.' I loved being someone else while I was at the club. Anyone other than who I really was would do.

"You certainly work magic, Margo," I said, pressing two twenty-dollar bills into her hand. "Thank you."

"No magic needed for you Diamond. You got the look going."

We were interrupted when a high-pitched, whiney voice demanded Margo's attention. It was Garnet, the petite, red-haired dancer who worked the same shift as me.

"Can you spare a few minutes to work on me, Margo?"

Her tone was all about irritation. She gave me a quick glance, then mentally dismissed me. I wasn't sure what I'd done to earn her dislike, but it was evident in her dismissive attitude towards me.

"Sure, Garnet. Take a seat."

I left to finish dressing. My dance was coming up and the place was fairly packed. I wasn't going to let Garnet's whiney-ass attitude dampen my mood.

My mood always seemed to escalate when I was dancing at the club. I loved it.

The money was pretty damn good too. I'd been shocked when I counted my tips up after the first couple of nights I worked. I'd made a little over four hundred dollars my first night, and nearly six hundred my second one. After that, I pretty much averaged anywhere from five to seven hundred per night. Not too shabby for doing something that I absolutely loved doing.

I heard my name being announced as next up on the dance floor. I moistened my lips, smoothed my sequined boy shorts into place, and checked that my garters were straight.

Showtime.

I'd finished my number and was headed back to the dressing room to change when Janine intercepted me.

"Hey, got a customer that wants to buy you a drink, Diamond. He's over at table six."

I still wasn't totally comfortable with this part of the job. It wasn't that any hanky-panky took place. Janine and the bouncers were really strict about that. It was simply a matter of my being out of my comfort zone. I was a dancer, not a talker. It went with the territory, though, and I needed to get used to it.

"Sure thing," I replied, turning back and heading out into the crowded room.

Table six was close to the horseshoe bar nearest the entrance. I saw the lone gentleman sitting there. He smiled as I approached. He looked like he was in his late fifties, perhaps early sixties. He reminded me of someone that my father might associate with in his line of business. It was obvious the man was a businessman of some sort.

He stood as I got to the table, holding the chair next to him out for me to take a seat.

"Thank you," I murmured in the husky voice I used exclusively at the club.

"What would you like to drink, Diamond?" he asked, motioning Renaldo over. His voice was soft. It lingered on my name a bit too long, as if he liked the way it felt on his lips and tongue. My creep radar was out big-time.

"Club soda's fine," I replied. He placed our drink order, turning his full attention back to me.

"My name's Harry. I want to know everything about you, Diamond, every last detail."

This was typical of how these club one-on-one conversations went. Janine had clued me in to develop a fictional story, then stick with it.

"Well, Harry," I crooned huskily, "there's not a lot to tell. I was born in Kansas City. I lost my parents in a car accident when I was just three years old. My grandparents raised me on a farm. Needless to say, this girl wasn't about to be tied down on a farm for the rest of her life. So, after I graduated high school, I high-tailed it to Chicago. That's where I learned to dance. I've been doing it ever since. I came to Indy about three years ago. Chicago's not a safe place for a single girl these days."

"I can imagine," he said, his eyes were locked on my cleavage. I noticed his tongue dart quickly over his lips. He was totally creeping me out now.

Renaldo brought my club soda and Harry's martini. Harry didn't bat an eye when Renaldo collected the $50 from him for this round of drinks.

"What about you, Harry? Tell me a little something about yourself."

I gave him a smile, as if I was really interested in knowing something about Harry. The truth was, I was close to spitting my club soda down the front of him at this moment, hoping some of it would land in his crotch and dampen his spirits. I wasn't pleased that his hand was occasionally rearranging his junk while he ogled my tits.

I laughed inside, thinking about how much my demeanor had changed in three short weeks. The influence of the other dancers, bouncers, and even Janine had given me a hard edge that was new to me. I couldn't imagine saying *junk* and *tits* to Becky.

"So that's pretty much why I'm here in Indy. I'll be going back and forth to conclude business for the next couple of months."

Shit! I hadn't been paying attention to Harry's conversation; something about mergers and acquisitions, I think.

"That's so fascinating, Harry. You must really love what you do," I commented, as if I'd actually heard him.

"Honestly," he purred, scooting closer, "I find what you do much more fascinating than anything else. How much for a private dance?"

Thankfully, I was spared giving him an answer right then when a group of bikers came in through the entrance. I knew the bouncers would be congregating nearby.

Bikers weren't really the type of clientele that the club welcomed. There were about six of them. They took seats at the horseshoe bar. They all had the trademark black leather jackets on, which sported some type of insignia displaying proudly to which biker club they belonged.

Garnet was up on the stage. As she paraded her scantily-clad body just above them, it prompted loud whistles, hoots, and hollers from the bikers. She was eating it up. Garnet loved attention. It mattered little to her from where it came.

Harry was getting impatient, as I'd yet to respond to his question, since my attention had been diverted to the bikers.

"Well?"

"Well what?"

"I asked about you giving me a private dance, Diamond."

"Oh, yes. I mean no. I don't offer that service."

I could tell this didn't sit well with Harry. He frowned, as if he wasn't going to accept my answer. His body language was loud and clear.

"I'm almost sure that the last time I was in here, I was able to get a private dance from one of the girls," he continued, eyeballing me still.

"That may be so, Harry," I replied, "I'm sure Garnet, Ruby, Jade, or Pearl would be happy to provide that for you. I, personally, don't offer that service."

"Why's that?"

Relentless prick aren't you?

"I just don't," I replied, not bothering to mask my irritation at this point.

"I'll certainly compensate you generously, Diamond. Perhaps you'll reconsider?"

His tongue flicked over his lips again; his eyes were boring into mine. He was a determined son-of-a-bitch, I gave him that.

"Look, Harry," I said, smiling, "it's been fun chatting with you, but I do have to get changed for my next number, so if you'll excuse me, please."

His hand found my arm as I started to get up from the chair. He grasped it tightly, forcing me to gasp as I turned to face his angry eyes.

Uh . . . got bouncers?

I tried to tug my arm from his grasp. The son-of-a-bitch was stronger than he looked.

"Listen," he hissed, his voice having lost its softness…

33

"No, *you listen*, old man. Take your fucking paws off of her and do it now. I believe the lady has declined your invitation." The voice had a steely edge to it. It had come from behind me.

I turned to see who had come up to the table. I gazed up into the intense blue eyes of one of the bikers. He was tall and muscular, and his thick, dark hair hit just below the collar of his leather jacket. His face was rugged, yet young. He was gorgeous.

I felt Harry's hand drop from my arm. I pulled it back to my side, instantly aware of those magnificent blue eyes on me, taking a long, leisurely look, as if he was checking for damage. I felt my face flush.

"Are you alright?"

I started to answer when Vince, one of the bouncers, came up to the table.

"Is he causing a problem with you, Diamond?" he asked, nodding his head toward the biker.

I quickly looked up into those smoldering blue eyes and saw his mouth twitch into a slow smile.

God he's smokin' hot . . . God I sound like my daughter now.

"Actually no, Vince. He was assisting me with a customer who didn't understand that I don't give private dances."

Vince looked over at Harry, immediately sensing a good paying customer.

"So, are you clear on that now, sir?"

Harry nodded, giving all of us a frown. Vince turned his attention back to the biker.

"Look, dude, we don't need you butting into our business here. That's what I do. It's *my* job to work with the customers and provide clarification, got it?"

The biker didn't bat an eye at Vince.

"It looks to me like you were a little late on this one, *Ace*. Your customer there had his hands on the girl. Someone needed to step up to the plate here."

I could see that Vince was now totally pissed off at being taken to task by this biker. I needed to resolve the issue before it became a battle.

"Hey, I appreciate your help, Mr. . . . . . ."

"Slate," he said, his eyes locking with mine, "just call me Slate."

"Thank you, Slate," I said huskily, my heart skipping a beat.

"Any time, Diamond," he replied, giving me a sexy smile.

He turned, going back to his group. I watched as he sauntered away, totally mesmerized by his powerful presence. That was the only way that I could describe it. There was a sense of power he exuded, and it was sexy, damn sexy.

"Don't go there, Diamond," Vince cautioned. "Bikers are bad news, babe."

Chapter 7

The bus pulled over at my usual stop at the Park and Drive lot. The attendant was on duty until midnight, which gave me a sense of security. He waved as I walked past his station and went to my parking spot.

This is where I parked my car on the nights I worked at Jewels. There was no way I was parking my Mercedes in the club lot, not to mention putting myself in a position to explain why I drove a Mercedes to begin with and then worked as a pole-dancer. It was much easier this way.

I'd changed into my street clothes, leaving my hair and make-up intact until I got home. I had my wig case in the back seat.

Hopefully, I could get into the bathroom off of the main hall and wash the makeup off before I faced Jack, provided he was still awake. He accepted my excuse that this was a girls' night out with Becky and another mutual friend of ours, Annie. He hadn't seemed to give it much thought, one way or the other.

I had my routine down pat at the club. I parked my car downtown, then took a bus to the club, and caught the last one incoming at 11:15 p.m. One of the bouncers always walked me out. The bus stop was on the corner, and he waited until I was safely aboard. None of my co-workers knew much about me, with the exception of Janine. I didn't have to worry about her. She was simply pleased that I wasn't a twenty-something scatter-brain, as she put it.

My mind drifted back to Slate for perhaps the hundredth time this evening. I shivered thinking of the way his eyes had skimmed over me with an almost appreciative look. My God! What was I thinking? He was probably younger than me, maybe still in his twenties. I needed to get over it. Those days of getting butterflies by fantasizing about bad-boy sex were over.

Hell, for me they'd never begun. Maybe this was all about my lost youth. I quashed it from my mind for the time being.

Luckily, Jack was in bed when I returned home. I showered downstairs and got into a comfortable pair of jammies, curled up on the couch with the remote, and fell asleep. For some reason, I didn't want to sleep next to Jack.

I was up the following morning to the sound of Jack banging around in the kitchen. I heard him mumbling something, which clued me in that he wasn't a happy camper at the moment.

I went up to the kitchen from the family room where I'd slept. There was a guest suite right next to it. I'd been tempted to start sleeping in there, just to see if Jack noticed.

"Well," he said with a hint of irritation in his voice, "it appears that my wife did, in fact, make it home last night. I was beginning to think I'd have to file a missing persons report with the local authorities."

"Were you worried? That's new."

His head snapped up quickly to look at me. He hadn't expected that I'd get flippant. I actually hadn't intended for it to come out so sarcastically.

"Actually, no," he said, his tone every bit as sarcastic as mine had been. "I couldn't imagine what kind of trouble you could have possibly gotten into with Becky or Annie."

He gave a slight smirk and continued filling the coffeemaker with water. "What's for breakfast?"

I walked over to the fridge and opened the door. Thank God we had some eggs. I hadn't done much grocery shopping over the past couple of weeks.

"Scrambled eggs and toast sound okay?"

"I suppose it'll have to be, seeing that it looks as if you haven't been shopping in a while. What are you doing with your time these days, Sammie, besides working out and going to the tanning salon by the looks of it?"

"I'm not tanning. It's a spray tan that eventually wears off."

"Then what's the point?"

"I guess there isn't one, Jack. I just thought it kind of looked nice. It's just a healthy bit of color. I don't think the technician overdid it."

"Let me make my point, Sammie, since you have failed to make yours. I'm busting my ass working for your father's company to provide you with this home and a lot of extras. I don't think it's too much to expect that when I'm home the laundry is caught up, and there is food in the house. I had to run a load of towels through the wash again because you failed to put them in the dryer in a timely fashion. There was a mildew odor to them when I went to use one after my shower last night. I have four shirts that need ironing, and right now, I'd appreciate some breakfast. Those are your responsibilities and always have been. Do you understand?"

"Yep," I grumbled, turning away from him.

He hauled me back to face him. My eyes widened and I swallowed nervously. This was new territory for me. I couldn't remember the last time I'd made Jack angry. I'd simply never given him reason before, since my activities had always been oriented to seeing to his and Lindsey's needs, without delay or error.

"I'm not finished yet. I'll be traveling extensively the next four to five weeks. I'll be home by Christmas, but I have to do training presentations to the marketing groups at four of our sales facilities in order to compete for R & D money. You will need to step up to the plate and start handling the bill paying activities. I've just got too many other things on my mind."

I'll bet.

"Sure," I replied. "We can go over them before you leave again so that I can take over. Not a problem."

"Okay, then," he said, releasing my arm. "I'll have my breakfast upstairs in the study when it's ready."

I mentally flipped him off as he turned and went towards the stair case and then immediately felt bad about it. Jack was right. I hadn't been fulfilling my domestic obligations to him since Lindsey had left for college. I made a mental note to try harder on that front as I started preparing his breakfast.

By the end of the day on Saturday, I had all of the laundry caught up. Jack's shirts were ironed and hung up in his closet. The fridge and cupboards were well-stocked. I had a beautiful roast in the oven for dinner. I was going to please Jack, come hell or high water. I'd set the dining room table with good china and linens, and lit candles. I poured each of us a glass of fine merlot wine.

We ate dinner mostly in silence. Jack was still a bit perturbed with me. I asked questions about how the distribution center groundbreaking had gone, shared with him my most recent conversations with Lindsey, and told him that I'd been working out a lot at the gym, which, in essence, was sort of true. I'd decided there was no way in hell I'd ever to tell him about my job. That's all.

Finally, towards the end of the meal and three glasses of wine later, Jack seemed to ease up and become more cordial.

I cleared the table and loaded the dishwasher while he got comfortable in the family room with another glass of wine. Maybe Jack would finally be in the mood . . . for once.

I went upstairs to shower. I'd enjoyed a couple of glasses of wine at dinner. It was enough to make me just slightly giddy and bold. I decided that I was going to do exactly what Vonda had suggested. I was going to blow dry my hair, put some make-up and sexy lingerie on, and dance provocatively for my husband. Granted, we didn't have a pole from floor to ceiling in our family room, but I would make do with some props of my own.

After I showered and dried my hair, I found a black lacy bustier with red trim and a pair of black lacy bikini panties. I put on a black garter belt and black fishnet hose. I'd purchased these items specifically for the bedroom, hoping one day I would have need of them. That day had come.

I carefully made my face up, not nearly as drastically as Margo did, but it still took away that innocent, housewife look. I piled my hair up into a ponytail and slipped my feet into some four-inch spiked heels. I was ready.

I saw right away that Jack had switched to bourbon when I descended the staircase to the family room. He had his sleeves rolled up, taking a sip from a glass with bourbon and ice in it. He liked his bourbon straight. He did a double-take when he saw me. I took the remote and found a music channel that I used during the week when I practiced. The tunes were just right for erotic dancing. I watched as Jack studied me moving with the music. I danced over to him provocatively, allowing him ample view of my breasts that were bulging over the tight bustier.

I hovered over him, taking my knee and expertly spreading his legs. I then lowered myself in front of him and allowed my fingers to play against his chest and groin area to the music. I saw his face darken; the rage was unmistakable.

I froze in confusion. I thought my moves had been pretty damn good, seductive yet tasteful. That was what I was going for with my husband. It'd been months.

"What in the hell are you doing, Samantha?"

"I, uh, I just--"

"You just *what?* Wanted to come down here made up like a whore and strip for me?"

"I wasn't going to strip. I uh, thought......."

"Thought what? You thought *this* would get me in the mood, is that it?"

"Well, I mean it *has* been months for us. I thought......."

"The hell with what you *thought*, Samantha. I'm fucking sick and tired of you whining about not getting enough cock."

He was pissed - totally and royally pissed. I'd never seen him so angry before.

"If you want to act like a whore, by God, I'll treat you like one."

Before I knew what was happening, Jack threw his drink down and grabbed me, wrenching me to the floor. Suddenly, I was feeling a tad terrified. I mean, for the first time ever, I was afraid for my well-being. Something was wrong. Something was very wrong.

I tried to twist away from his grasp once he'd me pinned on the floor, but his strength far exceeded mine. He landed a hand firmly across my cheek by my left eye. I saw stars for a moment, and then I simply relaxed. I realized that the more I fought him, the more determined and rough he became.

He had my arms pinned down at my sides as he roughly ripped my lacy undergarments off of me. I squeezed my eyes shut tightly. This was something I could not fathom. Jack had never been a tender lover, but he'd never been a violent lover, up to this point.

"There whore, you're naked now. So, since you went to great lengths tonight to let me know what you're so determined to have, how about if I give it to you, huh?"

I tried again to squirm out from under him, trying like hell to bring my knee to his groin, but it wasn't happening. He quickly spread my legs open with his hands and raised himself up over me.

"No, Jack. Please......"

His erection plunged into me with a vengeance. I shrieked in pain.

"Oh, but this is what you wanted, isn't it Samantha? The *whore* in you wanted this and now you have it."

He continued to thrust himself in and out of me unmercifully, grunting like the pig that he was. I felt like I was going to split in half.

My mind was reeling. I was silently praying that I got out of this in one piece. Was it the alcohol that had triggered this? Or maybe he just hated me. All I knew was that this had never happened before. I won't lie; he'd never been a soft or tender person.

But this?

This was pure violence being unleashed upon me, and it wasn't about sex even. This was about pure and simple control. What in the hell had I done to make him feel as if he'd lost control?

I didn't have long to wonder as I finally felt him come. He moaned Susan's name as he emptied himself into me.

Oh. My God.

He then quickly pulled himself out and off of me. He didn't look me in the eye as I lay there in shock. The pain was gone, the numbness had taken over. He zipped his fly up and sat back down on the sofa. He picked the remote up and changed to a different channel.

"You probably need to get some sleep, Sammie. Go on to bed. I'll be up a little later."

I picked myself up off of the floor, totally naked, totally exposed. It wasn't as if I had to hide my nakedness from him because his attention had been diverted to the television. I had been dismissed.

I hurried out of the room, seeking refuge once again in our suite. I got into the shower and scrubbed myself clean of his anger, his abuse. My skin was flushed pink by the time I got out.

I quickly dressed in my conservative underwear and pajamas and crept underneath the sheets of our bed. I curled up into a ball and eventually fell asleep. I felt like a total piece of shit.

Chapter 8

I spent Sunday trying to avoid Jack, most of it spent in the bathroom, trying to cover up the shiner I had around my left eye. It was bruised and tender, turning dark shades of purple and black by the hour. I hoped like hell that it disappeared before I worked again on Tuesday.

Jack never mentioned once what had transpired the night before. He acted no differently than usual.

He sat me down in the afternoon to show me how he handled the bill payments on line. Jack was extremely organized with his file folders, Excel files, and logging payments in with confirmation numbers provided by the bank, once remittance was scheduled. He was meticulous and expected no less out of me, now that this household task had been relinquished to me.

He packed his suitcase and his garment bag late in the afternoon. Giving me a peck on the cheek, he was off to the airport. He told me he would be calling to check in. No mention of anything else. No apology. No explanation - as it there could possibly be one.

I phoned Becky and chatted for a while, trying to take my mind off of the obvious. I didn't dare mention what had happened between Jack and me, because she would've gone off about it and yelled at me for not reporting it to the police or getting the fuck out immediately, both of which were sane reactions. I needed to think this through on my own, to handle it in whatever way was best for me. I hadn't been up against anything like this before.

Tuesday finally came, and I was in the chair while Margo was doing her best with applying a heavy concealer around my left eye. She was being gentle, which told me that this wasn't the first shiner she had needed to conceal for one of the girls.

"Do you want to talk about it?" she asked cautiously, as she gently dabbed make-up over the concealer.

"Not really," I replied with a shrug. "It's no big deal."

"It's always a big deal, sweetie, but I respect your right to privacy, so I won't push. Hopefully, your perspiration won't wash it off."

I got through my first couple of dance routines without a hitch. Tuesday was generally a less-crowded evening. It was mostly regulars in during weeknights.

I'd just changed into another costume. It was shiny gold boy shorts, with a matching sleeveless gold vest. I accented it with four-inch black leather boots, and a glittery, sequined cowboy hat.

Kevin poked his head around the corner of the dressing room.

"Front and center, Diamond. There's a dance request for you, followed by a customer-purchased drink."

Please don't let it be Harry.

I knew immediately when the first chords of the tune blared out from the speakers that this request hadn't come from Harry. It was Steppenwolf's 'Born to be Wild.'

I took the stage and, immediately, my eyes met with Slate's incredibly blue ones. I saw the shadow of a smile cross his sensual lips as I took the pole and twirled to the beat of the song. My heart fluttered as I watched him watching me. None of his biker buddies were around. He must have been flying solo.

The song ended, and I descended the three steps from the stage to the main floor. Slate was on his feet, nodding toward a table near the back. I saw Vince nearby. He was making sure Slate didn't touch me. Vince seemed much more attentive when the gentleman was a biker instead of an old geezer, like Harry.

He held a chair out for me, as any perfect gentleman would have done. Renaldo took our drink order. Slate ordered bourbon straight up, and I requested my usual club soda. I was nervous, for some reason. His presence unnerved me.

"You have some nice moves, Diamond. Did the song justice out there. I like that."

"Glad you got your money's worth, Slate," I said in my husky club voice.

I watched as he cocked an eyebrow, a slight smile gracing his lips. "I'm not sure about that, Diamond Girl. I guess that remains to be seen."

I gaped at him, feeling myself flush. He didn't talk like any biker that I'd seen around the place. There was a quality to his voice. His choice of words hinted at something more than biker lingo. I was certainly no expert on bikers. And maybe I was basing my opinion on stereotypical impressions.

The several moments of silence between us was making me more self-conscious.

"So, Slate, tell me about yourself? Where are your biker buddies tonight?"

"I really don't give a shit where they are. We have separate lives, you know?"

"I'm sorry. I didn't mean to……."

"Insult me? You didn't. I'm used to the stereotypical comments. I'm sure you're used to them in your line of work, right?"

Point well taken.

"Yeah, you got that right," I said with a throaty laugh.

"How long have you been dancing in clubs like this, Diamond?"

"Not long," I said with a sigh, "kind of new to this circuit."

"You're not from Indy?"

"No, Kansas," I replied, "And then Chicago, and now here. How about you, Slate?"

He took a sip of his drink that had just arrived and shrugged.

"I'm from all over. I really don't call anywhere home for long."

It almost seemed as if Slate had a script.

Like me…

Or maybe it was a macho biker thing.

"So, are you a member of the Outlaws?"

"Do you see an OMC patch on this jacket?"

"No, but then, I'm no expert on biker gangs, either."

"They're called clubs, not gangs, Diamond."

Whatever.

They were mostly criminals, from what I'd observed.

"So, what do you do outside of the club?" I asked, cautiously.

"I manage," he replied with a shrug.

"Well, you must work. How else can you afford to make special requests and buy a dancer a drink at these prices?"

He laughed, shaking his head. "You aren't going to get rich off of me, baby. Maybe that old geezer can hook you up. He didn't seem to lack for money."

What the hell?

"Fuck off, Slate."

His blue eyes were locked on my green ones. All humor had left his face. His eyes were as cold as ice instantly. He perused me up and down, and I saw his jaw twitch as his gaze came to rest on my left cheek bone. His eyes darkened.

He lifted his hand to my face. His thumb lightly caressed my outer cheekbone underneath my eye. Vince was immediately in the vicinity.

"It's okay, Vince," I called over my shoulder. Slate removed his thumb from my cheek.

"Who fucked you up?" he asked.

His gaze was now burning into me, waiting for an answer. I didn't owe him a response, let alone an explanation. I finished my club soda, turning my face away from him.

"I asked you a question, Diamond. Who the hell left that mark on you? I want to know who it is that I need to fuck up."

"My husband," I replied, returning my gaze to his. "It was my *husband*, okay?"

I saw a quick look of disbelief cross over his face. He turned his head, rubbing the back of his neck with his palm.

"Christ," he muttered. "What the hell's wrong with you, Diamond? You put up with shit like that from your old man?"

"It's none of your concern, Slate. Is our time up yet? I need to have my make-up touched up before the next set."

"Yeah, babe. We're done here."

I scooted my chair back and hurried away from him. He was making me feel like trash. How in the hell could some biker dude make me feel like trash? But he had. I was certain he hadn't meant to, but at the moment, it was how I felt. I also felt out of sorts with my departure. I realized it was when he said we were "done here." What had that meant?

I quickly banished those thoughts from my mind. What the hell did it matter? I was certainly not going to get involved with some young biker. I headed into the dressing room as Margo was finishing up with Jade.

"Need a touch up, hon?"

I nodded, too frazzled by the brief time I'd spent one-on-one with Slate to try and make small talk with Margo.

"I saw you out there with the hottie biker," she said, as I took the chair that Jade had just left. "I poked my head out when I knew your number was up to see who your admirer was. Just so you know, I can be nosy that way with dancers that I care about."

I eyed her warily. I couldn't help but smile when I saw the way she fussed over me like a mother hen. We had to be around the same age.

"Is he a regular here?" I asked.

"I wouldn't say that. I've seen him in here before, though. He just started hanging around with the others, I don't know, maybe around last spring, I guess. The dancers here sure are crazy about him, especially Garnet. I think the old Diamond used to hang with the bikers before she was fired. Hell, that was probably her downfall. She started living a different life after she got involved with Slash."

"Who's *Slash*?"

"I think his real name's Jamie. He's one of the Outlaws, been in the club for a while. He took to the previous Diamond. He still comes in with the others sometimes. I think he's one of the higher-ups in the Indy club. He acted like he owned her. That was her fault for letting it happen. I know he used to take her tips from her, the lazy son-of-a-bitch. Then he used to bruise her up nicely, if he thought she was dancing too provocatively for one of the customers. That girl was in a no-win situation. Janine banned them all from here for a while. She lifted the ban once she fired Diamond. She won't stand for any of the dancers getting involved with that bunch, though."

"I don't intend to get involved with *anyone*," I said to her bluntly.

"This is the first time I've seen him ask for a private drink with any of the dancers, though. He might have plans for you."

"Please, Margo. He's got to be a twenty-something biker. What could he possibly want with me?"

"Hmm, that's a tough one. Couldn't be your looks or your body. I bet it's your *money* he's after," she said, snickering loudly. "Yeah, that must be it."

I gave her my version of a dirty look. I wasn't especially good at those yet. I was still learning.

"Bikers around here are bad news, Diamond, even after hours. I don't think you're the type to fit in with that group. I'm no expert, but I've done enough time in clubs like this to know a little something. I don't see you as a biker bitch, not even for someone as hot as Slate. He seems to have earned the respect of his colleagues, but I've heard stories about how bikers treat their chicks, you know? Pass them around to their buddies, discipline them in violent ways. Of course, maybe I'm not telling you anything you don't already know, by the looks of that eye. Did a biker do that to you?"

"Of course not, Margo. Damn, give me some credit, please."

"I'll be glad to, darlin' just as soon as you tell me that whoever gave you that shiner is missing a gonad."

I lowered my eyes from her expectant gaze. Now, I was not only feeling like a piece of trash, but a pitiful one at that.

"There, finished," she said, spinning the chair around so that I could see the repair job.

"Thanks, Margo," I replied, softly. "Hey, don't worry about me. I don't intend to let it happen again."

"That's my girl," she said, smiling for the first time at me this evening.

Chapter 9

I hadn't seen Slate on Thursday or Friday as I worked my usual shifts. Some of the other bikers, along with their girlfriends, had been in the club, acting extremely rowdy. Janine had kicked them out for the evening, after taking a bunch of shit from them.

The biker chicks seemed to bring out the nastiness in the guys. Their behavior was much more belligerent, except with their men. They were fairly subservient to them. They would stand while their men sat, fetch their drinks, and speak only when spoken to. It kind of reminded me of my life with Jack, only without the sex and leather.

I'd done pretty well in tips this evening, bagging $585. I'd been tucking my tips away at home in a metal lock box. I wasn't sure what had prompted me to do that because Jack was never home. I guess I considered it part of my secret life; the one that I had locked away from everyone else.

I'd changed into a pair of tight, ragged jeans, a pullover sweater, and leather boots. I grabbed my sweatshirt hoodie from the hook, shrugging it on over my head. I slung my shoulder bag over my arm and headed out.

I didn't see Vince or Ethan on the floor. The other bouncer, Jay, was busy keeping some guy who was totally wasted from climbing up onto the stage where Emerald was dancing. Emerald was twenty-two years old, black, and extremely petite. She'd relocated from Detroit with her boyfriend, Ivan, about six months ago. Ivan had lost his job at one of the automotive plants. He was currently working as a millwright at one of the factories here in Indy. I knew Emerald missed her family terribly. Margo and I'd both taken to mothering her. There was something very fragile about Emerald.

Jay seemed to have the situation well under control, finally grabbing the drunk by the scruff of his neck and escorting him out the front door. This had brought a series of booing from his cohorts, who were still ogling Emerald. Jay saw me as I approached the door to leave.

"I'll walk you to the bus stop, Diamond."

"No, that's okay. You need to stay here and keep an eye out for Emerald. I have a feeling those idiots over there are going to make it tough on her, since you booted their buddy. Where are Vince and Ethan?"

"Ah, fuck, there was a major fight over on the other side. Some of those bikers were roughing up their chicks. Vince and Ethan are waiting for the cops to show."

"Really, I'm good," I said. "Keep your eye out on things here, okay?"

"Be careful, babe." With that, Jay turned his attention back to the floor, and I made a swift exit out into the dark night.

It was clear out. For late November, the weather had remained above normal temperatures. It was cold and chilly, but well above freezing. There was no cloud cover so the stars lit up the night sky.

I was nearly to the corner where the bus stopped when I heard the loud and vicious sound of a motorcycle next to me. I kept walking, looking straight ahead, even as I heard the engine slow down to a not-quite-so-loud idle. Undeterred, I continued on my way and, finally, I heard the engine shut off completely.

I didn't slow my pace, and I ignored my peripheral vision. I finally heard a male voice call out.

"Diamond, hey! What's your fucking hurry? Got to get home to that violent, piece-of-shit old man of yours?"

I stopped and looked over into the beautiful, totally amused blue eyes of Slate. He was untying his do-rag, shaking his hair free. I noticed then that he had a pierced ear. It was totally sexy.

I glanced over at him impassively, shrugging my shoulders.

"Maybe I am. You wouldn't want to hold me up now and make him mad if I miss this bus? It's the last one."

"So, you're telling me that the rat bastard doesn't even bother picking you up? You ride a freakin' bus home?"

"Who's to say he isn't watching our three kids?"

I watched as a slow grin spread across his handsome face as he contemplated what I said. His muscular arms were crossed in front of him. His leather jacket couldn't hide the fact that he was totally buff.

"Naww," he said with a grin. "That body of yours doesn't look like it's been through childbirth, baby. Way too firm and way too slender. It does have a way of making a guy want to plant his seed, though, I give you that."

Oh wow...

"So, how about it, Diamond?" he teased, re-tying his do-rag into place.

"How about what?" I tried to make my husky voice sound icy cold, but I wasn't sure that I was pulling it off.

"You want to carry my baby?"

"Maybe later," I answered dryly, continuing to walk towards the corner.

Slate was rolling his motorcycle along side of me in the street, next to the curb.

"Hop on," he said. "I've got a helmet strapped on for special passengers."

"Isn't that for your biker bitch?" I asked, putting my hand on my hip.

"That position hasn't been filled yet. Are you applying?"

"I'll pass," I replied. "One asshole in my life is quite enough."

I heard him laugh genuinely. He had a nice laugh. It was sexy, like everything else about him. I looked over at him and noticed for the first time that he had a dimple when he smiled widely…just one more thing identified in his sexy-attribute inventory.

"Come on," he urged, giving me a wink. "I can take you anywhere you want to go. You don't need to take a bus with all of those perverted freaks riding around on them this time of night."

I stopped and turned to face him.

"I think I'll take my chances with the perverted freaks on the bus rather than the ones on motorcycles this evening, thank you very much, Mr. Slate."

"It's just Slate, baby," he said with a chuckle. "I presume your name's something other than 'Diamond.' What shall I call you?"

"Mrs. Diamond," I answered as the bus pulled over to the curb and I stepped aboard. I heard Slate's gorgeous laugh as the door to the bus closed behind me.

I took my seat and watched out the window as Slate revved his motorcycle back to life. He turned it around and headed back in the direction from which he'd come. I was thoughtful as I watched him disappear.

He didn't seem like a typical biker, not that I had all that much knowledge or experience with them. Still there was something powerful about him, yet not frightening or repulsive. His grooming was different. He had the five o'clock shadow thing going, the longer unkempt hair, the pierced ear, yet there wasn't anything disgusting about his build or grooming. His teeth looked well taken care of and incredibly white and straight; no tobacco stains or missing teeth.

There I had gone with my stereotypical thinking. I'm sure he had his own opinion of dancers. He probably thought I was a "clap-trap" or an easy piece-of-ass that had been done by many until my abusive husband took me in. He probably figured I waited on my hubby hand and foot and looked forward to his occasional attention, if nothing more than a slap across my cheek to let me know I was his possession. Yeah, I got it. We both had a lot to learn.

The ride to the Park and Ride went quickly. I entertained myself with thoughts of Slate. I thought of his beautiful blue eyes, his sensuous lips, and how they might feel on mine. I thought of his hands touching me. I actually was getting moist down there thinking about him!

What the hell is my problem?

I departed the bus, digging for my keys in my purse as I passed the attendant station. I gave my usual wave to the attendant as I passed. I hit the remote to unlock my car and opened the door, ready to climb inside and head for home. I was exhausted. Right before I closed the door of the car, I heard the sound of a loud motorcycle as it peeled out from the curb across the street from the Park and Ride.

Something about the sound of the bike's engine caused me to shiver and wonder if it was him.

Chapter 10

Thanksgiving Day was like any other day for me this year. I nuked a turkey and dressing Lean Cuisine, eating it in front of the television, while I watched the Thanksgiving Day parade. I'd talked to Becky earlier on the phone. She'd wanted me to come to their house for Thanksgiving dinner, but the truth was, I didn't want to pig out on turkey and make small talk with Becky's family all afternoon. I had to work my Thursday shift at Jewels tonight. I certainly didn't want to go there gassy.

I hadn't seen Slate in the club on Tuesday when I worked. Of course, none of the other bikers had been in either. I mentally kicked myself in the ass for finding myself looking for him when I was on stage. I needed to take Margo's advice and keep clear. Janine wouldn't tolerate it at the club and I certainly wasn't cut out for the type of life a biker would provide. Aside from the obvious: I was married. I didn't need to cloud the issue of dealing with that by forcing some idiotic distraction to get into the way.

I'd purchased a new dance outfit for tonight. It was a white opaque unitard that had long sleeves and a plunging neckline. I had gold, sparkly four-inch spiked heels, and a white feather plume intertwined into the mass of brown hair piled loosely on top of my head. There was something extremely classy about my outfit tonight. Even Margo made a comment, as she put the finishing touches on my make-up and gold glitter, about how stunning I looked.

"Looks to me like you're trying to impress someone special tonight, chica. I don't need three guesses to figure out who it is." Her tone was slightly admonishing.

"Margo, sometimes you act way older than your years. You do realize you and I are about the same age, right?"

"I don't give a damn. You're still a babe in the woods, and girls look after girls. That's just the way it is here."

"I'll be fine. I just want to class it up a bit tonight. It's a holiday. Wait until you see my Christmas costume."

"Diamond, you're a rarity around here. I hope you know that."

"Is that a good thing?" I asked, giving her a sly grin.

"Absolutely, chica. Hey, I think they're calling your number, sweetie."

I'd selected my first number for my shift. It was "Girls, Girls, Girls" by Motley Crue. I'd worked out a perfect dance to it and had practiced all week long. I took the stage as the chords of the song started the upbeat.

On my third twirl, as I climbed the pole to execute my first upside down decent, I saw him. He was alone at the bar. For whatever reason, the flame-haired Garnet was sitting next to him, sipping a drink.

What the hell? Did he freaking buy her a drink?

They seemed to be in a deep conversation. He barely noticed me as I continued my routine, eyeing them both whenever my dance allowed me to look that way. When my number was over, I flounced off the stage, ripping the feather from my upswept hairdo.

"What'd I miss?" Margo asked, her expression clearly puzzled. "Did you slip? Land on your ass out there?"

"No - nothing like that. Not much of an audience out there. Isn't Garnet on the clock tonight?"

"No, her shift was earlier. She switched with Emerald. She said she had a hot date."

"I see," I said, seething.

I wasn't sure why the hell it bothered me. Slate and I were nothing to each other. He most likely fucked a different bitch on a daily basis. Why did it have to be Garnet, though? She was such a *skanky* bitch.

I went to my locker and got another outfit out for my next dance, which wasn't for another forty-five minutes. It was much skimpier...pure glittery trash in red. I chose red because that was one color Garnet couldn't wear with that hair color of hers. Maybe it'd be enough to distract Slate from his attentive conversation with Garnet. I was actually counting the minutes until it was my turn to go back out on the stage. I still had another thirty.

I was in the dressing room as Emerald was preparing to go out next. She looked so sexy in her black fishnet body stocking with built-in bikini crotch less panties and pasties covering her nipples.

"When are you out?" I asked her.

"Right after Ruby. She's on now."

"Which stage is next?"

"Center," she replied.

That was the horseshoe bar where I'd spotted Slate with Garnet.

"Want me to take a dance for you?" I asked Emerald.

"Hey, I could use a longer break," she admitted. "I'm so freaking premenstrual. I hope like hell I don't start tonight. These outfits can't even hide a tampon," she remarked, laughing.

"It's settled then," I replied, smiling. "You take it easy. I've got this one covered."

"Thanks, Diamond. I owe you," she replied.

She ran out and told the announcer that I was switching dancing order with her so that I would be announced when the next song played.

A couple of minutes later, I was announced to center stage to the tune of Whitesnake's, "Here I go Again."

How fitting.

The beat was awesome to display many of the moves and additional gymnastics I'd added to my repertoire. I made sure I strutted my stuff right in front of Slate, who was still sitting next to Garnet, though I clearly had his attention now. I preened about like a peacock in front of him. Garnet's displeasure was obvious as I ascended the pole and spun and twirled like she wished she could.

"Just another heart in need of rescue; waiting on love's sweet charity…"

This song tugged at my heart, at my pride. It said all of the things that I felt inside of me and had for so very long. My dancing was my means of getting it out there, dealing with it in a healthy way. I lost myself to the music and the lyrics.

As the song ended, I wrapped myself around the pole and slid downward, allowing myself to segue into the splits right in front of where Slate was sitting, his eyes not moving from me.

I saw the hateful look that Garnet was directing my way. It didn't faze me a bit. I raised my head up to look directly into Slate's sapphire blue eyes. I saw something there as well. It was indistinguishable, but somehow I felt that he got it. He got me. I wasn't someone to be toyed with, and he understood.

I rose up from my floor position and left the stage amid the loud applause, wolf whistles, and male shout-outs. This had been one of my best performances. It had been all about the song, and all about Slate. I truly didn't know why.

I returned to the dressing room and quickly went to my locker. This was my last set for the night. I wanted to get into my street clothes and get the hell home. I changed into a pair of jeans and a hoodie, trading my four-inch heels for a pair of brown leather boots.

I told Janine I'd collect my tips tomorrow night when I worked. She was fine with it.

"Is everything alright, Diamond?" She had that motherly look of concern on her face.

"Yeah, everything's good. It's just hard, you know, with both Lindsey and Jack gone. It's kind of lonely, I guess."

"Okay darlin', you take care. I'll see you tomorrow night then."

"Yeah, until then," I replied, heading out the door.

I didn't bother with getting a bouncer to walk me out. I left through the back, not wanting to face Slate, who was probably still sitting with Garnet and hoping to score for the night. I was certain he would have no problem. Garnet made no secret she would offer her pussy up on a silver platter for Slate.

I'd left the building through the back and was nearly to the corner where the last bus of the night would pick me up, when suddenly, out of nowhere, strong arms grasped me from behind, whirling me around. My heart plummeted to my stomach. I immediately let my instincts kick in and took a defensive stance, one that I'd learned in kick boxing.

My eyes fell upon my attacker's deep blue eyes. It was Slate.

"What the fuck are you doing?" I hissed, my adrenaline pumping, poised to protect myself.

"What the fuck are *you* doing walking out here by yourself at night? I thought the bouncers saw you out safely after your shift."

"You seem to know quite a bit about what goes on here, don't you?" I was lashing out at him, not sure why.

He cocked an eyebrow at me quizzically. He wasn't getting that I was out of sorts with him. Neither was I.

"Look," I said, trying to normalize my tone and body language so as not to appear to really give a damn about this man who, for some odd reason, intrigued me. "I'm fine. I'm nearly at the corner. The bus will be by shortly, no worries."

"I'll wait with you," he said firmly.

"Why?"

"It's not *safe* for a girl to be out by herself this late and in *this* neighborhood."

"Yeah, I know. Lots of biker riff-raff hanging around lately, I've noticed."

He gave me a sardonic look with a slight rolling of the eyes, definitely not a biker reaction.

"So you have something lined up later with Garnet?"

"What's it to you, babe? Do I sense some jealously going on?"

"Yeah, right. That's close," I murmured.

"Hubby waiting for you at the crib?"

"Maybe."

He smirked, shaking his head. "You know, if you were my old lady, I wouldn't let you outta my sight."

"Why's that?"

Before he could reply, the bus was slowing down and pulling towards the curb. He moved swiftly, pulling me up against him. His hand roughly tilted my chin upward. His mouth covered mine, his lips taking full possession of mine. I struggled against him momentarily, until my mind was fuzzy with desire and I didn't want to resist.

His tongue traced my lips and then entered my mouth, thoroughly exploring it with a sensual rhythm. He lightly nipped at my bottom lip. I laced my arms around his strong neck as I heard the hydraulic door to the bus open. He shoved me away gently.

"Go home, Diamond Girl. You don't belong around here."

With that, he turned on his heel and headed back to the club. I saw Garnet standing at the door of the entrance. She'd been looking for him...that was obvious. I turned and stepped onto the bus with shaky legs. His kiss had left me wanting more. I wasn't sure why.

Chapter 11

I heard from Jack on Friday afternoon as I was lining up my dance costumes for my shift that evening. He wanted to make sure that I was keeping up with bill payments and to let me know he would be coming home for a week on Sunday afternoon. It was a short break in his schedule. Then he would be off again until he came home for Christmas.

My parents were expected back before Christmas. I felt guilty for not staying in touch with them. My mother had always done everything my father had told her to do, and had done it exactly as my father had wanted it done. It bugged me as an adult, having seen how that felt. I resented the fact that my mother had never carved an identity out for herself. She had never instilled that need in me while I was growing up.

Right now, I needed to concern myself with how I was going to get through the week with Jack home, while still showing up for my shifts. I'd totally decided against telling him I had a part-time job…period. I would talk to the girls to see if I could get one of the late shift girls to take my shift for three nights next week.

I sat down in Jack's office at the computer and pulled up the Excel spreadsheet he'd created for me that was titled, "Samantha's Financial Records." It was kind of an odd file name, but Jack was anal like that. He'd shown me how to go into our online banking with the password and pull up our joint account. I saw where a recent electronic deposit had been made for $9213.77. That seemed odd to me.

I clicked on the transaction number to get the detail. It simply said "Cash" and referenced that it was an ATM deposit. The location was Manassas, Virginia. I decided it was probably one of the sales offices where Jack was conducting training. I wasn't sure why a cash deposit of that amount had been deposited into our joint account. I made a note to ask him about it when he was home.

I went through the Excel file and selected the payees who had a "Due Date for Payment" current or within the next three days and highlighted them. I then submitted payment amounts required on the on-line tool for our account, and posted the confirmation number in the column marked the same.

There, I was finished with that.

No reason for Jack to bitch or smack me around.

I powered off the computer and put the files away.

I took extra care with my bath this afternoon, as I prepared for work. I shaved and waxed, plucked a couple of errant eyebrow hairs, and selected one of the new outfits I'd purchased by mail order. I was now on a first-name basis with the UPS delivery guy.

Tonight, I was going to wear a black lace, layered mini dress. The front was a princess, Lolita-style neckline. It had an open back, and a matching, black lace G-string was worn underneath. I was going to wear my black, leather, four-inch, spiked heels with ankle ties. My nails were painted a bright red.

I was in need of some male attention tonight. I was in need of Slate's attention.

Ever since the kiss, it'd been difficult to get him out of my mind. I chastised myself for even considering getting involved with someone that reckless, dangerous even. What the hell? I was entitled to some temporary insanity after the lackluster existence I'd had with Jack over the past eighteen plus years.

Margo noticed the change in my demeanor almost immediately when I got into the chair. Maybe it was the new dance costume, and the bright red nails. Or maybe, it was when I requested she use longer lashes for tonight and do up my green eyes in smoky dark grey shadows, with black liner and no glitter.

"It looks like someone has plans for tonight," she remarked, pulling my brown locks up on top of my head into a long ponytail. "Maybe Garnet will have something to say about that."

I looked at her reflection in the mirror. Our eyes met.

"What's that supposed to mean, Margo?"

"Just seems to me that the both of you may be hot after the same dude, that's all."

"And your point would be?"

"The point is, I like you, Diamond. I like you way better than Garnet, but you're outta your league if a bitch fight's on the horizon over that biker."

"What biker?" I asked, innocently.

"Don't play me," she said. "Garnet's rough and she's ruthless. And the bottom line is, she's been here longer than you. Janine doesn't like fighting amongst the girls. If push comes to shove, you're out honey and Garnet's in. Ain't worth it, darlin'."

I gave Margo a prize-winning smile.

"You've done a beautiful job on me, as always, Margo," I said, pressing $40 into her hand. "Thanks."

I heard her call after me as I went into the lavatory. "She left here with him last night, Diamond. I just thought maybe you should know."

I was glad the door to the bathroom had shut behind me once her words had sunk in. My legs immediately turned to jelly. I sought refuge in one of the stalls, her words continuing to reverberate in my mind over and over again.

I felt my stomach knot up with a feeling that wasn't familiar to me. It was a mixture of anger, jealousy, and a little bit of hurt and disappointment thrown in for good measure. I had no reason to feel those things. I had no right to feel those things. Slate was nothing to me. I was nothing to Slate. I needed to stop allowing insane distractions to keep me from dealing with the real issue: my disaster of a marriage, better known as the big lie.

I dabbed at the corner of my eye with a piece of toilet tissue. I refused to let this bit of news cause me to ruin the awesome make-up job that Margo had just completed. I managed to regain my composure and finished up in the bathroom.

My first number out was a request from one of the regulars that came in to the club. His name was Joey, and he was a nice enough guy. He'd never activated my creep radar. He was a lonely, married guy in his early forties, not too bad on the eyes, either.

The tune he selected was "Feeling Good," by Michael Bublee. It was a slower tune, with an almost "striptease" beat to it: a very bold and sensual arrangement.

Once I took the stage, I saw Slate sitting with his biker buddies at the next horseshoe stage. This was perfect.

I slowly danced over to Joey, using the music to move my body sensually as I went to the pole in front of him. I did a slow fireman's spiral around the pole, arching my back so that I could feel the tip of my ponytail hit my scantily-clad ass.

I did a slow, seductive climb and hitched my leg around the pole, arching my back as I twirled downward in front of him. I left the pole and danced seductively over to the edge of the stage where Joey sat, his eyes glued to my cleavage and crotch. As I rolled my hips provocatively, I raised my right leg up parallel with the bar, and allowed myself to spiral slowly around it.

I noticed from beneath my nearly closed lashes that I had Slate's attention. He'd stopped in mid-sentence to gaze over at me.

I licked my red lips for Joey, dropping down to kneel in front of him, and presenting him with an unobstructed view of my pushed-up breasts. I did a side roll, sweeping my outside leg around so that I was now in an outstretched position on the stage, my torso less than a foot away from Joey's face.

As the song ended, I could feel the heat of Slate's stare on me. I loved the fact that he was bothered. I could feel his vibes from the next stage over.

I smiled at Joey. His eyes had widened in pleasure at my slow, sensual dance for him. He licked his lips, smiling back as I blew him a kiss. I whispered I'd meet him at table six in the back as I left the stage. I heard some loud applause along with the usual cat whistles as I descended the steps and went behind the curtain.

Pearl was up next.

"Wow," she said, "you're a hard act to follow tonight, girl. Give the rest of us a break, huh?" She was smiling at me.

"Thanks, Pearl. You'll do great, as always," I assured her as the music started and she was announced.

I made my way out the side entrance to the main floor and was immediately greeted by a scowling Slate. My first instinct was to simply walk by and ignore him, but that would only prove to him that I was jealous or trying to make him jealous, which was the truth. I quickly decided another strategy was in order.

"Hi, Slate," I greeted with a smile. "I don't think Garnet comes on until later."

"What the fuck did you think you were doing out there?" he hissed, not bothering to hide his anger.

"What I'm paid to do, baby. What's it to you?" I asked, putting some heat in my voice.

"Dancing like that's going to give you more than you bargained for around here, Diamond. You need to take it down a notch."

"Joey seemed to like it," I snipped, starting to walk away. He grabbed my arm, spinning me around.

"This isn't a game, Diamond. This is for real. You're bringing way too much attention to yourself and it's not safe to do that in a place like this."

"I think I can take care of myself, Slate. But thanks for worrying." I saw Ethan approaching at the same time Slate did.

"Don't be stupid, Diamond," he snapped, before walking off.

I nodded to Ethan that everything was fine. His touch had electrified me. He had an astounding effect on me and I'd be damned if it didn't piss me off.

I found Joey waiting for me at table six with my usual glass of club soda. We chatted for about ten minutes, and all the while I was thinking of Slate and what he'd said to me. Maybe this had nothing to do with jealousy. Maybe it was something more ominous than that. Now I was bothered by what almost seemed like a warning.

Chapter 12

I was counting my tips from Thursday and tonight. I'd brought in a little more than seven hundred dollars. I had dressed in my street clothes and was waiting for Ethan to walk me to the bus stop. Slate had hung around the club for a while.

I noticed he hadn't acted interested whatsoever when Garnet came in before her late shift. I found that a bit puzzling. Perhaps the sex hadn't been that good for one of them. He was gone by the time my shift was over.

Ethan came up to where I was standing at the door, shrugging his jacket on.

"Let's do it," he said, opening the front door for me as some bikers were on their way in.

"I swear to fuck, I wish Janine would ban all of them from this place. They don't fucking pay me enough to put up with the shit that always seems to be going down with those fuckers. It wasn't enough they got the former 'Diamond' hooked on coke and Oxy."

"Come on, Ethan, you know she had a choice in that, don't you think?"

He shrugged, pulling a Marlboro from his chest pocket and lighting it. Ethan didn't mind doing bus stop detail with me because it gave him a smoke break.

"Lilly was young, impressionable, you know?"

"Lilly?"

"Yeah, that's her real name: Lilly. She's only twenty-two. It's pretty fucked up. She got all starry-eyed over Slash. He's like the local chapter's ringleader. He's pushing forty, man."

"Yeah, that's way old," I said with a sigh.

"It is for a twenty-two year old from Sioux City, Iowa. She had "daddy" issues, I guess. Her old man threw her out when she turned eighteen. She has brains, you know? She was trying to put herself through community college while working here. Then she gets involved with Slash. He turns her on to coke. She says it helps her stay up for school and then work, just another tragedy waitin' to happen. She falls one night at work and fucks up her ankle. That's when ole Slash turned her on to Oxy. There was no turning back after that," he said, taking a drag off of his cigarette.

I started to ask Ethan which one was Slash when we were interrupted by a male voice behind us.

"Diamond, can I walk you the rest of the way to your stop?"

Ethan and I both turned to see Slate standing behind us. I knew Ethan was ready to spout off. Something told me that wouldn't be a good idea.

"Ethan, it's okay," I said, touching his arm. "Slate's a friend."

"Humph," Ethan replied, not bothering to hide the contempt in his voice. He hesitated, torn about leaving me with a biker that he obviously despised, like all of the rest of them.

"Really, its fine," I assured him with a smile.

"If we don't see you again, Diamond, I'll let the cops know the name of the scum you called a friend."

With that, he turned and headed back to the club.

I was looking at Slate now, taking in his tall, strong build, the tightness of his jeans, his expertly polished boots, and black leather jacket. He'd changed his earring. It was now a dangly skull with crossbones. How appropriate.

"Can we talk, maybe get a coffee?" he asked.

His hands were hooked in the pocket of his jeans; his weight was shifted to one side and he had a slight slouch going on that I found totally sexy in a James Dean sort of way. His eyes were intense.

"This is the last bus --"

"I can take you wherever you need to go, Diamond. I can give you a ride home, wherever that is, or I can take you to the Park and Ride."

My head immediately snapped up to look into his eyes. He'd followed the bus to see where I'd gotten off. Why? He saw the alarm in my eyes.

"Relax," he said. "I admit it. I followed the bus on my bike that night to see where you went. I was worried you were undercover. It's instinctual for someone like me."

I eyed him warily. How much more did he know?

"I saw you get off the bus at the Park and Ride. I kind of figured it out for myself."

"Figured what out? Did you follow me?" I asked him, narrowing my eyes.

"I didn't have to," he said with a shrug. "I told you, babe, I'm instinctual."

I looked up at his gorgeous face.

"Your old man doesn't know that you dance, right?"

I nodded and remained silent.

"He probably thinks you have another type of job, maybe waitressing at some greasy spoon, or working the at some dive bar near the Park and Ride. I'm betting he doesn't know the kind of tips you're pulling in, does he?"

I nodded my head again, confirming that he was on target.

"I'm guessing you're tucking that money away, probably saving up a little nest egg to get away from the violent bastard."

I didn't respond as my bus was coming, and I moved toward the curb. I didn't know why he wanted to talk to me or what he really had planned, but it wasn't worth the risk of being front page news the following day for having been found in some ditch with my throat slit.

"Wait," he said gently, taking my hand.

I was forced to look into those smoldering bold eyes. "I really don't mean you any harm, Diamond, just a cup of coffee and some conversation, please?"

My mind raced for what to do. If he was telling the truth, he hadn't waited around to see me leave the lot in my Mercedes. Therefore, he hadn't followed me home. He didn't appear to pose an immediate risk. There was a purpose to his wanting to talk to me. I was curious about that. I looked up and nodded at his expectant gaze. He waved the bus on by.

This was it. The choice had been made. I was at Slate's mercy. I only hoped that my instincts about him posing no danger to me were on target.

I turned from him, searching the parking lot we had just traipsed through and both sides of the street.

"Where's your bike?"

I looked up into his amused eyes.

"It's almost December, Diamond, and its freaking cold out. I have my pick-up."

I followed to where he was pointing and saw a black Ford Ranger pick-up truck parked by the curb. It wasn't brand new, but it certainly wasn't a clunker either.

We walked over to the truck, and he pushed his remote, unlocking the doors. I headed toward the passenger side, expecting him to open my door for me. He was circling around the bed of his truck to get into the driver's side.

Once we were inside the cab of his pick-up, he instructed me to fasten my seat belt.

Really, Slate?

"So, where do you want to go for coffee?" he asked, glancing over at me.

"Seriously?"

He gave me a puzzled look. I almost wanted to laugh but thought better of it.

"I'd rather have a drink."

"I didn't know you drank, Diamond. I've only ever seen you have club soda."

"That's because I'm working. I'm off work and I'd like a drink. Somewhere not seedy, please."

"You've got it, babe," he replied.

He pulled his pick-up truck into a small, neighborhood-type bar about a mile-and-a-half from the club called "The Crystal Pistol." It wasn't as seedy as most of the clubs around it, only because it didn't draw a young, rowdy crowd, mostly a group past fifty that were, thankfully, un-rowdy at this point in their lives.

Slate and I slid into a booth in the corner. Our server took our drink orders. I ordered a double tequila shooter, and I noticed Slate's raised brow. He ordered bourbon on the rocks.

"So," I said, "what do you want to talk about?"

"Diamond," he started, and then quickly got a look of irritation on his face. "It would help if I knew your real name. Do you mind?"

"Yes, I do. I'll give you my first name only. It's Sunny," I lied.

I mean, seriously? Did I truly believe his given name was Slate?

"Thank you," he responded, piquing my curiosity at his manners. "That helps. Sunny, I know I don't know you very well. Hell, you don't know me, either. You have no reason to trust or to even believe me, but you remind me of someone, a person that I used to know and care about. Anyway, all I'm trying to say is that I don't think it's safe for you to continue dancing at Jewels. As a matter of fact, I think you need to quit."

Our server brought our drinks, and I downed mine, ordering another. God, it tasted so good.

"Slate, forgive me if I've got this stereotypical thing going here, but for the love of Jesus, I can't believe a member of the Outlaws has taken it upon himself to worry about a pole dancer at a somewhat seedy gentleman's club."

"First of all, I'm not a patched member of OMC yet. I'm what they call a 'prospect.' I was patched into a club in Virginia called the Mongols before coming to Indy. The Outlaws recruited both my buddy Taz and me. We've been here about six months. We're checking it out and deciding if the OMC is what we want."

"Excuse me for being ignorant on all of the biker lingo and politics, but exactly what's the difference between being a Mongol and an Outlaw?"

I saw the smile cross his face. It was pure sexy. He took my hands in his large ones, his thumbs caressing my fingertips gently.

"Hmm, great question. Let me see if I can put this into chick terms. I guess it's kind of like shoes. I've noticed you have a thing for shoes. So, let's say that OMC is Prada and Mongol is Stride Rite."

I totally got it. He knew that. I could tell by his sexy smile.

I had a couple of more drinks and was feeling totally buzzed when it finally dawned on me that we needed to finish the conversation he'd started about me working at Jewels.

"Slate," I halfway slurred, "you've explained all of this shit about the Mongrels and now the Outlaws… . . ."

"Mongols," he corrected me, with slight agitation.

"Whatever," I said, waving my hand dismissively, "but what you haven't explained is why you think it's dangerous for *me* to work there. I don't get involved with those bikers. So what is it?"

"I just don't think you belong there, Sunny. I'd prefer it if you found another job, something that doesn't involve that type of clientele."

"You mean clientele such as yourself?" I asked, my index finger waggling at him.

"Yeah, exactly. I'm no good for you, and the rest of those assholes sure as hell aren't good enough for you. Take this as a friendly warning to someone I don't want to see hurt. Humor me, please?"

I took the final swig of my latest drink, and then looked him straight in the eye, sort of. I was starting to weave a bit.

"You're awfully bossy, aren't you?" I asked with a giggle. I then leaned over closer, my voice a husky whisper. "What's in it for me, Slate?"

He could tell that I was shit-faced. His demeanor changed abruptly to one of no-nonsense. His hand reached across the table, gripping my upper arm tightly.

"I'm serious, Sunny. You need to go back to whatever trailer park you came from. Trust me; you're out of your league here."

His voice was calm, yet highly authoritative. I kind of liked that.

For whatever reason, I started giggling. He thought I was trailer trash. How ludicrous was that? A biker was looking down his nose at me. I couldn't stop, even when I looked over and saw his extremely somber expression.

"You're fucked up. We're outta here. Come on, I'm taking you home."

He left two twenty-dollar bills on the table, and pulled me out of my seat across from him in the booth. He helped me with my jacket and led me out to the parking lot where his pick-up truck was parked. Just before we got to his truck, I felt the ground underneath of me start to spin.

Oh God - I'm going to heave...

The next thing I knew, I was leaning over in the parking lot and tossing my cookies all over the pavement.

I vaguely remember Slate helping me into his truck and me accusing him of slipping me a roofie. I vaguely remember him chuckling and saying, "I don't think so, babe."

He took me to a motel and got a room.

This was it. I was now going to know what it felt like to be raped by a probationary member of the OMC, as opposed to being raped by my husband. Hell, my money said Slate would be gentler.

The last thing I remembered was Slate peeling my clothes off until I was down to my thong underwear and push-up bra. He pulled the bedspread back and got me under the covers, checking first to see if I thought I was going to heave again. I gave him the all clear signal and promptly passed out, seeing him sitting on one of the chairs next to the bed, channel surfing with the remote.

God, he's gorgeous.

Chapter 13

I awoke the following morning with a headache and cotton mouth in a strange room. It took me a couple of minutes to think back and fast forward to where I was.

I sat up in bed abruptly, looking around the room. I was alone. The door to the bathroom was open, so I presumed Slate wasn't in there. I didn't see his jacket strewn anywhere, just my clothes.

My cheeks felt flushed when I recalled him undressing me before I passed out beneath the sheets of this hotel room bed. The clock radio on the bedside table said it was 8:43 a.m.

I got up and out of the bed, wondering why in the hell he'd simply left me here to fend for myself. I wasn't even sure where the hell I was, as far as where this motel was located. I saw a piece of paper and some cash on top of my jacket, which was on one of the chairs. It was a note from Slate.

Sunny,

Call yourself a cab when you get up. I needed to leave. Here's some cash for the cab. Remember what I said. Call Janine and let her know you won't be back. It's not safe for you to be there. Please listen to what I'm saying to you, Diamond Girl. I care.

-Slate

What the hell? Nice guy.

I went to the bathroom sink, splashing cold water on my face and rinsing my mouth out thoroughly. What in God's name had I been thinking getting trashed like that with a biker that I hardly knew?

I hurriedly dressed and gathered my stuff. I wasn't sure why Slate had left cash for me. I had all my tips in my purse, unless he'd ripped me off and had enough of a conscience to leave cab fare. I checked my purse; the wad of bills was still rubber-banded together at the bottom. I was thankful that I kept my billfold with all of my identification in it, along with my cell phone, locked in the glove box of my car.

I called a cab to take me to the Park and Drive lot. I was home before ten. I had a million things to do before Jack got in the next day. I wanted to make sure the laundry was done to his expectations. I needed to make sure the refrigerator and cupboards were well-stocked, and that the ironing was caught up for his majesty.

My first order of business after I'd showered and dressed was to get one of the other girls to take my shifts for me next week. I found the list with their cell phone numbers on it in my billfold and started calling. Emerald agreed to take my Tuesday and Thursday shifts. Opal, another new hire, jumped at the chance to take my Friday shift. I let Janine know of the switches. She was fine with it, asking no questions.

By the time Jack rolled in the following afternoon, all remnants of my secret life were safely tucked away and the house was in perfect order, just the way he liked it. I'd made a roast chicken for dinner. Our conversation was the typical above surface discussions about Lindsey, the house, his work, and my answering his numerous questions about this or that.

He went up to his office after dinner, as I cleaned up the kitchen, and he remained there until nearly eleven o'clock. I'd fallen asleep on the sofa in the family room. Jack woke me and instructed me to come to bed. I felt my stomach turn at the thought of him touching me. I had no desire for him after my attempt to seduce him the last time he was home had resulted in violent sex and a black eye.

I lingered in the bathroom getting ready for bed, taking an extra-long shower and giving myself a facial. I breathed a sigh of relief upon entering our room and finding Jack sleeping soundly.

I crawled quietly into our bed, the bed that had become mostly mine for the past couple of months. I found that I liked having the whole bed to myself. I turned on my side, away from Jack. I thought about those piercing blue eyes that continued to haunt me. I thought about how I wouldn't mind sharing a bed with him.

The week ahead seemed to drag on for an eternity. I was anxious for Jack to be back out on the road so that I could resume the life (and identity) that had come to be mine. I realized it was a sick existence, to some extent. For now, it was my therapy until I could feel comfortable in making the break I knew I needed to make. I was going to discuss it with Becky this week. We were having lunch on Friday.

Jack had checked my job performance on the handling of our finances since he'd delegated it to me. He actually complimented me on my accuracy.

"You did really well on handling the books," he said, coming into the laundry room where I was ironing his fifth shirt.

"Jack, I saw an electronic cash deposit made through an ATM in Virginia come through. I wasn't sure how you wanted me to post that on the Excel file, since typically the deposits are payroll or transfer. Was this a one-time thing?"

"Oh, that," he replied, turning to head back out to the family room. "One of the company cars was involved in a collision. I meant to deposit the check from the other driver's insurance company into the business account for that branch office while I was down there. I cashed it by mistake. It had been made out to me. I'm glad you reminded me. I need to issue a check from our personal account to Banion Pharmaceutical Eastern District Office. I'll do that now."

By Friday afternoon, my nerves were frayed as I headed out to meet Becky for lunch. It wasn't as if Jack had done or said anything. It was simply the fact that I missed the life I'd carved out for myself in his absence. I was back to being lackluster Samantha. I was bored and I missed dancing, but mostly, I missed Slate.

Becky noticed right away as the waitress left with our order.

"Okay," she said, "what's Jack done now?"

"He hasn't done anything. He's just home."

"And that's not a good thing, why?"

"Because I finally realized something, Becky - something I should've realized a long time ago. I don't want to be married to Jack anymore. I probably never really did."

Her eyes widened as she looked at me in disbelief.

"I don't know why you're acting all shocked, Bec. You've never been a fan of his. I believe you refer to him as a mannequin most of the time."

"Yeah, I get that, but what brought you to this realization? I mean, you always seemed satisfied with the…mannequin."

I shrugged. "I've gotten a taste of being on my own, making my own money, and not having to answer to him - to anyone. I like it."

"Would you like to clue me in on what the hell you're talking about, Sam? I know we don't see each other as often as we used to, but we talk at least once a week. You've never mentioned a thing about making your own money. Did you get a job?"

There it was. I needed to confide in my best friend. She would either think that I'd gone off the deep end and was in dire need of medication and psychotherapy, or she'd be happy that I'd finally started to live. Either way, she would be honest with me, no holds barred. I told her everything.

Once I'd spilled everything to her, I sat back and waited for her reaction. It took her a couple of minutes to digest everything. I saw her mind coming to terms with what I'd told her about the club, Slate, and even Jack's abuse.

She finally broke the silence.

"Sam, when I encouraged you to get a hobby or take classes, or get a job, it was more along the lines of making pottery, taking a cooking class, or working part-time at Bed, Bath & Beyond. I'd no clue you'd go and create some wild-child alter-ego and live on the edge."

"So, you don't approve?"

"I don't think it's *my* place to approve or disapprove. You're my best friend and I don't judge you like that. I *can* be concerned though. I guess that's what I am: *concerned.*"

"Concerned that I've lost my mind?"

"Now, I didn't say that. Don't put words into my mouth. I'm concerned about where you're working and the clientele that you seem to be drawn to, at least one of them. What do you know about Slate?"

"Not much," I admitted. "All I know is that he totally fascinates me, despite the age difference."

"How old is he?"

"I'm not sure. I'd guess mid-to-late twenties, maybe."

"Seriously, that's the least of your worries, Sam. He's a biker in a gang, a notorious one at that."

"They aren't called gangs, Bec. They're a *club.*"

"Whatever," she said, waving her hand impatiently. "The point is that you're literally flirting with danger. It's unsafe. Are you telling me the truth about this being the first time ever that Jack physically abused you?"

"Of course. Why would I lie?"

"Okay. So now that you've told me all of this, do I get to have an opinion?"

"Of course."

"Am I allowed to verbalize it?"

I nodded at her, rolling my eyes.

"I think you need to take Slate's advice and quit that job for your own safety. I fully support whatever you decide. I seriously hope you leave that bastard you married, and find a life somewhere in-between."

"In between what?"

"In between that "Stepford Wife" existence you've lived for the past nineteen years and the "Easy Rider" life you've got going on now."

"I *knew* you wouldn't understand," I said, rolling my eyes at her once again.

"I *do* understand, Samantha. I understand that your marriage is a farce and that you realize that now. But this isn't the answer, you know?"

I remained silent...getting my sulk on.

"Hey, I'm all for you being with a younger guy, if that's what you want, but get rid of Jack first. Don't enter a new relationship with the old baggage still attached. I also think you need to find a different type of guy. Do you really see yourself with a member of the Outlaws? I think that's something that spawned from the fact that you never got to be a teenager. You never got to go through that phase where bad-boys were all that attracted you."

"Oh, and like *you* did?" I asked incredulously. "You've been with George, *forever.*"

"We met in college, Sam, and not until my junior year. My freshman and sophomore years? Hey, I was all about dating the bad-boys. You were happily ensconced in your imaginary Stepford life of bliss. We didn't talk much, but I was dating some real losers."

"Yeah? So why am I just now hearing about it?"

"Wasn't one of my proudest moments, those couple of years," she replied. I could tell she was thinking back on them now.

"How bad were they?"

"Well, let's see. They were all *townies*, of course. Most of them were high school drop-outs. The first one I dated was Ritchie. God, we were together for like six months. He'd self-tattooed his body in places that shouldn't ever have tattoos. He had the names of every person he'd ever fucked tattooed on his body."

"No shit?"

"Yep," she said, shaking her head. "I used to find new ones all the time. The day I found the name "Marvin" tattooed on his left thigh was the day I knew it was over."

"Oh my God!"

"After that came Butch. He worked at a gas station near campus. I loved his sultry, pouty, chip-on-the-shoulder look. He was great in the sack, too. We did it every way and everywhere. Once we did it in the cemetery during a full moon. That was totally erotic. I used to tell my roommate in the dorm all of the lurid details. She thought I was making it all up. One night, I got back early from a night class, and I found Butch doing my roommate in our dorm room."

"My God, Becky. I had no clue."

"So you see what I'm saying though, right? With some girls, going out with bad boys is like... . . . a rite of passage. You never got yours, Sam. I'm just saying it's ludicrous to think that I would've ever *married* one of those idiots. It was just a phase."

"So, you think my attraction to Slate is *my* postponed bad-boy rite-of-passage phase?"

"I think so, Sam, but it's something that you'll likely need to do in order to get it out of your system."

"Then you wouldn't like *disown* me as a BFF if I did?" I couldn't believe that I was even considering it. I'd never considered cheating on Jack. Ever. I mean I was certain that Jack was cheating now with Susan; and maybe he had in the past as well, but still two wrongs and all that jazz didn't give me a free pass. Still - there was just something about . . . Slate.

"Honey, you don't need my permission to fuck some young bad-boy. I'm just saying you need to be careful. He comes from a whole different world than my college bad-boys."

Chapter 14

I felt like a giddy teenager as I prepared for my Tuesday shift at the club. I took extra care with my waxing for my first night back since Jack had hit the road again.

I packed another new dance outfit in my garment bag for tonight. It was a silver-sequined cutout, one-piece monokini swimsuit. The cutout was in front and the sparkly material only covered the barest of necessities.

I'd been getting Brazilian waxes over the past month. That was one reason I was glad Jack hadn't wanted sex. He definitely would've wondered about my baldness down there, not that he ever really *looked* at what he fucked.

Jack had never cared for being the provider of oral sex. He enjoyed the recipient role only. He was a taker and always had been. Tonight, I was in the mood for both.

Margo was happy to see me back. She said that no one knew why I hadn't been in last week. That was her way of prying it out of me. I simply told her I needed a break to take care of some personal business. She fussed over my hair and make-up; styling my long-tressed wig into an exotic bunch of loose curls that framed my face. She added matching extensions to it, so it went down nearly to my waist.

I got into my 4-inch spiked heels and added my silver grip gloves that were attached to wrist cuffs.

"Has Slate been in?"

"Yep. I saw him in last Friday with that wild bunch. He was sitting with Slash, that fucking dirtball."

"Slate?"

"No, Slash. I hate that mother-fucker for what he is and does. Don't get me started on that fuckin' pill pusher."

I honored her request. It wasn't often I saw Margo get that steamed up about someone.

Opal came in just then. "You're up, Diamond."

"Thanks," I said, handing Margo her money. "See you in a few."

My first dance was dancer's choice for the music. I'd told Kevin I wanted "Slow Dancing in a Burning Room" by John Mayer for my first dance. It was a slow, sensual song. I loved the lyrics. It was my message to Slate. I prayed that my bad boy was out there. I heard the first chords to the song start as I slipped onto the stage.

There he was, sitting along the side of the stage where my dance was being performed. There were four or five others with him, all in the signature leather jackets and colors of OMC. He did a double-take when Kevin announced me as I walked out. Whoever was sitting next to him let out a low growl as I danced seductively for Slate. His face darkened. He was pissed. Even from where I was, I could see the muscle in his cheek twitch.

Oh, shit...

I didn't take my eyes from Slate. Even when his buddy tossed several bills on the floor in front of me, ordering me to bend down and pick them up, I kept my eyes on him.

Typically, the money was put in a large glass jar on the side. This biker asshole was trying to make a point. I wasn't going for it. It wasn't about the money for me; it'd always been about the dance. I was the only one that knew that.

I continued my graceful, seductive moves, taking the pole and doing slow, sensual slides, wrapping my leg around it, and twirling to the melodic music of this song meant for Slate and no one else.

The biker dude that had tossed the money was starting to get a bit louder, more obnoxious. I noticed his denim vest had quite a few emblems on it. Maybe he was the big kahuna. One patch was of a skull and crossed pistons. The top read "Outlaws" and the bottom portion read "Fort Wayne." There was another patch on the front that was a white diamond-shaped emblem trimmed in red that had "1%" on it.

I wondered if the Indianapolis chapter was hosting visitors from Fort Wayne this evening. I certainly didn't appreciate the guy's big mouth. He was getting pissed that I hadn't interrupted my dance to bend over and pick up the handful of twenty-dollar bills he'd tossed on the runway.

"Come on, baby," he yelled. "Bend over and pick up the cash. We want to see some tits!"

I tried my best to ignore the comment. I didn't want it to throw my rhythm off. I could see Slate's demeanor worsening by the second. What had started out to be my dance for Slate was turning into a free-for-all with the barbs and cat whistles amongst the group.

"Come on, Bunny! We want to see if those are bolt-on's you got there!"

I'd taken all of the lip I was going to from this ass-trap. I didn't give a shit what type of violent, abhorrent behavior he was capable of unleashing. The freakin' bouncers weren't addressing the issue, and they sure as hell needed to! They were probably intimidated. I could see Slate saying something to the loud mouth right now.

Fantastic. Now Slate's jabbing his finger into the dude's chest...

I strained to hear over the music what was being said. Finally, I heard motor mouth give Slate a half-assed apology.

"Chill, Slate. I didn't know the chick was your Betty, man."

Who in the hell is Betty?

I was never so grateful for a song to be over. I hurried off the stage behind the curtain. I saw Garnet in the chair getting ready. She smirked as I walked by to the restroom. I found a stall and sat on the commode. I was shaking. I'd been humiliated out there. I'd been treated like female trash by that loud-mouthed, piece-of-shit biker from Fort Wayne.

I stayed hidden in the stall, licking my wounds when Margo finally poked her head in and asked if I was okay.

"I'm fine."

"Uhh, well Kevin came back looking for you. Slate bought a private drink for you."

"Tell Kevin to return his money. I'm not having a drink with that S.O.B."

"Diamond, you know how Janine feels about turning those down. It's a lot of money for the club."

"Hells bells, I'll pay it out of my tips then, Margo. I'm not going back out there until my next number."

"Okay, okay," she said, soothingly. "I'll pass the word along to Kevin."

Forty-five minutes later with my pride semi-intact, I went out to wait behind stage for my next number. I heard Kevin announce the next song was a request for Diamond. It was "Bad Girlfriend" by the group Theory of a Deadman.

Shit. I knew it was Slate. This song was something else, difficult for pole-dancing for the style that I liked because it was loud and fast; there was no pause or smooth transitioning. He'd done this to punish me. I wasn't sure if it was for not quitting the club, or for refusing his private drink.

I took the stage and immediately saw his eyes burning into me. He regarded me coldly. It was as if I'd somehow humiliated him and now it was payback time. I swallowed nervously as I took the stage. I tried like hell to keep up with the beat of the song. I was distracted by him and the others.

As I descended the pole in a fast, upside down twirl, I saw Slate toss a one-dollar bill on the floor next to me. His eyes looked at me in pure anger.

Tossing a one-dollar bill at a dancer was the worst kind of insult. It was along the lines of leaving a penny as a tip for a server. It sent the message to the recipient that he or she was a piece-of-shit. That was Slate's message to me.

I felt the tears well up in my overly made-up eyes. He expected me to pick it up. That was the price for his forgiveness. I somehow understood that without having to be told. I was expected to acknowledge his insult so that he could save face with the rest of his biker cronies.

What the hell?

I climbed the pole and arched my back doing a downward spiral. My arms were free, and as I neared the bottom, I picked up the dollar bill. I looked at Slate and saw the smug look of satisfaction cross his face. In that instant, I hated his guts. His comrades seemed pleased with his dismissive treatment of me. The big mouth from Fort Wayne was clapping him on the back as he downed his beer.

Fuck them all and the bikes they rode in on.

Blessedly, the song was over. I went back stage and asked Opal if she would cover my last dance for the night. I gave her fifty bucks to do it.

I went to the locker room and quickly got out of my costume and into my jeans and sweater. I pulled my new Ugg sweater boots on and got my purse and jacket out. I was outta there.

Hopefully, there was a bus due shortly. I slipped out of the back door and ran across the parking lot towards the corner where the bus stopped. I was nearly there when I felt strong arms grab me from behind.

I started to scream before a hand clamped firmly over my mouth, and I was hauled over to the sidewalk near the curb. I recognized Slate's pick-up truck. I saw the lights flash as the remote was activated, unlocking it. I was in Slate's arms, I realized now. That didn't make it any less scary for me.

Chapter 15

I was in Slate's truck. I wasn't sure where we were going, but he seemed determined that we were going somewhere.

He was still obviously pissed. For whatever reason, the personal humiliation he'd doled out to me with his song choice, then tossing the one-dollar bill for me to pick up hadn't fully assuaged his need to punish me.

I finally broke the steely silence.

"I hope you know that kidnapping is a major felony," I spat. "Of course, it may be *minor* compared to what you do on a typical day."

"Not a word, Sunny. Not *one fucking* word until we get where we're going. Do you understand?" It was a quiet threat.

"Where are we going?"

His hands tightened the steering wheel. "You can't listen to a goddamn thing I say, can you?" His voice was still measured, spoken in an almost careful way. And that was somehow scarier than if he had raised his voice.

I didn't answer his question because I knew he'd explode. Several blocks later, he pulled over to the curb. It was in an older neighborhood. There was an alley running along the side of the building that he'd pulled up near.

"Get out," he ordered gruffly.

I scrambled to get the passenger door opened and jumped down from his truck. I was now following him around to the side of the building. It looked to be a neighborhood carry-out store. On the side of the building there was a wooden staircase leading up to an apartment. I actually wondered if I was in for some type of biker gang-bang. My legs were wobbly, but there was no way out of this. I had to trust my instincts about Slate.

Slate turned around briefly to make sure that I was still behind him. He mounted the exterior staircase taking two steps at a time. He was already inside the door by the time I got to the top of the landing.

"Get your ass in here," I heard him bellow from inside.

I quickly opened the storm door and went in. I heard the interior door slam shut behind me. The sound of the deadbolt lock being put into place followed.

I turned and faced my gorgeous kidnapper. He must have seen the look of uncertainty in my eyes at that moment, and he must've sensed that I knew I was at his mercy.

He took my shoulder bag from my arm and tossed it onto the kitchen table. I looked around quickly. This must be his apartment. We were in his kitchen. In one quick movement, he had me in his arms.

"Sunny," he breathed against my wig, "What the fuck did you think you were doing tonight, babe?"

I raised my head to look into his incredibly blue eyes. The anger was gone. His eyes were searching mine now. He really needed an answer.

"I just wanted to dance for you, Slate. It was just for you. I didn't mean to make you mad." I heard my voice tremble with the truth. There it was.

"Oh, baby," he breathed, cupping my face in his strong hands. "You shouldn't have come back to the club. I thought you'd taken my advice when I didn't see you last week."

"I don't want to quit, Slate. I wouldn't see you anymore if I left."

He considered me for a quick moment, his eyes still searching mine. "You don't even *know* me, Sunny. You don't know what it is that I do. You don't *fit* into my world, baby."

"Maybe I could," I said, realizing how pathetic that probably sounded to him. I had to remember that he thought I was trailer trash.

He lowered his lips to mine, his fingers under my chin, tilting my face upward. His eyes were smoldering with something. It wasn't anger. He kissed me softly, my lips eager to respond to his. I felt him nipping and gently tugging at my bottom lip. His tongue caressed my upper lip, tracing an outline slowly and sensually. I felt myself tingle in anticipation of what came next. Where were these feelings and sensations coming from? This was foreign to me.

I'd never been kissed like this before and my pulse quickened as his tongue slipped inside of me, exploring my mouth, and teasing my tongue. I laced my arms around his neck tightly, and pressed myself into him, answering his kiss with a passion of my own, one that up until now, I hadn't known I possessed. I was dizzy with his closeness, his taste, his touch, his scent. His hands were brushing against my hips, drawing me into him even closer, massaging the back of my thighs in a circular motion. I released a soft whimper, my hand now fisting in his hair.

He pulled back, gazing down at me with hooded eyes. But his thick eyelashes still couldn't hide the inner war I saw behind them. And when I felt his hands suddenly grip the back of my thighs, lifting me up. I wasn't sure if he'd won or lost.

He carried me effortlessly into another room off of the living room, his mouth still working mine.

God this man can kiss.

Suddenly, I felt a soft mattress underneath me, and his arms were no longer locked around me as he took a step back. I looked around the darkened room, and knew instantly that this was Slate's bedroom.

He licked his bottom lip, dragging his teeth over it as he seemed to be sucking on my taste. "Get undressed for me," he ordered softly, his eyes flickering over my now-flushed face and neck.

I moved quickly to obey him, kicking off my boots and raising my sweater up and over my head. I unfastened my jeans, lowering them down past my hips until they fell into a heap on the floor. I stepped out of them. I unclasped my bra, in front, letting it slip from my shoulders. All that remained on me was the silky black thong I wore.

"This too," he said, coming up behind me, snaking his arms around my hips, and hooking his thumbs into the elastic band on the thong. I shimmied it down to my ankles with his help, feeling his hardness pressed up against my backside as I stepped out of it.

I heard his boots hit the floor behind me as he took a seat on his bed. His leather jacket followed, landing on a chair across the room. I hadn't turned back around, frightened, yet fascinated by what I was allowing him to do.

"Sunny," he said, "Turn around, babe. I want to see you."

I turned around slowly, raising my eyes to his as he stood there now, completely naked and totally unaffected by having my eyes studying him from top to bottom and then back again.

Jesus!

His muscles bulged beautifully in all of the right places. He had an impressive tattoo of a snake winding up a sword on his back shoulder; another one of the Celtic symbol on his left upper arm. A silver cross on a chain hung around his neck. His stomach was firm and muscular. It was male-model flat.

Damn!

He looked as if he *could've* been a model, *should've* been a model, not a biker who lived a life of crime. I mentally told myself not to think about that part. Not now at least.

Slate's eyes were resting below my bare hips. I watched as he brought his hand up to his rock-hard cock, and began to slowly stroke himself. I was mesmerized by the movement.

"Come here," he gently ordered in a dark voice. "I want to touch your pussy. I want to see if it's worthy of my cock."

I obeyed, moving to stand in front of him, watching his face so that I could see some sign of approval.

He kept his eyes on mine, refusing to let me look away as I felt his thumb and forefinger from his other hand traced the cleft of my pussy. I sucked in my lower lip and watched as his eyes immediately latched onto my mouth.

"You shave your pussy. I like that."

I felt my face flush under his unrelenting gaze.

He stopped stroking his cock, grabbed my hand, and brought it to the hot skin of his shaft.

Reflexively, I fisted it, and had to hold back a moan as I heard his gravel-like growl when he leaned into my touch. All the while, he was using two fingers to rub the lips of my pussy in an almost teasing way. I wanted them inside me, so I tightened my grip on Slate's cock and began a hard stroke.

"Fuck," he exhaled, his hips rolling up as I pumped him. His thumb strummed over my clit, and he sank a thick finger into me. My breathing became a little more broken, and a bit shallower as he used it to match the rhythm of my hand.

I rested my forehead against his shoulder, biting back a moan. His teeth scraped the shell of my ear. "When you're on stage," he said in a rough voice, "you want to know what I think about, Sunny?"

I barely nodded. He rewarded me by pulling back his finger, curling it up as he did so, and returning with *two* fingers. I let out the moan I was holding back earlier, leaving it on his skin.

"I think about this," he pressed his thumb down hard on my clit. "About what you'd look like riding my hand...my face...my dick."

My hand was stroking him a little faster now, and I was trying to keep up with his fingers. He was so hard. I couldn't even make my fingers meet around his length.

I lowered myself to my knees in front of him, and took his full length into both of my hands. I knew from experience, if only with Jack, what to do orally to please a man.

I ran my tongue up and down the length of it several times before taking his cock fully into my mouth, swirling my tongue around it over and over again. I heard Slate's sharp intake of breath once again as I went from top to bottom sucking and swirling it alternately, my hands gently kneading his balls. He moaned. I hummed in gratification.

His hands were on my breasts, rubbing and massaging them with his clever fingers. He captured each nipple between his thumb and forefinger, squeezing them until I flinched with pain that was quickly followed by pleasure.

He pulled me up from where I was now vigorously sucking his cock and brought my face up to his, plunging his tongue inside of my mouth, tasting himself. He lifted me up, placing me on my back in the middle of his bed. His muscled thighs straddled my torso his erect cock teasing my erect nipples. He leaned over and pulled a condom from his bedside drawer, ripping the foil packet open with his teeth.

"I'm going to fuck you." He told me, brushing his thumb across my lower lip. "Because I need it, and you want it. Don't you?"

"Yes," I answered, "I want it."

I watched as he expertly rolled the condom onto his swollen cock. His thigh parted my legs as he lowered himself down and guided himself into me.

His lips were on mine, kissing me hungrily and passionately. With one strong thrust, he buried himself inside of me. The fullness was sweet to me. The fact that he continued to kiss me while we fucked was new to me. It was intimate and sexy. I loved it. My legs instinctively wrapped around his hips, pulling him deeper inside of me as I rolled my hips back and forth, side to side. My fingernails dug into his muscular back as waves of pleasure found me. My hands felt his sinewy muscles flex with each forceful thrust. It had never felt like this with Jack.

He rocked himself in and out of me, his hips swiveling so that his cock was hitting places deep within me that I hadn't known existed...until now. I heard myself moan in pleasure.

"You like that, don't you, baby?" He whispered the question into my ear, and his warm breath gave me chills as my fingers dug into his back. All I could do was moan as he plunged himself into me again, going deeper.

I felt his tongue now circle the inside of my ear, and then he gently nibbled on my ear lobe, which sent shivers through me. One hand was kneading my breast tenderly. His mouth was once again on mine as he groaned with pleasure.

"Your pussy's so fucking sweet. That's it, keep fucking me just like that, Diamond."

I wasn't sure if it was his sensual sex talk, the rhythm of his thrusting, or his magical fingers and the things they were doing to me; maybe it was all of the above. All I knew was that something extremely pleasurable and explosive was building up deep within my core. This was new also. I wasn't sure how long I'd be on the brink of something that felt like a much-needed release.

My breathing quickened as I whimpered with the pulsating pleasure that began unfolding within me. My thrusts quickened with his; my whimpers turned into moans of ecstasy as my first full-fledged orgasm exploded around me. I pulled him to me so tightly, I felt as if we were one.

"That's it, baby. Just let it come. I'm right there with you."

He arched his back and continued to thrust deeply within me, supporting his weight on his forearms on either side of me. His tongue was exploring my mouth again with a fury; his teeth nipping at my lips. I felt his muscles tense as he gave one final thrust and released his climax into me.

I was still gripping him tightly against me as he relaxed on top of me. My skin tingled everywhere in the aftermath of my orgasm.

My God, I've been missing this all along?

I felt tears rolling down my cheeks. I'd never felt as fulfilled as I did right now. I wasn't sure what the tears were about. I certainly didn't feel guilty. I felt cheated by my husband.

His lips were now soft against my sensitive skin as he kissed my shoulders, my neck and my earlobes gently and playfully. His fingers stroked my cheeks coming in contact with my tears. He rose up and gazed down at me quizzically.

"What is it? You wanted this, yeah?"

"I did. I do."

"Why the tears, babe?"

"You kissed me while we fucked. You gave me an orgasm. I'm emotional, I guess. Those are both firsts for me."

He pulled up and out of me, sitting next to me on the bed, his arms crossed over his knees as he gazed at me.

"Sunny, are you saying that your rat-bastard husband never kisses you when you make love?"

"I don't honestly think that we've ever made love, Slate."

"Okay then, when you fuck?"

"It's a rare occurrence, even more-so now, since the whole incident with the black eye, but he never has kissed me during sex."

"And you've never had an orgasm?"

"Not until today."

"What about when you pleasure yourself?"

I turned crimson under his scrutiny. "I don't do that," I mumbled, embarrassed.

"Jesus Christ. What the hell's his problem?"

"I thought it was me," I answered honestly.

He let out a sound that was somewhere between a growl and a laugh, "It's not you, babe, at least not with me it isn't. Your pussy was *made* for my cock."

He propelled himself off of the bed and removed the condom. I watched as he tied it in a knot and tossed it over into a trash can. He swaggered over to a dresser in the room and pulled out clean boxers and a tee shirt.

"I'm grabbing a shower. You sit tight. When I get finished, you and I are going to have a discussion. I'm going to educate you as to what's acceptable behavior, now that you're *mine*."

Chapter 16

It had been a little more than three weeks since Slate had made me his. I hadn't been sure what that would entail when he laid the rules out for me that day. Now, it was perfectly clear.

I was at his beck and call. I no longer worked at Jewels. I wasn't even allowed to go in there. He explained to me that Jewels was his turf and that I wasn't to invade it.

He bought me a prepaid cell phone. He'd presumed that my rat bastard husband didn't allow me to have a cell phone, so this was his means of communicating with me. His communications were generally text messages, kept short and sweet: "My place in an hour. We need to fuck."

Occasionally, he'd give it a more intimate touch by actually calling me on it. I'd hear his husky voice on the other end: "My place in an hour. We need to fuck." It was followed by radio silence.

I'd always accommodate him. I dressed the way he expected me to dress, kept my hair long the way he insisted. (He hadn't figured out it was a wig, which was probably because I never spent the night.)

He respected the fact that I was married and said he wasn't looking to steal another man's wife, even if the other man was a rat bastard.

He made a rule that I couldn't ask or expect him to share personal information about himself or what he did to occupy his time. I insisted the same rule apply to me. He agreed, with one exception: if I needed to find another job to support myself, he needed to know where it was in advance and approve of my working there. He absolutely forbade me to dance anywhere.

I was never to come by his place without having first received an express order to do so from Slate. I was to notify him by text when my period started so that he knew I'd be "out of commission"' for a few days. (That one had made me blush with embarrassment.)

I wasn't to phone him at all; text messages only. If the rat bastard was around, I was to shut my phone off. That was the only excusable time I was permitted to power it off.

I wasn't to have sex with Jack, unless refusing to do so posed imminent physical danger, in which case, I was to lay there like a limp rag doll and endure it. (I had wanted to burst out laughing when Slate had given me that rule. Jack didn't care if he *ever* touched me again.)

I was instructed to text him the words "Code Red" if the rat bastard left another mark on me. He would then text me specific instructions on when and where to go, with my husband in tow. There'd be peeps there to take care of the rat bastard and make it look totally random. (That one had sent shivers down my spine.)

Of course, the obvious and major rule was that no other man could touch me. He was the only one who could do that, and he intended to do so at every available opportunity.

I'd asked him if the same applied to him and other women. He said it did, as long as our relationship was deemed active. He would decide when it was over. (That one made me feel a bit sad.)

I wasn't to get tattoos, body piercings, or change hair color without obtaining his permission in advance. I was to work out to stay in shape.

He inquired what type of birth control I was using, as he didn't want to continue using condoms since we were to be exclusive. I told him I had a diaphragm. He didn't need to know any more than that. The truth was, I did still have my old diaphragm in the bedside drawer gathering dust. It had barely gotten any use. He told me to make sure I carried that with me when I was meeting him.

He assured me that he was clean as far as sexually transmitted diseases went, and he'd asked me to confirm the same to him. That had prompted a trip to the county health clinic that had weekly free screenings. I'd decided with Jack's travels, it wouldn't hurt to be sure. Everything had come back fine.

All in all, it was a fairly simple and uncomplicated relationship. I'd decided that I'd go with it as long as I was getting something from it, and I was: the best damned, toe-curling, orgasmic sex that I could ever have imagined. There was nothing Slate wouldn't do to make sure I was satisfied multiple times.

I'd received Slate's booty call about fifteen minutes prior. I was now slathering my make-up on and trying to get those fucking false eyelashes in place. Margo had always done it so easily. There, I finally had the second one in place. I finished applying generous amounts of the smoky, gray eye shadow from my brow line down. The eyeliner and mascara were midnight black.

I'd put my diaphragm in after my bath this morning, as I figured I was due for a call. It'd been three days. I tucked my own hair under the wig cap and securely put my long, shiny, brunette wig in place, wearing it down. I secured some extensions to it so that it was even longer. Wearing the extensions had proven a deterrent in keeping Slate's fingers out of my hair, therefore protecting my wig's identity.

I pulled a black, long-sleeved spandex top with a plunging neckline over my head. I pulled a pair of my tight Calvin jeans up, and shrugged a pair of brown leather boots on. Once I put my jacket on, I was good to go.

I always parked at the same Park and Ride lot and then took a bus to Slate's. His apartment was a half-block from the bus stop. It was a freezing cold day. There were light snow flurries as I walked the distance from the bus stop to his house. Just as I approached the staircase, two bikers were coming down the steps. I recognized the OMC badged one as Slash, the main dude for the Indianapolis chapter. The other one had the same badging as Slate. It was his buddy, Taz. He recognized me from the club.

I waited for them to get to the sidewalk before continuing towards the steps. Taz gave me a nod as they passed. I breathed a sigh of relief. I wasn't comfortable around bikers, with the exception of Slate. I just never knew when they might fuck with me.

Slate had the door open for me when I got to the top. He was in the kitchen in front of the sink washing out his coffee cup. He was wearing jeans with no shirt or socks. His hair was damp, which meant he was fresh out of the shower. I loved the way his jeans hung low on his hips. He was so freakin' hot.

He turned as he heard me come in, and that's when I saw the butterfly stitches over his left eyebrow. There was a huge gash beneath them.

"Oh my God, Slate! What happened?"

I hurried over to where he was standing to get a better look.

"Just a little misunderstanding with a couple of business associates the other day. It's no big deal."

"It looks like a big deal to me," I said. "I think you need real stitches on this, Slate. It looks deep."

"The mother-fucker had a ring on, snagged me pretty good. Trust me, babe, he's in worse shape than me right now."

I frowned at him. "Still, I think you need to go to the hospital and have it sewn up. What about a tetanus shot?"

"It's fine."

"Do you have any hydrogen peroxide here?"

"Sunny - stop fussing over me. That's not why I called you over here."

I'd already headed into his bathroom, opening the medicine cabinet where I found a bottle of hydrogen peroxide and a box of cotton swabs. I headed back to the kitchen.

"Sit," I instructed him in my no-nonsense tone.

He rolled his eyes, but complied, straddling one of the two kitchen chairs at the table. I soaked one of the cotton swabs with the peroxide, squeezing out the excess. I dabbed it gently against the wound, carefully cleaning off some of the dried, crusted blood. I got another clean swab and repeated the process until it was pretty well cleaned up.

I dug through my shoulder bag that I'd thrown on his kitchen table upon my arrival and found my make-up bag. I knew I had a small tube of antibiotic cream in there from when I'd scraped my heel against an exposed nail in the dressing room at the club. I squeezed out some of the antibiotic cream onto a fresh cotton swab and dabbed it gently on the wound.

"There," I said. "Hopefully that'll keep it from scarring. I'm going to leave this here with you, so keep applying it several times a day until it's healed, okay?"

"Yes, bossy," he said, getting to his feet and coming towards me. My heart fluttered at his nearness. He pulled me against him, his chin resting on my head.

"Thanks, babe," he said softly, holding me closely against him.

He kissed my lips softly. My tummy did flip-flops. My hands rubbed his muscular back, loving the feel of his skin against mine. He pulled back, taking me by the hand. We headed into his bedroom.

Slate stood in front of me and undressed me slowly and methodically. I shivered as he hooked his thumbs into the waist band of my jeans, once he'd unfastened them, and tugged them downward. They fell into a heap at my ankles. He instructed me to raise my arms so that he could pull my black top over my head. He was careful not to snag my extensions.

I was standing before him in my black lace bra and matching panties. He unhooked my bra, cupping my breasts roughly in his hands, massaging them. He pulled my bra off then hooked his forefinger in my panties and lowered them so that I could step free.

He pulled his jeans off. He was totally naked standing next to me.

"Sit on the edge of the bed," he instructed.

I did as I was told. Slate knelt in front of me, spreading my legs with his hands. He grabbed a pillow, lifting me to place it underneath my ass. He placed each of my feet on each of his shoulders, and pulled my hips closer. I arched my back instinctively.

I felt his fingers touching and exploring my cleft. Pretty soon his lips and tongue followed, tracing a hot path of pleasure beneath the folds of my sex. His tongue continued to roll and explore my clitoris, flicking it gently, and his fingers were probing inside of me now. I was soaking wet, partly from him and partly from me.

"God, your cunt tastes good, babe," he said, his warm breath against it sending waves of pleasure through me.

My hips gyrated in a circular motion as his tongue now joined his two fingers going in and out of me.

"You like it when I fuck you with my mouth don't you, Sunny?"

"Mmmm, I love everything you do to me," I moaned softly, thrusting my pelvis into his face, which was now wet with my arousal.

He kept it up until I knew I was going over the edge into major orgasmic pleasure. I felt myself contract as I whimpered and writhed beneath his touch, my body taking control as my climax unraveled around me.

His mouth continued to work my sex, more gently now as I enjoyed the last remnants of my orgasm. My face was flushed, as was the rest of my body, post-climax.

He lifted me gently and pulled the covers back, placing me on the sheet of his bed. He was right beside me, kissing my lips, my neck, and then moving downward to my breasts. He brushed his lips across each one. My nipples became erect for him immediately. His tongue played and teased my nipples. I arched my back wanting his mouth fully on them.

"My sweet girl's greedy," he teased, taking his time and enjoying my impatience.

His tongue lingered on a nipple, circling it over and over again before taking it into his mouth. He suckled it roughly. I liked when he did that. A few minutes later, he moved to the other breast, teasing and then sucking it fully.

He straddled me, moving up my torso. This brought my hands instinctively to his ass, pulling him towards me as he guided his stiff cock into my waiting mouth.

It was my turn to suckle, and I did so with pleasure, loving the feel of him and the control it gave me. His hips gyrated back and forth as his cock moved in and out. I watched the pleasure revealed in his face. His blue eyes were hooded; his breathing was coming harder and faster.

In an instant, he pulled himself from my mouth and flipped me over onto my belly. I pulled my legs forward and raised myself up on my forearms. Slate's fingers were splayed underneath on my abdomen, raising my backside to tilt in front of him.

"Diaphragm in, babe?"

"Yeah," I answered huskily.

He plunged his cock into me deeply. I cried out in pleasure. He backed out and then slammed into me again and again.

His hands were braced on my hips as he continued to rock in and out of me. I was moaning with each deep thrust. He was groaning loudly as he increased his momentum. I felt his hands dig deeper into my hips as he braced me for his orgasm. Mine was close behind.

I rolled my hips in a circular motion, allowing him to hit my special spot. We came together in our usual frenzy. I could feel his cock throbbing as his warm jism squirted inside of me. My pussy was contracting around it, squeezing every last drop out of him.

He pulled out, collapsing on his back beside me.

"Fuck, that was good," he said breathlessly, his hands running through his still-damp locks. I curled up next to him, breathing in the smell of our sex that permeated the room.

My fingers traced along his treasure trail, then northward towards his chest. I gently fingered his silver cross that lay across his chest.

"Something you want to say, babe?"

He knew me so well for not knowing who I really was at all.

"Did we make love today, Slate?"

"We *fucked* baby. That's what you and I do. We *fuck*. And today we did it pretty damn well."

He was so freakin' careful about never letting his feelings show. My woman's intuition told me it was more than just "fucking" with him. He was simply not clued in on that yet. I wouldn't let it spoil my afternoon with him. I hadn't given my heart to him yet. I probably never would.

Several hours and three orgasms later, I dressed to leave. As I sat on Slate's bed putting my socks back on, I heard him holler out from the bathroom where he was taking a leak.

"You have family plans for Christmas, Sunny?" Christmas was the day after tomorrow. Lindsey would be home this evening; Jack tomorrow.

"Sort of," I replied. "My period's due that day."

I heard the toilet flush followed by running water in the sink.

"Good," he said, emerging from the bathroom drying his hands and smiling. "I guess that kills two birds with one stone then."

"How's that?" I asked, frowning as I zipped my leather boot up.

"I'm going to be out of town. So I guess I'll see you after the New Year."

"I guess," I shrugged, acting way more impassive than I felt. "Have a happy holiday."

I went to the kitchen and picked my jacket up from the chair, shrugging it on. Slate was putting his jacket on as he followed me out. He always walked me to the bus stop and waited until the bus got there.

It was already starting to get dark out. I needed to beat a fast path home to shower and scrub this make-up off before Lindsey got in. Her best friend, Julie, was picking her up at the airport. I'd offered to, but she said she and Julie needed to catch up.

We walked in silence to the corner. There wasn't a lot to say outside of the bedroom. So many topics were off limits between us.

"Can I ask you a question, Slate?"

"You can ask away, but it doesn't necessarily mean you'll get an answer."

"How old are you?"

He turned to look at me, quirking a brow. "Doesn't that break our "no sharing of personal information" rule?"

"I guess it does," I replied, looking downward as we reached the corner. I could see the bus coming down the street. I stepped to the curb.

Slate's arm reached out and hauled me back. He lowered his face to mine, searching my eyes with his.

His lips found mine as he kissed me sweetly and tenderly. His fingertips tilted my chin upward so that I could see his beautiful eyes. He kissed my lips a couple of more times quickly as the bus pulled over.

"Twenty-six," he said to me softly. "How about you Diamond Girl?"

I hesitated momentarily. "I'm a little older than that, Slate. Merry Christmas."

I boarded the bus and took a seat by the window.

He was still standing there, watching me from the corner. The wind was blowing through his thick, dark hair. His brooding eyes locked with mine.

Damn. He's only twenty-six.

Shit.

Chapter 17

I got through the Christmas holidays by the grace of God and having Lindsey home. Jack always acted more sociable when she was around.

My parents had come home on Christmas Eve. We had dinner with them and exchanged gifts. They were all excited about leaving for Florida before New Year's Eve. They would be there until the end of March, like always.

My dad was full of questions for Jack about Banion Pharmaceutical. He wanted every detail pertaining to the new distribution center, sales growth forecast for the following year, and the R & D budget proposal.

Even though my father was retired, he was still the Chairman of the Board. I could see that Jack liked telling my father exactly what he wanted to hear. That's what everyone had done for as far back as I could remember.

Lindsey and I'd decorated the tree at our house Christmas Eve morning. She'd been a bit surprised that I hadn't gotten to it yet.

"What's been keeping you so busy, Mom?"

"Oh, I don't know, this and that I guess. I've had Christmas shopping to do." That wasn't altogether a lie.

I'd hurriedly done all of my shopping by catalog, having it shipped next day air through a courier service. It had arrived the evening I'd returned from Slate's. I'd hurriedly wrapped them all before Lindsey got home from the airport.

Christmas morning, I made our traditional breakfast of bacon, eggs and waffles. We then went to the family room to open presents.

Lindsey loved all of the clothes I'd bought for her. I'd also given her an assortment of gift cards that she could use at school. Jack gave her the next generation iPad tablet that had just come out.

Lindsey bought me an assortment of CDs with Hits of the 1980s on them. She knew that I loved that genre of music.

Jack opened his gifts from me. It was always the same thing every year: shirts, ties, cologne, and a new wallet. It was what he wanted and I didn't dare disappoint him.

Jack was now showing Lindsey how to download new applications on to her iPad. I was looking under the tree for my gift from Jack. There weren't any more packages to unwrap. He finally looked up; a smug smile crossed his face.

"I didn't forget you, Sammie. Merry Christmas, darling."

He handed me a green envelope with a card inside of it that said, "To my Wonderful Wife at Christmas." I opened the card. There was a stack of one-hundred dollar bills clipped together.

"There should be five thousand dollars there," Jack said.

"Thanks, Jack," I said, puzzled at his generosity.

"I figure you can pick out whatever you want, honey."

"Let's shop, Mom," Lindsey said with a laugh.

Lindsey helped me in the kitchen with getting the turkey into the oven. She was telling me about her classes at Cornell. Apparently, she'd met a guy and they'd been out a couple of times. She claimed it wasn't all that serious, yet.

"I can't believe how great you look, Mom. I know you said you'd been working out, but you're hot. You could hold your own on campus, I bet."

"Yeah, right. You're silly, Lindsey," I teased.

"I'm serious, Mom. The guys would definitely call you a MILF."

"A what?"

She leaned close, whispering in my ear the definition of "MILF."

Mother I'd Like to Fuck...?

"Lindsey," I gasped, halfway shocked, "I can't believe that you said that to me."

I couldn't help smiling at her, though. I guess we were more like friends these days. Becky had been right.

"Is a MILF the same thing as a cougar then?" I asked, curious to know if I qualified.

"Only if she takes him up on it," she laughed.

Oh Christ!

We had our Christmas meal in the evening. Lindsey was then going out with Julie and a couple of the other girls that were home from college on Christmas break.

As predicted, my period had started earlier in the day with a vengeance. I felt crampy and a bit of irritability was sinking in at being home with Jack, now that Lindsey had gone out for the evening.

I pacified myself by taking a leisurely shower. I then dressed in some warm pajamas and curled up in bed with a book.

I remembered that my track phone was stashed in my bedside drawer, along with my diaphragm. Since Jack was busy on the computer in his office, I decided to power my phone on to see if I had any messages.

I immediately saw the symbol that showed that a voice mail was in my inbox. My stomach did flip-flops as I waited to hear it. My skin tingled as soon as I heard Slate's sexy voice on the message:

"Hey babe, hope you're having a nice Christmas. Was Santa good to you this year? I'll see you in a few days. Be a good girl, okay?"

I texted him a message back:

'Got your msg. Hope your Xmas is going well. I look forward to seeing you soon. Of course I'm being a good girl! XOXO'

I hit the 'send' button, instantly worried that Slate might not like the hugs and kisses symbols I'd put in the text. He wasn't one for romantic or sentimental shit...that was obvious. Oh well, I couldn't worry about that now. Perhaps it would be forgotten by the time he came back to town from wherever the hell he was spending Christmas.

I was getting ready to power my phone back off when I heard a 'beep' indicating that I had a text message.

Oh shit.

I looked at his message and smiled.

'I'm glad to hear that, babe. XOXO'

I powered my phone off, vowing that I would never erase his text message or his voice mail from that phone. I could pull either of them up whenever I missed him, like now.

I snuggled under the covers and fell asleep. Hearing from him had been my best Christmas gift of all.

Chapter 18

Jack left for Charlotte on January 2nd. Lindsey went with him. She didn't have to be back for classes until the second week in January. Jack had thought she might enjoy the warmer weather and they could spend some quality time together.

A year ago, the fact that Jack would have asked Lindsey to travel with him on business and not me, would have injured my feelings. It didn't faze me now.

I'd miss my daughter for sure. The rat bastard? Not so much. Slate referred to him as that so often that it had worn off on me. I had to watch to make sure I didn't use the 'RB' nickname in front of Lindsey.

I went up to Jack's office to pay bills and update our account balances to reconcile with the online figures. I'd posted everything to the Excel file, and balanced the personal checking account, but the figures still did not match.

Our bank account online showed over $9000 more in it than the Excel spreadsheet. I went over the figures again, now checking by check number or payment reference number to see if payments had cleared the bank.

I finally found the difference. It was the check that Jack had written to Banion East Coast District Office in the amount of $9213.77 that hadn't cleared. That had been over a month ago.

I pulled out the check ledger with our numbered checks. The check number referenced on the Excel file for that payment was gone. The carbon behind it showed that Jack had written and signed it. That was strange.

Maybe he'd forgotten to mail it or take it into the controller when he'd last been in Virginia. He usually made the trip to that branch office whenever he was in Charlotte to check the progress of the construction on the new distribution center.

I made a mental note to ask him about it the next time he called. I saw where Jack's electronic payroll deposit had gone in on January 1st. The previous one was received on December 15th. He got paid twice a month. I didn't see any withdrawals made for the five grand he'd gifted me for Christmas.

I clicked on the link to our joint savings account at the top of the screen. It required a separate password. I hadn't recalled that being necessary before. It had been a while since I'd been in that account. There was always more than enough money in the checking to cover our bills. I knew that Jack had transferred some in to pay Lindsey's tuition for the first half of the school year back in August.

I put in the same password we used for the checking account. I received an error message for that one.

Jack must have purposely set up a separate password for our savings account. Now I was extremely suspicious.

I looked around his desk, and through the drawers to see if, by chance, he'd written it down. He'd shown me where he kept the password to our checking account if I should forget it. He'd assigned an alpha-numeric password that had Lindsey's initials, plus his birth year behind it. I didn't think I would have a problem remembering that.

I searched everywhere, but didn't find anything with his handwriting that looked to be a password. There was one alternative that might work. I needed to see if I could get the password reset. I would simply have to know the answers to the secret questions he'd selected.

I clicked my cursor on the option that allowed a password to be reset, if forgotten. There were three questions I needed to answer before I would get an email with a temporary password.

The first question was to identify Jack's favorite sports team. That was easy enough as I typed in "Yankees." Jack was a baseball lover.

Correct!

The next question was to name his favorite vacation spot.

Oh hell. When was the last time we'd taken a vacation?

I racked my brain trying to remember. Jack and I hadn't taken a vacation in forever.

Then I remembered that he'd taken Lindsey on a trip to Disney World back when she was ten years old. He'd not been able to make it home for her birthday that year and she'd been devastated. He'd told her he would take a week off and she could choose to go wherever she wanted. That had been her choice. I'd stayed behind because my mother was having surgery at the time and I needed to care for her.

I typed in "Orlando."

Correct!

The last question was to type in his mother's maiden name.

How in the hell would I know that? They hadn't spoken in years. I myself hadn't seen her since Lindsey was born. Jack had only seen her a couple of times before she had up and moved to New York City a few years after that. I wasn't sure if Jack even had a phone number for her.

Then I remembered the Bible that Jack had been given at his baptism. It might have that information inside of it.

I dashed to our closet and pulled down the metal box containing Jack's personal records. I turned the key that he always left in the lock and opened the lid. I rooted around through papers, blue ribbons, newspaper articles from his football days, and his diploma. My hand touched the leather bound book.

Bingo!

I looked inside and saw his pertinent information in the back that showed a family tree. There it was: Mother's Maiden Name: Rafferty.

I raced back to the office and typed it into the field.

Correct!

Moments later, I heard the computer beep that an email had come in. I went in and clicked on the link, typing in the temporary password that had been given. It then prompted me to type and retype a new password. I made it match the one for our checking account. I was in.

It only took me a moment to figure out why Jack had blocked me from our savings account with a separate password.

What the hell?

We had more than $400,000 in our savings account.

I pulled up all of the transaction activities for the last eighteen months. I started a new Excel worksheet to post it so that I could study the activity in depth.

There were all kinds of cash deposits from ATMs around the country for various amounts. All were less than ten thousand dollars. I saw the cash withdrawal of five thousand which was likely my Christmas present.

There were also deposits of checks made to the account. The checks were written to and endorsed by Jack.

They were from insurance companies: State Farm, Allstate, Motorists Mutual, and Cincinnati Insurance. The checks were from different agencies around the country. There were a couple from Virginia, one from South

Carolina, two from Indiana, and one from Illinois. Those deposits totaled over one hundred thousand dollars!

There were miscellaneous withdrawals, generally done a couple of days after each deposit. The withdrawals were always half of what the deposit had been.

I also noticed that the savings account wasn't paying interest. Jack didn't want to report interest income on our tax return. He clearly didn't want me or the IRS to know about this nest egg or where the money was originating from.

I was startled when my cell phone vibrated in my pocket. I had a text message:

"Get your ass over here. We need to fuck."

I smiled as I typed a reply to Slate.

"Be there in an hour. Be naked and ready."

I shut the computer down, and put the check ledger away. I would review this more later. Right now, I had something more important to do.

Chapter 19

I was on the couch facing Slate. I was on his lap, his cock buried deeply inside of me.

My legs were wrapped around his back as I rode him up and down, my hips circling clockwise as I pressed in deeper with each of his thrusts. I arched my back and leaned backwards, letting my long hair flow down to the floor as he grasped my hips and pumped in and out of me.

I felt the orgasmic build-up deep within me. This had all of the markings of a mind-blowing orgasm. It'd been damn near two weeks since he'd fucked me and my body was in need of him. I sensed he was in need of me as well. As he neared his climax, he moaned my name over and over again. That was the tiny push I needed. He pulled me up; cupping my face in his hands as his lips devoured mine while we climaxed together.

"Oh Sunny," he rasped, as he was winding down. "I fucking missed this."

My heart fluttered, but not as much as it would have if he'd said he fucking missed *me*.

I fisted my hands in his thick mane of hair, my lips now moving to his face, kissing him all over. I whispered in his ear softly, "I fucking missed *you*, Slate."

He immediately lifted me off of him, and sat me down beside him on the couch. His eyes were burning through me; a look of anger was on his face. He raked his hands through his hair, and then finally looked over at me again. Most of the anger was gone now. It was replaced with a look of compassion and concern.

"Sunny," he said gently, taking my hand into his, "that's not what we're about. You know that, right?"

"What are you talking about?"

"About all of this shit like, 'I missed you, Slate, or I care about you, Slate.' We're not going there. You do get that, right?"

I totally fucked up. I'm a freakin' idiot...

"Well, sure. I know that. What I *meant* was that I missed you - you know? Our *fucking*. You're the only one that I allow to do that, right?"

He nodded his head affirmatively. He wasn't convinced that my last-minute save was really the truth. He was worried that I was starting to get attached to him and that just wasn't in the plan.

He continued to look at me warily and I was pretty sure he was going to say something else about it when I diverted his attention by looking at my wristwatch.

"Oh shit, I have to go," I said, getting up from the couch and picking up the clothes that he'd literally ripped off of me and tossed on the floor as soon as I'd walked in.

I headed towards the bathroom, trying my best to save face as the tears stung my eyes.

"What the hell? You're leaving already?"

"I have to Slate. Jack has plans for this evening. We're having dinner with friends," I lied.

I could tell he was royally pissed. It was good for him, I thought, as I got dressed and did my best to keep the tears from rolling dow-n my cheeks.

I forced myself to hum a little tune while I dressed and repaired my just-fucked hair.

When I returned to the living room, Slate was dressed and wearing a scowl that hadn't been there when I arrived. I pulled my jacket up off of the kitchen chair, shrugging it on.

"I kind of thought we would be spending the day together," he mumbled. "I went to the store and bought steaks. I was going to cook dinner for us."

If I didn't know better, I would have sworn he had a full-fledged pout going.

"I'm sorry," I said, trying to sound contrite. "I didn't know that you'd be calling today. Can I have a rain check?"

"Whatever, Sunny," he said, not bothering to hide his pissy attitude.

He pulled his jacket on and opened the door for me. We descended the stairs and walked in silence to the bus stop.

Just as the bus pulled up, I moved closer to the curb. I turned to tell him goodbye and he was right there, mere inches from me. He pulled me against him, bending my head back as he devoured me with his sensuous mouth. His tongue invaded mine, as he thoroughly kissed me.

I heard the hydraulic door to the bus open. The driver cleared his throat loudly. I pushed against Slate, breaking our lip lock.

"Slate, I gotta go."

"Don't you fucking let that rat bastard touch you, Sunny. I'll be able to tell, and I won't be happy which means you won't be happy. Got it?"

I took a breath; my heart was pounding.

"Yeah, Slate. I've got it," I murmured softly, turning to board the bus.

He stood there, watching me, as I took a seat near the window. I looked out at him standing there with a major scowl on his face, his smoldering eyes boring right through me.

I raised my hand up and gave him a little wave. His eyes were still boring into me. He finally raised a hand and gave a slight wave, never once taking his eyes off of me. I shivered as the bus took off.

The image of him was with me for the rest of the night as I nuked a Lean Cuisine and ate it in front of the television.

Becky called later, as we hadn't talked during the holidays. George had taken her and the kids to Aspen for the holidays. She had skied for the first time and had quite a story to tell me. She then asked how the holidays went for me. I filled her in, up to and including, what had happened this afternoon with Slate.

"So, you're still fucking the bad-boy biker, huh?"

"Yep. I figure I have a lot of orgasms due me."

"You know," she said, chuckling, "I can't believe you never told me you hadn't had an orgasm. Jesus Christ, Sam, that's kind of a major thing, you know?"

"Oh, come on, Bec, when did we really ever go into detail about our sex lives?"

She was quiet for a moment. I could only guess that she was thinking back to high school…to the time when I got knocked up by Jack.

"You know, you're right. I mean you never even went into detail about the night at that party when Lindsey was conceived. The first I heard about it was when your period was late. Good Lord, I know you were a virgin, but even with that, I mean didn't he sort of get you all lubed up so at least you were willing to bear the pain, just to get it over with?"

"It wasn't like that at all, Bec. He was drunk. We made out. The next thing I knew, he'd pulled my skirt up and ripped my panties off. I didn't have much choice in the matter."

"Whoa, hold up there for a second. Are you telling me that Jack date-raped you?"

"Well, I'm not sure *date-rape* is the correct term, Bec. We weren't actually on a date. Come on, he was drunk, we were making out. It just got out of hand, that's all."

"No, that isn't all. Did you at any time tell him "no," Samantha?"

Becky was notorious for going off on tangents because she was a woman of principle. She believed in causes and I had a feeling that this was one of them.

"I don't remember. Possibly. Probably. But he was drunk, you know? He was all hot and bothered. I probably shouldn't have even put myself in a position like that. But what can I say? I got Lindsey out of it, right? She's worth ten of the rat bastard."

"The rat bastard? So, is that what you're calling him now?"

"Actually, Slate came up with that name. It's fitting, though."

"Your marriage is *so* over. Why don't you just go ahead and file, Sam?"

"Uh, Becky, don't you think I should at least discuss it with Jack? I don't think the answer is to blindside him like that. What purpose would that serve?"

"Sometimes the element of surprise can work in your favor," she replied. "It gives you the power initially. We both know that Jack is all about power and control. In most cases, I'd agree with you, but not with him. Think about what I'm saying, okay?"

"I will Bec. I promise."

Chapter 20

Over the next three days, Slate summoned me each day to come by. Each day I texted back that I was unavailable.

It wasn't that I didn't want to see him. I missed the hell out of him. I was still smarting from that whole "this isn't what we're about, Sunny" speech. He was actually right. Knowing that, I needed to distance myself just a little bit, so that I wasn't left picking up the pieces of my heart.

On the fourth day, I got a phone call, not a text message this time from Slate.

"What's up, Diamond?" he asked. His voice was terse.

"Hey Slate," I said, "Just doing some domestic shit here, you know? Gotta keep my hubby happy."

I could almost feel his scowl over the phone.

"Well, you're not doing shit to make me happy, babe," he said flatly. "Maybe I need to do some trolling to see what I can do about that."

I wasn't going to play this game with Mr. Twenty-Six-Year-Old Biker Hottie. That was for damn sure.

"Do what you've got to do, I guess," I sighed.

"I will, *babe*," he said, doing his best to enunciate the word "babe." I heard the silence of his ended call.

I guess that was that. It was over. In Slate's words: we appeared to be no longer active. I wasn't going to piss and moan about it. I'd promised myself that from the get-go.

I mean, don't get me wrong, I'd miss the great sex and the mind-blowing orgasms, but I had to face the reality that this was all that he was willing to give me. And I wanted more. I wanted it from Slate, but I'd likely be old and gray before that ever happened. He'd made that perfectly clear to me on more than one occasion.

If nothing else, I now knew that I was capable of enjoying great sex. I knew that I yearned for intimacy and closeness. That was something that neither Jack nor Slate was willing to give me. I certainly wasn't going to act like some over-the-hill matron that was all dried up. At least Slate had given me the self-assurance that I still had some good years ahead of me in that arena. He'd made me feel sexy and attractive. Plus, he had taught me so much. I needed to take my mind off of him because already I felt an emptiness knowing it was over and that I'd never had a choice in that.

I decided to go back to work. I wanted to dance. There were other clubs in Indy; clubs where I'd never have to worry about running into Slate or any of those fucking OMC club members. I was going to start looking immediately.

I'd started back with my Pilates and kick-boxing classes at Foxy's. Vonda was tickled to see me again.

"You look fantastic, girlie! My sister was flipping out when you quit Jewels, you know? She said you were one of the best. What was up with that?"

"Oh, you know, just got tired of living a secret. I was afraid my hubby would get wind of it eventually and then I'd have hell to pay."

"I hear that," she remarked, nodding her head. "Well anyway, sweetie, it's good to see you back here."

I worked out extra hard all afternoon. I had tons of frustration and conflicting emotions gnawing me up inside. I needed to deal with them constructively. I was exhausted by the time I pulled into my driveway.

It had been over a week since my last conversation with Slate. I checked my cell phone and a wave of disappointment swept over me when I saw that I had no text messages or voicemails. I suppose that he'd moved on to someone else. Perhaps it was Garnet.

I erased his text messages and voicemails. I changed the name on his contact number from Slate to "Asshole." It somehow made me feel a bit more in control.

I shoved all thoughts of Slate and Garnet from my mind as I grabbed clean underwear and pajamas from my dresser and hit the shower. I took a nice, long, cold one.

Later, as I sat in front of the television munching on a salad and sipping a glass of wine, the local news ran a story about several secret indictments being handed down by a federal grand jury which may implicate several members of the Outlaws Motorcycle Club in racketeering and conspiracy.

The news reporter was doing a live telecast standing on some corner in Fort Wayne, Indiana, which, apparently, was that chapter's clubhouse.

My mind went back briefly to the big-mouthed, asshole biker from Fort Wayne, that had been in the club the night I'd tried to dance for Slate. Slate had been royally pissed at me for still working at Jewels.

It had been the night that he'd thrown a one-dollar bill on the floor for me to pick up. It was the first night we had fucked; the night of my first orgasm. If truth be told, it was the night that I started falling in love with Slate, a road to nowhere.

The following week, I heard about another opening for a pole-dancer at a club nowhere near Jewels. I'd seen something posted on the bulletin board at Foxy's. There was no way that I was going to let Vonda know that I was going to apply for it. I wasn't sure how close she and Janine were, but probably close enough that it would get back to the girls at Jewels and I couldn't risk that happening.

The name of the club was Sharkey's and it offered the lower class clientele, though it was purported to be biker-free. That was good enough for me.

I was only able to pull two shifts per week for the hours I wanted. It was enough. I worked both Thursday and Friday from 5:00 p.m. to 9:30 p.m. It was on a bus route, so that would work out fine.

The dancers there also had stage names, so I simply stuck with Diamond. I'd called Becky to let her know I was back in the work force. I knew she wasn't pleased about it, only because she worried about me, but she didn't voice her opinion other than to say, "Whatever makes you happy, Sam. I know you've been kind of down lately."

She knew that Slate and I were no longer fuck buddies. She hadn't hid her relief about that from me at all.

I showered and waxed Thursday afternoon in preparation for my debut at Sharkey's. I'd taken my wig out of mothballs, shampooing and styling it at home.

This club didn't offer any help with hair and make-up, so I brought my case of cosmetics from home to store in my locker there. I was fairly certain I could handle my own make-up, having watched Margo go through the paces many times.

I selected one of my dance costumes from the trunk of my car where I kept them in a wardrobe bag, and headed to the bus stop from the Park and Drive.

Sharkey's offered private dancing rooms for customers willing to pay the high dollar amounts. There was a glass partition that allowed the customer to see the dancer; however, the dancer could not see the customer.

I wasn't particularly thrilled about that part of it, but Juanita, the manager, had assured me that no customer requests for stripping or fondling by the dancer should be tolerated. Plus, there was no way that some pervert could get to the dancer, because of the glass-enclosed compartment. There was just enough room to do some simple glides, and then climb and twirl the pole in the center.

I asked Juanita if the customers who bought this individualized service pleasured themselves while watching. Her response was simply, "Don't think about it. Just dance."

Oh yuck!

My first evening on the job, I had three private dance requests. The customer would pick the song and, as the music started, a black velvet curtain would open so that whatever customer was on the other side of the glass could see me on the lighted mini-stage take the pole.

The private dances cost eighty bucks. The dancers received a flat rate of fifty dollars for each dance; the club got thirty. The customer could then put an additional tip in the slide-in drawer at the end of the dance, if he (or she) so chose.

I received a total of eighty dollars in tips for those three requested dances. It wasn't so bad by the third dance. In some ways, it was almost better than having to dance in front of horny, sweaty men that you could see.

By the end of my shift my first day, I'd collected about three hundred dollars total. Definitely not as good as what I'd netted at Jewels, but I was new, and needed to build a following. Juanita assured me that I had what it took. She expected my Friday cache to be much larger. It really wasn't about the money with me. I didn't need to share that with her, though.

As predicted, Juanita was correct. My haul for Friday was over five hundred dollars. I was starting to get into the groove there. I liked the other dancers as well.

Most of them were college girls, just barely past twenty-one, which was different than those who danced at Jewels. They didn't make me feel ancient, though. They were sweet and looked to me more as if I was their big sister.

The second week working at Sharkey's, I'd received a call from Jack. The minute I picked up the phone, I could hear the cold anger in his tone.

"Why did you change the password on our savings account, Sammie?"

I immediately froze, my throat constricted by fear, but then I realized there was nothing Jack could do to me over the phone.

"I think you need to answer that question first, Jack. What are *you* trying to hide?"

"I have multiple business dealings going, Sammie. I simply needed to ensure that I was the only one having access until I finalized them. I didn't want you thinking that the money was at your disposal for bills or other expenditures, until I had an opportunity to see how my investments were panning out."

So much freaking bullshit.

Jack obviously had me pegged as an idiot. Maybe for now, that was safest for me.

"You mean that some of that massive amount of money in our savings isn't really ours?"

"Correct. I deposited some cash that I received as a result of some independent loans, promissory notes that I signed. So those funds are strictly for re-investment opportunities to cover the repayment of the notes with interest, plus profits made from the investments targeted."

Yeah right...lying bastard.

"Oh, okay. I guess I understand," I replied. "You know me when it comes to being as well-versed as you are with financial matters. I was just trying to see if we had enough funds for paying off the rest of Lindsey's tuition this year, since it was after the end of the semester."

"Yes, Sammie, that's fine. I transferred funds from the savings into the checking account that will more than cover that so you can go ahead and pay that to the registrar. You will find all of that information in the file marked "Cornell" in the desk drawer."

"Okay, will do. What's your schedule look like?" I asked.

"I'll be traveling for another four weeks, then I'll be back in Indy for Lindsey's spring break."

"Fantastic," I said, genuinely relieved for the additional reprieve.

"So, don't worry honey," he said. "I'll continue to handle any necessary transfers from our savings to checking, okay? You don't have to worry about that part of it."

"Okay, Jack," I said cheerily. "That's fine with me."

We chatted for a few more minutes, mainly small talk. Jack wanted to see if I'd bought his story on the savings account issue. I gave him no reason to think that I hadn't.

I knew without checking that he'd changed the password, and come up with new security questions that I, in no way, would ever be able to answer.

What Jack didn't know, was that I'd downloaded all of the activity on both the savings account and checking accounts for the past two years into an Excel file which I then zipped and e-mailed to Becky. I'd asked her to save it to her hard drive for me. She did so without question.

I needed to take an afternoon or two and sit down and analyze the activity of both accounts and try and figure out what type of a shell game Jack was playing. Becky could be a huge help with that. I made sure that I cleared all of the cookies and deleted my activities in case Jack was monitoring me on our home computer.

The following Thursday, I was putting make-up on in the dressing room when Juanita informed us that a new dancer was starting this evening and would be here any minute. She asked that one of us show her the ropes, commenting on her way out, "She better already damn well know the poles."

Several minutes later, I nearly dropped my lipstick when I saw the cute, tiny, dark-skinned, Emerald walk in to the dressing room.

"Oh, my God, *Diamond?*" she shrieked, running over to me for a hug.

"Emerald, what the hell? You left Jewels? Why?"

"Probably for the same reason you did. I was getting way too much heat from Ivan about those bikers being in there all of the time. It worried him sick, even though he knew that I was just all about making money for the family. Ivan doesn't make the money he made in Detroit. He hates that I even have to work, but dancing, it's just a thing with his pride, you know?"

In a way, I did understand what she meant. I knew that Slate hadn't wanted me to dance there, or anywhere. It just wasn't for the same reason, though, as Ivan's. He truly loved Emerald. They were a perfect example of a team.

"Hey, what about you?" she asked. "Is that why you left?"

"More or less," I replied.

"I don't mean to be nosy, girl, but was it because of Slate? You can tell me it's none of my business."

"It was, in a way," I said. "It's kind of complicated."

"I know you don't see him anymore," she remarked softly. "All of us could tell that he'd had his heart broken. He can be a real ass in that place. There were a couple of brawls in there this past month. That was the final straw for Ivan, even though it didn't involve me. Ivan said something wasn't right there…not with those bikers."

I thought about what Emerald said. How in the world had she come to the unlikely conclusion that Slate had a broken heart?

"Emerald," I said quietly, "can I ask you two questions?"

"Sure girl, ask away."

"Have you seen Slate with any other women since I left?"

"Not a one," she replied, "but then, I only worked the three nights."

I breathed a small sigh of relief. That was something I guess.

"Emerald, would you please not tell anyone else that I'm working here? It's important."

"Not a problem," she assured me. "Is it okay if I tell Ivan, though? It might make him feel a little better about me being here if he knows I have a friend like you. He knew you always had my back at Jewels."

"Sure," I said with a smile.

Emerald and I both caught the bus after our shift. I led her to believe I lived close to the Park and Drive. She got a transfer to a different bus once she got downtown.

She had liked her first day at Sharkey's, though she too, voiced reservations about those private-viewing dances behind glass.

"I mean, I just don't like not *knowing* who's on the other side," she complained, as she brushed mascara onto her lashes.

"I just try not to think about it, Emerald. By the way, do you care if I call you by your real first name?" I asked, putting my earrings in.

She laughed. "I can't believe we never got around to that, though the other girls said you were extremely private, so I never wanted to cross that line with you. My name's Jackie."

"Hi, Jackie. I'm Sunny."

Chapter 21

It was Tuesday and it was Valentine's Day.

Jackie had asked if I would take her Tuesday shift for her. Ivan had gotten the evening off, and wanted to do something special with her for Valentine's Day. I told her that, since I had no life outside of the club, I'd be happy to do this.

I'd bought a new costume special for Valentine's Day. It was a red sequined pair of boy shorts with a black sequined, low cut camisole top. The top had a big red heart in the middle of it, outlined in gold. It was festive.

I'd asked one of the other dancers to help with my hair. She'd arranged it up in a high ponytail, with red glitter sprinkled generously over it.

"My God, I never knew that was a wig," she said, as I'd pressed my fingertips into the area near the hairline as she brushed it up into a ponytail to keep it in place. "It looks totally real, especially with the fine little wisps of hair cut all around the hairline."

"Thanks," I said, smiling. "It certainly cost enough."

I'd replaced the one I had worn at Jewels. I'd spent about two grand on it. It was worth it. I loved the look.

I was first out on the stage for second shift. It wasn't really crowded yet, but there were some special events planned for Valentine's Days to draw men in who would typically be taking a wife or girlfriend out for the evening.

One of the promotions offered the private booth dancing at half price, meaning the dancer would get forty bucks, the club zip, in an effort to make sure the girls scheduled for tonight were taken care of financially. Juanita was pretty cool that way.

The club had three separate private dancing booths, and from around six o'clock until near the end of my shift, they were in constant use. I'd already earned close to five hundred dollars, between dances and tips. I'd performed six private dances so far this evening.

It was close to 9:30 p.m. when Juanita approached me to let me know that I had a private dance request in booth one.

"Damn, I'm almost off the clock," I halfway whined. "Can't Lauren take it?"

"Dude wants you," she said. "Suck it up."

I was really tired. I'd danced more tonight than any night before at either Sharkey's or Jewels. One more dance, then I could hit the road to home.

I went to the back door of the private, glass-enclosed booth and waited for the music to start, which would move the curtain aside. I always pretended that no one was sitting on the other side of the one-way glass, so that I didn't have to imagine what they might be doing to themselves as I moved sensually and seductively on the pole to the music.

My heart dropped to my stomach as soon as I heard the first few chords of "Bad Girlfriend" blast from the speakers.

Good God, it's got to be a coincidence. It can't be...

I forced myself to focus on the music and not who was on the other side of the glass. I took the pole, moving and spiraling to the beat of this song. The song that Slate had picked for me before; the song he used to punish me.

The words and the melody were now familiar to me. It was if they were ingrained in my mind.

'She likes to shake her ass; she grinds it to the beat;

She likes to pull my hair when I make her grind her teeth;

She's a bad, bad girlfriend......'

Somehow, through the grace of God, I made it through the song without fainting or falling on my ass. I convinced myself that it wasn't Slate. It was someone else that liked this hot song. It was a great song for pole-dancing, if you liked it fast. I liked it slower.

As the song ended with the final chords, the curtain closed and the automatic drawer was sent in with my tip. It was a one-dollar bill.

Oh, holy shit!

My pulse quickened. I felt faint. I sat down on the floor and buried my face into my hands. He couldn't hurt me if I didn't leave this booth. Within several minutes, Juanita was pounding on the door to the booth.

"You alive in there, Diamond?"

I got to my feet and unlocked the door. She was standing there looking confused and concerned.

"Are you alright?"

"Juanita, can you find out if whoever paid for my last dance is still in the club?"

"You know the rules on that, sweetie. The identity of our customers who make these private requests and pay good money is protected."

"I don't want to meet him for Chrissake! I'm afraid of him. I need to know he's left the building, you know? To make sure he's not lingering around."

"Calm down, sweetie," she said, taking me by the arm. "Come with me."

Juanita led me to her office and unlocked the door. She flipped the light on and told me to take a seat.

"You sit tight here. I'll check with Damon to see if the customer's left. I'll have him check out in the parking lot too, okay?"

I nodded.

She came back twenty minutes later with my street clothes and a cold bottle of water.

"Here you go, sweetie. You relax and drink some water. Get dressed at your leisure. Damon will walk you to the bus stop when you're ready, okay? There was so sign of him inside the club or out in the lot."

I nodded, taking the water from her and downing it.

I took my time getting dressed. I knew the bus schedule and I'd already missed my normal bus. The next one around would be the last one for the night. I didn't want to make Damon have to stand outside in the February cold, waiting with me any longer than necessary.

I was dressed and ready twenty minutes later. Damon walked me to the corner and waited until the bus picked me up. I found a seat near a window and relaxed back against it. The gnawing fear in the pit of my stomach had subsided.

I'd practically dozed off when I realized we were nearing my stop. I hurriedly scooted out of my seat. The driver knew me well enough to pull over.

"Nite," I said, stepping down onto the curb.

"Take care," he answered, as always.

The bus pulled away, and as I stepped forward to hit the button for the crosswalk light, I was suddenly snatched up from behind. I opened my mouth to scream, but a hand was immediately clamped over it as I was lifted and pulled backwards to the dark and sinister confines of an alley.

My fight or flight reflex was in full force, as my muddled mind finally registered danger. I quickly thought back to what I'd learned in self-defense training, and not sure of what possible disease I might contract, made the decision to clamp by teeth down as hard as I could on the flesh of the hand that covered my mouth.

Immediately, I heard a loud curse, and the hand that had been restricting my ability to scream, left my face. I took this opportunity to launch a scream, until I was whirled around. My face was within inches of Slate's.

"Shut the fuck up," he hissed.

Chapter 22

I'd been slammed not-so-gently against the side of a building that bordered the alley Slate had ducked into. I could feel the rough edges of the uneven bricks against my back. His face was in front of me.

As my eyes adjusted to the darkness, I could see his blue eyes were blazing into me with something I didn't recognize. It wasn't really total anger. It wasn't really total lust. It was a combination of the two.

"What in the fuck do you think you're doing, Sunny?" he asked in a low, controlled voice. His arms were on either side of my head, trapping me.

"What I'm *not* doing, Slate, is holding someone against their will."

He brought his lips to where they were centimeters from mine. "Seriously? That's all you fucking have to say for yourself?"

"What the hell do you want me to say? You don't own me." I raised my chin, defiantly.

"I believe I told you before that I'd be the one to decide when it's over. I've never once told you that I'd come to that decision. Why haven't you returned my text messages or voicemails?"

He had me stumped there. I hadn't checked my cell phone in a few weeks. I'd presumed it was all a done deal for us. This took me by surprise.

"What are you talking about?" I asked, blinking cluelessly.

"I'm talking about the numerous text messages and voicemails I've fucking left for your ass that have been ignored. That's unacceptable, babe."

"I haven't checked my phone. I assumed we were over."

"Oh, yeah? Well as I said before, I'm the person to make that decision and it's not been made," he said, nuzzling my jaw line. I had to let in a quick breath when I felt his tongue graze over the soft skin beneath it.

His closeness was melting my reserve. God, I so wanted the feel of him again; his nakedness, his passion, his body entwined with mine.

Stop it - I can't do this again...

Before I had a chance to shove him away or to try and escape, he brought his lips down to mine. He sucked hard on my lower lip, owning it. I relaxed my mouth, not responding; not giving in.

When he caught on to my tactic, he swiftly changed his. He gently bit down on my lip, rolling it with his tongue. I let out a gasp at the feel of it; and he used that as an opening to steal inside, licking deeper into my mouth. Slate brought down one of his arms to cradle the side of my face, his thumb resting below my ear as his other fingers tugged on the hairs at the nape of my neck.

He worked my lips and mouth in the way that only he could. And it was splintering my self-control, because he would alternate between sucking hard on my tongue and kissing my lips gently. He'd finish by pulling back slightly, to see if I would finally take the initiative and kiss him back. The first strand of times, I wouldn't. He'd then just start over, never getting frustrated. He would just continue slowly fucking my mouth with his.

"Give in," he said, pulling back once again. He faintly brushed his upper lip over my bottom one. My hands were shaking. My body was fighting the silent battle that my mind was trying to win.

Slate brushed my hair behind my ear, and leaned in again. His teeth nipped my sensitive earlobe, "Just one, Sunny." He soothed the bite with his tongue, "Kiss me once, and *then* try to tell me you're done."

He pulled back. Softly resting his forehead against mine, he waited for my next move.

Before I had the chance or the opportunity to reinforce my resolve my body, the traitor that it was, defied my better judgment. My arms laced up and around his neck. My body melted into his. My lips parted and accepted his tongue; my tongue explored him. I felt his body pressed into mine now. I felt the rock-hardness of his erection against me. My body was aching for the fulfillment that I knew he could provide.

I fisted my hands into his thick mane, sighing audibly as I capitulated to his touch. I pulled him even closer, making no secret of the fact that I wanted him right here, right now, no matter what. I had to find some strength against this man. My self-preservation depended upon it.

"Slate, no," I pleaded, breaking off from our passionate kiss.

"Baby, your lips are sayin' no, but the rest of you is screaming hell yes," he said, stepping back.

"I don't want you to hurt me," I said, bowing my head in shame.

"Sunny, I'd never do anything that you didn't like," he replied, totally clueless.

"I'm talking about my *heart*. I'm talking about what I feel for you that you don't feel for me. Please?" My eyes were imploring him to understand, to get a clue.

He moved back from me almost immediately. He raked his hands through his hair, turning his back to me as if he was ready to go off. His frustration was apparent as he whirled around, facing me once again.

"You're too good for me, Sunny. You don't need the aggravation of what my life involves. Can you please trust me on that?"

I looked into his intense blue eyes, and all I could see was sincerity and pain. His admission hadn't come easily. I wanted to be back in his arms again.

"Slate," I said softly, "can't you let me be the judge of that? I can't fuck you and not love you. I'm sorry, that's just how I am."

He wasn't comfortable with my words. It was fairly obvious. I didn't care. I wasn't going to dance around the issues any longer.

My feelings had to count for once. If they didn't, then I'd learned *nothing* from the past nineteen years of marriage to the mannequin. I was done being the type of person who allowed someone else to define their existence.

Done.

"Jesus Christ, Sunny," he growled. "I'm not that person. I'm sorry."

"Then please let it alone, Slate. Please don't break my heart."

His gaze penetrated me totally as he took several moments to consider what I had said.

"Babe," he said softly, "Come here."

I obeyed and moved closer to him. His strong arms reached out and pulled me against him. He held me tightly, his chin resting on the top of my head. We rocked back and forth in the embrace. The cold February wind brushed against us.

"Can I ask you something, Slate?"

"Go ahead," he replied, tucking another lock of hair behind my ear.

"How'd you know I was working again?"

I wanted to make damn sure that Jackie had kept her promise to me and not told anyone.

"Indy's a small town, Diamond. Your private-viewing dances are somewhat notorious with certain patrons of both clubs. I have good hearing and I listen. I had to see for myself. But I don't want you dancing, babe."

"I know you don't Slate, but it's not really for you to decide."

"Can we reach a compromise?" he asked, his expression softening.

"What do you mean?" I asked warily, wondering what he had in mind.

"Can we spend a day together this weekend? We're supposed to have record high temps for February. I want to take you out on my bike. I want to feel you behind me as we travel the roads together and just hang out. What do you say?"

My mind was racing. There was no reason to not go, with the exception of the major issue of my heart being broken.

"If I agree, will you please lay off about my working and agree that we go as friends and not fuck buddies?"

"I can do that," he said, his wide grin allowing the appearance of his sexy dimple. "Well, I mean, I can do that for *one day*."

I had to smile back at him. He was so freaking cute and hot at the same time.

"Okay, then," I said, returning the smile. "What time?"

"My place? Around ten in the morning?"

"I'll be there," I replied, a hint of amusement in my voice. He sure as hell was an expert at getting his way.

Chapter 23

It seemed to me as if Saturday would never arrive.

True to the weather forecast, Saturday dawned sunny with the high temperature projected to be in the mid-sixties. A warming trend had started on Thursday, and was to carry though into mid-next week.

I fussed over what I was going to wear. I finally decided on a pair of my skinny jeans, a cotton tee, a comfortable hoodie, and boots. I did my make-up carefully, and put my wig on, making sure that I wore it tied back so the wind wouldn't tie it into knots.

I'd taken my cell phone from the drawer earlier in the week, and listened to the multiple voicemails that Slate had left. I decided that we would definitely address the language that he'd used in the later messages.

He'd also left several text messages that weren't quite as graphic. I erased them all, not bothering to change his name on my contact list from "Asshole" just yet. As I put the phone back into the bedside drawer, I spotted my diaphragm case.

What the hell?

I stashed it into the pocket of my jeans.

Better safe than sorry.

Slate was waiting for me at the bus stop when I got there. I couldn't help but smile inside at the fact that he was looking forward to our day together as much as I was.

I even saw a slight smile grace his rugged good looks as I stepped off of the bus. He was right there, putting his arm around me as we walked to his apartment.

His bike was out and ready to roar.

"You ready to ride, babe?"

I nodded, genuinely enthusiastic about spending some time being that close to Slate. His nearness made me tingle inside.

"Let's get a lid on you," he said, as we approached the bike.

What the hell is a lid?

I understood once he reached for the helmet that was perched on the back bar thingy on his bike. Slate handed it to me and I situated it onto my head, having no clue how to fasten it properly. I heard his smirk as he gently brushed my hands aside and fastened the strap to fit snugly.

He quickly tied his do-rag into place and then motioned for me to climb up behind him as he fired the engine up. I wondered why he'd insisted I wear a helmet, when he didn't. I suppose it was a "club" thing. At any rate, the helmet was much better when wearing a wig, I decided.

I climbed in back of him, wrapping my arms around his torso as he revved the engine a couple of times before we took off into the unknown together.

Slate took a route out of town. We headed out into the country northward from Indianapolis. I'd never been on a motorcycle before. I loved the feeling of freedom that came with being out on the open road, feeling the sun and the wind around me, and pressed up against Slate as he kicked the bike into higher gears.

We'd been on the road for a while before Slate pulled off the main highway onto a county road that was winding and remote. It was a beautiful day. It seemed like spring, not winter. The road continued on up around hills and woods. I knew this area from years back. We were getting close to Forest Woods Reserve. It was comprised of hundreds of acres of woods with trails, streams, cliffs and waterfalls.

It was a gorgeous, well-preserved area that offered year-round activities for those who wished to escape from the city and enjoy remote nature.

I was beginning to wonder just what Slate had in store for me. This area was extremely remote and secluded.

He continued on until we were out of the park reserve and turned on to another county road. A couple of miles into it, he turned off into a gravel parking lot in front of a log building that had a flashing sign that read, Katy's Café.

Slate cut the engine and hopped off the bike. He turned to me, unfastening the chin strap of my helmet, lifting it off and affixing it to the back of his bike. Wordlessly, he started off towards the door of the café.

"Uh, Slate?" I called out, not budging from where I was standing.

He turned and looked back at me, seeing my questioning gaze.

"You like chili, Sunny?"

I nodded.

"Come on then, best in the state," he replied, waiting for me to catch up.

I followed behind him as he entered the café. It was dark and faintly musty. There was a big stone fireplace against one wall that wasn't going because of the balmy February day.

The inside of the café was rustic, with a long bar that spanned one whole side of the café. There were tables and a few booths along the opposite wall. Several patrons were seated at the bar and another couple at one of the tables, eating.

A tall, dark-haired woman, who looked to be in her mid-fifties, came bustling out of a swinging door behind the bar which, I could only guess, led to the kitchen. She had two steaming bowls of something on a tray, which she promptly delivered to two of the customers at the bar.

She looked up, a smile and a look of recognition crossed her face.

"Slate," she said, grinning, "It's been a while. Where have you been keeping yourself these days?"

"Oh, you know, Katy, busy with stuff in the city."

"Uh huh," she replied, rolling her eyes. "Up to no good is my guess, handsome. Who do you have there with you?"

Slate looked over at me with a look of warmth.

Wow! That's different.

"Oh, this is a friend of mine, Sunny."

"Hi there, Sunny," she greeted. "It's nice to meet you. I'm Katy, the owner of this establishment. Slate's my favorite customer. Any friend of Slate's is welcome here."

She was extremely friendly. I was having a difficult time in drawing a connection between bad-boy Slate and this seemingly warm and friendly woman who knew him.

"You two sit anywhere. As you can see, there's plenty of room."

Slate headed over towards a booth in the corner. It was a little more private. Katy was eyeballing me. I could see it out of my peripheral vision.

Slate ordered for both of us, which didn't surprise me, since he seemed to have the need to control everything.

What the hell had his mother done to him? He ordered two bowls of chili and grilled cheese sandwiches.

"You're gonna love Katy's chili," he promised me.

Katy brought us two tall glasses of iced tea.

"How do you know about this place?" I asked, taking a sip of my tea.

"Oh, I've been coming here for years," he replied. "I guess I don't remember how I first found it."

"But I thought you moved around. Didn't you say your last home was in Virginia?"

Slate looked at me suspiciously. "I thought we had the rule about personal stuff," he remarked.

"Okay, fine. It's going to make for a pretty boring day if we can't make small talk," I griped, taking another sip of my iced tea.

His hand reached over taking mine, gently caressing my fingers with his. He played with my wedding band, frowning.

"So, has the rat bastard been on good behavior?" he asked.

"What about our rule?" I chided.

"How about we amend the rules just a little bit?" he offered, giving me a sexy wink.

"Oh, I get it. I have to answer your questions, you don't have to answer mine," I replied, rolling my eyes.

I actually was surprised to see a smile spread across his face. Don't tell me my bad-boy biker had a sense of humor buried somewhere deep down inside.

"No, smart ass, we simply keep it to generic type stuff; no names, no specifics, no family history."

"What the hell's left?" I asked.

"Plenty," he said. "Now answer my question."

"He hasn't bothered me physically or otherwise, okay?"

"Good," he said. "Where does he think you are today?"

"He's out of town. He travels quite a bit with his career."

"I see. What is he? A truck driver or something?"

"Yeah," I lied, "something like that."

Katy brought over our chili and sandwiches. I was surprised at how hungry I was. We dug into our food. It was silent for several minutes.

"Okay, my turn," I said, wiping my mouth with a napkin.

Slate stopped spooning chili into his gorgeous, sexy mouth, looking over and cocking an eyebrow at me.

"Have you ever been married?"

"Nope."

"Engaged?"

"Hardly."

"In love?"

"That's enough questions for you. My turn."

He's been in love. He clearly avoided answering.

"How often is hubby on the road and for how long?"

"Often. It depends. Why?"

"Just wondering why you always run off afterwards," he replied with a shrug.

I'm going to have some fun with this.

"Afterwards? I'm not following you, Slate."

"The hell you're not, Sunny. You know exactly what I'm talking about. After you and I.... ... *fuck.*"

The fact that he had to put emphasis on the F-word totally pissed me off. He sure as hell was making sure I was clear on that.

I shrugged. "Maybe he was home those times, I can't really recall. I don't remember you asking me to stay, anyway."

"That's not my thing. I don't want you staying at my apartment when club members can stop by without an invitation."

"Oh, I see. They're allowed to come by without an invite, but I'm not?" I was giving him a semi-glare.

"That's right," he replied smugly.

"Then what exactly was the point of your question?"

"Just wondering why you've never suggested your place." He gave a non-committal shrug, spooning the rest of the chili into his mouth.

"Hey Slate, wait a minute here. I believe you're the one that outlined the rules. It was never on the table."

"So, what about now?"

"What about it? Don't you think it's kind of a moot point since you want to sport fuck and I want some feelings in the mix?"

Why is he so. . . . . . clueless?

"I *never* said that I didn't have feelings for you, Sunny," he retorted briskly.

"You never said you *did,* either," I countered, giving him a stare.

He rolled his eyes, and shifted in his seat. "You know - it's just that I'm not into all that bullshit about *feelings* and *caring.* I prefer to let my actions speak for themselves. I treat you good."

Compared to what?

He reached into the pocket of his leather jacket, and pulled a small box from it. It wasn't wrapped. He set it on the table and slid it over in front of me. I looked down at it, not sure what he expected.

"That's for you. Happy Valentine's Day."

I was in shock and awe at this unexpected gesture.

I carefully lifted the lid and pulled a beautiful sterling silver, dual chain bracelet from the pillow of cotton. It had a ring and T-shaped skull ends that served to fasten it. It was pure biker jewelry, but it was lovely and I loved it because Slate had given it to me.

"I don't know what to say," I said softly, looking up into his eyes. "I mean, what does this mean, Slate?"

"It *means* that I want you to have it. Here, let me fasten it for you."

He put it around my wrist and fastened the clasp.

I fingered the bracelet gently, looking back up at him. "It's beautiful. Thank you."

I could tell he wasn't comfortable with the tender moment.

"Now, I gotta make a pit stop. So, this is your chance to use the head before we hit the road."

"I'm good," I replied softly, still fingering my bracelet.

When Slate returned, he paid the bill and we said our 'goodbyes' to Katy. I climbed back behind him on the bike and we took off.

I felt closer to him on the ride back to Indy. Maybe it was because of the brief moment of sweetness he'd given me when he presented the bracelet to me at the café. I leaned into him closer now, resting my head against his back. I felt better than I had in a long time.

It seemed as if we were back in Indy too soon. I wasn't sure what Slate had in mind for the rest of the day. It was only around 3:30 in the afternoon. I could see it on a bank clock as we skirted the business section close to his neighborhood.

Slate had stopped for a traffic light at a busy intersection when the sound of thunder seemed to surround us. There were at least six other bikers from OMC that had pulled up alongside and behind us. I could almost feel Slate's back tense up as he looked over at Taz, whose bike was closest.

Holy hell, what's this about?

Taz gave him some sort of signal. Slate nodded. When the light changed green, the bikers turned and Slate went straight ahead, pulling down the street to the garage next to his apartment. He parked the bike outside, shutting off the engine.

He helped me remove my helmet, fastening it back onto the rear of the bike.

"Sorry babe. I've got to go to the clubhouse. Some unexpected business issues need to be taken care of immediately."

"What?" I stood there in confusion.

"I need to *go*. You need to go home."

"You mean our day together is... ... over?"

"Looks that way. I can't wait with you until the bus comes. I need to jet now. You'll be okay, yeah?"

"Of course. Don't worry about me," I replied snippily, turning from him and heading to the corner.

"Hey," he shouted after me. "What the fuck's the *problem*?"

"There's no problem, Slate," I replied, turning to face him. "I just thought that maybe we were going to... ... ""

"Going to what?" He was becoming impatient at my holding him up.

"Never mind," I snapped, feeling the flush of embarrassment cross my face.

"I'll be in touch," he replied, slamming his foot down on the pedal to start the engine again. He gave me a wink and off he went, leaving me standing there, totally confused, in his wake.

Chapter 24

It was two days later before I heard from Slate again.

I'd been sleeping with my cell phone placed on the nightstand. When I wasn't sleeping, I had it in my pocket on vibrate. I was determined I wasn't going to miss his next call or text message. Hopefully, there would be a next call or text message. Come hell or high water, we were going to fuck again, my pride be damned!

When my phone vibrated as I was doing laundry, I snatched it up to my face and answered immediately. I heard his deep voice on the other end.

"What'cha doing, Diamond?"

Why's he calling me Diamond?

"Laundry," I replied flatly. "What's up?"

"Just wondering if we're still *friends*?" His voice had some cockiness to it. I was so down with that.

"We are," I stated honestly. "Friends with benefits."

"What?" I could picture his eyebrow cocking with that one.

"I'm coming over, Slate. We're going to *fuck*."

I heard silence. I could feel his smirk over the phone. I held my breath waiting for him to tell me 'no.' I fucking dared him.

"See you soon, babe."

End call.

I flew into prep mode as I showered, shaved, inserted my diaphragm, applied make-up, dressed and donned my wig that I'd just washed and put into a fancy French braid.

Slate was waiting for me at the bus stop when I arrived. I shamelessly flew into his arms as soon as I stepped down onto the curb.

"I *fucking* missed you," I said. "And I don't want to hear *shit* about it, either."

He laughed softly, as he wrapped his arm around me, pulling me close against him as we walked to his apartment.

We were like two savages that hadn't been fulfilled for months, rather than a couple of weeks. I tore at his clothes, and he tore at mine. He unceremoniously lifted me from the pile of clothes that had been shed, and placed me on his bed.

I watched as his gorgeous blue eyes studied the length of me. His desire was evident as my eyes took in every inch of him, noting his full erection bulging from beneath his jeans. He quickly finished discarding the rest of his clothing.

He lowered himself to the bed, gently gathering me into his strong arms where he kissed me softly all over. His lips grazed my lips, my neck, and then moved to capture a breast. His tongue gently and thoroughly blazed a path from my breasts to my wet pussy, where his fingers had been expertly finger fucking me to near orgasm. I writhed beneath him, my hips thrusting upward in response to his tongue and his fingers. I was now pulling at him, trying to force him closer to me, moaning softly as he brought me to the brink of climax.

"What, baby?" he asked, as he rose up and then sat back on his haunches watching me in my near-frenzy state, wanting him inside of me and now ready to scream because he'd withdrawn his tongue and his fingers, leaving me teetering on the brink.

I watched as his hand moved from my pussy. He brought his fingers up to my lips.

"Lick," he said, pushing his wet fingers against my lips. "I want you to taste yourself."

I took his fingers into my mouth, sucking the salty wetness from them, licking them clean of my scent. He pulled them from my mouth and I watched in fascination as his hand closed around the thick expanse of his cock.

His eyes penetrated mine as he slowly and methodically stroked his shaft in front of me, his tongue tracing his bottom lip, his eyes shuttered. He was teasing me, tantalizing me as he continued to pleasure himself with the part of him that I desperately wanted inside of me. Right now. I whimpered softly, my fingers now replacing his at my apex.

He moaned softly, squeezing his eyes shut as he continued his strokes in faster rhythm, drawing out his erection fully.

"Tell me what you want, baby?" he asked, his voice a hoarse whisper.

"I want your cock inside of me," I murmured, my eyes pleading, now that he was again watching me as he continued stroking himself.

"Take your fingers out of your pussy," he instructed, nodding towards me.

I did as he ordered.

"Roll over," he said. "I want you up on your knees."

Once again, I did as instructed.

I felt his hands bracing my hips as he thrust his hardened cock inside of me from behind. I moaned in pure pleasure as Slate rocked in and out of me. His hands traveled from my ass to my hips and up my back as I tilted myself up to receive him again and again.

His fingers found my clit from underneath as I rolled my hips and pressed into his abdomen to meet his powerful thrusts. He rolled my clit between his fingers, applying just the right amount of pressure to make me come apart.

"That's it, baby," I moaned, not caring how bold it sounded. "Fuck me like that Slate; keep it going. This is mine and no one else's."

His rhythm was deep and forceful. My hands fisted the bed as I continued rocking back and forth, meeting his thrusts with my own.

I heard him moan loudly, saying my name, telling me that I was his forever. I loved it. I wanted it. I only prayed that he meant it.

"God, Sunny," he groaned, his momentum picking up even more. "Oh, God, baby."

He cried out, as did I, when the force of our climaxes sent us both spiraling into pure, pleasurable oblivion. Our orgasms seemed to go on forever, which was fine with me. I was moaning and telling him how good he made me feel.

"I need you, Slate," I moaned as we transcended into complete rapture.

It took several minutes for us to wind down after the explosive climaxes we had both enjoyed. Slate had pulled me into his arms that were now wrapped protectively around me. Our breathing returned to normal. His fingers were gently caressing my post-orgasmic skin.

My thoughts were returning to normal. Then it dawned on me what I'd said to him only moments before.

I didn't move. I didn't say a thing, hoping that perhaps he hadn't heard me. After all, he'd been pretty damned caught up in his own climax…maybe it had somehow slipped past him. I could only hope. I didn't want my admission of how I felt to interfere with our relationship.

I felt his long, lean fingers cup me beneath my chin as he turned my face to meet his. His eyes were even bluer at this moment. Perhaps it had to do with the blood flow increase during orgasm. Whatever had caused it, it was hot.

I looked into his eyes and I waited for him to say what he had to say to me. I knew he was going to put me in my place once again, so I braced myself for the sting of pain I was going to feel when he did.

"I need you too, Sunny."

He lowered his lips to mine, kissing them softly and gently over and over again. Then he pulled me closer to him and we fell asleep entwined together. We were satisfied and content. It was a great feeling for me; one that I'd never felt before.

I'm not sure how long we napped before I was awakened by Slate's phone ringing. He mumbled a sleepy curse as he disengaged himself from me and picked his cell phone up from the nightstand.

"Yeah," he greeted the caller. "What time? Uh huh, will Slash be there? What about the inventory discrepancy?"

Do I even want to know what this conversation is about?

Somehow I felt that, if I did, I'd be an accessory to something.

"Okay. See you in twenty."

Slate ended the call then turned to look at me. His expression was all business; the tenderness was gone as he smacked my bare behind.

"Time for you to roll on out, Sunny. I've got to be somewhere in a few."

I watched him saunter over to the side of the bed and gather his jeans up off of the floor, pulling them on over his narrow hips and muscular ass.

"Aren't you even going to wash up?" I asked, feeling myself blush at the question.

"Why would I want to do that?" he asked looking over at me while he zipped up his fly. I was struggling to get my clothes back on.

I shrugged, feeling kind of stupid for asking.

"I want your scent on me just like I expect you to keep my scent on you, got it?" He seriously wanted an answer.

I nodded, and then asked. "For how long?"

His mouth broke into a slow smile. "You're really a trip, Diamond Girl."

Now I really felt stupid. I could feel my cheeks flush.

I turned away as I finished dressing. By the time I had my boots on, Slate was fully dressed. He was tying his bandana around his head like a 'do rag.'

"Slate," I started, "why do you only wear that when you're meeting your buddies or on a ride with the club members?"

"I don't know," he shrugged. "I really don't care for having something wrapped around my head like that, I guess."

"Well, I mean, isn't it a requirement or something that it's worn all of the time? I mean I notice that Taz is always wearing his 'do rag' whether there are other club members around or not."

"That's Taz, babe. He's living the dream."

I thought his response was kind of strange, living the dream? Being part of a biker club was living the dream?

"Aren't you living the dream, Slate?"

"Sometimes, babe. You're asking a lot of questions. How about we get you going, huh? I can't wait with you for the next bus. I need to jet."

"I can stay up here until the bus is due at the stop. I'll lock up behind me."

He gave me a sardonic smile.

"I don't think so, babe. I'm not having you snooping around my shit like chicks do and then asking me all kinds of questions. You ask too many as it is," he teased, kissing the tip of my nose.

I was hurt that he didn't trust me to be alone in his apartment, though he was right, I most definitely would have snooped, given the opportunity to do so without the risk of getting caught.

I feigned insult at his comment as I brushed past him and put my jacket on.

"Fine," I said stiffly. "I'll just stand down there on that corner and freeze my ass off waiting for the goddamn bus."

"You'll live," he chuckled, giving me a swat on the ass as we headed out the door.

He pulled me against him as we reached the sidewalk beneath the stairs. He gave me a fantastic 'don't be mad at me' kiss, tilting my chin up so that I was gazing into his incredibly blue eyes.

"Don't be mad at me, Sunny. I mean it."

"I'll think about it," I replied, rolling my eyes at him. He then got his bike from the garage and sped off, giving me a nod.

I walked the half-block to the bus stop and waited. The sun was out. It wasn't all that cold today, or maybe it was. I was still feeling the warmth of having Slate wrapped around me in his bed, feeling the warm flush of my skin against his, savoring his scent that was still part of me.

I was still in my totally satiated, dreamlike glow when I walked into the entry hall of my house and was greeted by a cold and extremely angry Jack. It took him all of five seconds to see by my long-haired wig and excess make-up that I'd been up to no good.

"Well, I see that my *whore* of a wife has decided to come home. No doubt with another man's stench on her. Come here, Sammie."

My defense mechanisms were kicking in heavy duty now. Jack had trapped me, which meant that he'd been suspicious of something; but what and how? I quickly thought back replaying the last few months in my mind. I could think of nothing I'd done that would've made him suspicious.

Or just maybe it was something that I hadn't done.

The only thing I could think of was that I no longer bothered him for sex. In fact, most of the time, I tried not to sleep in the same bed with him. Surely, he'd have attributed that to the whole 'raping of the whore' debacle, though.

He was moving toward me with a menacing look on his face.

"You're wondering how I knew, right?"

"It's not what you think," I stammered, slowly backing away from him. "I've been pole-dancing, that's all."

"You've been doing a hell of a lot more than that," he spat, his lip curling up in distaste. "Why do you think I introduced you to Susan?"

Huh?

He was prepared to answer that question with his next statement.

"Susan's much more than my administrative assistant. Susan looks after my interests when I can't. I know about everything you've been up to, including the fuckfest you've been having with that biker named Slash."

Slash?

I didn't have time to consider the possibilities before Jack's fist came forcefully in contact with my face, the swift blow knocking me into darkness.

Chapter 25

When I came to, I was laid out across our bed in the master suite. The contents of my purse had been emptied out onto the bed.

No doubt, Jack had rifled through everything, trying to find out what else I may have been up to over the past few months. Thank God, I'd left my cell phone in the drawer of my night stand.

My head was pounding; my mouth was dry as I sat up and placed my fingers on the knot I had right under my left eye socket. I dreaded looking into the mirror, fearing the worst. I was going to do exactly what Slate had instructed me to do. It was time to text him a 'Code Red.'

I struggled to sit up. I felt groggy. I opened the drawer of the nightstand, my hand feeling around for the phone.

"Is this what you're looking for, Sammie?"

I was startled by Jack's menacing voice as he came into the room. He was holding my track phone in his hand. He had a snide look on his face, as if he was always one step ahead of me. Maybe he had been.

"I take it this is how you and Slash communicate?"

I nodded, swallowing nervously.

"Is it usually by text or by voicemail?"

"Text," I whispered hoarsely.

"Okay, then. Guess what? You're going to send him a text right now. I'll compose it, if you don't mind. Looks like you're in love with the piece of trash. I like your pet name for him by the way, 'asshole,' huh?"

"I think you've officially won that title now, Jack."

"Ooh, gotten kind of lippy now since you've been fucking a biker, I guess," he replied with a sneer.

"You don't know shit about Slash and me," I said, laughing at how truthful that statement was.

His face went rigid as he stepped towards me, ready to deliver more punishment. I didn't cringe.

"Do it. Go ahead and do it and then watch. Because I promise you that I'll bring down the wrath of Slash and the rest of the club on you. You can't keep me a prisoner in here forever."

"What have you become?" he asked, his voice steely cold and harsh.

"My own person."

"We'll see about that, Samantha," he snarled.

"What name does he know you by? I'm presuming that you had enough sense not to tell him your true identity or where you live. I don't think you've totally flipped out. If nothing else, you wouldn't want to sully the good name of your father's company."

"Diamond Girl," I replied, turning from him.

"Catchy," he said with a smirk. "Here we go then."

Jack pressed the letters on the keypad to type up the text message that he would send on my behalf to Slate. He held it up when he finished, just outside of my reach.

"Do you want to proofread this, Sammie?"

I looked at what he'd typed:

'We r done, asshole. I decided to take a walk back on the side of sanity. Go fuck yourself! I'm too good for you. Diamond Girl'

I looked up at Jack and saw his evil smile as he pushed the 'send' button.

"What makes you think he'll believe that I sent that?"

"Because Sammie, he has no other way to contact you now."

Jack tossed the phone to the floor and smashed it with his foot.

"I have all of your cell phone records, along with our landline records. You haven't called him from either phone. He hasn't contacted you on either phone. The computer's e-mail account shows you haven't sent any e-mail messages to anyone for months."

I breathed a sigh of relief that I'd erased my outgoing message with the attachment to Becky.

"Again, who are you to think I can't get in touch with him whenever I want? There are other ways, you know." I was trying to take a cocky stand with him.

"Oh, I know. But you won't. Because if you do, I'll make damn sure your daughter and your parents know exactly what it was that you've been up to these last few months. I'm sure they'll be impressed with your private dancing skills at Sharkey's. Did you know that one of those dances you gave in that private booth was for Susan? Yep, she videotaped it on her smart phone. I can make sure your daughter sees it and maybe your parents too."

He was truly a monumental piece-of-shit. He had the upper hand, for the moment. I needed to bide my time. I needed to appear to acquiesce to his directives. I had some ammo of my own to sort out, and now was the time to do that.

I certainly didn't want him showing that video to Lindsey or my parents. However, I was sure that, while he might have all of the bargaining power at the moment, which could change, I needed to keep my wits about me.

"You wouldn't dare do to that," I snapped back.

"Of course I would, Sammie. So I need to hear it from you, right now. Are you through with Slash?"

I took a few moments. I had to make it look as if it was a tough decision. I blinked back tears that I'd forced to materialize. I threw in a sniffle for good measure.

"Yes, Jack. I'm through with Slash. I promise."

"Time will tell," he laughed. "Don't worry, that recording of your dance is in a safe place, for now."

Fucking double-rat bastard.

"Go clean yourself up. Then call your employer and quit. Do you understand?"

"Yes."

I hurried off to the bathroom, slamming the door behind me and locking it. I assessed myself in the mirror. I had quite another shiner, courtesy of my not-so-loving husband.

I tore my wig and clothes off, and stepped under the hot shower. I washed all of Slate's scent off of me, tears now rolling down my cheeks. I scrubbed all of the make-up off, trying to be as gentle as possible around the bruised, puffy area under my left eye.

I dressed in clean sweats and a tee shirt. I shampooed my wig, then conditioned it for storage.

I blew dry my own hair. It was actually to my shoulders now. I pulled it up into a ponytail and dabbed some concealer underneath my eye. I put my Nike's on and pulled a hoodie on over my tee shirt. I descended the stairs where Jack was sitting in the living room, pecking away on his laptop.

"Where the hell do you think you're going?" Jack hollered.

"For a run. You're welcome to come with me."

"Maybe later," he sneered, shaking his head. "For now, you stay put inside where I can keep an eye on you. Did you call Sharkey's and quit?"

"Not yet."

"Do it!" he bellowed, causing me to jump.

"Okay, okay," I said, going to get my cell phone on the counter. It'd been smashed to smithereens.

What the...?

"Oh, sorry. My temper sometimes gets the best of me. You'll have to use the cordless landline. I have it here beside me. Tell them you and your hubby are working things out, something to that effect."

"So, is this how it's going to be, Jack? Are you keeping me a prisoner here, not allowing me to communicate with family or friends?"

"Just for a few days until I'm sure all of this has really sunken in, Samantha, and to make sure your bruise heals up nicely," he replied with a smirk.

I phoned Sharkey's and left a message with Damon that I had to quit without notice. When he asked why, I simply repeated what Jack had instructed me to say. He didn't press me further.

Chapter 26

Four weeks later

~ SLATE ~

It had been a month since Sunny sent her 'Dear John' text to me. At first, I'd laughed it off. She was just pissed that I'd sent her on her way from my place without giving her a proper good-bye fuck or waiting with her at the bus stop like some drooling, pussy-whipped medieval knight.

Fuck that! She had no clue what was at stake here. She knew nothing about my life. I hadn't wanted her to know. It was safer that way.

After a few days without her answering my text messages, I'd tried to call her. The calls went straight to voicemail indicating her phone was off. I'd figured the rat bastard was home.

Another full week had passed without my being able to get in touch with her. I'd worried that maybe he'd busted her. I might've misjudged the stupid fuck. It seemed unusual that he would have been in town for such a long period of time. Hadn't she said he drove a truck for a living?

I'd stopped in at Sharkey's a couple of times. She hadn't been working. All I'd gotten when I asked about her was a fucking 'deer in the headlight' look. I guess they had to protect the chicks who worked there by playing ignorant. They wouldn't tell me shit.

On my fourth visit to the shithole, just a week before, I'd literally bumped into that cute little black girl who'd danced at Jewels on my way out.

"Emerald?"

She had looked up at me and, I swear, she looked afraid.

"Hey, take it easy," I had told her. "This ain't my type of place or the rest of the club's. I'm on a personal mission. I'm looking for Sunny."

"I haven't seen Sunny since she left Jewels," she lied.

"Is that right? Then how in the hell did you know who the fuck I was even talking about?"

She was busted, big time. I fucking knew Sunny hadn't shared her real name with those other bitches at Jewels.

"Okay, okay," she replied, still looking scared and intimidated. "All I know is that Sunny called in and quit without notice. She told one of the staff that she and her husband were trying to work things out."

There it was: bam! How fucking stupid had I been once again? Chicks will fucking burn you every damn time they get a chance. Fuck that! Fuck her!

"Slate, are you okay?"

Emerald had seen that I was zoning out on this piece of information she'd just shared. I'd shaken off my rush of emotions, burying them back inside of me, where they would stay safe and quiet once again, maybe forever this fucking time.

"Yeah, I get it. Emerald, do me a favor, will you?"

"If I can."

"If you should ever see Sunny again, will you pass this along for me?"

She nodded.

"Lean closer then. I don't want anyone else hearing this but you."

She had hesitantly leaned in closer so that I could whisper exactly what I wanted her to tell Sunny if she ever had the opportunity to do so. I swear to God, I'd never realized black people could blush. I'd been fairly certain that Emerald had.

"Got that?"

She had nodded slowly, indicating 'yes.'

"Take care, Emerald."

I brushed it all from my mind now. What good did it do to dwell on the past? Sunny was definitely filed away there.

She joined the ranks of 'poor judgment on my part' experiences. Hell, what was that old saying? 'What doesn't kill you only makes you stronger'? I had the strength of Hercules these days. I was done with distractions like that. I had club business to take care of, which had to take priority over fickle chicks.

Just then, I heard someone knocking on my door. I pulled the blind up. Speak of the fucking devil.

"What's up, Garnet? Did I invite you over and forget about it?"

"Don't be like that, Slate," she gushed, trying to be all flirtatious with me. "It hurts my feelings that you aren't happy to see me. I figured you just might be feeling lonely these days, you know?"

"Well I'm not," I lied. I had no desire to be with another chick just yet, and definitely not with Garnet…ever.

"Our relationship seems like a one way deal," she whined, walking into my living room and tossing her jacket on the couch.

She was dressed in jeans so fucking tight they looked like they were painted on her. Her top wasn't much different, pushing her tits up so high you could almost see the nipples. Her body didn't do it for me, not like Sunny's could. Fuck! There I was again, thinking of Sunny.

"So, Slate baby," Garnet crooned, "what say I help fill the void that Diamond left?"

As if you ever could, you low-life clap-trap.

She was all up on me now, her titties rubbing against my bare chest, her fingers trying to dip underneath the waistband of my jeans. It was damn-near pathetic.

I wriggled free of her and turned away. That pissed her off monumentally.

"What? You don't think I'm good enough for you, Slate? I'm better than Diamond could ever fucking be! Maybe I just won't hear things anymore and let you know. Then you wouldn't be so high and mighty in the OMC would you?"

I wasn't in the mood for Garnet's shit. I already regretted opening the door for her, but she did have a point, unfortunately.

"What the fuck do you want from me, Garnet?" I asked, not bothering to hide my exasperation.

"Your cock."

Holy Christ! She isn't making any boners about it either. Oh hell - why not?

I turned back around to face her, placing my hands on her shoulders. I pushed her down in front of me so that she was on her knees.

She fumbled with the zipper on my jeans, eager to spring my cock free. It took her all of a nanosecond. God damn, she did want it bad.

I closed my eyes pretending that it wasn't Garnet's lips and tongue on my prick. I wanted it to be Sunny's. Sunny's full, beautiful lips taking the length of me into her sweet mouth; Sunny's soft moans as she kissed, licked and made it hers. I heard soft moans, only they weren't coming from Sunny - they were coming from Garnet and it wasn't even close.

I peered down at her from beneath my eyelashes. Damn! She was going to town. The girl kind of liked giving blow jobs.

"Umm, Slate, your cock's the best. It's so fucking hard and huge."

Yeah, yeah; just suck it, bitch.

"I sure would like to see how that bad boy feels inside of me."

"It *is* inside of you, Garnet."

"You know what I mean. Inside my pussy."

No fucking way…

"Maybe next time. I'd like to finish this way."

"Mmmm, okay. I want to taste your cum anyway. I bet you have quite a load to give."

I wasn't too sure about that. I'd been on a marathon jack-off bender since Sunny had left. I only jacked-off when I thought about her, which was once, twice, or a dozen times a day. My fucking hands were blistered up good.

For now, I focused on my nut. I closed my eyes again, rocking back and forth on my heels as Garnet put her suction into overdrive. At least I was able to give my hands a rest as I thought about Sunny.

Damn, this was feeling good. I felt the familiar throbbing of my cock as I was ready to blow. I heard my own moans as my release was ready to explode. Garnet was ready and waiting for me to fill her mouth with my warm cum.

I timed it perfectly. Just as I was ready to spew, I pulled my dick from her mouth and released my climax. Warm, salty cum squirted out of me and onto her face, hitting her hair, eyes, cheeks and chin. She squeezed her eyelids shut, screeching as the salty liquid burned her eyeballs. Her hands flew up immediately, trying to rub where it burned, making it worse.

"You fucked up son-of-a-bitch! Why the hell did you do that?"

She was flipping out; totally furious with me. She blindly got to her feet, staggering into the kitchen to rinse her eyes and face off with cold water at the sink. I calmly put my cock back into my pants and zipped up.

"Hey, Garnet, I'm sorry. It was an accident."

"Accident my ass! You've got issues, Slate."

Oh, really?

She was slowly calming down as she was able to rinse the stinging, salty cum from her eyes. She had a dish towel, patting her skin dry.

She grabbed her jacket from the couch, shooting me dirty fucking looks.

"You know, I've covered your ass more than once. I didn't deserve that just now. See if I cover for you again, you bastard!"

She started for the door. I was right behind her as she flung it open and started down the outside staircase. I was barefoot still, only wearing jeans. Spring was here, but it was still pretty chilly. I finally caught up with her halfway down the steps, grabbing her arm, and whirling her around to face me.

"What in the hell are you talking about?" I asked, glaring down at her.

"I'll fucking tell you what I'm talking about. Some bitch named Susan was nosing around a couple months back. She was asking a whole lot of questions about your precious *Diamond*. I figured her old man was somehow involved. So here I am, wanting to make sure that no harm came to you because I liked you, Slate. I really did. I thought you fucking liked me, too. I told the bitch Diamond was with Slash; that they're real tight and have been for a while. I pointed her in the wrong direction, just to save your ass from the drama," she spat.

Now I totally felt like a piece of shit. I wasn't sure who this Susan was, but if she was nosing around about Sunny, it couldn't be good.

I pulled Garnet close, giving her a hug. "I'm sorry, Garnet, I really am. It's just all about Diamond right now."

She nodded her head that was now buried against my bare chest. The sound of tires screeching from the curb across the street caused my head to snap up and look over.

A blue Accord peeled out from where it'd been parked and sped past to the corner, it hadn't bothered to make a full stop at the sign. It hung a fast right and disappeared from sight. I could've sworn the passenger had long, streaky brown hair. It could've been Sunny's twin.

It had been a month since Jack had blackened my eye and broke things off with Slate on my behalf. I now knew what it felt like to be a prisoner in my own home, and paranoid to wander from it.

The week between the incident and Lindsey coming home for spring break had proven to be extremely tense. Jack hadn't let me out of his sight. He'd destroyed my phone, of course, and what was worse, he'd locked the office which had our desktop computer in it so that I could not access it. He'd kept our wireless landline phone next to him at all times, even when it was on the charger.

Becky had called once and he'd told her I was in bed with the flu. He told her I'd get back with her just as soon as I felt up to it.

If I balked or challenged him with anything, he held up the cell phone that contained the video recording of my dance for Susan. It was extremely provocative, proof that he wasn't bluffing. There was no way in hell that I wanted my daughter to see it. I didn't care so much about my parents, but not my Lindsey.

The ten days that Lindsey had been home for spring break had been filled with family activities. I was never out of Jack's sight. When I was, I was with Lindsey doing some pre-arranged thing that Jack had set up. He'd kept my Mercedes remote in his pocket so that I couldn't arbitrarily leave to go on an errand.

When Lindsey and I would go somewhere, he invariably called me back on the pretense of him not getting his kiss from me. He'd then whisper a reminder of what would happen, should I stray from the plan.

"You and Daddy seem closer than ever," Lindsey had remarked with a smile. "I'm so glad, Mom."

"Yes, he's been home for a while," I replied.

I'd kissed Lindsey at the airport as she headed back to Ithaca to school. I hugged her tightly, not wanting her to leave me alone with the monster that was both my husband and her father.

"Don't cry, Mom. The semester will be over before you know it. I'll be home for the summer and you'll be sick and tired of me before fall semester starts."

"I doubt that very much, baby girl," I'd sobbed. She was so precious to me. I loved her so much.

The following week after Lindsey had returned to college, Jack remained at home. He'd spent hours upon hours in the office on the computer. He had multiple hushed conversations with someone that I could only presume was his right-hand bitch/nark, Susan.

I'd spent my time cleaning, cooking, and working out in the yard, since it was time for spring clean-up. I had no means of communication unless Jack allowed it.

He'd allowed me to call Becky a couple of times. She had wondered what in the hell had happened to my cell phone. I had lied, telling her it went through the laundry and I was waiting on a replacement. Jack would sit right there while I was on the phone, listening.

He created a world of paranoia for me with each passing day, leading me to believe that, even when he did hit the road again, there would still be eyes and ears on me no matter where I went, or what I did. It was a mind-game of huge proportions. It was working.

I called Becky from my land line the day after Jack left to go back on the road.

"Hello stranger," she laughed when she answered the phone.

"Hi, Bec. You busy?"

"Just the usual shit: cleaning, laundry - stuff like that, why?"

"I just thought it'd be nice to have lunch or something. We haven't seen each other in a while."

"Is something wrong, Sam?"

"No, not at all," I lied, figuring Jack was likely tapping the phone. "I just feel cooped up. I'd like to get out for a bit now that it's starting to warm up."

"Okay, I'm game. Where do you want to meet?"

Uh oh.

Jack had installed some type of GPS in the Mercedes where he could tell where I traveled and how long I stayed. I didn't want to fuck with it.

"Could you pick me up, Bec? I misplaced my remote to the car. I don't feel like tearing the house apart looking for it at the moment."

"Sure," she said. I breathed an inaudible sigh of relief. This paranoia was crippling. "Be there in about thirty, how does that sound?"

"Perfect."

I took a quick shower, putting my long-tressed, brunette wig on over my own hair. I was ready by the time I heard Becky's Accord out front honking. I hurried outside and got into the car.

"Nice hair," she commented wryly. "Are you going incognito for a reason?"

I was ready to let the tears roll. Becky saw it.

"What the hell is wrong?"

I immediately burst into tears. "Just drive, please? Get us the hell out of here. Jack could have cameras or a fucking tracking satellite on me for all I know."

She drove the car out of our drive and down the road about a half-mile before she pulled over and turned off the ignition. She turned to face me; her face was serious and concerned.

"For the love of Christ, Samantha, what's going on?"

I told her everything in between my sobs and bouts of hysteria. She looked at me as if she thought I'd gone off of the deep end. If Becky didn't believe my paranoia was warranted, who else would?

"You need to get in touch with your parents."

"I can't, don't you see? If I do, Jack will ruin my relationship with them, but more importantly, he'll ruin my relationship with Lindsey," I wailed, now starting to hyperventilate.

"Calm down, Sam. Take deep breaths and calm down. We'll figure this out together, okay?"

I nodded, too afraid to speak. She unfastened her seat belt and put her arms around me, giving me the BFF hug that I so desperately needed.

"Can we let George in on this, Sam? I really think he might be able to help."

I wasn't sure if I could trust anyone, with the exception of Becky. I was so scared of what Jack might do.

"If you're worried that George will judge you, there's no need. He thinks you hung the moon and, for whatever I think of Jack, I guaran-damn-tee you that George thinks one hundred times worse. Please?"

"Okay," I said sniffling. "But there's more, Bec."

"Just tell me, sweetie. It can't be worse than anything you've just told me."

"My period's late, really late."

"Holy fuck. Déjà vu all over again. We're hitting a drug store, then to my house to test, okay?"

I nodded again, pulling a tissue from my purse to blow my nose.

Becky went into the CVS Pharmacy a few blocks from her house, and came out with an E.P.T. package. We rode in silence to her house. The kids were at school. George was at work.

I made my obligatory pee contribution then reclined on her couch while she set the timer. I needed to relax and calm down. Being hysterical wasn't going to change the outcome of the test as she'd so eloquently pointed out.

I'd nearly dozed off when I heard Becky come back into the room. I could tell by the look on her face the news wasn't what I wanted to hear.

"I guess congratulations are in order, Sam. You're going to be a mother, again."

Chapter 28

I sat on Becky's couch, feeling nothing but numbness. It's strange that numbness can even be felt, but it can. I was in a numbing fog. I wasn't sure why I was even numb or surprised. My periods came like clockwork. This one hadn't.

My mind drifted back to my last time with Slate. It had happened then, the afternoon that we had slept entwined with one another afterwards. It had happened on that magical afternoon when I'd told Slate that I needed him, and he'd told me the same.

I felt the warm, salty tears roll down my cheeks. Becky was sitting beside me on the couch. She had an arm around me, trying to give me best friend comfort.

"Sam - you're my best friend. You know that I'll support you in any decision you make, right?"

I nodded.

"I mean, if you want, I can make the arrangements for you. I'll drive you there and stay by your side throughout the whole...*procedure*."

Procedure?

She saw my cluelessness immediately. Then it dawned on me what she'd meant. I looked over at her, not bothering to hide my horrified expression.

"I can't believe that you would even suggest that to me, Becky," I said. I pulled myself away from her and stood up. I was pacing now. I was furious.

"Look Sam, I didn't mean to make you angry. You do have options, though."

"That," I hissed, "is *not* an option for me!"

"Okay, I'm sorry. What are you going to do? You know Jack will figure it out soon enough."

"Jack and I aren't together for the long haul. That much you already know. This changes a lot of other things as well. This baby deserves my protection every bit as much as Lindsey does. If I have to tell Lindsey the truth about everything, then that's what I'll do."

"Let's not cross that bridge just yet," she suggested. "Don't you think there's someone else you need to tell first?"

Oh God. Slate.

"Let me think for a minute, Becky. I need to sort this out."

She left the room, coming back in a few moments later with a hot cup of Chamomile tea for me. I accepted it from her gratefully. I sipped it slowly, allowing the calming effect to seep in.

"Will you drive me over to Slate's? I have to do this now while I have the opportunity and the nerve."

"Sure," she said, grabbing her keys. "Let's go."

I gave her directions to Slate's apartment. It was a good twenty minutes away by interstate.

I thought about the things a mother thinks about when she finds out she's expecting. Our baby would be due in December. I would be thirty-six years old when it was born. My birthday was July 12th. I wasn't sure how old Slate would be. We had never shared birthday information with each other. That had gone under the heading of 'personal' information.

I thought about what I would say to Slate. Would he even be open to talking to me? Could he have believed what Jack had typed in on that final text message? Even if he'd doubted its origin, the fact that I'd not contacted him for a month spoke volumes.

I directed Becky to the neighborhood once we had exited the freeway. As she pulled down his street, I instructed her to park across from his apartment and down a couple of houses. I needed to scope out the situation, to see if it looked like he was even home; to make sure none of the other bikers were loitering nearby. I asked Becky to lower her window a bit to see if I could hear anyone.

I gazed back and forth across the street and down the alley. It appeared as if he had no visitors. There were no bikes or trucks present. I couldn't hear his stereo blasting from his apartment. His truck was parked up next to the garage. I gathered my courage, nodding to her that I was going to do it.

Just as my fingers touched the door handle, we both heard the upstairs door to the apartment fling open. I froze as I watched Garnet descending the wooden stairs from his apartment. Slate was right behind her. He was only wearing jeans. I saw the silver cross on the chain around his neck glisten in the sunlight. I sucked my breath in sharply. A pain had formed in my chest and was quickly spreading throughout my body.

We both watched as Slate yanked Garnet around to face him. Some loud words were exchanged. I couldn't make out what they were saying. The next thing I saw was Slate pulling her against his bare chest. He was soothing her. She buried her head into him.

"Get me the hell out of here - now!"

Becky wasted no time in putting the car in gear and peeling out from where we were parked. She made a quick right at the corner. She drove several blocks at a high rate of speed, as if that would change anything, or erase what we had witnessed.

"Who the hell was that girl?"

"Just a fucking bitch named Garnet," I replied. "I'm glad that Slate was able to move on so quickly."

"Fuck him!" Becky was pissed. That's what best friends say when someone has hurt their BFF.

"Slow down, Becky. Please pull over now."

She did so without asking why. As she pulled to the curb, I flung my car door open and stepped out on to the grassy strip next to the sidewalk. I vomited into the newly blooming grass there. I waited a few minutes to make sure that I was done.

I got back into the car. Becky handed me a tissue so that I could wipe my mouth and blow my nose. She handed me her unopened water bottle. I took a nice long drink, washing down the sour taste in my mouth along with the memory of what I'd just seen.

"Yep," I said. "Fuck all of them."

Chapter 29

It was the first of May. Spring was gorgeous and, after getting over the initial shock of what I'd witnessed a few weeks prior, I'd accepted the reality of what my life was now. I'd also decided what my life wasn't going to be going forward. I wasn't going to allow Jack to bully, beat or blackmail me.

Becky had taken George into our confidence. He now knew everything pertaining to Jack's treatment of me, the financial concerns that I had, and the fact that I was pregnant by someone else.

I'd begged Becky not to divulge the details to him of my short-lived gig as a dancer along with my even shorter role as 'cougar whore' to a biker. Becky said those things were strictly on a need-to-know basis, and George didn't need to know that aspect of it.

George had spent several hours going over the Excel files that I'd downloaded a few months back and emailed to Becky. Since Jack's discovery of my secret life, I was no longer taking care of the bills. In fact, Jack had moved the desktop computer to his office at Banion. I presumed Susan was handling our finances for him at the moment, among other things. I didn't really give a shit.

Jack was due home tomorrow. I was trying my best to prepare myself for his return. I'd replaced my cell, complete with new number.

Jack had attempted to cut me off financially by having Susan handling our finances. The bills were being paid in his absence, but my bank card had been cancelled. I still had the rest of my credit cards to use as I wished, though I knew damn well everything I purchased would be scrutinized or cancelled.

I dug into my hidden cash reserve from all of my dancing tips and purchased my own phone. I discovered I had a significant stash tucked away. I didn't want Jack to know shit about what I was doing. I prepaid my phone service out for a full year so that my monthly charges could not be viewed by Jack. There would be no paper or electronic trail whatsoever. I didn't want him to have my number or to be able to track any of my comings or goings.

I took my Mercedes to the dealer and had them remove the GPS apparatus that Jack had them install. I moved all of my clothes to a spare bedroom and had a locksmith install a dead-bolt lock on the interior side of the door.

Becky had phoned earlier. She wanted me to come by their house. George had someone he wanted me to meet regarding the bank information I'd downloaded. I was just heading out the door when the landline rang. I checked caller I.D. It was Jack.

"Hello?"

"Sammie, I understand from a phone call I received that you took it upon yourself to have the GPS disengaged on your car. Did you think I wouldn't find out? You really are a dumb bitch, aren't you?"

"Maybe, Jack, but I don't think so."

"What the hell does that mean?"

"You'll find out," I smirked, showing more courage than what I actually felt at the moment. I hung the phone up and hurried out of the house.

When I got to Becky and George's, there was a 'fiftyish' looking man there in a business suit. He looked nerdy, but professional. George introduced him to me as Alan Krause.

"Samantha, Alan's a forensic accountant for the law firm we use at our company. His expertise is being able to analyze, reconstruct and detect various types of criminal activity such as money laundering, fraud and tax evasion. I really think it's prudent at this time to have a set of eyes on what you have provided to ensure that if any type of illegal activity has been transpiring, you're not implicated."

"George, you're scaring me," I replied. It was the truth. What the hell had Jack been involved in over the past couple of years?

"Mrs. Dennison," Alan started, "I'll do my best to untangle what I can with the records you have provided for this time period. If I cannot come to any viable conclusion, I'll make contact with the county D.A.'s office and offer these records for their inspection to see if, in fact, they may coincide with any current investigations. Hopefully, by doing this under your approval, any subsequent criminal charges wouldn't be lodged against you. In other words, you're offering evidence that could be linked to criminal activity that you're unaware of. Having said that, the D.A. would hopefully ascertain that you were not a party to it."

"You're saying 'hopefully' Mr. Krause. That means there's no guarantee."

"There are never any guarantees, Mrs. Dennison. However, in my judgment, this is the best route to take."

I looked over at George. He nodded his head which told me I needed to take this as my best shot for proving my innocence to whatever type of activities Jack was involved in.

"Okay," I said. "Please keep me informed of your progress."

"Very well, Mrs. Dennison. I have the records for examination. I'll contact you in a few weeks."

While I was on pins and needles about what this forensic accountant might discover, the fact that I'd done something proactive made me feel as if I was taking back some of the control I'd relinquished to Jack. It felt good.

The accountant had cautioned me not to let Jack know that anything was being investigated, and to hold off any mention of terminating our marriage until such time as the financial shell game Jack was playing yielded some results. He said once divorce lawyers got involved in determining assets, the whole financial picture could become even more skewed. That was going to be the hardest part for me. I would have to test my skills as an actress.

The next day, Becky and George were both at my house when Jack made his entrance. He was immediately taken aback by their presence. We had discussed how we were to handle it amongst ourselves the evening before. Jack tried to recover from his initial surprise by putting on a congenial façade.

"Hey George...... Becky, nice to see you both. How have you been?"

He walked towards me, preparing to give me a husbandly kiss, as if he'd missed me.

Yeah, right.

"Cut the crap," I snapped.

His demeanor immediately changed to one of being stunned.

"George and Becky know everything. I've told them all about it. Now, why don't you take a seat so that I can fill you in on some things you don't know?"

He gave me a look of pure hatred. He clamped his lips together in a thin line and took a seat across from me. George and Becky didn't take their eyes off of him. I loved watching him squirm emotionally...not having the upper hand at the moment.

"First of all, I'm pregnant. Oh, and in case you get confused, we're happy about it. I'm having the baby and it makes no difference to me whether people know that it's not yours. That includes my parents and Lindsey, got it?"

He shook his head up and down slowly.

"I've taken my own room downstairs, for which I've installed a lock. You'll respect my privacy. You'll also never, ever lay a hand on me again, is that understood?"

Again, he nodded.

"Good," I said, continuing, "our marriage needs to be repaired Jack. I realize that this can't happen overnight. For now, I want an internal separation of sorts. We can explain it to Lindsey by saying my pregnancy is a difficult one and I need my own space, that is, of course, dependent upon whether you also want this marriage to work at some point."

God! I so wanted to gag as I spoke these words. I had to keep reaffirming in my mind that it was for the greater good…I had to protect myself and my children from whatever criminal activity Jack was involved in.

"Oh Samantha, you know that I'll do anything to save our marriage. I'm so sorry for how I've behaved. I know I was despicable," he lied. "Can you ever forgive me?"

"It will take some time," I lied right back.

He was starting to resemble a whipped dog as he hung his head and nodded once again.

"And Sammie," he continued, "as far as this baby goes, I want to raise him or her as my own. I'm partially to blame for all of this, but I'll love the baby, I swear."

Of course you will, you demonic droid.

"Jack, you don't know how happy that makes me feel to hear you say that."

"I really mean it, Sammie."

You lying bastard.

"I believe you."

I just vomited in my mouth…

Once I'd said everything as we'd rehearsed, Becky and George stood up to leave. George had something to say to Jack before he left.

"Jack, both Becky and I have witnessed everything that was said today. We both wish you luck going forward, but please know this: if we get any inkling that you've done anything to injure Samantha, we will involve the proper authorities. She's our one and only concern right now, do you understand?"

I watched as Jack grew contrite right before my own eyes. Christ, what a chameleon he was. I must've really put his shit into the wind for once.

"George and Becky, I absolutely understand. I thank you both for being there for Sammie. I know damn well that I've failed her as a husband. Please understand that I can't undo the past, but I'll damn sure make certain that I don't screw up our future. I would expect no less from either of you. I know that she comes first in your book."

"Damn straight," Becky said in her no-nonsense tone. "Remember that, Jack."

"I will, I will," he promised.

I truly wondered why Jack was making this so damn easy.

After George and Becky left, Jack got settled into our old suite. I retired down to my new room, which had a bathroom attached, though not nearly as large as the master suite. I continued to put my toiletries away that I'd packed up in boxes during the move. I came across the case that held my diaphragm, along with the nearly empty tube of spermicidal jelly that was with it.

I took it out of the case, examining it closely. It looked fine to me. I opened the tube and squeezed an average amount of the spermicidal jelly onto my fingertip, coating the inside of the diaphragm, as per the instructions. Once finished, I put the concave diaphragm up under the bathroom faucet and let the water drip into it until full. I then held it up in front of the mirror, checking for leaks.

Damn!

There it was: several different locations were dripping water droplets out of the diaphragm into the sink. I guess it hadn't dawned on me that these contraptions needed to be replaced occasionally.

I showered, making sure that my deadbolt lock was in place, in case Jack had a change of heart about how things had gone earlier. I dressed in a clean nightgown, brushing my teeth and combing through my damp locks.

As I crawled under the clean sheets on my new bed, I couldn't help thinking about Slate. He was going to be a daddy. He would probably never even know. I thought about what kind of father this OMC biker would make. A pretty damn good one was all that I came up with, which puzzled me because I had no reason to believe that, based on having no point of reference. It was my instinct, I decided. Slate would be a good and proud daddy; of that I was sure.

Chapter 30

Lindsey got home from Cornell the last week of May. I was ecstatic to see her. Her hair had somehow gotten lighter.

"What did you do to your hair?" I questioned.

"I just had it highlighted. I've been spending a lot of time in the sun with spring soccer, so it has lightened up. Do you like it?"

"Lindsey, my darling, you know I think you're gorgeous, right?"

"Mom, you're so obligated to say that," she laughed.

"Maybe so, but in your case, it's the absolute truth. How are things with your boyfriend, honey? I'm sorry, I keep forgetting his name."

"Don't worry about it, Mom. You're free and clear to continue not remembering his name because it's over."

"Oh, honey, I'm sorry."

"Don't be. It would have never worked out anyway. I've been spoiled. I want to have the same kind of marriage that you and Daddy have."

Oh hell to the no.

"Speaking of which," I replied, segueing into the perfect opening to what I needed to tell her, "Your father and I have some great news for you."

"Really?"

"Yes," I said, excitedly. "I wanted to wait for him to get home from the office, but maybe this is better. Women are so much more enthusiastic about this sort of thing, I think. We've been blessed with an unexpected surprise. You're going to have a baby brother or sister in December."

"What?" she shrieked totally caught off-guard. "Are you serious?"

"Uh huh," I responded happily. "I'm due on December 7th. It's official."

"Oh, Mom," she cried. "I think that's so wonderful. I have to tell you, I was worried about you and Daddy after I went off to school. I mean, it just seemed as if you two had really grown apart. I'm so happy to see that you two have had a fantastic resurgence in your relationship. That's so healthy for middle-aged people."

"Well, thank you, I guess."

"You know what I meant," she laughed.

"Lindsey," I replied, "I'm just so happy that you're happy about it."

"Why wouldn't I be, Mom?"

"I don't know. I guess it's just because you've been an only child all of these years. I wasn't sure how you would take it, I guess."

"Well it isn't as if we have to share a room or compete for attention, you know? I always hated being an only child. I wish you and Daddy would've done something about that sooner, but I'm happy about it, really."

In that instant, I knew that she was. My Lindsey was so precious to me. Only child or not, she had a heart of gold and I loved her for it.

"Oh, Lindsey," I said, "I love you so much. Thank you for being happy about this."

"Mom, I love you, too. I only wish I wasn't going to be away at college when my brother or sister arrives. I want to help you as much as I can."

"You don't worry about that now, sweetheart. Daddy will be here to help," I lied.

I so hated lying to my beautiful daughter. She was mine; not Jack's. There was no evil in my baby girl at all. I hoped that there never would be. I didn't want his evil DNA to ever show its ugly head in Lindsey.

"What do you have planned for this summer?" I asked, wanting to skirt away from the issue of her father and me for the moment.

"Well, Daddy has an internship position for me at Banion," she said. "I'm kind of looking forward to being able to work closely with him. I miss both of you so much."

"That's great, honey," I lied. "It'll be great experience for you."

"I think so too. You know, since I've not decided on my major yet, Daddy thought it'd be beneficial to assign me to the R & D lab. I think he wants me to see how interesting testing of new medications and experimental drugs going through the FDA process will be. He says it's a complicated and lengthy process."

"That's great, honey. I'm sure that you'll learn a lot at Banion."

I only hoped that Lindsey kept her soul, unlike Jack. He'd lost his soul a long time ago if, in fact, he'd ever had one.

Lindsey started her internship at Banion the following Monday. I drove over to hang out with Becky for the day.

It was a sunny and warm early June day, beautiful in Indianapolis. I passed several motorcycles on the way over to Becky's. It brought Slate to my mind for the hundredth time since I'd discovered I was carrying his child.

It didn't do any good to dwell on it. What was done was done. He would never know about this child because I wanted no part of him in my life or the baby's.

I pulled into Becky's driveway and immediately saw another car there. It looked like the one that Alan Krause had driven when we had met the first time.

Becky swung the front door open before I had the chance to press the doorbell. She appeared a bit anxious. A look of relief graced her features as I walked through the door.

"I'm glad you're here. Alan needs to talk to you, Samantha."

I went into the living room and recognized Alan right away, there was another man seated next to him. They both stood up immediately upon seeing me.

"Alan," I greeted, reaching out to shake his hand.

"Samantha, I would like you to meet special agent Craig Donovan. He's with the Department of Alcohol, Tobacco and Firearms."

The Feds? What in God's name has Jack gotten us involved in?

I shook Mr. Donovan's hand. A feeling of numbness had crept over me.

"Please, take a seat, Mrs. Dennison. There are matters of grave importance and concern we need to discuss."

Chapter 31

~ SLATE ~

Someone was banging on my front door. Fuck! It seemed like my head had just hit the pillow. I opened one eye, squinting into the sunlight that was now streaming through my bedroom window. The bedside clock read 9:37 a.m. Shit! It was later than I thought.

I threw the sheet back and got out of bed, pulling a pair of boxers on. I opened the door, knowing full well that it was Taz. He was going to chew my ass for not being up and ready by now.

"What the fuck, dude. You still crashing?"

What'd I say? Taz is predictable, if nothing else.

"No, man. I'm wearing my boxers on today's run."

"Smart-ass. Out late again, I presume?"

"Maybe," I replied, rinsing my face in the bathroom sink. "Last time I looked, I didn't have a curfew, or a wife."

"Yeah, well maybe you fucking should, Slate. I mean you're going to lose your edge if you don't fucking clear your mind of that chick. You being out all hours going from one dive to another to see if she's dancing...What the fuck?"

"It's my business what I do, okay?" I threw him a dirty look.

"Yeah, well I'm pretty sure that Slash is going to make it his business pretty damn soon. He ain't happy with you bagging out like that on a couple of the rides recently."

"Yeah, well he'll get over it," I said, squeezing toothpaste onto my brush.

I knew as soon as I started brushing, Taz would take that opportunity to rerun his usual lecture. I'd learned to mostly tune them out.

"I mean, if the chick wanted to be found, she knows where the hell you live, right? Accept the fact that she got tired of taking a walk on the wild side, and went back to her trailer park to have vanilla sex with her old man in their mortgaged-to-the-hilt trailer. End of story."

I rolled my eyes while brushing my teeth, leaning over to rinse and spit. Damn, I did look like shit as I caught a glimpse of my reflection in the mirror.

"Just roll with it, Slate. Shit, you have 'Garnet the Mouth' here once or twice a week sucking your dick and happy to do so. Why in the hell do you need some high-maintenance townie to make things complicated, huh?"

I cocked an irritated eyebrow at him as I pulled a tank top over my head. Taz didn't know shit about how I felt. I wasn't even sure how I felt anymore. All I knew was that Sunny had done a fucking number on me. At this point, I'd have liked nothing more than to return the favor tenfold.

I'd initially searched for her to make sure she was okay. Who the hell knew how crazy that fucktard husband of hers might be? Having hit every dancing dive in the city, it now appeared as if Sunny had simply dumped me like her text message had read.

I pulled up my jeans and then located my boots under the bed. I'd bide my time. My instincts told me I'd see the prick tease again. Then I'd have some sweet revenge. This was the last fucking time a woman was going to get one over on me.

"So what's the plan today, Taz?" I asked, pulling my leather bike boots on over my socks.

"Slash says he met with his supply chain contact yesterday. We've got a nice gross of unstamped Percocet to pick up north of town. New supplier, so there's to be no one-on-one contact. The financials will be handled once we move the inventory and collect. Make sure your saddlebags are empty. There are six of us riding up there for the drop. The stuff's bagged up to fit inside our saddlebags."

"Are they tens?" I asked.

"Yep, street value fifty thousand. Sweet deal Hammer arranged. Half of them are going on to Fort Wayne. Flush is moving those."

"What's the split?"

"Sixty-forty."

"Shit and we're taking all of the fucking risks in distributing. How fucked up is that?"

"It is what it is," Taz said with shrug. "Sure beats an eight to five though, huh?" He gave me a wicked grin.

"Whatever."

We headed out the door just as Garnet was about halfway up the steps.

"Oh shit," Taz moaned, continuing on down the steps, brushing right past her towards his bike

"What's up, Garnet? We're rolling out at the moment."

"I just wanted to stop by and see you," she said, her eyes not hiding for a second what she really wanted.

I'd never met anyone who liked giving head as much as she did. She had whined a few times about wanting me to fuck her. I'd quickly told her that wasn't an option. She had accepted that and was satisfied with sucking me off, as long as I didn't give her any more jism facials. It worked out pretty well 'cause I knew she was blowing and fucking Slash too. She liked to share information with me that she referred to as "pillow talk."

I looked at her for a second, debating whether I should simply send her on her way. I called down to Taz. "See you at the club house in about twenty."

"Christ, you're fucking unbelievable," he said, shaking his head as he started his engine.

She followed me inside the door, closing it behind us.

"We've got to make this quick," I said, unzipping my fly as she knelt down in front of me, wetting her lips.

"I'll do my best," she purred, taking my cock into her mouth, and beginning her oral assault. She liked to be rough, which was fine with me these days.

I watched as her tongue and mouth licked and swirled up and down the length of me. Her fingernails were digging into my ass, pulling me closer, deeper. This chick liked taking it all. I was almost positive she had no gag reflex.

I thrust my hips back and forth, fucking her mouth as she sucked in rhythm to my movements. She was moaning now, her teeth lightly nipping around the sensitive ridge of skin near the head. I heard myself moan, which totally turned her on. She was motivated by it to suck deeper and faster, bringer me closer.

I fisted her hair, pulling her head in to me as I felt the familiar, pleasurable throbbing. She knew the signal. She braced herself for the liquid rush that was coming. There it was.

I moaned as I emptied myself into her waiting mouth. She swallowed and swallowed, moaning as if I was pumping some sort of heavenly nectar down her throat. I counted five good swallows. I stilled as she then ran her tongue along the head, licking up every last drop that dribbled out.

"Mmmm, your cum tastes so much better than Slash's, baby." She was still licking her lips, enjoying it to the last drop.

"My pleasure, Garnet. I've got to go now though, babe," I said, tucking my glistening dick back into my jeans. "Come on. I've got to lock up."

"See you tomorrow?" she asked tentatively.

"We'll see," I replied, tying on my do-rag. "Bring me some 'pillow talk' and it's a definite."

The rest of the riders were waiting for me at the clubhouse when I roared up. We took off heading north to the pick-up point. It was Taz, Nate, Red Dog, Gramps, Flush, and me. The pick-up point was remote, near the edge of the Forest Woods Reserve.

We pulled our bikes over the hill and down into a shallow ravine. In about fifteen minutes, a dark van pulled in on the road along the ravine. The back door opened, someone tossed a cardboard box from the van. It went end over end down into the ravine. Flush went over to grab it.

He pulled a switchblade from his pocket, and cut along the taped flaps to open. We all filed up and got our big baggie full of Percocet to tuck away into our saddlebags.

As Flush handed me that last bag of one thousand pills from the box, I saw the logo imprint on the side of the box. It was the fancy 'B' with the 'P' positioned underneath in a different color so that the bottom loop of the capital 'B' was also the top loop of the capital 'P'.

Banion Pharmaceuticals. This is definitely getting interesting.

Taz and I took off from the clubhouse after Slash verified inventory and sent a team of three on their way to Fort Wayne with the split. He and Hammer were working on a deal with a shitload of hand guns that had had the serial numbers filed off. They were discussing the means of moving them out of state.

Garnet had traveled with them to Chicago to collect the handguns after one of those police-sponsored gun buyback programs, no questions asked. Apparently, a couple of cops up there had no problem being bought off to part with the weapons before they were crushed at a salvage yard.

Taz followed me upstairs to my apartment, talking about the ride that was scheduled tomorrow. Once I reached my door, I nearly didn't notice the small hole in the glass that had been cut out in a perfect circle in order to allow someone's hand to slip through and unlatch the deadbolt.

I nudged Taz, nodding my head toward the hole in the glass, and put my finger to my lips for him to be cool. Sometimes Taz could be excitable. I lowered my hand to where I had my switchblade strapped around my inner thigh and pulled it out.

Taz jiggled the door knob. It turned easily and quietly in his hand. He swung it open and I checked both sides of the doorway before going in. Once inside, we heard a voice from the living room.

"Sorry about the door, Slate. I needed to get inside quickly and unseen."

"Jesus Christ, Donovan, you scared the shit out of us."

"Need to talk to both of you. I've got news."

∞ ∞ ∞ ∞ ∞ ∞

I'd dozed off on my couch when I heard the pounding on my front door. Shit! I didn't get up right away, hoping that whoever the hell it was went away.

Bang! Bang! Bang!

No such fucking luck!

I peeked out between the slats of the mini-blind.

Shit!

It was Garnet and she'd been fucked up. I opened the door, pulling her inside. I looked around on the darkened street. I didn't see anyone else out there.

"How the hell did you get over here?"

"I took a freaking cab. Is that all you can say? Notice anything different about me?"

"I was getting to that. Who fucked you up?"

"Who the hell do you think? Slash, you ass!"

"Calm down, Garnet. Sit down so I can clean you up."

"Fuck that," she yelled. "My fucking life is in danger now because of you!"

I was in the bathroom, gathering first aid shit to treat her cuts. She had dried blood caked on her face from the lacerations.

I returned quickly with cotton balls, hydrogen peroxide, and the rest of the antibacterial ointment that Sunny had left for me.

Despite her anger and protestations, she finally allowed me to treat her abrasions. Once finished, I sat back on my haunches and looked at her. Damn, she was a mess. Had I caused this? Was I responsible for what Slash had done to her?

"You wanna tell me what happened?"

"Yeah. Slash doesn't like the fact that I've been blowing you. Someone's been running their mouth about that, amongst other things. Plus, someone ripped off one of those bags of a thousand Percocets from the club house. Slash blamed me for running my mouth. I fucking bet it was Taz."

"Whoa, wait a minute now, Garnet. Taz wouldn't say anything about that. He's like a brother to me. We go way back."

"Hope you're sure about that," she hissed. "Here, this is for you."

She tossed a patch at me that had been rolled up in her right hand.

I could see the threads that had once attached it to a vest, hanging from it making it obvious that it had been ripped off in anger. I recognized it immediately as being one that had been sewn onto the front of Slash's vest. It read: 'Snitches Are a Dying Breed.'

I looked over at her.

"Yep, Slash gave it to me after he smacked me around. I figure you deserve it more than me. I won't be back, Slate. I'm leaving Indy. If you're smart, you'll leave and not come back either."

Chapter 32

It had been more than a week since I'd sat numbly and listened to what special agent Donovan had told me at Becky's house.

Once again, I'd left there reeling from the information he'd divulged, though I knew it was probably just the tip of the iceberg. There was an ongoing investigation. Apparently, Jack was in the thick of it.

I thanked God and my best friends for putting me in touch with Alan. I was fairly certain that Donovan knew that, whatever Jack had done, clearly was without my knowledge or participation.

From what Donovan relayed, there appeared to be some money laundering and insurance fraud going on within our personal account. He wasn't sure to what extent, if any, Banion Pharmaceuticals was involved.

He seemed to think Jack was likely working with people outside of the company, but couldn't be sure until further undercover investigations took place. I was going to be more than furious if Jack had, in fact, put my father's company at risk.

Donovan cautioned me to keep everything confidential. He assured me that he would keep me updated as appropriate. He asked that I keep him informed of Jack's traveling agenda, and anything else I could glean without drawing suspicion. I assured him that I would.

Jack was spending more time in Indianapolis these days. I suspected part of it was because Lindsey was home and working at Banion for the summer. For all of Jack's nasty traits, I couldn't deny that he'd been a good father to Lindsey.

She enjoyed her job in the lab. She was working with a few other interns and seemed particularly fascinated with a student named Eric. He was in his final year of the Masters of Pharmacy program at Purdue. She said he'd changed his major a couple of times before deciding on Pharmaceutical Science.

"It's definitely a growing field that can't be outsourced," Jack commented, while we were having breakfast. "What about you, Lindsey? Have you decided to declare a major at Cornell?"

"Yes," she said, smiling. "I've decided to major in Sociology."

I thought Jack was going to choke on his coffee.

"Really?" I asked. "Why Sociology?"

"Exactly," Jack commented, wiping his mouth with a napkin.

Lindsey frowned at him before continuing. "Daddy, did you know that most Fortune 500 companies are hiring Sociology majors over Business majors?"

"It's probably because they can get them cheap," he said with a laugh. It was my turn to shoot him a dirty look.

"I think it's wonderful, Lindsey. It sounds as if the degree program will make for a well-rounded individual."

"Exactly, Mom. I'm glad that you understand my rationale here, even if Daddy doesn't."

Chalk one up for Mom.

"Lindsey, as long as you're happy, we're happy. You'll always have a position waiting for you at Banion. It isn't as if you will ever have to support yourself by stripping or pole-dancing."

That's a zinger and a half.

"Geez, Daddy! Where in the heck did that come from?"

"I'm just reiterating the fact that you have opportunities available to you that most people would love to have."

"Yes," I joined in. "You can thank your grandfather for that, too."

Lindsey looked back and forth between us. "Am I missing something here?"

"No sweetie," Jack said, giving her a dazzling smile. "Your mother's right. Your grandfather *has* provided you with a wonderful legacy."

"Well, I'm grateful, but I may choose to live somewhere other than Indianapolis, you know?"

"Not a problem," Jack replied. "Banion has locations all over the U.S. You simply need to pick one."

"Eric says that people who have their lives planned out for them in advance end up being slaves to someone else's dreams."

"I suppose one of Eric's previous majors was philosophy then?" Jack asked, his tone not hiding his irritation.

Lindsey shrugged, getting up from the table. "I don't know, but it makes sense to me." She left the kitchen to get dressed for work.

Jack looked over at me with a scowl.

"I hope she isn't starting to go through some rebellious stage. God knows I'm going to be saddled with the spoils of your belated one here before too long," he snapped, looking at my baby bump with disgust.

Jerk.

I caught Lindsey on her way out the door.

"Honey," I said, "I just want you to know that whatever path you choose to take is yours to take. I want you to carve your own career path and identity for yourself, okay?"

"Okay, Mom. I love you for that. Eric says that any man who would stifle a woman's individuality is simply using his control over her to carve an identity for himself. Is that what Daddy did to you, Mom?" She was watching me, waiting for an explanation.

"Oh, honey, I guess it's a little more complicated than that, but I think you get the picture. I don't think you have a thing to worry about."

She leaned in, giving me a kiss on the cheek. "See you this evening, Mom."

"I'm looking forward to it. Maybe you'll have to invite this new man in your life over for a cook-out soon."

She cocked an eyebrow in confusion.

"Eric?"

"Yeah, right," she giggled, "Eric's a little too old and worldly for me. I do like the way he thinks though. Maybe I will." She flashed me one of her own dazzling smiles and was out the door.

I swung by and picked Becky up. She was going with me to my monthly appointment with my OB/GYN. I was to have an ultrasound today. I hadn't decided whether or not I wanted to know the sex of the baby. I was four months pregnant and, so far, no complaints.

"So, how's Jack been treating you since the big talk?"

"He's still the rat bastard but only with his mouth. He hasn't argued, hasn't touched me and seems to be comfortable that no one is poking into his life of crime."

"I suppose that's the best we can hope for at the moment."

I was chewing on my lower lip without thinking about it when Becky caught it.

"What's stressing you now? I haven't seen you chew on your lip for ages."

"Becky, how's Lindsey going to take this when whatever happens to Jack happens?"

"First of all, we don't know the extent of what the charges might be, if any. They might not be interested in prosecuting Jack if he offers them names of the higher-ups in all of this."

"What if Jack *is* the higher up, maybe even the highest?"

"Then, that was his choice, Sam. Lindsey will see her father for what he is. She was bound to eventually when you divorced his ass."

"Divorce is one thing; going to a federal penitentiary is another."

"Damn it, Samantha. You did nothing to deserve this. Lindsey did nothing to deserve this. I guess you'll have to make her understand that her father is a criminal and will be punished for his crimes. I know that sounds awful, but I'm just glad your dad will finally get to see him for the schmuck he is. It's pissed me off all of these years the way your father gave him so much power and trust within that company."

"Don't you think Daddy did that for me, Becky?"

"Then why didn't he give the gilded career to you instead of the rat bastard?"

I giggled. Even Becky was now referring to him as the RB.

"You know my dad. A woman's place isn't in his corporate world."

"Hmmph," she snorted. Becky's father hadn't been nearly as old-fashioned as mine. Plus she had three sisters so, what choice did he have?

Everything went well at Dr. Bailey's. I decided to have the doctor let Becky know the sex of the baby. I would decide later whether I wanted to know. She was certainly playing the poker face after getting that little piece of information.

"It's another girl, isn't it?" I asked her on the way out to my car.

"I'm not telling you unless you sign a waiver, witnessed by George that you will cause bodily injury to me unless I tell you the sex of your baby. That was our agreement, remember?"

"Whatever," I said, waving my hand dismissively at her as I got into the car.

Fifteen minutes later, Becky noticed when I didn't get off at the usual exit of the freeway.

"Where are we going?"

"I just want to make one quick stop in town," I said.

She looked out the window. It took her about five seconds to figure it out.

"Are you serious, Samantha?"

"Why not?"

"Do you remember how upset you were the last time we stopped by his apartment?"

"Uh huh, but I never got to talk to him, Bec. He needs to know the situation. I mean Jack totally fucked this up. I need to set Slate straight. He'll understand about what the rat bastard did. I want him to know."

"I can't stop you, but I don't think it's a good idea."

I pulled up next to the alley that bordered Slate's apartment. My heart fell when I saw that his pick-up truck wasn't there. Maybe I could leave him a note with my new phone number on it. I grabbed my purse, locating a pen and a scrap of paper from a receipt. I scribbled a quick note to him.

'Slate - I stopped by to see you. We need to talk. It was the rat bastard that sent that text to you. It wasn't me. Please call me! Here is my number: 317-555-0182. -Sunny'

"Be right back," I said to Becky, getting out of my Mercedes.

I traipsed up the wooden staircase to his apartment. As soon as I reached the landing outside of his door, I knew that I wouldn't be leaving the note.

The blinds to his kitchen door were raised up. I peered inside and it was obvious the apartment was empty. There was a 'For Rent' sign on the inside door with the words, "Inquire at Folsom Realty."

My heart dropped to my knees. Slate was gone. I had no clue as to where he went. I wasn't going to contact Folsom Realty. Knowing Slate, he'd left no forwarding address. I hurried back down the staircase and got into my car.

"What?"

"He's gone," I said, my voice quivering with disappointment and sadness. "His apartment's empty. I'll never see him again."

The tears started flowing immediately. I felt so alone and empty, knowing that I'd never see this bad boy that I was now convinced I truly loved.

"Honey, it's just as well —"

"I love him, Becky. I fucking love him!"

"Samantha, stop. Honey, you don't even know him. How could you think you love him? You were just infatuated with him, remember? We talked about your need to go through your 'bad boy' stage that you never had the opportunity to do. It's just hormones, sweetie."

"It wasn't! He was mine and now he's gone."

Becky forced me to switch places with her so that she could drive. By the time we reached her house, I'd stopped the wailing and was now simply expelling involuntary sobs from the hysteria.

"Listen," she said to me in her concerned, BFF tone, "come on inside and let me fix you some herbal tea."

"I don't want herbal tea. I want Slate," I wailed again.

"Okay listen, listen to me. He's gone, Sam. If it's meant to be, then he'll find you somehow."

"You know he can't," I snapped "He doesn't even know who I am. That's how fucking duplicitous I was with him. It's my fault. It's my entire fault. My baby girl will never know her daddy."

"Honey, it's not a girl," she said quickly, forgetting that I wasn't supposed to know.

"Fuck!" she said, pissed at herself.

"A boy?"

She nodded.

I wailed even louder. "My baby boy will never know his daddy… … ."

Chapter 33

For the next day and a half, I took to my bed at home. I told Lindsey I wasn't feeling well and needed to take it easy. Jack didn't even ask. Lindsey tended to me like the mother hen that I was supposed to be to her. My mother called and Lindsey filled her in the on the 'good news.'

I knew that my mother was going to be royally hurt that I hadn't shared the news with her before now.

They were coming back from their condo in Maui to be here for my birthday on the 12th, and stay through Lindsey's birthday on July 30th. They weren't planning to head out again until mid-August when they left for San Diego, where they vacationed until mid-October.

Lindsey had brought the phone to me so that I could speak to my mom. I shook my head lip-syncing to tell her I was napping. Lindsey frowned, but complied with my request. I knew she hated lying to anyone.

"Mom, what is it with you? You don't even want to talk to Grandma?"

"I'm just not up to her million questions as to why I haven't told her yet."

"Well, Mom, it's a good question. Why haven't you told her?"

"I don't know," I replied with a shrug. "I guess I just don't want her fussing over me like you are," I lied.

Lindsey rolled her eyes, fluffing my pillows.

"Can I get you some soup or maybe some tea, Mom?"

"Tea would be great honey, thanks."

She left my room to get the tea. When she returned, she had made a cup for herself. She sat down on the bed next to me, handing me my cup as I sat up in bed.

"Mom," she said, tentatively, "Why aren't you and Daddy sharing a room anymore?"

I knew that question was going to be asked sooner or later. I'd prepared an answer in advance.

"Well," I started, "this pregnancy's been tough on me. I'm restless and, to be honest, it was a real surprise for both of us."

She was looking at me strangely now.

"I'm just more comfortable having my own room, sweetie."

"But Mom, you and Daddy should be closer than ever now. I mean, I know how Daddy can be, but I'm certain he understands that maybe you're not in the mood for - well, you know --"

I felt myself blush and then, thankfully, her cell phone rang.

"Hi," she said, smiling from ear to ear. "What's up?"

She paused, listening to whoever was on the other end talk.

"Well, yeah. I think that sounds great. I'd love to go. What time?"

Another pause while the time was set for whatever activity she'd agreed to attend.

"Okay, see you then."

She got off the phone, beaming.

"What?" I asked, glad to be off of the previous topic.

"That was Eric. We're going to see a movie tomorrow and then have coffee afterwards."

"That's nice, honey," I replied, genuinely pleased. "I'm really glad that you're getting out. You've been so busy with work and now trying to mother me, you need to have some fun."

"Yeah, I'm actually comfortable with him. I can hardly wait for you to meet him. Do you need anything else, Mom? I'd kind of like to wash my hair and do my nails."

"You go right ahead, sweetie. I'm going to finish my tea, read, and then go to sleep."

"Okay," she said, leaning over to give me a kiss on the cheek. "See you at breakfast?"

"Absolutely."

She left me alone in my private refuge where I'd been for the past two days, wallowing in self-pity. I needed to snap out of this funk.

Becky was right. If it was meant to be, then Slate wouldn't have left. I needed to get on with life and see how things unfolded with all of Jack's shenanigans. Lindsey would most likely have a lot to face in the near future.

Hopefully, her budding relationship with Eric would cushion the blow for her. I still worried about what all of this would do to her once it all came to light.

I finished my tea then took a shower and got into a summer nightgown. I opened the window, letting the cool night breeze filter in. I was sleepy now. The tea had done its magic for calming and relaxing me.

I curled up underneath my cool sheets and started to doze off when I felt a flutter in my womb. Our baby was moving; the baby that Slate and I had made was moving. It gave me comfort and sadness at the same time. I placed my hand on my abdomen and fell asleep feeling the fluttery movement that felt like butterflies spreading their wings.

Chapter 34

~ LINDSEY ~

I was really looking forward to the end of my shift at Banion Pharmaceuticals. I'd washed my hair and done a manicure and pedicure last night in my room. I was so looking forward to going to the movie tonight with Eric.

His invitation had caught me a bit off-guard. I wasn't sure that he'd regarded me as dating material. I was only going into my sophomore year of college. He was at least six or seven years older, by my estimation. I based that on all of the time he'd spent in college changing majors.

I loved talking to Eric. He seemed to know a little about almost everything, and a lot about certain things. I'd almost come to regard him as a big brother type, only hotter. He was definitely hot!

Maybe the older thing was where it was at. I'd certainly struck out with my high school boyfriend, as well as Matt, the guy that I'd been seeing briefly at Cornell. Matt had been too much of a partier and a player on top of it all. After catching him in his hundredth lie, I made the decision to tell him to 'fuck off.'

Eric swung by the lab after he clocked out for the day. He crept up quietly behind me as I was signing off on some scrapped raw material.

"Are we still on for this evening, Lindsey?"

I jumped, totally caught off-guard by his presence.

"God!"

I heard his sexy laugh. "Hey, I'm sorry. I didn't do that on purpose."

"Yes," I laughed, my heartbeat returning to almost normal. "We're still on. You have the address, right?"

"Absolutely. What do you have there?" He asked, looking at the scrapped material that was bagged up.

"Oh, it's just some expired raw material that I was told to tag out. It will be written off the inventory and disposed of with all of the other expired stuff, I guess."

I affixed the red label with the chemical identification, batch number, and date of disposal to the container.

"So, I'll be by around sevenish to pick you up, Miss Lindsey."

"Don't keep me waiting, Eric. My parents are looking forward to meeting you," I replied with a wink.

He rolled his eyes as he turned to leave. "Yeah, that's always been my *favorite* part," he mumbled.

"You'll do fine," I called out after him. "My father will love you for going into pharmaceutical science…period."

"Later, Lindsey."

I sighed after he left. What a sweet, although a bit serious and uptight, guy. It was no big deal. We were just friends . . . for now.

Once I clocked out, I hurried home in my VW Bug to get ready for this evening. I'd already decided what I was going to wear. I'd bought a cute pair of khaki capri pants. I'd also purchased a peach-colored, cotton v-neck tee. My new heeled sandals would look great with the ensemble. I mentally reminded myself to accessorize with a light gold chain and bracelet.

I took a quick shower when I got home and declined dinner with the folks. Mom balked at that a bit, but I was too busy trying to look great for Eric.

There I went again, presuming this was going to lead to a romance. I wouldn't even see him after I returned to Cornell. Still, there was something to be said for a summer fling. I blushed at the thought.

Chapter 35

It was quarter to seven, and I was just finishing up in the kitchen. I brushed a stray wisp of hair back from my face. I'd put my hair into a ponytail as the day had heated up. Even with the air conditioning going full blast, I seemed to have issues with my bodily thermostat these days.

Lindsey had been in and out of the kitchen at least a half dozen times wanting my opinion on this or that for her movie date. Every time I referred to it as a 'date' she got pissed.

"It's not a date, Mom. We're co-workers, barely friends. He doesn't know anyone around here, that's all."

Yeah, yeah, yeah - right!

For all of her denial, she'd certainly been fussing at Jack and me to make sure we looked presentable for 'Eric the friend.'

"Mom, you're going to change your top, right?"

"Bermuda shorts, Daddy? Really?"

I'd changed into a summer dress and sandals, putting some blush and mascara on; dabbing a bit of color on my lips. Working in the yard had given me a light tan, so this was as good as it was going to get. Lindsey had finally nagged Jack into putting on a pair of summer Dockers and a polo shirt.

I heard the doorbell ring. Jack called out that he had it. Lindsey came down for one last nod of approval from me. As she walked down the hallway toward the entry, I caught a glimpse of Eric from behind. He was tall, had dark hair that was neatly cut and was dressed eerily like Jack.

In that split second I hoped to God that Lindsey wasn't looking for someone like 'dear old dad'.

Jack was introducing himself, shaking his hand as they heard us approach. He turned to us, with his fake, congenial smile.

"Here are my girls," he said, giving Eric a dazzling grin. "Of course, Lindsey, you already know. This is my wife, Sammie."

"Samantha," I corrected, smiling, holding out my hand as Eric turned to face me.

I felt my smile freeze.

Those incredibly blue eyes took only a nanosecond to register recognition and then they froze up like blue ice. His smile never faltered.

"Glad to meet you, Mrs. Dennison," he said. "I'm Eric."

His hand captured mine and, for a moment, I felt the brutal squeeze as he let me know that he'd made the connection, as if I couldn't already tell that by his arctic glare.

"Eric," I repeated, as if in a daze. He still hadn't released my hand, even though I was attempting to pull back. In a couple of seconds, it was going to be obvious to Jack and Lindsey.

"I didn't catch your last name, Eric."

"I'm sorry, ma'am."

Did he just refer to me as a 'ma'am'?

"Slater," he said. "Eric Slater."

I was finally able to pull my hand from his grasp. Instinctively, I crossed my arms in front of my belly, anxious for his eyes to move on to anything or anyone but me. They didn't though.

I saw his gaze lower to my rounded little baby bump. It registered as his eyes returned to mine. Ever so slightly, his right eyebrow cocked questioningly. I hurried to break our gaze.

"Eric, Lindsey tells us you attend Purdue? Are you from that area?" Jack had blessedly forced Slate's attention from me.

"No sir," he answered politely. "I actually grew up in Virginia. I came to Indiana for college."

"I see," Jack replied. "Well, since tomorrow is the 4th, please come by for a cookout, won't you?"

I could see Lindsey beam at the idea. I wanted to puke.

Eric/Slate gave one of his slow, lazy smiles to Jack. "Thank you, sir. I'd love to."

He turned his attention to Lindsey.

"You look great, Lindsey. Ready?" he said to her in his slow, sexy voice that I thought had only been for me.

"Yep," she replied smiling up at him. "Good night Daddy. Good night Mom."

"You kids have fun," Jack called after them as they crossed over the threshold. I wanted to strangle him with my bare hands.

I noticed Slate had his hand on the small of Lindsey's back as he escorted her outside to his waiting vehicle, the pick-up truck, no doubt. At that point, I wanted to strangle him with my bare hands as well.

"He seems like a nice enough fellow," Jack commented after they'd gone.

"Hmmph," I said rolling my eyes. "A little too old and worldly for Lindsey at this stage in her life."

"How can you tell that by the thirty seconds you were around him, Sammie?"

"Call it mother's intuition."

I didn't care to discuss it any further with the mannequin, so I retreated to my bedroom downstairs. I immediately phoned Becky.

"'Sup girlfriend?" she giggled.

Becky had obviously been starting her July 4th celebrating a day early.

"How many margaritas have you had, Bec?"

"I don't know, two…maybe three, why?"

"That's not nearly enough for you to handle what I'm about to tell you. Guess who's coming to dinner tomorrow with Lindsey?"

Chapter 36

I played it over and over again in my mind as I made the potato salad the following morning, and the deviled eggs, and the baked beans. I continued to play it over and over again as I filled a Jell-O mold of the American flag using red, white and blue Jell-O.

What in the hell was Slate doing? Was this some sort of twisted revenge? Had he played me all along? If so, why?

Lindsey finally sauntered into the kitchen around 11:00 a.m. She was still in her summer pajamas.

"Can I help you with anything, Mom?"

"I've got everything pretty much done, sweetie. As soon as the brownies come out of the oven, I'll give them a dusting of confectioner's sugar and that should be it. You were out kind of late last night, weren't you?"

She poured herself a glass of orange juice from the fridge. "Gee, I don't know, Mom. I don't think 11:30 is all that late."

"It was more like 11:45," I replied.

"Were you waiting up for me?" she asked, with a smile crossing her face. "I'm almost nineteen you know."

"I know how old you are, Lindsey. I was there, remember?"

"Just sayin'."

"Did you have a nice time?"

"Sure did. Eric's nice and so funny, too."

I wondered if Slate had suddenly acquired a sense of humor after parting with his long locks.

"What do you mean, funny?" I asked.

"He said that you and I look more like sisters than mother and daughter. Isn't that a hoot?"

"A laugh riot," I commented. "Maybe he's trying to impress you by complimenting your parents."

"Maybe," she said thoughtfully, "but he didn't have any compliments for Daddy. Said he looked kind of uptight. He sure was surprised when I told him you'd be thirty-six in a week or so."

I choked on the iced tea I was sipping.

"You told him my age?"

"Sure, why not? It's not a secret, is it?"

"Honey, once past thirty, it isn't polite to advertise someone's age. Speaking of which, isn't Eric a bit old for you?"

"Geez, Mom. We're not getting engaged or married, just hanging out a little bit this summer. Eric says he can't commit to anyone until he gets through with all his schooling and interning. I get that."

"That sounds sensible to me," I agreed. "So, he didn't get fresh with you or anything last night?"

"No *mother*, he didn't get fresh. I can't believe you'd even ask me that."

Lindsey was clearly getting irritated with my questions. I needed to chill. I had to figure out what Slate's deal was without putting Lindsey in the middle. I'd be furious beyond reason if I discovered he was, in some way, using Lindsey as some pawn in a scheme. None of this made sense.

Becky had been too tipsy the night before to offer much help or speculation. Perhaps I needed to find out directly from the source. I would try to get Slate...Eric; whoever the hell he was these days, alone, to find out exactly what he was up to and why.

Jack had been out most of the afternoon. He still hadn't returned. He was only supposed to be getting beer, wine, hamburger, brats and hot dogs. I couldn't figure out why it was taking hours to do this. My parents arrived at 3:00 p.m. They were early (as usual). The cook-out wasn't scheduled until 5:00 p.m.

I'd showered earlier in the afternoon. I was wearing my hair up on top of my head with a few wispy tendrils hanging down. I dressed in another sun dress that did a bit more to hide my growing baby bump. I certainly didn't want Slate's attention to be focused on that the whole evening.

I noticed Lindsey had dressed in some tight little shorts and a tank top that accentuated her cute figure. She kept her hair shorter than mine. It was cut really cute. It fell just below her ears. She looked cute and wholesome. There was no doubt about it. Slate had better leave her the hell alone.

As soon as my parents had greeted Lindsey, they headed down the hall and into the kitchen where I was making up a relish tray of snacks.

Daddy gave me one of his notorious bear hugs as soon as he walked in, telling me how proud he was of the fine job that I'd done with Lindsey, reiterating what a good man Jack was.

I wanted to puke for the second day in a row.

"Where the hell is he, anyway?" he bellowed. "I could use a cold beer."

"Should be here anytime, Daddy. Take a seat on the patio. Lindsey's getting the lawn chairs out of the garage. When Jack gets here, we'll start the grill."

"Okay," he hollered back. "Need a cold one before long, though."

Mom wasted no time cornering me in the kitchen as I made a fresh pitcher of lemonade. I knew that she was going to lay a guilt trip on me as only a mother can.

"Well, dear, I'm glad you decided to share the good news about the impending birth of a new grandchild with everyone, with the exception of Daddy and me."

Guilt properly laid.

"Mom, I'm really sorry. The truth is, you guys travel so much, I can't keep up with where you are one minute before you're going on to yet another vacation spot."

"That's nonsense, Samantha, and you know it."

This is so not like Mom.

"Mom, I don't know what else to say, other than I'm sorry. It was thoughtless of me, I know."

"Can I ask you something, Samantha, and will you promise to be totally honest with your answer?"

I looked over at her as I poured both of us a glass of lemonade. She had a serious look on her face. It was if she'd wanted to ask this question for a long time, but dreaded the answer.

"Of course I will."

"Did your Daddy and I make a mistake in forcing you into a marriage with Jack?"

I had no clue why my mother was acting so out of character; trying to delve deep into something . . . but what? And why?

"Mom," I said, hoping the sincerity in my voice made up for the fact that there wasn't an honest answer I could give that wouldn't tear her up. "You and Daddy did what you thought was best for all concerned. Jack's been a wonderful father to Lindsey."

"That's not an answer, Samantha," she snapped, almost loudly. "You promised to tell me the truth."

I sat down across from her at the kitchen table and took her hand into mine.

"I'm not sure if I can answer it honestly. I'll try, though. I don't know for certain if Lindsey would've turned out so well had she not had Jack's love and attention. I also don't know whether Jack would've given her as much love and attention had we not married and had he not been given his position at Banion, which afforded us things for the family. I can tell you that I don't love Jack, though I was fully prepared to love him. I can also tell you that it's doubtful Jack has ever loved me."

"I knew it," she said with a sob, hanging her head. "I knew it was a mistake on our part. Forgive us please, Samantha? I know your father will never see that as being a mistake, but I did. Can you forgive me for not standing up to him for once in my life for my little girl?"

"Oh, Mom," I said, leaning over and hugging her to me. "There's no need to ask me for forgiveness. I had choices after that I could've made, should've made, and didn't."

"No," she said, still upset, "parents should never put their children in a position to be hurt like that. It was wrong. Just know that whatever you do in the future, you'll have my total support, okay?"

I nodded, wiping a stray tear from my cheek. She leaned in close as if she had a secret to share.

"This baby isn't Jack's, is it?"

Her eyes almost looked hopeful; as if by some chance it made my escape from Jack easier, which perhaps it did. I smiled back, squeezing her hand.

"No," I replied. "This baby isn't Jack's. He had a vasectomy years ago. Lindsey doesn't know this yet."

She patted my hand as I saw her smile for the first time since she'd come in to see me.

"Your secret's safe with me for as long as it needs to be, Samantha."

Chapter 37

~ ERIC/SLATE ~

I'd been a fucking wreck all night after seeing Sunny..... . . Sammie, whatever the fuck her name was, when I went to pick up my little co-ed friend.

Jesus Christ! How in the hell was I supposed to process this turn of events? I hoped that I'd maintained my cool.

Lindsey hadn't acted as if anything was wrong. My head was spinning upon leaving the multi-million dollar mansion the Dennisons called home. What the fuck? I had no clue Sunny came from Banion money. No wonder she traveled incognito. Being rich must be a burden, one that I'd never know.

I could barely focus on the movie. Coffee afterwards had seemed to drone on and on. I was pretty sure that Lindsey wasn't suspicious of the questions I asked about her mother. I'd been picking her brain for a few weeks about her dad. That had been much easier. I simply made it look as if he was a mentor of monumental proportions to someone like me, just coming up the through the ranks. She'd loved talking about Daddy.

She said her mom was getting ready to turn thirty-six. I had to smile. I bet Sunny had a hissy fit when, and if, she found out that Lindsey had shared that info with me. Chicks were funny about aging.

What the fuck? Sunny looked to be more like twenty-five than thirty-five. I could almost guarantee that she'd grilled her poor daughter about our 'faux' date.

I'd wanted to kick the rat bastard's ass all over their ten acres when I put two and two together last evening.

What a fucking wasteroid, hitting his wife, like I knew he had in the past. I was certain that Lindsey hadn't a clue about that part of it. I couldn't see her loving Daddy so much if she knew how he treated her mother.

The truth was, this was the part of my job that I hated more than anything; duping nice people to find out information.

Lindsey was a nice kid; an only child for Chrissake. She was sweet and innocent, but there's no way I'd given her any indication I was anything other than a friend or confidante. I figured a kid growing up as an only child needed as many confidantes as possible.

Hanging with Lindsey at Banion had given me plenty of opportunities to study the processes and procedures. It was my way in for getting into areas typically not accessible by interns, simply because she worked in those restricted areas.

All I had to do was press my face up against the glass door of the test lab and wave to her; she would immediately buzz me in.

We talked, well mostly she did the talking, while I observed and asked questions. She was happy to answer them all. She was a sweetie, for sure. I knew there was no way in hell Lindsey knew anything about her father's criminal activities.

Therein lay the problem. I couldn't say the same thing about Sunny. Since I'd mistakenly assumed that Sunny was married to a truck driver, and lived in a trailer park, I wasn't prepared to honestly and objectively assess her involvement, if any, in these activities.

My thoughts were in turmoil. My emotions were right there, too, though I fucking hated admitting it. I thought if I ever set eyes on the prick-tease again, I'd feel nothing but the need to lash out at her…seek some sort of verbal revenge. I felt none of that now and it pissed me off in all honesty.

My tumultuous thoughts were interrupted when my doorbell sounded. It was Taz and Donovan. I had summoned both of them to my apartment.

I opened the door and they both filed in, looking none too pleased.

"You know this isn't typical protocol, right Eric?"

"Yeah, yeah, have a seat. I wouldn't have called you here if it wasn't a matter of grave importance. I'm not a rookie, for Chrissake."

They both eyed me warily, and then took a seat on my overstuffed leather sofa.

"Sorry for the inconvenience, Agent Matthews," I said with a smirk.

"Just get to the point," Taz griped, twisting his 'do-rag' back into place.

Taz fucking loved his role as mean biker gang member. I actually thought he was going to regret it when all of this shit was over, which was supposed to be fairly soon. Now, I wasn't so sure. They were both waiting for me to say what I needed to say.

"I think I may need to take myself off leading this investigation, guys."

"Are you crazy?" Donovan snapped, unable to contain his anger.

"Hey, I'm the senior officer," I snapped back. "Watch your fucking mouth, Craig."

"Both of you chill," Taz interjected. He was forever the calm one.

Donovan and I'd had our share of disagreements. Still, it wasn't his fucking place to question a senior investigator. I knew that there was a major conflict here. Protocol said that I needed to make it known to the other operatives. I'd already communicated this to my senior operative in D.C., first thing this morning.

"What's going on?" Taz asked, his forehead breaking into those premature frown lines he got when worried. He was too damn young for frown lines. He hadn't earned them, but I had.

"Guess who the douche bag is married to?"

"No…"

"Yep. Diamond Girl."

"Who?" Donovan asked, clearly clueless.

"Jack Dennison is married to the dancer Slate was fucking for a while, Diamond Girl, a.k.a., Sunny."

I threw Taz an immediate glare for describing Sunny as simply a fuck buddy. It was way more than that and he damn well knew it.

"That's impossible," Donovan breathed, now feeling totally stupid that his investigative information was less than mediocre on such a high profile case. "I've met with her several times. She was cooperative, forthright and I know that there's no way in hell that soccer mom's a dancer."

"Well she is - was," I corrected. "And she's pregnant with what may turn out to be my child."

"What?" they both said in unison. "Did you also report that?"

"I did. So you can see why this is a total conflict of interest for me. If, for one minute, the attorney defending her husband or those fucking bikers got wind of my involvement, it could blow the federal prosecutor's case into oblivion."

"So, what are your instructions from DC? We were supposed to serve the warrants on the 5th."

"We're to hold tight for a couple of days until revised instructions are provided. In the meantime, gentlemen, I have a 4th of July cookout to attend."

"You aren't seriously still going out with the daughter are you?"

"We aren't going out," I replied tersely. "I cultivated a friendship for the purpose of gaining information. That's acceptable within the parameters of our jobs here, last I heard. I haven't been instructed to do anything otherwise, at the moment. I wanted to fill you two in on the developments and to confirm that the 'sit tight for now' instructions are followed by you and the others. Do you understand?"

Donovan and Taz both nodded. They were disappointed that things wouldn't be moving as quickly as they would have liked. Neither of them were too keen on the fact that this case, which had consumed a great deal of our time for better than two years, first in Virginia and now here in Indiana, was stalled once again.

They departed with their hang-dog demeanor and my commitment that I would be in contact as soon as I received further instructions.

I dressed in my preppy college garb for the cook-out. I looked at my haircut in the mirror. I was so fucking glad that I'd been finally able to cut those long locks off. I didn't appreciate the hair covering my neck with summer coming.

I'd removed my earring, and kissed that fucking bandana good-bye, once and for all. Taz still loved playing that scene. I'd been done with it after leaving Manassas, Virginia when our first huge bust went down nearly two years prior.

That one had been up close and personal for me. I'd taken great pleasure in putting those pieces of garbage away for life. They'd taken someone very close from me. They'd taken my sister, Laney, with their drug dealings, extortion and violence. I had a personal stake in that one. I had no clue that, two years later, it would lead me back to Indiana, back to where I'd been raised all those years ago.

I grabbed the keys to my pick-up truck and headed out. It was a good half-hour drive to the Dennison estate.

I almost chuckled to myself as I thought about how off-base I'd been in my professional assessment of Sunny. I prided myself on reading people quickly and being able to assess their personal situations. I'd totally missed the boat on that one.

She had reminded me a little bit of Laney. She looked innocent and out of place at that club...like she needed someone to watch out for her. I'd fallen right into that role, whether I wanted it or not. I couldn't help myself where she was concerned.

My first impression was one of awe and appreciation. I saw Diamond-the-dancer, who looked like an angel, and danced like a born seductress. I'd gotten a hard-on just watching her dance. Innocence and lustiness all rolled up into one beautiful chick that could move her body in perfection to the music. I was intrigued. I was more than intrigued; I was fucking amazed by her.

I needed to shake it off. This wasn't about me and her at the moment. She had some explaining to do, but only after I was absolutely sure that she wasn't involved in the criminal shit her ass-hat husband had going.

Donovan had called her a soccer mom. I wasn't about to take his word for shit right now. I'd have to find this out for myself. If Sunny was involved, Sunny would go down with the rat bastard and all of the others. I'd see to that.

My instincts told me that Sunny was innocent of criminal activities. My heart was counting on it.

Chapter 38

My mother and father had finally left. I hated to sound that way, but my father could wear anyone out. He'd done a fairly good job of it this afternoon. First with me (in front of Slate, naturally) going on and on about my pregnancy and hoping for a grandson…and it's about god-damn time Jack had me barefoot and pregnant again. I'd literally felt my cheeks glow red with that remark. I didn't dare look over at Slate. I wasn't sure if he'd figured it out yet. As far as I was concerned, the S.O.B. could think this baby *was* Jack's.

Then Daddy had kept referring to Slate as 'Lindsey's Young Man,' which had made her uncomfortable and kind of pissed me off at the same time. I'd made a point of checking out Slate's reaction through my peripheral vision. He'd remained cool, calm, and collected.

Jack had simply managed to get drunk and laugh at his own stupid jokes, while constantly checking his cell for messages.

Slate had been eyeballing Jack. I busted him a couple of times, throwing him a hateful glare when he thought no one was looking. I could tell it pissed him off when Jack would tell me to fetch him another beer, or when Jack made a big production of grilling me about the potato salad.

"Are you sure you used your regular recipe on this batch, Sammie? It tastes like something is missing."

"Missing something? Like what?"

"How about flavor?" he said, guffawing at his own nasty barb.

"Perhaps the alcohol has dulled your taste buds today."

Jack had given me a hateful glare, turning to look at Slate.

"Hey, Eric, don't feel as if you have to clean your plate there, buddy. Somehow, Sammie has made her potato salad taste bland. No one will be offended."

Slate had given him a look, purposely digging into the bowl and putting more of it on his plate.

"Tastes fine to me, Mr. Dennison," he said with a wink.

"Jack - call me *Jack*," he said once again, tossing back the rest of his beer. "I guess it's all in what you're used to buddy. Me? I have a taste for the finer things."

My father cleared his throat loudly after that exchange and then stood up.

"Come on, Joan. It's about time we head out to the club if you want to watch those fireworks."

My mother helped me with the last of the clearing, then caught me in the kitchen.

"Remember what I said, Samantha. We'll support you in any decision you make. I hope you make one soon."

With that, she kissed my cheek and left me standing, somewhat stunned, in the kitchen. Wow, my mother was more intuitive than I'd ever thought. Why now, though?

I peered out the kitchen window to the deck. Jack had gotten up and was out in the yard with his cell phone up to his ear. Lindsey and Slate were heading into the house.

My heart fluttered as I wondered if he was taking her out this evening.

"I'm going to give Eric a tour of the house, Mom. He really likes your decorating."

Slate gave me a warm smile that betrayed nothing.

"I really love your place, Samantha," he said. "I can't tell you how great it's been spending time here today."

"Why, thank you, Eric. I suppose your family lives out of state somewhere?"

"Here and there," he said, in his typical evasive manner.

"Let's start downstairs," Lindsey interrupted, taking him by the arm.

Thirty minutes later, Lindsey and Eric came out onto the deck where I was sitting with Jack.

"Mom, Eric's getting ready to leave. He wondered if he could take some of your potato salad home. I'm going to fix him a plate."

I looked up at Slate and caught the warmth in his eyes as he smiled down at me. I blushed, caught off-guard by the moment.

"Hell, Lindsey," Jack called after her, "have him take it all with him. It probably does taste good to a bachelor."

Jack killed the rest of his beer, then handed me his empty bottle. I started to get up to go fetch him another one. Slate's eyes met mine briefly and, with one look, I could tell he wanted me to stay put. I sank back down in my chair.

"Yo Lindsey," he hollered, "grab your dad another brewsky on your way back, yeah?"

"Sure thing," she called out.

When Lindsey reappeared, she had her dad's beer and a foil-covered plate for Slate.

"Mr. and Mrs. Dennison, thank you so much for having me here as your guest today," Slate said. "The food was fantastic, and the company was mostly great."

He smiled at me when he spoke, his dimple making a rare appearance.

Jack stood up and shook his hand. "Glad you enjoyed it, Eric. You're welcome anytime. Don't be a stranger, you hear?"

"Absolutely, sir," he replied, with a wink.

Oh my.

"I'm going to walk Eric out," Lindsey said, her face not showing as much enthusiasm as earlier.

"Good evening, Eric," I said, as they turned to go.

I looked back over at Jack. Something was on his mind. He'd been terribly distracted all day. He generally didn't pound beers the way he'd been pounding them all afternoon, either.

"Jack," I started, "is everything okay?"

"Sure it is," he said with no conviction. His voice was empty. "Everything is just fine, Sammie." His eyes were blank as they looked out over towards the setting sun.

I took time in the shower, lathering my skin up and letting the cool water rinse over me. I shampooed my hair and stood under the stream of water, contemplating today's events. The only way to possibly describe it was strange, incredibly strange.

I never had the opportunity to catch Slate alone. It was if he'd choreographed it that way, always sparking a conversation with someone when they were on their way out of the room, just so we would never have the chance to be alone, even for a brief moment.

After my shower, I combed out my hair and dressed in a pair of silky shorts with a matching cami top. I slathered lotion on my legs as I sat on the bed. My cell phone rang. It was Becky.

"Can you talk?" she whispered.

"Yes. Why are you whispering?"

"George is in the other room. I've been dying to know how it went today. Spill it now."

I relayed the events of today, including the unusual conversation that had taken place between my mother and me.

"No shit? Really? That's so uncharacteristic of your mom, isn't it?"

"It really is. I hope everything's okay with her and Daddy."

"Oh, I'm sure it is hun. Maybe she finally sees what a bastard he is, Sam. It definitely sounds as if she's dealing with guilt over the whole thing after all of these years."

"Yeah, but why? I need to get her without Daddy some time for lunch or something. There's more to all of this. I'm sure of it."

I sat on the bed and talked to Becky for another half-hour while I painted my toenails. She was hysterical about the whole incident with the potato salad.

"You see, Sam. That's so 'Jack' in the way he talks to you. I'm glad Slate put him in his place without appearing to do so. It sounds like Jack was getting kind of trashed."

"Yeah, no shit. I'm definitely keeping my deadbolt locked tonight."

"What do you think all that was about?"

"He's worried about something. I don't have anything concrete to give Donovan, though. I mean, he has been sticking close to Indy these past few weeks. He never freaking leaves his cell phone around. I think he sleeps with it under his pillow and that's no exaggeration."

"Just be careful, okay?"

"Yep. Got to. I have to take care of Dalton."

"Who the hell's Dalton?"

"That's the name I've picked out for the baby."

"Oh geez! You'll have that name changed fifty million times before that baby's even born. I remember what we went through with Lindsey, don't you?"

"There weren't that many names," I argued.

"Really? Let's see: Jessica, Emily, Justine, Kylie, Jillian, Jamie, Zoë, Hannah, Rebecca, Anna - need I go on?"

"No, please don't," I laughed. "Okay, I'll keep the name to myself until such time as the baby's here and I have my final choice."

"Thank you," she said. "Hey, gotta go. George wants to go to the end of the street. We can see the fireworks from the empty field."

"'Kay, talk to you later."

I checked my toenails to make sure they weren't still tacky before I crawled under the sheets of my bed. They were good.

I got up and brushed my teeth, then checked my deadbolt lock, making sure that it was securely in place. It was close to midnight. I was fairly certain Jack had crashed in front of the television in the master suite we no longer shared.

As I pulled my comforter back to fold it at the foot of the bed, I saw the silver bracelet that Slate had given me for Valentine's Day on the pillow. It had been in my jewelry box on the dresser. I didn't wear it when Jack was around, not wanting to draw his attention to it.

I picked it up and saw the note folded underneath.

My heart fluttered as I opened up the folded piece of paper. The dormant butterflies in my stomach suddenly came to life. They were swarming as my eyes read the words in his neat script:

'Leave the door from your bedroom onto the terrace unlocked. I have the need to taste the finer things tonight. -S.'

I crawled under the cool sheets of my bed after I'd left the French doors leading from the outside terrace to my bedroom unlocked.

I sure as hell wasn't going to allow Slate to taste *anything* until he told me what the hell was going on and I was certain that he was the 'good guy' in all of this, although I couldn't see how *that* was possible.

I was determined to stay awake until he arrived. I glanced at the clock on my nightstand several times. I was listening to the Bose system that I'd turned down softly. It generally lulled me to sleep. Tonight, I had it on a classic rock station as I lay back against my soft, down pillows and waited for Slate.

I glanced at the clock on my nightstand. It read 1:16 a.m. I listened to the sounds of the Rolling Stones and the classic tune, 'Gimme Shelter.'

It's just a kiss away; it's just a kiss away...

I drifted to sleep with the sound of those lyrics in my head. Then later, I felt my mattress sink down with the weight of someone else. I opened my eyes and willed that they adjust to the darkness, though I knew who it was.

I felt his presence right next to me. He said nothing, but he knew that I was awake. He molded himself next to me in my bed. He was dressed in black like some 'summer' Ninja: black wife beater shirt, black jeans and ever so quiet and panther-like in his movements.

I started to say something. It was if he could read my reaction before I had a chance to know how I would react.

His mouth covered mine, silencing me for the moment. No, this wasn't going to work, Slate. I refused to melt to his kiss as his lips were on mine, working them with his expertise. His tongue invaded my mouth, exploring and tantalizing me, slowly and methodically wearing my resolve down to nothing.

I laced my arms around his neck, pulling him in closer to me, meeting his kisses with no reservation now, wanting him now more than ever. His kiss grew rougher. I felt his teeth tug at my bottom lip as he broke the moment. He pulled back, placing his hands on my shoulders so that he could study my face.

"So, *Samantha*, was everything you ever fucking told me a *lie?*"

His eyes were boring into mine with something akin to anger and irritation…neither of which I understood.

"I could ask you the *same* thing, *Eric.*"

He rose to a sitting position, pulling me up with him. He switched on the small lamp on my nightstand so that he could look at me in the light.

"I know why I wasn't upfront with you. What's your excuse, Mrs. Dennison?"

"Why don't you go first, Slate? You still have me in the dark, clearly that's to your advantage at the moment, but you're on my turf now and I need some answers."

He gazed at me with an intensity that gave me chills. I sensed he wanted to provide me with the answers I needed, but there was reluctance to do so.

"I'm not a biker," he said, with a slow smile.

"That much I figured out on my own. What's your involvement with my daughter? Were you trying to get back at me for something?"

He immediately pulled me against him. He was pissed.

"I didn't even fucking know she was *your* daughter. The Intel I was provided said she was the daughter of Jack and Samantha Dennison. Besides that, what reason would I have for wanting revenge?"

"Then you must be working with the authorities," I said, trying to put the scant information he'd already provided into some semblance of order. "Are you like an undercover cop or something?"

"Yeah, something *like* that," he replied softly, brushing my hair back from my face. "I swear that in no way would I do anything to hurt Lindsey. In fact, I won't be working at Banion any longer. My participation in this investigation will be changing soon. I told Lindsey this evening when she walked me out that I was returning early to West Lafayette to take a late summer class."

"Then you must be investigating whatever it is that Jack's involved with. You must think it involves Banion Pharmaceuticals, right? But how are the Outlaws tied into all of this?"

"Babe, I can't tell you anything that could compromise this investigation. I just need to ask you right here and right now whether you're involved in any way. If you tell me now, I can probably offer you some immunity from prosecution. But you have to be upfront with me. This is a one-time, get out of jail free pass, babe. It's now or never."

Now it was my turn to be pissed. How could he possibly think that I would participate in whatever it was Jack was doing?

"Slate," I said, "I'm the one who took the financial records to a forensic accountant as soon as I knew something was wrong. I even talked to an investigator named Donovan and gave him access to everything. Jack has kept me in the dark most of our marriage, but I don't think whatever he's involved in has been going on for more than a year - two years tops. I guess if ignorance makes me an active participant in whatever his crimes turn out to be, then I'm guilty."

"No, babe, ignorance under these circumstances, makes you *innocent*. I just had to ask. I thought maybe the reason you broke things off with me was because I *had* blown my cover," he said chuckling. "Now I guess I have to face the cold truth that you simply broke things off."

"I didn't, Slate. Jack sent the text message. He was waiting for me when I got home from your place that last day we were...... together."

"What - he came home unexpectedly?"

I nodded.

"Did he hurt you?" he asked, his eyes getting darker.

"No, nothing like that," I lied. "He had someone keeping an eye on me: his administrative assistant at Banion. Her name is Susan Reynard. She saw me dancing at Sharkey's, and took a video for him. He threatened to show the video to my parents and to Lindsey. He found my phone in the nightstand. Somehow, though, he was under the impression that I was involved with Slash," I said. "I didn't tell him any different."

I saw a look of recognition cross his face when I told him that. He graced me with a half-smile.

"What?"

"Garnet said there was a chick in the club asking questions about you named Susan. She's the one who threw Slash's name out there."

At the mention of Garnet's name, I immediately froze up. I recalled the day seeing Garnet on the staircase leading from his apartment, and then him following her down the steps and pulling her around to face him. He'd hugged her against him. It had been an intimate scene.

Slate noticed the change in my demeanor.

"What's wrong?"

"Nothing's wrong, Slate. It just seems to me that it didn't take you long to find a new fuck buddy, did it?"

"What the hell are you talking about, Diamond?"

He hadn't called me that for a long time.

"I'm talking about seeing her leave your apartment one day a couple of months ago, seeing you go after her and pull her close to you in a hug. That's what I'm talking about. I was parked across the street."

He looked at me and saw that I was pissed. I was hurt by the thought that he'd so easily replaced me.

"It's not what you think, babe. She's nothing to me. She provided some inside information now and then, but that's over now, too."

"What do you mean 'too'? So, you *were* fucking her, right?"

I twisted away from him, scooting across the bed so that my back was to him.

"Hey," he said, circling around the bed and coming to stand in front of me. He pulled me up so that I was now standing within inches of him.

"Garnet was nothing to me. She was an informant without knowing who I was. I played the part, Diamond. That's part of the job."

"Was I part of the job too, Slate?"

"Actually, no. You're what they call an 'impediment' to the job. You distracted me. I fucked up a bit. I put myself at risk, along with the investigation, momentarily. I don't usually do that. In fact, it was a first. Now, I'm tired of talking about it. That's not why I'm here."

"Why are you here?"

"Why do you think?"

"I think you're freaking crazy if you think I'm going to *fuck* you, not knowing who you've been with since me. Forget it."

"I haven't been with anyone since you, baby. I wouldn't put you at risk that way. I wouldn't put my baby at risk that way either."

"I see," I said, pushing away from him. "How are you so certain that this is your baby?"

I saw the spark ignite in those incredibly blue eyes. He cocked an eyebrow as he moved towards me with the grace and litheness of a panther. His arms pulled me into him, and his fingers lifted my chin so that I was now focused on his beautiful, perfect face.

"Because, baby, Jack Dennison's medical records show that he had a vasectomy in 1999. I know damn well you haven't been with anyone since me. That's not your style."

"Hah," I laughed. "You thought I was trailer trash, Slate. How is it you're suddenly an *expert* on my style?"

"Fine," he said with a shrug. "Tell me I'm wrong about it then."

I stared at him with his cocky look going on, his slight slouch with his thumbs hooked in his jean pockets, his lean, muscular body right there in front of me. I ached for him, but he'd not convinced me what his involvement had been with Garnet.

"You're not wrong about it. The baby's yours. But I'm still waiting for an answer as to what went on between you and Garnet."

He rolled his eyes and looked away from me for a moment. That meant there *was* something. He raised his hand to his forehead, his thumb rubbing against an eyebrow.

"I never fucked Garnet. I haven't fucked anyone since you. Garnet sucked me off a few times, and that was the extent of it."

"Oh, my God," I hissed, turning from him.

His arm reached out and gently hauled me back around. "Does it make it any less repulsive to know that I always thought about you when she did?" He gave me a cocky little smile and before I had a chance to answer, his lips came down on mine, kissing me with a passion that I'd missed these last couple of months.

As much as I was pissed about Garnet, I still couldn't resist him. And at the moment, I didn't want to resist him.

I laced my arms back around his neck, pulling his face down even closer to me. He lifted me up and placed me gently on my bed.

He pulled his shirt up over his head and unfastened his jeans, pushing them down and stepping out of them. Somehow, his boots were off and he was totally naked in seconds.

He straddled me, tugging my shorts down past my hips, maneuvering them off. He leaned down and helped me pull my camisole top off. His lips found mine again as he thoroughly kissed and explored my mouth with his tongue.

His hands fondled my breasts gently, bringing my nipples to erection. He lowered his face southward, kissing my neck, my shoulders and then finding his way to my breasts. He ravaged them with his mouth and tongue. His fingers massaged them roughly, his teeth capturing my nipples, inflicting just a hint of pain that turned to pleasure once he began suckling them.

His hand had moved to my baby bump. He was so gentle, lingering there to allow his fingers to trace the roundness. His mouth moved there. He tenderly kissed my stomach, his tongue rolling across it, sending shivers up my spine.

"When's our baby due, Diamond?"

"December 7th," I whispered huskily.

"And do we know yet whether we're having a son or a daughter?" he continued, as his mouth was now sliding down to my extremely wet pussy...

"A boy," I said, my voice now bordering a whimper as I waited for his tongue to arrive.

"Umm, excellent," he whispered against me, as his tongue rolled around my clitoris. I was squirming in pleasure, whimpering in delight.

"You need to keep quiet when you come, baby. Can you do that?" he asked, continuing to administer exquisite pleasure to the sensitive folds of my sex.

"I'll try," I replied, now reaching the moaning phase of my response to him.

I felt his smile against the lips of my pussy. His fingers were inside of me, pressing all of the sensitive spots he knew so well.

"We can't wake Lindsey or the rat bastard, baby. You're going to have to be quiet when you come. I know how difficult that is for you. You like to scream things out...dirty things when you climax."

I felt myself getting close, but he wasn't inside of me yet and I knew that's how we would reach our peak together.

"I know, baby. I know what you need," he whispered hoarsely. "But I need to know that you'll be a good girl and not scream. Do you promise?"

"I promise," I said gritting my teeth, arching my back.

I heard him laugh quietly as he moved his face back to mine. His mouth was on mine. I could taste the salty sweetness of myself on his lips.

He drew himself up onto his knees, straddling me. I could see his impressive erection. The thought of Garnet sucking on it came to my mind. It was as if Slate could freaking read my mind.

"Stop it," he said. "You need to quit thinking about what Garnet did to my cock. It was a release for me, baby. It had nothing at all to do with you. Do you understand?"

I nodded, my body aching for the fullness of him. I watched as he put his hand around his erection and hovered over me, ready to guide his cock into me.

"So, we won't have any further discussions on the matter? You understand that I did what I had to do, right?"

I nodded again, tracing my lips with my tongue. He was watching me with his smoldering eyes; challenging me to make an issue of it, knowing full well he would withhold pleasuring me if I didn't agree.

"Yes, Slate."

"That's my girl," he whispered, guiding his cock into me with one quick thrust.

I moaned and his lips captured mine to silence me. My legs wrapped tightly around his hips. My toes dug into his firm, muscular ass. I kissed him fervently, my tongue exploring his mouth, whimpering softly against him.

His thrusts were deep. His penetration fulfilled my need for him. We rocked back and forth together, totally entwined within each other. He rotated his hips in a circular motion, making sure he hit my special spot that brought even louder whimpers from me.

"Quiet baby," he breathed into my ear, his warm breath sending shivers through me once again.

His thrusts increased in rhythm. I could feel beads of perspiration on his smooth back. He was totally into this every bit as much as me. I felt the silver cross on the chain he wore around his neck brush back and forth against my breasts as his momentum picked up.

"Come on, baby," he urged, his voice thick with lust. "Let's do this together."

That was all he needed to say. My climax unraveled around me as I met him thrust for thrust, trying my best not to cry out.

His mouth, once again, covered mine to silence me. He was having difficulty keeping silent as well. I heard several low moans escape from him as he pumped his orgasm into me. I contracted around him which drove him to groaning deeply as he finished emptying himself into me.

We lay intertwined together for several minutes afterwards. He lightly traced my damp skin with his long, lean fingers. He planted soft kisses all over my face and neck, whispering how sweet and perfect I felt to him.

All too soon, he raised himself up and out of me, leaving the bed.

"Where are you going?" I whispered loudly to him. He was gathering his clothing from the floor, getting dressed.

"I've got to go, babe. I shouldn't even be here."

"But we still have to talk," I continued. "I need to know more about what's going on with Jack."

"Donovan's your contact for that," he replied, pulling his boots on. "Remember, Diamond, I *wasn't* here. This *didn't* happen."

"Okay, okay," I whispered back, rolling my eyes at him. "Can you at least tell me when '*this*' is *not* going to happen *again?*"

He came over and sat down next to me on the bed. I got a dimpled smile from him on that one. He pulled me to him. I was still naked.

He tilted my face up and kissed my lips softly several times.

"I don't know. Keep your door unlocked each night though. I'll visit when I can, okay?"

I nodded; a feeling of sadness was creeping back in.

"Hey," he said softly, "take care of my son, baby."

With that, he disappeared quietly into the darkness of the July night. I might've thought it had been an extremely lovely sex dream if I hadn't spotted the nice, big hickey he'd left on my right boob.

Damn.

Well, at least it wouldn't be noticeable to anyone else.

Chapter 40

I didn't see Slate for several days, even though I'd left the doors leading from my room to the terrace unlocked each night. I fretted about how he was. I had no clue what part he was playing in this investigation.

I was betting Donovan was his boss. I knew there was no way I could mention Slate to Donovan. He'd been extremely adamant that whatever contact we had was to remain just between us. There was no way in hell I'd put Slate in danger from the Outlaws or his boss. Still, I missed him constantly.

Lindsey had been moping around a bit the days that followed our July 4th cookout. I asked her if anything was wrong. She shrugged it off as simple boredom at her job with Banion.

"How's Eric?" I asked, cautiously.

"Who?"

"Lindsey," I said, shaking my head and feeling totally like a shit. "Did you two have a disagreement or something?"

"No, nothing like that. He went back to Purdue, I guess. Said he was taking a late summer course. I think he was simply bored with Banion Pharmaceuticals or maybe just bored with me."

My heart went out to her; such a beautiful and talented girl she was. She would naturally think it had something to do with her. For whatever reason, Lindsey needed a wake-up call for her own self-esteem.

What the hell? She was just like me in that respect. I could blame Jack for that, but the truth was Jack only did what I'd allowed him to do. Guess it was time to blame 'Mom.' I certainly didn't want Lindsey blaming me. I needed to give her the best advice that I could.

"Lindsey," I said in my admonishing tone, "you need to give yourself some credit. If Eric said he needed to go back to school for a summer course, then why would you doubt his honesty? Besides, you yourself said it was a friendship."

"I know, you're right," she admitted. "It isn't really about Eric at all. It's more about the fact that I can't seem to maintain a relationship with a guy, at all. Is there something wrong with me?"

"No, not at all, sweetheart. You're only nineteen, honey. Not even officially nineteen yet. What's your hurry?"

She looked at me with a hangdog look, so unlike Lindsey.

"I know that I'm in no hurry to marry, but it's just sort of like when I'm ready, I'd like to know that a good and decent man will be interested. So far, even my high school and freshman college relationships have been a failure. Mom, can I tell you something and you won't judge me?"

Was I prepared to hear this? Was she going to tell me she'd let some jock screw her because she felt she owed it to him? Worse yet, was she going to tell me that Lance had gotten her 'in trouble' and she had taken care of it?

"Of course, sweetheart. I'm your mother, you can tell me anything. I love you unconditionally."

"I'm still a...*virgin!*" she choked, tears filling her eyes as if it was a confession of shame.

My sweet baby girl.

"Oh, honey," I said, giving her a hug. "There's absolutely nothing wrong with that. It simply means that you've used good judgment and are saving yourself for the right man."

"Please don't take this the wrong way, but I've been able to do simple math since first grade. I mean, I know that you and Daddy were... . . . intimate when you were way younger than me. I know that you were pregnant when you married. I mean, how did you know that he was the right man?" She was looking at me expectantly. Wanting an answer that just didn't exist.

"Honey, I'm going to be honest with you because you're a woman now, and you deserve to be treated like one. You're right. I was young and I felt 'pressured' to have sex way earlier than I should have. Luckily, it worked out for me. I had the most wonderful child anyone could ever have wanted. The truth is, your father and I have had our share of differences."

"I can see that, Mom. I can see that you aren't really close at all. I mean what's the deal with separate bedrooms? I don't for one minute think it's because of your pregnancy. Then there's..... ."

She suddenly stopped talking. She was looking extremely uncomfortable with where the topic of conversation was headed.

"There's what, Lindsey?"

"It's just that Daddy seems inordinately interested in his assistant, Susan. I've noticed it at work. It's really starting to piss me off. I think you should call him out on it."

Lindsey loved her father regardless of his indiscretions. Hopefully, she would continue to love me the same way once she learned of mine. Now wasn't the best time to find out though.

"Lindsey, it's complicated. Please trust that I'll do the right thing?"

"I think there's much more to this, Mom. If you truly believe that I'm an adult - a woman - then why can't you be upfront with me about it?"

I was torn as to how to answer my daughter. She was old enough to handle the truth, most of it anyway, yet she loved her father. I didn't want her feeling pressured to take sides. She'd opened the door for this, perhaps it was an opportunity.

"Okay, Lindsey, if you want the truth, you shall have it. I only hope you can handle it."

She nodded, taking a seat at the kitchen table. I took a deep breath, opting to just spit it out, short and simple.

"Your father and I don't love each other. We probably never have. We both love you very much and always will. I'm pregnant with another man's child."

There it was…the Reader's Digest version. She would either continue to love me, or she would hate me forever. It needed to be said, though.

I watched Lindsey's face as she digested the news. I saw no shock or disbelief at all. Had she always suspected? She reached across the table and took my hand in hers.

"Oh Mom," she said softly, "does Daddy know about the baby not being his?"

I nodded, tears welling up in my eyes. "I suppose you think I'm the worst kind of mother," I said, half-sobbing.

"No," she said softly, giving me a hug. "How could I possibly think that about you? All of these years, the years when I became aware of things between you and Daddy, I wondered how you had hung in there for so long."

"What do you mean?"

"I wasn't blind, Mom. I had friends that I spent time with, going to sleepovers and camping trips with their families during the summers. I saw the way their parents interacted with each other. It was way different than the way you and Daddy interacted. I never actually saw you laugh together, or hold hands, or even kiss. I don't mean to hurt you Mom, but I see Daddy laugh with Susan. They talk all the time, have lunch together. They've invited me, but I politely decline."

"Oh, honey, I'm not hurt that you've told me that at all. I figured as much. In your father's defense, he was up against my father when I found out I was pregnant. He was pressured into the marriage. He wasn't pressured into loving you, though. Please know that."

"I do know that, Mom. I know that both of you love me and have always put me first. That's why I have no problem at all with you putting yourself first for a while. I know how Granddaddy can be. He's extremely set in his ways and domineering. I have one other question for you, though."

"Go ahead," I replied, nodding. I mean how bad could this be? The worst part was over.

"Do you love the father of the baby?"

How can I explain this to her?

She didn't ask for an explanation, though. She asked a simple question.

"Yes, Lindsey. I love him."

"Does he love you, Mom?"

I didn't have to think long or hard about that question. Slate had never given me any reason to believe that he loved me, though I knew he cared about me. Those were two different things altogether.

"I don't know. I truly don't know."

Chapter 41

It was two days before my birthday. I was lying on my back with my feet up in the stirrups waiting for Dr. Bailey to come into the examination room.

I had the paper sheet across my knees, offering a small bit of privacy to protect what dignity I still possessed. I'd learned quickly when I was pregnant with Lindsey, that modesty goes out the window when it's all said and done.

I thought about the discussion that Lindsey and I had the previous day. I was relieved to finally get it out there. She hadn't pressed me for any further info on the baby's father. I wasn't ready to divulge all of that anyway.

I did ask that she not let her father know that I'd shared this with her. I explained it was a matter of pride for him. She understood. The truth was, I couldn't tip Jack off that the marriage was over. Though I hadn't specifically told Lindsey that, she knew it was inevitable, given the circumstances. She assured me that she would keep everything confidential for as long as necessary.

The nurse had been in and taken all of my vitals. Everything looked fine. I looked up at the ceiling and giggled at the sticker that had been placed near the light fixture. It read, "Smile - your doctor is watching you."

Just then, I heard a bit of a commotion out in the hallway.

"Sir, excuse me, you can't go in there," the nurse's voice called out.

What the…?

"You said exam room three, right?"

Oh dear God. That's Slate's voice . . .

"Are you Mr. Dennison, sir?"

"No," he said with a smirk, "I'm the father of the baby."

My cheeks were flushed a rosy pink by the time the door opened and Slate sauntered in, as if he had every right to invade my privacy. He shut the door behind him, not bothering to notice that he'd shut it in the nurse's face.

"Nice position you're in babe," he said. "Wonder if we can buy one of these tables for your room."

"What the hell?"

The nurse pushed through the door just then, extremely upset.

"Mrs. Dennison," she started, "I'm so sorry-"

"It's okay; he can stay. He *is* the baby's father."

There, it was out now. I could officially be thought of as a skank at my OB/GYN's office.

Whatever.

She backed out through the door, telling me Dr. Bailey would be in shortly.

I looked over at Slate. He was thoroughly proud of himself for the commotion he'd caused.

"How did you know I was here, Slate?" I was perturbed at his smugness. No - I was pissed.

"I know every move you make, Diamond."

"Why in the hell are you still calling me that? You know my name now."

"I won't call you Samantha. It's too hoity-toity."

"Hoity-toity? Is that a real term, Slate?"

"Okay, how about *pretentious* then?"

"I'm impressed. Then call me 'Sammie' like other people do."

"That's what the rat bastard calls you."

"How about I tell Jack that he can't call me that anymore; that he has to use my pretentious name of Samantha, will that satisfy you?" I asked.

He smiled, gracing me with that scrumptious dimple. "If you promise you'll enforce it with him, then yeah, I'm down with that."

He sauntered over to where I was still laying on my back, feet up in stirrups and lifted the paper cover up to take a peek.

"Slate, for crying out loud, a little privacy would be appreciated here."

"Aww babe, it's not like I haven't seen, touched or tasted it all before," he smirked. He put the cover back down and leaned over, giving me a kiss on the lips.

"Why are you here?"

"Just being supportive of you, babe, in your delicate condition. I want to hear what the doctor has to say, make sure that you're doing everything that you're supposed to be doing and that things are progressing like they should."

Just then, Dr. Bailey came bustling in with my chart. He was in his late fifties, a no-nonsense type of man with snowy white hair and bushy eyebrows to match.

"Well, Samantha, I see we have your husband with us today."

Holy crap.

Dr. Bailey hadn't been my OB/GYN with Lindsey, though he had all of my records from my earlier doctor who had since retired.

He held his hand out to Slate. They shook hands. I hoped like hell that Slate didn't blurt out anything inappropriate.

"Pleased to meet you, doctor. I wanted to be here to make sure you have all of the information you may need."

Dr. Bailey clearly looked perplexed at the moment, glancing over my chart once again.

"I'm not sure if the record shows that my blood type is O negative. I know that's important information if Sammie has a negative blood type," Slate explained.

Dear God - Slate could've simply asked me that himself and saved me from . . . this!

Dr. Bailey was scratching his forehead now, turning over various sheets contained within my file.

"Your wife's blood type is B positive. You didn't know that, Mr. Dennison?"

Here we go . . .

"No, Doc, I'm not Mr. Dennison. I'm the baby's father."

At that moment, I very much wanted to bury myself under the paper sheet. I seriously thought about just pulling it up over my head, but then realized it would leave my crotch area exposed for everyone to see.

"I see," Dr. Bailey replied, with a slight frown. "Well, now that we've cleared that up, there's no cause for worry then Mr. - ?"

"You can call me Slash."

Oh. Dear. Lord.

"Ok then, Mr. *Slash*," he said, turning towards me now, giving a slight nod of his head as if clearing his mind of confusion.

The doctor pulled the paper sheet down a bit, squeezing some of the warm, clear gel onto my abdomen, rubbing the wand around so he could pick up the baby's heartbeat.

"Nice and strong," he said.

I watched as Slate caught the sound of it and noticed a look of pure joy flicker across his handsome face.

The nurse came into the room, signaling that it was time for Dr. Bailey to do my pelvic exam.

"Mr. Slash, if you'll step outside for just a moment, you can return once the nurse leaves and I'll be happy to answer any questions you may have."

"Sure, Doc," he said, giving me a wink. "Be right back, Sammie."

As soon as Dr. Bailey finished, he snapped off his latex gloves and instructed me to sit up. I wrapped my paper sheet around my lower half as Slate re-entered the examination room.

"Everything looks good and on schedule," Dr. Bailey reported. "Your weight gain is appropriate. Your vitals are perfect. You have no complaints, so I would say just continue doing whatever it is you're doing and I'll see you next month."

"Doc," Slate started, "I do have a question."

Dr. Bailey looked up from where he was making notations on my chart. "Yes, Mr. Slash?"

"Is it safe for us to continue having sex regularly?"

I. Am. Going. To. Kill. Him.

I actually saw Dr. Bailey blush. Slate didn't bat an eye waiting for an answer. Dr. Bailey cleared this throat.

"Yes, Mr. Slash, it's safe to continue having sex as long as Samantha's comfortable with it. I would caution against anything too... . . . rough or strenuous."

"Got it," he said. "Thanks, Doc."

Dr. Bailey left the room. Slate stood there with a dopey grin on his face. I was fuming.

"Would you mind waiting outside for me? I'd like to have some privacy while I get dressed," I hissed at him.

"Are you pissed, babe?"

"Nooo," I said with an exaggerated sigh. "Why in the hell would you think I was pissed?"

"We'll talk outside," he replied, slipping out the door.

Once outside, Slate was on my heels as I headed to where my Mercedes was parked.

"Hey, slow down, Sammie. Want to tell me what the hell has you in a snit? Is it some type of hormonal thing?"

I clicked the remote unlocking the car door and opened it. "No, Slate, it's not a 'hormonal' thing. It's more of an 'assholey' thing. You made an ass out of yourself in there and embarrassed me to boot."

I started to get into the driver seat, but his strong arm reached out and pulled me back to him.

"Hey," he snapped, "I didn't mean to embarrass you Sammie, but my mother told me that I should find out if your blood type was negative, too. She said it could cause complications with the baby."

"Okay, so now your *mother* knows about this?"

He nodded, as if that was the most normal thing in the world.

"Why couldn't you just have asked *me* about my blood type?"

"Because I haven't seen you since I talked to her about it."

"Whose fault is *that*?"

"Oh, I see. You're pissed 'cause I haven't been by to *service* you," he chuckled.

"That has *nothing* to do with it, Slate. It was you barging into the exam room, making sure that everyone knew you were not my husband, asking about having sex and calling yourself Slash for Chrissake. Of course it pissed me off!"

"Okay, okay," he said, pulling me to him. "I'm sorry babe. I really am. I can't blow my cover though. You understand about that, right?"

I nodded against his chest.

"I'm going to be there for you, Sammie. I guess I didn't tell you that before. I mean, if you want me there, that is."

"I do, Slate," I replied softly, hugging him. "Just maybe a little more low-key, though?"

"You got it, babe."

He kissed my lips softly several times, giving a low groan as I pulled away to get into the car.

"Have you been keeping the door unlocked for me?"

"Yep," I said. "For all the good it has done."

"I'll be there when I can. I miss you, too."

With that he was gone, quickly and quietly disappearing around the corner. It was almost magical, at times, the way he would turn up unexpectedly. He could disappear the same way. I sighed as I started the car and headed home.

Chapter 42

I'd slept restlessly all through the night. I wasn't sure if it was because I kept hoping Slate would pop in and surprise me with a mind-blowing orgasm, or because I was simply on edge and had no clue why. I finally drifted off to sleep around five in the morning. I was dozing somewhat peacefully at 10:30 a.m. when my cell phone rang. It was Becky. I was still in somewhat of a sleepy fog when I answered.

"Sam, turn your television on right now to the local news on Channel Seven. You have got to see this." She hung up before I had a chance to ask her what the hell was going on.

My hand felt around for the remote on my nightstand. I switched the television on, and rolled over on to my side to watch as I hit the buttons for Channel Seven. Apparently, whatever was happening had pre-empted the regularly scheduled programming.

There was a man in a suit and tie talking into a multitude of microphones attached to a wooden podium. At the bottom of the screen, lettering was scrolling by which identified him as U.S. Attorney General Joe Hodgett. He was addressing a roomful of press and media reporters. It looked like there were local authorities in attendance as well.

"Ladies and Gentlemen," he began, "earlier this morning, federal agents and special task forces executed a number of search and arrest warrants in Indianapolis, Fort Wayne, and Ohio. FBI agents, along with the assistance of U.S. Marshalls and local law enforcement personnel have arrested and taken into custody forty-two members of the Outlaws Motorcycle Club, both in Fort Wayne and Indianapolis; one warrant remains outstanding for a club member who remains at large. In the following days, it's expected that additional indictments will be handed down as the investigation reveals the identification of others who may have been involved in these criminal activities. These indictments include racketeering, mail fraud, money laundering, extortion, drug trafficking, insurance fraud and various federal firearms charges."

I stopped listening to what this guy was saying as my attention was drawn to the video that appeared on the backdrop screen behind the podium.

I recognized him by his lean, muscular build and his swagger as he led one of the bikers over to a paddy wagon in cuffs.

He had on a navy blue tee shirt that had large, white letters across the chest that read: 'F B I.' He had on a matching navy blue ball cap with the same insignia. I had to smile. Only Slate would wear the ball cap turned backwards on his head, like some gangster agent.

I watched in awe as he went back inside the clubhouse and came out with another one in cuffs. I recognized this one as 'Hammer.' He used to come into Jewels with Slate and the others.

Another FBI agent caught my eye as he was struggling with a biker. It was Taz! Holy shit! Taz was an agent as well? He seemed to fit in so perfectly with the OMC. I remembered Slate saying that Taz was "living the dream."

I watched as my G-man loaded the paddy wagon with more members of the club. This had to be big, really big. Chills ran through me as I watched the agents and task force members corral the bikers into several paddy wagons. There was yellow crime scene tape surrounding the entire property.

The voice of U.S. Attorney Joseph Hodgett once again caught my attention:

"In conclusion, the ongoing investigation will likely take weeks, if not months, to identify everyone involved in what has been termed one of the largest and most extensive criminal networks in Indianapolis and throughout the Midwest. Today's initial arrests reflect our dedication in dismantling a criminal organization that pumped a deadly mixture of drugs, violence, and fraud into this city. These charges also serve as a reminder that if you're involved in organized crime in Indianapolis, if you assist these groups in any way, you will wake up one morning soon to the sound of federal agents at your door."

Once again, I felt shivers run up and down my spine as I wondered how much of a role Jack had played in this criminal network. He was at work now. I wondered if he was even aware that this had taken place. My cell phone rang, and I jumped. It was Becky again.

"So, did you recognize any of them?" she asked excitedly.

I'd shared with Becky that Slate wasn't interested in Lindsey after the July 4th cook-out. I'd not shared anything else, per his instructions to me. As far as Becky knew, Slate had left Indianapolis to take care of some pressing business and would be back at some point. She still considered him to be 'shady' as she put it.

"A couple of them, yeah," I replied. "I think one of them was called 'Hammer' and I definitely saw 'Flush' too."

"As in he can "flush" the rest of his sorry-ass life down the toilet?" she asked, laughing.

"Yeah."

"Didn't recognize anyone else, though?"

"What do you mean?"

"Hmm, I don't know. Just thought maybe one of those guys in the FBI shirts might have caught your eye. They are so damn sexy, aren't they?"

Becky couldn't possibly have recognized Slate. The one and only time she'd seen him was for about ten seconds. That was months ago, plus his hair was longer back then. She was simply fishing.

"Becky, I'm not following you. What in the hell are you talking about?"

"Never mind, Sam. Just be ready when you wake up one morning to the sound of federal agents at your door."

"That's so not funny, Becky. I haven't heard a damn thing in days from Donovan. Did you happen to see him there during the footage?"

"No, and I was looking for him, too. Relax though, whatever Jack has been doing doesn't implicate you. If anything, you have assisted the authorities."

"You know that and I know that, but who's to say they'll believe I had no knowledge of it all along?"

"Hey, I'm sorry, hon. I was just kidding about the knock on the door. I'm sure all the evidence resides at Banion."

That didn't make me feel a whole lot better when I considered that it was my father's name on that company and the shame that might be brought to it because of Jack. I was really feeling depressed.

I showered and dressed for the day after I got off of the phone with Becky. I managed to eat some fruit and granola, and then set about keeping busy with household chores.

My mother called late in the afternoon to see how I was feeling. I told her about my recent visit to the doctor, leaving out the part about Slate barging in. I told her that everything was going well and the doctor was pleased.

"That's good to know, Samantha," she said. "Your father and I wondered if you wanted to go out for dinner tomorrow for your birthday."

"Does Jack have to go?"

"That's entirely up to you, sweetheart."

"Can I call you tomorrow to let you know, Mom?

"That'll be fine, Samantha."

She asked if I'd been watching the local news at all today. I told her that I had. She wanted to talk about the big bust at the biker club. She claimed she'd heard from several ladies at 'the club' that more arrests were to be made that included several prominent businessmen in the Indianapolis area.

I wanted so much to warn her about the impending disaster, but I knew that I couldn't. It tore me up inside.

"Listen, Mom, I have to go put the clothes from the washer into the dryer. I'll call you tomorrow about dinner, okay?"

"Okay, Samantha. Talk to you then."

I finished up the laundry and got dinner started. Lindsey got home at her normal time. She told me that Jack had said he was stopping at the gym so not to hold dinner for him. She rolled her eyes when she gave me the information.

Lindsey and I sat down to dinner alone. She didn't seem to be upset about anything, so maybe things were slowly falling into place for her with the understanding that her parents would be splitting sometime in the near future. She told me that she was going to hang out with Julie later in the evening. They were going to the mall and then to the club for a late swim. Frankly, I was glad that she seemed to be getting back into the swing of things.

She cleaned up the kitchen for me before going upstairs to shower and get ready for the evening. It was just past 7:30 p.m. I'd just settled down in the family room, turning the television on when the landline rang. It was Jack.

"Sammie," he said, "I'm on my way to the airport to catch a flight to Charlotte. Some things have come up and it's urgent I get there as soon as possible for damage control."

"What happened, Jack?"

"The general contractor over the project was skimping on building materials; wiring, piping, things like that. The building inspector caught it early, but all construction has halted until we can get it sorted out and up to code. I may be there for a week or more."

"Fine."

"I'm sorry I won't be here for your birthday, Sammie. Is there something I can do to make it up to you?"

"Yes, there is. Please don't call me 'Sammie' anymore. Call me Samantha. Got it?"

There was a silent pause as Jack tried to figure out where the hell I was coming from on this.

"Sure thing," he replied. "I'll call you in a couple of days when I know more."

"Goodbye, Jack."

Chapter 43

I was sleeping peacefully beneath my sheets, dreaming of Slate. I felt his lips on mine as I welcomed his mouth with my own. I could smell his masculine scent. It was a mixture of soap and aftershave that was his alone.

"Happy birthday, baby," he whispered against my lips, his tongue tracing my lower one.

My eyes flew open. I wasn't dreaming. He was right here beside me in bed. His warm, muscular body was molded up against mine. I closed my eyes, moaning with happiness and pleasure. He was kissing my lips, the tip of my nose, my eyelids.

"You're really here," I said, smiling up at him. His hands were now all over me. I pushed myself up into a sitting position.

"Where you going?" he asked, pulling me back against him.

"Slate, please. I need to tell you something. It's important."

He pulled himself up so that he was sitting beside me. I had his full attention.

"What is it, babe?"

"I saw you on the television yesterday morning. You were in a dark blue 'FBI' shirt, ball cap on backwards, leading 'Hammer' to the paddy wagon."

He nodded, still watching me.

"So, didn't that blow your cover?"

"It's kind of a moot point at the moment with the bikers."

"But what about Jack? What if Jack has seen that clip and recognized you?"

"Sammie, it was a brief clip. I doubt very much that he'd have recognized me with the FBI garb and ball cap pulled down on my forehead."

"I recognized you, Slate. If I did, then he could have, too."

"Babe, do you have reason to think that he did?"

"Nothing concrete, it's just a feeling. He told Lindsey to tell me he was going to work late last evening and not to hold dinner. Then he called a little after seven and said he had to take a late flight out immediately to Charlotte; something about the construction being stopped on the distribution center that's underway for Banion. He made it sound like he could be gone for a week or more."

"Shit," he said, pulling his cell phone from his jean pocket and hitting a speed dial number.

"Donovan, who's watching Dennison?"

There was a momentary pause. Slate rubbed his thumb back and forth on his forehead waiting for an answer.

"What's that? His car is still there in the parking garage?" He looked over at me, covering the mic on his phone.

"Have them check to see if Susan Reynard's car is still there. She drives a new, black, Ford Mustang convertible," I instructed.

Slate relayed the instruction to Donovan who relayed it to whomever was on the other end of another phone or radio.

I could tell Slate was on edge. I was certain that Jack had eluded them and slithered out by way of Susan's car. He probably had crouched down in the back seat, like the coward he was.

"What's that? God damn it," he snarled. "You tell Agent Hatfield I want to see him at field headquarters at zero eight hundred hours. Send Daugherty to the airport to see what he can find out. I'm sure it's too fucking late at this point."

Slate shut his phone off. At that moment, I felt fortunate that I wasn't Agent Hatfield.

He turned back to me, raking his hand through his thick, dark hair.

"Call Jack right now on his cell phone," he ordered, none too gently.

I jumped to grab the landline phone and pushed the speed dial to Jack's number. A recording came on stating that the cell phone number was no longer in service. I held the phone up so that Slate could hear it.

"Fuck," he said. "Is there anything else you can think of to tell me?"

"Yes, there is. You need to know right now that I'm afraid. You don't tell me shit because of blowing your cover, then I fucking see it on the local news. I'm clueless as to how deeply Jack is involved in this whole mess. Am I going to have to find that out on the local news as well? Am I going to be one of those people that wake up one morning to the sound of federal agents at my door?"

"I actually prefer sliding in through the unlocked terrace doors to your bedroom, in case you haven't noticed, babe."

"It's not funny, Slate. This is my life we're talking about here. This involves Lindsey's life, too. You're not telling me shit about anything."

I was pissed now and making no bones about it. Tears of frustration were building up. I felt like kicking and screaming. I might have done so, except for the fact that I'd heard Lindsey come home a little after midnight and I didn't want to risk waking her.

"Hey, come here," he said gently, pulling me up into his lap. He gently stroked my hair with his hand. "It's because I can't, baby. Do you trust me?"

"What choice do I have?"

"You have a choice, Sammie. Everyone has a choice. Now do you trust me?"

"I guess I do. I'm just not sure that you trust or believe me."

"Why do you say that?"

"Because, Slate, you've never once told me that I have nothing to worry about, that I'm not under suspicion, that Jack hasn't somehow involved me in this by the mere fact that we are married and have joint accounts. You've never once assured me that my baby won't be born inside some woman's prison," I sobbed to him, burying my face into my arms that were wrapped around my knees.

"Hey, hey," he soothed, kissing the top of my head. "I'm sorry, baby. I guess I didn't think how this might be affecting you. I've never doubted your innocence, okay? This is my investigation. I'm the lead on this and trust me, I've seen my share of evidence and, in no way does it implicate you, or your father's company as an entity. I can tell you that much."

"What about the biker that's still at large. Can you tell me who it is?"

"It's Slash," he replied, kissing my face. "He can't get to you, don't worry."

"Did Slash have any direct dealings with Jack?"

"No," he replied. "It was all indirectly done through an intermediary in Fort Wayne, okay?"

I nodded, but I was worried once again.

"Is Slash after you?"

"Probably. I'm not worried, though. I don't want you to be worried that he's followed me either, understand? I'd never put you at risk. Besides, Slash is more worried about saving his own hide at this point than retribution."

I wiped the tears from my cheeks with the back of my hand.

"So, are we good then?"

I raised my face up to his and we kissed.

"Maybe," I said, starting to feel better.

"Hmm - only maybe?" He cocked an eyebrow at me, his eyes full of amusement. "How can I change that maybe into a definitely?"

"Hmm, well maybe my G-man can make nice to my G-spot," I said, squirming away from him on the bed. I pulled my nightgown up and over my head. Slate was naked within seconds. We dove underneath the sheets together.

"I think that can be arranged for the birthday girl," he whispered, as his hands expertly started their exploration.

When I awoke, Slate was gone. I pulled the sheet up under my chin, and bit my lower lip, like I always did when I worried about something.

We had made love several times throughout the night. I didn't give a damn what he said, it wasn't fucking this time, it was love. I worried that somehow this piece of happiness I'd found would disappear as suddenly as it had arrived. I really did love him.

I got up to use the bathroom. I had to pee more than usual, which was to be expected as my pregnancy progressed. I was officially thirty-six years old, I thought, as I glanced in the mirror to see what that looked like.

I didn't look any different than I had the day before when I was still thirty five - with one exception: I now had a large hickey over my left boob.

I had to smile as I thought about my Slate. His hickeys were the equivalent of a male dog marking his territory. It really was kind of cute.

I showered and dressed. As I pulled the bracelet that Slate had given me out of the jewelry box where I stored it, I found something new in there. It was wrapped in tissue paper. I opened it carefully and found a pair of beautiful diamond stud earrings. There was a note folded up beneath it. I opened it and read:

'Happy Birthday, Diamond Girl. - Love, S.'

Chapter 44

When Lindsey got up, I was already in the kitchen making breakfast.

"You sure seem chipper this morning, Mom. Is it because it's your birthday?" she asked, with a wicked little smile on her face.

"Ha Ha," I said, flipping a pancake onto her plate. "You're so funny, daughter. No, I just slept well, that's all."

"Well, Happy Birthday. How are we going to be celebrating your birthday anyway?"

"Oh," I said, setting a glass of orange juice down in front of her. "Your grandmother called yesterday and wondered if we wanted to get together for dinner this evening."

"Sounds good to me," she said, sipping her orange juice. "Where's Daddy? Has he already left for work?"

"Well, no. Actually he called while you were in the shower last evening, Lindsey. I didn't see you before you left, but he had to fly to Charlotte on a late flight. Apparently there's some trouble with the construction in Charlotte."

"How long is he going to be there?"

"He said it might take up to a week or more to get it straightened out with the county inspection people."

"Hmm," she said, digging into her pancakes. I got the distinct impression that she wasn't buying it either. It was uncanny how perceptive Lindsey was, even about the father she loved dearly. It made me wish I'd possessed the same gift at that age. Things might've been a whole lot different now.

She finished up her breakfast and got ready for work. She wished me a "Happy Birthday" again before she left, letting me know she would be home by six.

I'd just finished cleaning up after breakfast when my cell phone rang. The caller identification came across as "G-Man"?

"Hello?"

"Hey baby," the soft, sexy voice said.

"Slate?"

"Who the fuck else would be calling you that?"

"Did you program your number into my cell phone?"

"Uhh, yeah. Is that a problem?"

"No," I said with a laugh. "I just don't remember you having access to it."

"Baby, I can get access to about anything I want. Don't you know that by now?"

I rolled my eyes, laughing at his cockiness.

"Hey," I said, "thank you for the earrings. I found them this morning. I love them."

"You're welcome, babe. I thought they'd look great on you. Listen, this call is about business. The Intel that we received this morning confirmed the fact that Jack wasn't on any flight to Charlotte. He was, however, booked on a flight from Indianapolis to Dallas, then a connection from Dallas to El Paso."

"El Paso?"

"Yeah, it's a border town. Most likely, he's crossed over into Mexico."

"I don't understand. Jack has a passport. Why wouldn't he simply fly into a city in Mexico?"

"Because babe, he's there illegally and doesn't want a record of it. He's a fugitive from justice. There are outstanding warrants for him in the U.S. He got wind of it and booked. I need for you to meet me and Donovan at your bank. We need to check your accounts and, with your permission, it will be much quicker than getting a subpoena. Bring your identification and meet us there in thirty, got it?"

"Yeah, okay, Slate. See you then."

Donovan and Slate were already there when I got to the bank. I knew Slate must have thought it strange that I couldn't access my balances from the home computer. But there were two problems with that: Jack had taken the home computer out of the home, plus he'd changed passwords on the savings and checking accounts. I'd basically been using my debit card with no consideration given as to whether the charges would clear. They always did. Jack hadn't wanted me poking around in our finances since my last run-in with him. I hadn't pressed the issue for obvious reasons.

We immediately got with the branch manager and sat down to go over the balances in the joint accounts. Jack had cleaned the savings out, leaving a token $500 balance in it out of good faith. I would have had to sign something had he fully closed it out. Our checking account had a total of $5000 left in it.

Fucking rat bastard.

The branch manager printed out the detail on transactions for the past month when the majority of the withdrawals had been systematically processed. As near as I could tell at a glance, Jack had cleared out nearly a half-million dollars. We were broke. Correction: I was broke.

I was reeling as the reality of my situation sunk in. I was stunned, numb with the realization that Jack didn't give a rat's ass about Lindsey either. It was one thing for him to have no concern about me, but how could he have done this to his daughter?

"Hey, you okay babe?"

"Not really, Slate. I have to think about what I'm going to do. I need to let my parents in on this. My father is still the Chairman of the Board for Banion Pharmaceuticals. I have a responsibility to let him know that Jack has fled."

I looked at Slate. He was without expression. I couldn't understand how he managed that - it must be his gift.

"So then, you're not going to tell me that I'm blowing anyone's cover or compromising your investigation?"

He shook his head. "You do what you need to do, Sammie. We have operatives on the inside who have been cooperating. Your father may be aware of that, at this point. I agree that you need to let them know because financially, you need some help going forward."

I was a bit taken aback by Slate's attitude. I wasn't running to Mommy and Daddy for financial support. I needed to let them know at least what I knew.

"Fine," I said, turning from him and Donovan. "Keep me informed if any of your 'operatives' locate my rat bastard husband."

I phoned my mother as soon as I got home. She wished me a happy birthday and mentioned going out to dinner. I asked if she and Daddy could have dinner here with Lindsey and me. There were things to discuss. She was a bit puzzled, but not enough to question me further. She said that they would be over around seven, which meant six-thirty.

When Lindsey came through the door at four-thirty, I knew that something was up. Our talk was going to begin immediately. I could see that she'd been crying. Her sadness had somehow morphed into anger at some point. Her anger was directed at me.

"How could you not tell me that something was going on with Daddy? I thought you and I had a better relationship than that, Mom," she sputtered, her tears spilling down her cheeks.

"Oh Lindsey, sweetie," I started, going to her and putting my arms around her. "I honestly didn't know anything other than the fact that your father's cell phone had been disconnected when you left for work this morning, I swear."

"But Mom," she wailed, "that's something isn't it? I mean that tells us that there's something wrong somewhere, doesn't it? I had to go into Banion and spend the better part of the afternoon being questioned by people I don't even know."

"Who questioned you?"

"Some detectives and special agents. I felt like I was under suspicion for something by the mere fact that I'm his daughter. What's going on, Mom?"

I pulled Lindsey down to sit next to me on the sofa. I held her hands in mine.

"Listen to me," I started calmly, "I'm not sure exactly what's involved in all of this and that's the truth. I was contacted by a couple of federal agents today as well. I was asked to allow them to check into our personal financial situation. Otherwise, they would have subpoenaed the information. According to the bank records, your father emptied our joint checking and savings accounts of about a half million dollars."

Her eyes widened in surprise. "A half million - I never realized Daddy made that kind of money."

"He doesn't," I replied. "That's why these agents are investigating the money trail to see where it originated. Honey, I first discovered something funny was going on in the savings account a few months back. Once your father realized that I'd accessed it, he changed the password on both accounts so that I had no access to the balances."

"Why, Mom? Why would Daddy do that?"

"Sweetie," I replied, "The authorities are pretty sure that your father has been conducting some illegal activities. The investigation's still underway."

She was sobbing now. All I could do was hold and comfort her.

"It makes sense now. There were all kinds of people in today. They were going over input and output records, taking inventory, checking disposal and scrap records. It was pure chaos at work. I can't go back there, Mom. I feel ashamed because of Daddy. There's someone else who didn't show up today at Banion."

"I'm going to guess it was Susan."

"Yep," she confirmed. "I bet she's with Daddy."

"I know, baby. I know."

"What will Granddaddy say when he finds out?"

"I'm not sure, Lindsey. I've a feeling we'll soon find out. They're coming over here for dinner this evening."

Chapter 45

The visit with my parents had gone better than expected. I'd put together a quick dinner of broiled salmon and salads. No one was very hungry after the conversation got underway.

As it turned out, my father had been apprised of the suspicions a couple of months ago. He said the most difficult thing for him was maintaining a normal attitude and demeanor around Jack. That's why they'd traveled so much during the spring.

When I informed my parents about Jack cleaning out our savings and checking, he'd wanted to rip his head off.

He explained to Lindsey and me that the Director of Security at Banion had been contacted by a federal task force unit once a connection had been made between the Outlaws Motorcycle Club and the distribution of unstamped pain tablets thought to have been produced at Banion.

My father knew of the outstanding warrants for Jack. He was also aware of the involvement of two chemists at Banion who were arrested today without incident. They were being questioned by federal agents and, hopefully, would provide more information in exchange for a plea deal.

Lindsey had become more upset as the realization settled in as to her father's involvement and initiation of these criminal activities. My mother finally convinced her to come and spend a few days with them at their condo. She'd worried that I'd need her here. I told her I'd be fine, instructing her to relax and let Grandma spoil her.

My father insisted on having a locksmith change the locks on the doors. He had one come out immediately. He also arranged for a security system to be installed the following day. He was going to come out of retirement to run the operations at Banion until such time as the investigation was concluded and Jack's position was filled.

"You know, Samantha," he said, "You're a major shareholder at Banion. If you have any financial concerns, you can always sell some of your shares back to me."

"Thanks, Dad, I'll keep that in mind. I need to get a handle on the finances. Jack has all of that information on his computer that he took. It'll be like starting from scratch."

"Nonsense," he replied. "I'll make any of the accountants at Banion available to sort this out for you. Just get copies of your bank statements and order a credit report. It won't take long to figure out your debt to resource ratio."

As they prepared to leave, my mother reached into her purse and pulled out a birthday card and handed it to me.

"I guess this hasn't been the best of birthdays for you, has it Samantha?"

"Oh, I guess I've had better, Mom. Thank you," I said, giving her a big hug and kiss.

"Where's mine?"

"Thanks, Daddy." He pulled me close to him in a firm hug.

"I'm so sorry, baby girl," he whispered gruffly to me. "I made a terrible mistake. I'm so sorry."

I felt tears well up immediately. That was so not my father to admit he'd ever made a mistake, much less apologize for one.

"I love you," I said sniffling.

After they left, I turned the outside lights off. Better start conserving wherever possible, I thought. The money Jack left wouldn't go far. At least Lindsey's tuition had been paid for the first semester in the fall.

I opened the birthday card from my parents. A check floated out onto the floor. I picked it up and felt my eyes widen. They'd given me a check for twenty-five thousand dollars for my birthday.

I showered and climbed into my bed, exhausted from the day. I heard some rustling outside as the drapes billowed out from the terrace door. The room was dimly lit from the light filtering in from the lamp I'd left on in the family room.

My eyes immediately went to where the noise originated. There he was, dressed in his black garb.

My Slate.

We said nothing to one another. He undressed quickly and quietly, climbing into bed beside me. He removed my clothes even faster so that we had skin touching skin.

His lips were on my mouth; his tongue playfully dancing with mine. I fisted my hands in his thick hair, pulling his face closer to me; framing it with my fingers. His tongue traced a path down the column of my neck, finding my breasts and gently circling the nipples.

His hand moved between my legs; his fingers exploring the folds of my sex. He inserted a finger inside of me, gently pressing and tapping the magic spot that seemed to be made of nothing but nerve endings. I moaned with pleasure, my body moving against his.

Slate lifted me up, sliding underneath me so that I was now positioned on top of him. His hands braced on each of my hips, raising me up so that he could position me just above his erection.

I felt myself being lowered gently down upon him. I sucked in my breath as I felt the pleasurable fullness of Slate inside of me.

"Umm," he moaned, as he started his rhythmic movements underneath me; raising me up and down with his hands at the speed and tempo he wanted.

I leaned forward a bit so that my breasts were brushing against his chest. My hands gripped his shoulders as the heat of our lovemaking increased.

He raised me up and down, up and down. My hips gyrated in a circular motion making sure the head of his beautiful cock was hitting my magic spot over and over again. My whimpers of pleasure were getting louder. His breathing was coming faster as he moaned my name.

"God, baby…"

We were there now; together our pleasure peaked as we spiraled into mutual orgasms that rocked our bodies as one. We came over and over again. I felt myself pulsate around him. He continued to groan in pleasure.

I collapsed against him, kissing his damp face and neck, his chin, his eyelids.

"I love you, Slate," I whispered in his ear as I kissed him there, too.

"I know, baby," he said. "I know."

Chapter 46

I was surprised when I awoke the following morning to find Slate sleeping next to me, his arm thrown across me like it was the most natural thing in the world for us.

In truth, it was the first time Slate and I'd ever actually slept together, other than the nap we had taken the day 'Grant' had been conceived.

I'd decided the name 'Dalton 'didn't go that well with 'Slater.' Of course, I was presuming that Slate would want the baby to carry his last name, but we hadn't actually discussed it. Grant Slater definitely sounder better than Dalton Slater.

I lifted Slate's arm off of my belly so that I could scoot out from underneath it to go pee. He immediately woke up. I felt him haul me back as I tried to exit the bed.

"Where do you think you're going?"

"Well, I kind of needed to relieve myself, if it's all the same to you."

"I don't think so, baby. You know having a full bladder makes a woman's orgasm about fifty times stronger?"

"Really?"

"Would I lie?"

"Prove it."

Since we had fallen asleep naked, no time was wasted having to disrobe again. We each popped a mint into our mouth from the supply I kept on the nightstand and commenced devouring each other once again. Twenty minutes later, covered in sweat and winding down from the best freaking, mind-blowing orgasm in the history of womankind, I knew that Slate had made a believer out of me.

"Wow," I said, still panting as I rolled over onto my back. I laid my wrist across my forehead as my heart rate slowly returned to normal.

"Didn't I tell you?" he said with a cocky grin, his head perched up on an elbow staring down at me.

"You were so right," I said, smiling up at him.

"Damn, I hope you didn't wake Lindsey. You made quite a racket with those lungs this morning."

"Braggart," I teased. "Actually, she's staying with my parents for a few days. Everything with Jack has left her emotions raw. She's had to face some cruel facts. It's been hard on her."

"How about you?"

"I didn't have the emotional investment in him that Lindsey did. I knew what he was."

"Did you ever love him?"

"I thought I did," I replied, with a shrug. "I didn't really know what love was, I guess."

"And now?" he asked, watching me intently.

"And now I know what it is, Slate. I meant what I said last night. I love you. I understand if you don't feel the same way about me. Does that have to affect the way I feel about you, though?"

He gave me a scowl as he raked his hands through his just 'thoroughly-fucked' hair.

"Christ, Sammie," he said, "I mean, what the fuck? I *know* that you love me. You think I can't tell by the way you treat me? You're having my baby, for the love of Christ. Can't you tell that this makes me so fucking happy?"

I nodded. "So, what's your point?"

"What's my point of what?"

"What's the point that you're attempting, but failing, to make, Slate?"

"I just think that you must *know* how I feel by the way that I treat you, alright?"

Where the hell is he coming from with this?

"Actually, I don't."

"You don't what?"

"I don't know how you feel about me."

"Oh, Christ," he said, totally uncomfortable with the conversation. "I think it's pretty *obvious*, Samantha. Use your head."

With that, he propelled himself off of the bed and swaggered into my bathroom to relieve himself. I managed to make it to the guest bathroom on the main floor without having pee running down my leg.

Thankfully, one of Jack's tee shirts was hanging on the hook in there. I pulled it on over my head so I didn't have to parade naked in front of Slate. I was starting to feel a tad self-conscious about my blooming belly.

When I returned to my room, Slate was zipping the fly on his jeans up.

"So, I guess you're taking off," I said, picking my panties up off of the floor.

"Aren't you going to make me some breakfast, babe?"

I gave him my best 'Are you kidding me' look. He chuckled, pleased that he'd managed to get a reaction of some sort to lighten the mood.

"Sure," I said, pulling up a pair of sweat pants and turning to go out towards the kitchen.

I felt his hand on my arm as he pulled me back and turned me around to face him.

"I was just *teasing*, Sammie. How about I take us out to breakfast, huh?" His thumbs were brushing each side of my face. His eyes were filled with something unfamiliar to me.

"Can I shower first?"

"Of course you can. Make it quick."

Thirty minutes later, Slate and I were headed out into the country, Slate behind the wheel of my Mercedes testing its horsepower.

"Where did you park your truck?" I asked.

"That's top secret information, little lady," he said with a wink. "I can't divulge information pertaining to my covert activities."

I rolled my eyes, shaking my head. I guess I was seeing the 'playful' Slate now. I wondered how many different personas he possessed.

"Where are we going for breakfast, Michigan?"

"No, smart-ass, we're not going to Michigan. We're going to one of my favorite places. Sit back and relax."

My stomach growled loudly enough that Slate heard it.

"Whoa, it sounds like someone's definitely hungry."

"Yeah, Grant and I are both ravenous."

"Grant?"

"Uh huh, that's the name I've picked out for the baby."

"Grant Slater," he said, considering it for a moment. "I actually like that."

"Don't get too attached to it," I advised him. "More than likely it's going to change."

Slate had no clue how I was about naming babies. Since this one would likely be my last, I expected it'd be even worse than with Lindsey and the host of names I'd given her prior to her birth.

I recognized where we were now. It was the same restaurant that Slate had taken me to for chili.

"Katy's has breakfast?"

"The best," he replied, pulling my car into a parking space. It was definitely more crowded this time than it was when we last visited.

Slate was even a gentleman, opening the car door for me and helping me out.

The aroma of freshly brewed coffee, bacon, and eggs greeted us as we walked through the door. Within moments, Katy had spotted us. She hurried over with a big grin on her face. I recalled that she had said Slate was one of her favorite customers. There was no hiding that fact at the moment.

She came up to him, planting a big kiss on his cheek.

"Where in the world have you been keeping yourself, handsome? It's been forever."

Slate actually looked like he was going to blush at the attention she was giving him.

"You remember Sunny?" he asked.

"Of course I do. How are you, Sunny?"

Before I had an opportunity to answer, Slate interrupted.

"Actually, she lied about her name. Her real name's Samantha. I call her Sammie."

I felt myself blush with embarrassment. Why the hell did he feel the need to share all of that with the restaurant owner?

I glowered at Slate, and then turned my attention back to Katy, who was watching me with amused eyes. Her gaze lowered to my growing baby bump. She was smiling, as if she was pleased with my condition.

"Sammie," Slate continued, with a smile of his own, "I'd like for you to meet my mom, Katherine Slater. You can call her 'Katy'."

Chapter 47

~ SLATE ~

What a fucking few crazy days had gone by. So much had happened...most of it good, from my perspective.

We'd made the bust. It had all gone down well, for the most part. I was livid that the rat bastard had slipped through the cracks. No one knew that better now than Agent Hatfield. He was given a written disciplinary action that would go into his permanent personnel file. Mistakes like that should never happen, not on my watch.

The bottom line was that Hatfield should've known better. He and I had both served together in the Army and had gone through Green Beret training together. Hell, we were on the same survival training for twenty-one days in the Mojave Desert. If you can't trust and assess the abilities of your lifeline partner in that situation, who could you depend upon? He'd gotten lax. He'd clearly fucked up. As his superior officer, I had to do what I did. Personal feelings couldn't enter into my decision. That's just how it was.

Then, of course, there was the issue of Sammie. How in the hell could I not let my personal feelings interfere with my best judgment?

Fuck! I was trained better than this - what the hell? She was under my skin in a big, big way. I'd let her distract me. I'd carried on with her even after I knew that she had no Intel to offer me. She had no value, for all intents and purposes in this investigation, as far as I knew.

What a fucking idiot I was for not being clued into the fact that she was "Mr. Big's" fucking wife? Oh yeah, don't think for a minute the title of "Mr. Big" that was given to him by the Outlaws, hadn't stuck in my craw once I knew who he was to Sammie. It had nothing to do with the size of one's dick. It was the fact that the title "Mr. Big" in and of itself denoted power. There was no way in fuck that this dude had more power than me. Period.

I thought about last night, the night I'd spent with Sammie all alone in that fucking huge house of hers. She was under my skin. There was no way that I couldn't think about the way she looked, the way she felt, the way she kissed and touched me, the way it felt to be buried deeply inside of her and hear her moan and feel her writhe beneath me. It hadn't been a line of shit whatsoever when I'd told her my cock was made for her pussy. It was the God's honest truth. I'd never ever had that before with a chick.

But then, the inevitable happened, the talk of love: 'I need you Slate; I love you Slate.' Christ, how in the hell was I supposed to deal with that? I'd never, ever told a chick that I loved her. Why? That was simple. I never, ever wanted to give them the pain that was associated with love.

My mind drifted back to when I was growing up, it was just me and my little sister. My dad did his share of partying and drinking. I was too young to understand the full ramifications of it. I figured that was just what dads did. I remembered him coming home drunk. Mom had made dinner. We'd eaten and then were sent to our rooms once he hit the door.

Mom would warm his dinner up and take it out to him, setting it in front of him at the dining room table. She would always wait and eat with him. She said it was important for a husband and wife to spend quality time together.

Laney and I'd be upstairs in our room. We only lived in a two bedroom duplex in Virginia. We had bunk beds, I remember.

Laney was younger, so she had the bottom bunk. She would lay there on her bunk and play with her stuffed animals, talking to them as if they were real. Pretty soon, the raised voice of my father could be heard. Laney would roll over onto her stomach and put her pillow over her head and start humming some nursery rhyme.

Not me. I'd strain to listen to what my old man had to say. It wasn't pretty.

"What kind of goddamn shit is this you're giving me to eat, Katy? It tastes like dried out dog shit!"

"I'm sorry," my mother would say patiently. "It was better when it was freshly made, Clint. I didn't know you were going to be so late in getting home. It's just a bit dried out."

Then the sounds of skin smacking skin could be heard, along with my father's chastisement that my mother should've had fucking sense enough to know how to keep a meal from tasting like dried out dog shit. The whole time, my mother would be apologizing. The slapping just continued, followed by my mother's crying and begging for him to stop.

I remember several times running downstairs and hollering at my old man, telling him to leave my mom alone. He had laughed, calling me a good for nothing little shit-stain and backhanded me so hard that I had flown against the wall. My mother would try her best to protect me...standing in front of me to take the blows he delivered.

The following day, she had come upstairs after he'd left for work. Her eyes were blackened and she cried, begging me not to interfere anymore.

"Mom," I had said to her, "I need to protect you from him. I don't want him to hurt you anymore."

"Eric," she had said in a solemn voice, "don't you see, son? You're not big or strong enough to protect me. All you're doing is making him angrier, and then he beats me harder when you interfere. Please son, I'm begging you to leave it alone."

At the end, I promised her that I'd quit interfering.

So after that, whenever it would happen I'd lay on the lower bunk with Laney and hum along with her as we tried our best to block out the sounds of my father and what he was doing to our mom.

Afterwards, my father would try to make up with my mom. He'd tell her that he did what he did because he 'loved' her and wanted her to be the best wife that she could be. He explained that if he didn't 'love' her, he wouldn't care that she didn't know how to cook properly or how to keep her man happy. He claimed it was all for love that he disciplined her. It felt sick to me. I wanted no part of love if that was what it entailed.

I thought about this morning when Sammie told me that she loved me. It came as no surprise. I was instinctual that way. I'd known for a while that she loved me. It was the greatest feeling in the world. I wanted to tell her that I felt the same way, and that I had for some time. I couldn't, though. It was an area that I had no experience with, other than with my own folks. I was scared that by saying it to her, I might become my old man.

My mother had suffered through years of his abuse. It had pissed me off so many times that she took it. She claimed my dad was ill; he wasn't in his right mind when he was drunk. I know, by today's terms, my mother was an 'enabler.' She loved the man despite everything. She didn't realize how much her 'love' for him had destroyed Laney.

When my mother wrote to me in 2003, while I was stationed in Iraq, that my father was terminally ill, all I felt was relief. When he died a few weeks later, I felt nothing at all.

My mother's life had finally become bearable for her, once he was gone. She had picked up the pieces, opened her restaurant and was doing well until, once again, she had to face despair with the death of Laney.

That one was difficult for both of us. Laney had claimed that she was in love with a biker from a rival group of the Mongols out of Manassas, Virginia a few years back. He was abusive and criminally involved like the others. Laney had become hooked on opiates.

My mom and I had reached out to her. We'd helped her to get clean. She'd been clean for six months when she wanted to do something to help the others like her.

She took it upon herself to become acquainted with some bikers from the Mongols. She wanted to provide me with information to help bust the drug ring that was fairly strong in the area. I was with the FBI by this time. I told her to leave it to us, we had agents that could easily infiltrate the club. I happened to be one of them.

That was the start of my undercover work with the FBI. I'd led the investigation two and a half years ago that had successfully sent Jake Rosiga (Milwaukee Jake) the National President of the Outlaws Motorcycle Club to prison for the next twenty years.

Through my infiltration of the east coast based club, the Mongols, I was able to connect with the club members of both the Outlaws as well as another rival club called the Pagans. In 2010, it came to a head at the Easyrider Bike Expo in Charlotte, N.C. There was a show of force, so to speak, with the Pagans and Outlaws joining forces to invade territory in Rock Hill, South Carolina that was traditionally 'Hells Angels' turf.

It had resulted in violent friction between the Outlaws and Hells Angels. Laney had been in the thick of it. She'd been found in a remote ravine outside of Rock Hill. Her throat had been slit.

Ultimately the investigation had led (through members ratting out other members) to the OMC club activities in Fort Wayne and Indianapolis. This thing was much bigger than anyone had initially imagined.

There was a multi-state network of bikers, rival or not, that still dedicated their efforts for the bottom dollar, as long as they got something out of it. My anonymous sources pointed to an OMC member in Indiana as being responsible for Laney's murder. I was fairly certain it was Slash.

During the subsequent investigation, starting in the fall and lasting through spring in Indianapolis, I'd met Diamond, a.k.a., Sunny, a.k.a., Sammie. She had blown my world apart...first reminding me of the innocence my sister had once possessed, then totally mesmerizing me with her sexiness and naivety - it was a potent mix, to be sure.

I thought back to the night I sat across the table from Diamond having a private drink. Despite all of the make-up she'd piled on, I saw her black eye. I was enraged as the memories came flooding back from my childhood that someone would've done that to her. Then I was disgusted that she would tolerate it; just the way I'd been disgusted with my own mother for tolerating it all of those years.

Laney and I had talked about it shortly before she died. She told me that, because I had no tolerance for those kinds of things, I expected everyone else to feel the same. She pointed out that I had unrealistic expectations where people were concerned. She suggested that I work on being a bit more flexible and compassionate.

I'd thought about that conversation after the night I saw Diamond with the black eye. It stuck with me. I was fascinated with her from the start. I ignored those little voices that had served as my barrier for many years and never allowed myself to get too close to a woman. I preferred keeping things superficial and carnal. I didn't want it that way with Sammie. I wanted more. I wanted it all.

Chapter 48

I couldn't wait to fill Becky in on my meeting Slate's mother. Katy was so bubbly and friendly. I'd liked her the first time I'd met her, before I even knew she was Slate's mom. I was touched that Slate wanted me to meet her. She, of course, had been de-briefed on my condition. She was tickled at the prospect of becoming a grandmother. She called 'dibs' on the name 'Nana.'

Becky had squealed with excitement when I filled her in.

"That's just too precious, Sam. I guess there's something to be said for today's youth." She cracked herself up with that one.

"Nice Bec, real nice. I already feel like a 'bloated' cougar, thanks for reinforcing it."

"You know that I'm just teasing. After all, what are nine or ten years, right? By the way, maybe he has already turned twenty-seven. Have you asked him what his birth date is?"

"No, we haven't had that much time to talk, if you catch my drift."

"Like I said," she replied with a heavy sigh, "there's much to be said for today's youth, but I think now you're just bragging."

"Hey, I have a lot of catching up to do at my ripe old age. If I'd known what I'd been missing, I would've pulled my head out of the sand much sooner."

"Speaking on that subject, have you heard anything at all about Jack?"

"Nope, last I heard, Donovan said that they had 'operatives' in Mexico looking for him and Susan. Of course, he also said that it's an entirely different ballgame south of the border. If you want to disappear, apparently Mexico is the perfect place for that."

"So, what about this Susan? Have they connected her to any specific crimes?"

"Not yet, but the forensic audit's still going on. According to Daddy, they should be finished by the end of this week and turn the findings over to the authorities."

"Unbelievable," she sighed. "You know I was never a fan of Jack's whatsoever, but Lord, a half a million dollars wouldn't be enough to make me drop off the face of the earth forever, you know?"

"Well, I actually don't think his grand plan was to disappear. I think he thought he could get by with it without raising any red flags. A half mil is just two year's salary for him. Granted, it'll go much further in Mexico than it would here, but he ran because he knew the jig was up. Plus, we don't know how much cash Susan had stashed, if she was involved as well."

"That's true," Becky replied. "Knowing Jack, he'll probably invest his money in some drug cartel in Mexico and continue his life of crime. How's Lindsey?"

"Staying with Mom and Dad for a few days. She's in shock, I think. She's going back to work tomorrow. She's going to need the money for her living expenses at Cornell."

"Wow, things sure have done a one-eighty from a year ago, haven't they?"

"You ain't a woofin'," I replied with a laugh.

"Careful Sam, you're showing your age!"

"Bite me, Becky."

Slate made his appearance later in the evening as I was making dinner. He spent an hour scoping out the security system that had been installed. He was impressed with the outside cameras that could be monitored from my new laptop. Slate sat down with me and went over it step-by-step, explaining it to me as if I were a two year old.

"Slate," I whined, "The guy from the security company already showed me this stuff. I know all about how it works."

"Oh really?" he said, cocking an eyebrow at me. "Well then, let's test it out, shall we?"

"What do you mean?"

"I mean I'm going outside. It's dark now, I'm in dark clothes. You lock all of the exterior doors and then check the panel to make sure all windows are secured and let's see if I can get in, okay?"

"I have something better in mind," I said coyly, pressing myself up against him. He squirmed away, placing his hands on my shoulders to hold me off.

"Time for that later; this is important."

"Whatever," I sighed.

He went out the front door and I locked the deadbolt behind him. I checked the back door leading to the deck, the terrace doors from my room, and the door from the garage leading into the lower level of the house. All were securely locked.

I went back up to the kitchen where my laptop was on the counter. There was a six-screen split showing the various sectors the cameras covered. The main panel in the kitchen showed everything was set, including the lower level motion detectors.

I sat on the kitchen barstool, staring at the computer screen. I could see the lights on cars going past the winding driveway on the main road. The driveway was clear, back patio was clear, east side of the property was clear, west side clear as well. This was B-O-R-I-N-G.

Several more minutes passed, and I was still not picking anything up on the cameras. I started to get up off of the stool to go outside and find Slate when I felt someone behind me. Naturally, I let out a blood curdling scream.

"It's me, it's me," Slate said. "Calm down, baby. It's me."

"What the hell are you trying to pull?" I yelled, placing my hand against my pounding heart. "You nearly caused me to have a heart attack!"

He pulled me against him, wrapping his strong arms around me and rocking me back and forth.

"I'm sorry, babe. I was just about to announce my presence when you started to get up."

"As if that would have been less frightening," I hissed. "How in the hell did you get in here undetected?"

"If you've calmed down enough, I'll show you," he replied. He instructed me to disengage the system so that we could move about without the motion detectors sounding.

He then took me by the hand, leading me downstairs to the suite I was using. He'd come in through the terrace doors, which should have sounded an alarm. He showed me how he was able to bypass that by simply detaching the wire that was embedded in the threshold with some little gadget he had in his pocket.

"What about the motion detectors?" I asked.

"Go back up to the main panel and activate the ones for down here," he instructed. Stay at the top of the steps and I'll show you."

I did as instructed. He turned the lights off and then pulled another thingamajig out that looked like a flashlight and switched it on. Immediately, the red ultraviolet waves were visible. All he had to do was to stay underneath them, which he managed to do very quickly and very well.

"Well I'm impressed, Slate. I don't feel very secure anymore, but I'm impressed."

"Babe," he said, "I'm not trying to freak you out. You just need to know that there are ways around this stuff. Granted, I learned this in the military, but think about how many other people learned the same thing?"

"So, what do I do?"

"Call the security company tomorrow and tell them you want your motion detectors upgraded so they scramble the rays. You don't want straight line signals. As far as the exterior doors, there's not a lot you can do about that. I recommend you change the sheets on the bed in the master suite the rat bastard was using and we move up there. That way, the motion detectors can do their work."

What he was saying made sense, except for one minor detail.

"Well, how will you get in at night?"

"Through the front door by ringing the doorbell, I presume. The rat bastard has fled the scene, remember?"

"There's still the matter of Lindsey, Slate. I simply can't spring you on her after all she's going through right now. It just wouldn't be right."

He threw his arm around my shoulder, and pulled me close to his chest, kissing the top of my head.

"I know, babe. We'll figure something out, okay? The most important thing is for you and Lindsey to be safe. I don't think you have anything to worry about, but with slime like Jack, you just never know who he may have pissed off."

"Are you hungry?" I asked.

"Starving," he said with his lazy grin.

"Slate, how did I not see you on the exterior cameras?"

"I was a green beret, Sammie. We have our ways."

Chapter 49

The following morning was Saturday, so I was graced with having Slate sleeping beside me once again. I stretched languidly next to him, a smile coming to my lips as I replayed last night in my mind over and over again. It had been delicious.

Slate and I had fucked with abandonment. There had even been food involved, at one point. I felt my face flush when I recalled how he had me straddle him with my back to his front as he sat in Jack's chair in the master suite. I'd ridden him up and down; the position allowed him to hit some very special places I hadn't yet discovered. I became extremely vocal. Slate said I was talking way dirty; directing him to keep stroking my 'you-know-what' with his 'you-know-what' until I 'f'ing' came all over him. I'd denied it when he told me, but I was sure he had no reason to lie. In fact, he had been extremely pleased about it.

I felt him stir next to me. He always seemed to sense when I was awake, even if I didn't move or say anything. I thought it probably had something to do with his special forces training in the military.

He pulled me up against him, splaying his fingers on my naked belly as we 'spooned.' I felt his warm lips kissing the back of my neck; his hand lifted my hair up so that he had access. I shivered against him. Just then, we both felt the baby move. It felt like a somersault, which wasn't all that unusual.

"Wow," Slate said. I could tell he was grinning. "He has some good moves, doesn't he?"

I rolled over to face him, gently kissing his lips.

"Yes, he does - just like his father. I hope 'Tate' looks just like you, Slate."

"Tate?" he asked, a puzzled frown appearing. "I thought it was Grant?"

"No, I changed my mind. I thought I told you I was prone to that."

"Well, be prepared to change it again then, baby. Tate Slater isn't a good combo. I can just hear the kids now calling him Tater Slater or some bullshit like that. No way, it won't be Tate."

"I'm the one carrying this baby. I'm the one that'll go through the pain of childbirth. I'll name him whatever I want."

"Think again, babe. I reserve the right of approval, got it?"

I squirmed in his arms, but he didn't budge. I looked at his face. He was serious and he wasn't going to back down.

"We'll find something we can agree on, I'm sure," I grumbled.

"Good," he replied, smacking my bottom gently as he rolled away from me. "Let's shower, and then we have work to do."

"What work?"

"You're calling the security company for the upgrade. Then we're going to go over Jack's cell phone detail that we subpoenaed. I need your help in identifying phone numbers you recognize."

I rolled my eyes, not anxious to be holed up all day going over phone records and being drilled by Slate to see if I recalled the numbers. Don't get me wrong, I definitely wanted to be drilled by Slate, but in other ways.

We'd spent about three hours reviewing the records. So far, I'd recognized Susan's number about a zillion times, Lindsey's cell number about a dozen times, my number a few times and about ten numbers I had no clue about. Slate said he'd get those numbers run to see to whom it was that they belonged; I was definitely getting bored.

We were now rummaging through copies of our financial records that Slate had been given to mark up expenditures on Jack's debit card. There were the usual charges for gas, restaurants, hotels, and a couple of major cash withdrawals were shown from an ATM located in Fort Wayne, Indiana.

That was strange, as I wasn't aware of any dealings he would've had there. Slate was going to check the ATM locations to see if the cameras revealed any other individuals being nearby when Jack made the transactions and to make sure that it was, in fact, Jack doing them.

By now, I was extremely bored. I sat at the table with my head perched in my hand, stifling a yawn. Slate was all about forging on. I didn't think I could take much more. He finally noticed.

"Are you tired, babe? Do you want to take a nap?"

"Uh huh," I replied smiling. "As long as you'll take one with me."

I saw his slow, lazy smile spread across his handsome face.

"I think that can be arranged," he said, taking my hand and leading me upstairs to the master suite.

Slate undressed me slowly and sensually, cupping my breasts in his hands, lowering his mouth to them to tease and tantalize them with his tongue. He hooked his thumb into the waistband of my panties and pulled them down.

He shed his clothes immediately, lifting me up and placing me on my back on the bed.

From there, he began his sensual journey down my body with his mouth and tongue. He pleasured me in every way possible, taking his time and savoring every inch of me. I moaned softly and moved my body rhythmically to his touch. His tongue explored the folds of my pussy, causing me to writhe beneath him impatiently.

"Are you ready for me?" he asked softly, as he prepared to thrust himself inside of me. I watched as he knelt out of my reach, stroking his hardened cock with his hand, taunting me with his movements.

"I want it now, Slate," I answered, wrapping my legs around his hips, urging him closer. He lowered his hips, his hand still encircled around his erection as he thrust himself into me, causing me to gasp in pleasure as he filled me with himself. I immediately dug my bare feet into his muscular ass while he rocked rhythmically in and out of me.

The house was empty except for us. I writhed in pleasure beneath him, crying out each time he thrust himself in and out of me. My pulse quickened, I was moaning loudly; he was bringing it home for me. I was quickly reaching my crescendo and being extremely vocal about it.

All of a sudden, the sound of the security panel that had been installed in the master suite started beeping. I could make out one of the red warning lights blinking. The computerized voice indicated an 'intruder in Sector 2,' wherever that happened to be.

Slate was up and off of me in a second. He pulled his jeans up and motioned for me to stay put. If I didn't punch a code in within thirty seconds, the authorities would automatically be dispatched. I realized that thirty seconds was a long time when one is riveted with fear. Slate was here. How much worse would it have been if it had only been me?

He slipped soundlessly from the room, whispering for me to lock the door behind him. I scrambled off of the bed and followed his instruction.

I made it a point to look at the clock on the nightstand. I had to get some sense of time in all of this. It read 12:49 a.m. At 12:54 a.m., Slate hollered for me to come down. I slipped my panties on and tied my robe around me. I unlocked the bedroom door and went down to the main floor, where Slate was checking various doors and windows.

I could see the flashing lights of the security patrol car that had been dispatched. Slate had the door open before the two security officers reached the threshold. I stood there in a semi-fog while he took charge of the situation.

He led them through the kitchen and dining room to the patio doors leading to the deck. That's where the 'perp,' as he termed it, gained entrance.

I followed them, listening to Slate's assessment.

God, he was such a 'G-Man,' I thought, as he pointed out that a small, perfectly round hole had been cut into the glass with a diamond wheel glass cutter. From there, the perp had reached in an unlocked the deadbolt. Slate pointed out several thread fibers that were stuck to the sharp edges of the hole in the glass from the perp's gloves.

Several minutes later, the county sheriff's deputies arrived to make a formal report. They spent about thirty minutes going over the outside of the house with flashlights looking for any other clues the perp had left. Slate concluded he'd been scared off by the blinking panel when he reached the kitchen area. He also noted that the laptop, which had remained on the kitchen counter, was gone.

Damn! That meant that the opportunity to access what the cameras had recorded and saved to the hard drive were gone, as well. I kicked myself for not taking the instructions I was given about hiding the laptop seriously. I'd simply left it out on the kitchen counter in plain sight.

The deputies said they'd send the crime lab out first thing in the morning. They asked that we steer clear of those rooms where the perp had been until it had been thoroughly dusted and analyzed. I knew they wouldn't find anything; so did Slate.

After they left, Slate and I climbed the stairs back to the master suite. I crawled under the covers, shivering, even though it was late July. Slate got naked and crawled in beside me.

"Who do you think it was?"

"I haven't the foggiest, babe. If I had to guess, I'd say it was someone who has a score to settle with Jack. He owes somebody something. We have to figure out who and what."

I curled up next to him, feeling safe now with his arms around me.

"Get some sleep, babe. You need to have Lindsey stay a while longer with your folks. I'm going to be staying here with you until we get a grip on this. I'm bringing a couple of my guns over here, too. I'm going to teach you how to use one."

"Slate," I started, "I don't - -"

"It's not up for debate, Sammie."

Chapter 50

The next week flew by quickly. I'd told Lindsey there had been an attempted break-in at the house. I told her to stay put with my parents until further notice. She wanted me to stay with them, as well. I told her I'd be fine. I had someone looking out after me. She didn't question me further.

As promised, Slate now carried his government issued 9 mm semi-automatic gun with him when he came to the house. He also brought a small 32 caliber snub-nosed handgun for me. I wasn't comfortable with it at all.

I'd never held a gun in my life. Slate taught me the proper way to handle it, load it, unload it and clean it. He'd taken me to the shooting range a couple of times, demonstrating the proper way to aim and shoot.

Slate was spending every free moment with me. He was there in bed next to me, on top of me, or underneath me each and every night. No new information had surfaced on Jack or Susan.

As expected, the crime lab wasn't able to pick up any prints from the break-in. The alarm system had been upgraded, per Slate's instructions. The new laptop was set up inside a locked cabinet, so anything recorded to the hard drive would be available, if needed.

I was getting dressed for a meeting with Donovan and some of the forensic accountants who had finished their investigation. My father was picking me up in about fifteen minutes.

I went into the bathroom where Slate was shaving.

It seemed so natural for him to be here now. I went over and kissed him on the cheek he'd already shaved. He was fresh from the shower, a towel wrapped around his hips.

"My dad will be here in a few, so I guess I'll see you later?"

"I should be back here before it gets dark, Sammie. I have a few leads that Taz and I are checking out. We'll be in Fort Wayne most of the day."

"Okay," I said with a sigh, "Lindsey's birthday is tomorrow. I'll probably be out the rest of the day shopping for her. I'll have my cell with me."

"Be careful," he said, pulling me closer for a warm kiss.

"*You* be careful," I replied, patting his ass. "By the way, when is your birthday, Slate?"

"September 3rd," he replied with a grin.

"So you'll be twenty-seven in September?"

He started to answer, and then his cell phone rang.

"Got to take this, babe. See you later."

My father was pulling up the driveway when I went out onto the front porch to wait. I got into his Lincoln Town Car, looking around the neighborhood as we pulled out onto the main road. I was still in the dark as to where Slate was parking his pick-up truck.

"How's Lindsey?" I asked.

"She seems to be doing okay. I think it's good that she returned to work. We usually eat lunch together every day."

"I'm glad. She needs a decent male figure in her life right now. I still can't believe Jack deserted her without a second thought."

The meeting with the forensic accounts and Donovan proved enlightening. It was about time some answers were forthcoming.

In a nutshell, the two former chemists at Banion had sung like birds in order to get the pending criminal charges against them reduced. They were still going to do some hard time.

Jack had enlisted their assistance in manufacturing unstamped Percocet and Vicodin tablets from the active raw materials that had falsely been written off as being disposed of by reason of expiration or scrapped due to arriving in damaged containers.

Obviously, the records had been falsified and inventory counts misrepresented over a period of time. The chemists had been receiving a nice chunk of change under the table, which likely explained those periodic miscellaneous cash withdrawals from our private account over the past year and a half.

Jack had then used the OMC as his primary marketing channel for distribution of the pills. As near as the accountants could tell, the total street value of the drugs involved over the period of time in question was approximately $1 million.

Jack, apparently, had an additional scheme going to help finance the operation. There were several different insurance claims submitted for company cars in various locations in the U.S. purportedly involved in collisions. The driver or passengers claimed medical damages and loss of income. The insurance companies had paid out on these claims; some involved Banion-owned vehicles as the claimant; other times they were the driver at fault's vehicle.

Donovan said that several of the 'non-Banion' claimants were members of the OMC in Fort Wayne. One of the claimants was Susan Reynard. She'd been driving one of the Banion company cars in Charlotte, North Carolina last fall when Jack had made his weeklong trip. That claim had paid out $50,000 to her for purported lost wages. Jack had signed off on the affidavit to Motors Mutual as her direct-line supervisor, validating the lost wages.

What a total crock of shit.

There were now outstanding warrants issued against Susan for insurance fraud, mail fraud, and racketeering. She apparently had acted as the intermediary between the OMC contact in Fort Wayne and Jack.

Several pieces of the puzzle were missing, namely records and data lifted by forensic examination of Susan's computer, which she'd attempted to wipe clean. The data pulled from the hard drive indicated that some type of deal had been underway involving the trafficking of assault weapons and cocaine. Again, the OMC was involved, but no specific names had been lifted.

My father dropped me back off at home. I immediately got into my car and headed towards the mall. The truth was, I didn't like being in my own house these days if Slate wasn't there. I was totally creeped out.

I spent the afternoon shopping, then stopped by Becky's house to give her the update on everything. I was home sitting out on the back deck sipping iced tea when Slate arrived. He'd come around from the side of the house, as if looking for me.

"Hey you," he said, coming up onto the deck. "I've been looking for you inside."

"I don't like being in there without you being with me," I said with a shrug. I knew it sounded 'needy' but it was the truth.

He pulled me up from my chair, wrapping his strong arms around me. He was comforting me. He'd been doing a lot of that lately.

"Let's go inside," he said softly. "I've checked everything, including the camera recordings. No one's been poking around at all."

"How long have you been here?"

"About an hour."

I hadn't heard him come in, but then I usually didn't. He was my 'Slate-ninja.'

We spent the rest of the evening talking about what I'd learned at the meeting this morning. I wrapped Lindsey's presents, while Slate pondered something. He'd become unusually quiet.

"How did things go in Fort Wayne?" I asked.

"Fine."

"That's it? Just fine?"

"Sammie," he used his warning tone with me.

I hated that he constantly kept me in the dark. If I learned anything, I had to hear it from Donovan. I was sure Slate already knew all about the findings that were discussed in this morning's meeting. He was such a stickler for protocol.

"Never mind," I said, getting up and heading towards the stairs.

"Where are you going?"

"To get a shower and then go to bed."

"Don't be pissed, babe. You know the routine by now."

"Doesn't mean I have to like it," I grumbled.

I showered, and then dressed in a light nightie, crawling beneath the covers. I was exhausted. The heat and humidity of late July seemed to suck my energy. The house was cool with the air conditioning going, but I looked forward to the fall every year by the first of August.

I felt Slate crawl into bed beside me some time later. I was still a bit miffed that he couldn't share anything with me. I knew that I could be trusted. Why didn't he?

He pulled me against him, circling an arm around me. I felt him kiss my hair, his fingers combing through my still-damp locks. I pretended to be asleep. If he knew I was awake, he would likely want to fuck and tonight I was just too tired.

I felt his hand lifting my hair up away from my neck. I felt him nuzzle his face against it, pressing warm, soft kisses on my skin. God, that felt so good. His hand settled on the swell of my belly. I was nearly five months pregnant. The baby's movements were getting stronger.

Slate kissed the back of my neck again. His hand gently rubbed my baby bump. Ever so softly, I heard him whisper, "I love you."

Chapter 51

It was the third week of August. God, I was so ready for summer to be over. The only bad part about fall was that Lindsey would be leaving to go back to Cornell.

She'd been staying with my parents, and, apparently, she had met a nice, young man at the swimming pool where they lived. I'd met him briefly at her birthday celebration. His name was Adam. He was a sophomore at Indiana University and as cute as could be. I could see that Lindsey was smitten. She was in no hurry to come back home.

I was sitting at the kitchen counter going over bills when I saw one addressed to Jack. On the outside of the envelope it was stamped 'Past Due' in red. The return address was a storage rental facility in Fort Wayne.

I slit the envelope open and pulled the piece of paper out. It was a letter basically stating that the checking account that had been used for automatic payments had insufficient funds. As co-signer for Susan Reynard, the responsibility for payment was being transferred to Jack.

What the hell?

The bill was for a refrigerated unit. July's balance (which had been due on the 15th) was past due; the charges for August were due now. The total amount due with late charges was $365. Evidently Susan had cleared out her account as well, when they fled.

I looked at my watch. Shit! I was going to be late for my appointment with Dr. Bailey if I didn't get a move on it.

Slate had left early. He said he'd do everything in his power to meet me at Dr. Bailey's. I made him promise not to embarrass me this time.

I set the alarm and locked up. It was a twenty-five minute drive to the doctor's office. If I didn't run into major traffic, I would make it.

I was five minutes into the drive on the county road leading to the interstate when I saw Slate's black pick-up suddenly on my bumper when I glanced in the side mirror. He was flashing his lights on and off, waving me over.

247

What the hell is going on now?

I pulled over to the side of the road. The front bumper of his truck had to be practically touching the back bumper of my Mercedes. I hit the button to lower my window as he came rushing up to the driver's side. Too late, I realized it wasn't Slate; it was Slash.

Panic set in immediately as I tried to power the window back up. Too late! My door flew open and Slash pulled me roughly from the car.

"Come on, bitch," he sneered. "You and I are taking a ride. We have some things to discuss."

Someone else had jumped from Slate's truck and was now in the back seat of my car. Slash opened the rear passenger door on the driver's side and pushed me in, slamming the door quickly and jumping into the driver's seat.

He peeled back out onto the road as the passenger in the seat beside me gave a toothless grin. He nodded toward his hand. My eyes followed as I saw what he wanted me to see: a revolver pointed directly at my baby bump.

"Hey, sorry for not making the proper introductions back there," Slash yelled from the front seat.

"Darrell, this here's Diamond, Mr. Big's old lady."

"Is that right?" Darrell said with a cocky smirk, his eyes boring into me. "You mean Slate's *whore?*"

"Yeah, that too," Slash replied. "She's gonna be helping us out today if she has plans on seeing tomorrow."

Somewhere, and I'm not sure where, I suddenly was filled with rage and fury. How dare they kidnap and threaten me? How dare that asshole point that gun towards my baby? I lashed out.

"You motherfuckers better not lay one finger on me. I swear on all that's precious, you're dead fucking meat!"

Somehow, I hadn't managed to pull it off. I felt the butt of Darrell's gun slam against the side of my head. Everything went black.

Chapter 52

When my eyes finally opened, they opened to darkness. I knew that it wasn't nighttime yet because, wherever I was, there was still sunlight streaming in through the cracks in the wooden planks. It looked to be some kind of a barn. It was hot, sticky and the air was thick with humidity.

My head was pounding. I felt beads of perspiration trickling down my face and back. My hair was damp, clinging to the back of my neck. I would have given anything for a cool breeze at the moment. My hands were tied behind my back; my ankles were tied together. The rough rope was digging into the skin on my wrists and ankles.

I looked around, my eyes adjusting to the darkness within. I saw my Mercedes parked over in front of a wide sliding barn door that was shut at the moment. My captors were nowhere around. I needed to clear my head, to think survival. That's what Slate would tell me to do.

I suddenly became emotional. Would I ever see Slate again? Or Lindsey? Or my parents? What did these bastards have planned? How was it I was expected to help them? Did anyone even know that I was missing yet? I had way more questions that I had answers. The sound of a squeaky door opening and the light that filtered in with it told me that I was about to get a few answers.

Slash and Darrell sauntered over to where I was sitting on a pile of straw in front of a long wooden crate of some sort. They took a seat on the crate, drinking from their water bottles. It reminded me of how thirsty I was.

"Well, what do you think, Darrell? You think Diamond there has been hog-tied and left in this sauna long enough she might be a bit more cooperative with us?"

"Guess we better ask her, man."

"What do you two want from me?" I hissed. "I had nothing to do with whatever it was Jack was doing."

"We know that," Slash said, taking another swig. "But we also know that Mr. Big left in quite a hurry. He didn't have a chance to wrap things up at the house, you know what I mean?"

"Not really," I replied.

"Well, let me make it simple for you, Diamond. We bought something from Mr. Big the day before he booked out of town, paid his fuck buddy 'Suzy-Q' cash on the barrel for it. It was a joint effort with two other chapters, so there's quite a bit of money involved, you see. Now, here's our problem. The day they split, Suzy-Q never showed up with the key or provided the password needed to get our goods. I'm betting that info's at your crib."

"Are you the ones who tried to break in last month?"

"Yeah, unfortunately that fucking computer we grabbed didn't have a damn bit of information on it. So, we need that information from you, little lady."

"I have no clue about any key, I swear to God. How do you know that information hasn't already been uncovered by the Feds?"

"You're *fucking a 'Fed,'* darlin'. If it'd been found, you'd be telling me that instead of asking me that, right?"

"No," I replied angrily. "Slate doesn't tell me shit. That's the truth."

"Well, we're gonna see about that," Darrell said, pulling my cell phone out of my purse.

I watched as he slid the battery back in. He powered it on and pulled up "G-Man's" number from my address book. He sent Slate a text from my cell telling him to answer the next phone call he received. He powered the phone off, removing the battery once again and slipping it into his pocket.

Slash untied my wrists. I massaged them with my fingers to get the circulation going. My fingers felt numb.

Darrell pulled a track phone from his shirt pocket, punching in Slate's cell phone number. Before he hit the 'send' button he instructed me on what to say. Again, the gun was flashed in front of me.

I nodded, as he handed me the phone.

"Sammie," he said, his voice strained.

"Slate - listen to me please. Jack was in possession of a key and a password that Susan was to give it to her contacts at OMC the day they split. You have to tell me the truth - has this been found in any of the stuff the Feds found at Banion during their search?"

"No," he said. "I'm being honest with you here. Nothing's been uncovered that sounds at all like what you're describing. Are you okay baby?"

"I'm fine, Slate, but I won't be if I can't help these guys. They're not going to release me until you show up with the key. They mean business, Slate."

"Tell me where to look, Sammie."

My mind was racing. I had to think like Jack at the moment. "Give me a second," I said, covering the mic on the phone.

"When and where was Susan supposed to meet your people to turn over the key?"

"Seven p.m. sharp at the corner of Eastern and Sixteenth."

That was near the gym where Jack worked out daily, either before or after work. That was where he'd told Lindsey he was going after work. He'd then called me later on his way to the airport. He had a locker there at the gym.

"Slate," I said, "you need to go to Sporty's Gym on Baxter Avenue. Jack has a membership there. You need to get into his locker. If he wanted to hide something, that's the only place I can think of where he might've put it."

"Let me talk to Slash," he said. I handed the phone to Slash.

Slash held the phone to his ear, rolling his eyes and grinning.

"You aren't in a position to threaten me at the moment, asshole. Just think about this while you're deciding whether being a Fed means more to you than seeing your baby born. I have nothing to lose if I get popped. I'm already going to serve more years than I have left on this planet. It wouldn't bother me one bit to add murder to the list. You involve anyone else and it's 'bye bye' to Diamond. You have one hour before we call back. Let's hope your little scavenger hunt goes well."

Slash ended the call and turned to me.

"You better hope your dude cares about you more than his career. He can't have both."

Darrell squatted down and tied my hands behind my back once more. Then, the two bikers exited the barn. I felt the tears well up, hoping that my hunch was correct and praying that Slate did care more about me than his career.

The puzzle finally fit. The key was to the storage locker in Fort Wayne, and the password was probably for the electronic gate that allowed access to the premises. They didn't know that I knew the location only because of the past due bill that had arrived in the mail just today.

How had they gotten Slate's truck? How would Slate get to the gym without his truck? I wondered where Slate was when I'd called him. I didn't dare ask any or say anything other than what they instructed. I was sick of having that revolver waved in front of me.

This hour would probably be the longest of my life. Maybe it'd be the last hour of my life......

Chapter 53

~ SLATE ~

The call ended with silence.

Fuck!

That son-of-a-bitch better not touch a hair on her fucking head. How'd this happen? How had I let some low-life mother fucker like Slash get one over on me? I'd been so freaking careful!

I knew immediately something was up when Sammie hadn't made her doctor's appointment that afternoon. I'd tried calling her cell phone a dozen times. It was turned off.

I'd raced from the doctor's office to her house in my truck, breaking the speed limit the whole way. I'd noticed a pick-up truck just like mine parked by the side of the road a couple of miles from her house. I stopped and called the plate number in to the locals. It'd been reported stolen that morning. That's when the hairs on the back of my neck stood up.

When I arrived at her house, I used my key. The doors were locked, the alarm had been set. I checked every room in the house and the garage. Her car was gone, so was she. I checked the camera video on the computer. The only activity was her leaving for the doctor's appointment at 2:12 p.m. She'd been running a little late, it seemed, for a 2:30 p.m. appointment.

I had sat down at the bar in the kitchen to try and get a handle on the situation. That's when my phone beeped that I had a text message. It was Sammie. I breathed a sigh of relief until I read the text. Several minutes later my cell phone rang. The caller I.D. was from Missouri; some fucking track phone. It was then I realized that Slash had gotten to her.

I listened to the message that Slash had instructed her to give me. The whole time, I was trying to figure out where she could be. I absently flipped through the mail she'd thrown on the kitchen counter. I listened to her instructions and then asked her to put Slash on the phone.

The mother-fucker knew he had the power at the moment and so did I. I listened to him yammer on as I picked up one of the envelopes that Sammie must've opened. It was a past-due bill that was addressed to the rat bastard. The letter folded up next to it told me exactly what type of key Slash was looking to find. It was why he'd attempted the break-in a few weeks back…a deal gone badly.

What kind of a stupid fuck doesn't pay a storage fee? Probably one who already has the money in hand and is on the run.

I was glad it hadn't been paid. I now knew where the goods from the deal gone badly were located.

I got into my truck and hauled ass to the gym. There was a young chick working the desk. I turned on the charm and showed her my badge, explaining that I needed to get into Jack Dennison's locker; that he was a fugitive from justice. She started some shit about a search warrant being needed. I told her she watched too much television. Federal agents didn't need search warrants, only local authorities. She bought the story and got the master key for me.

Once inside his locker, I emptied his gym bag out and there it was: a small envelope containing a key. There was a piece of paper wrapped around the key that had a pass code written on it. More than likely, the pass code activated the electronic gate on the premises.

I took his gym bag with the rest of his stuff in it and headed out. I had another twenty minutes before I would get the next call. I got on my phone and called Taz. I needed his help. I trusted him more than anyone.

The call back came in exactly one hour to the minute later. It was Slash.

"So is your Betty in luck, Slate?"

"I have the fucking key, *Delbert*," I said, putting the emphasis on his given name. I guess if I'd been named 'Delbert,' a name like 'Slash' would've suited me better too.

"Fuck you, pig," he sneered. "You don't wanna piss me off when I have your girl here no farther away than my hardened dick, right?"

My blood boiled at the thought of that piece of shit slime ball touching her. I needed to keep my cool *for her.*

"What's the deal, Slash? I give you the key, and you give me Sammie?"

"Not quite, Slate. There's a matter of trust here - or should I say, mistrust? Here's how this is gonna go down. I'll give you a drop-off location for the key, which I presume has a password with it?"

"Yep," I answered stiffly.

"Okay. Once we determine that no other feds or locals are involved and we collect the goods without incident, you'll get a phone call giving you the location on where you can hook up with your girl."

"What makes you think I trust you?"

"You really have no choice, dude."

I wasn't sure when Slash said 'we' how many others that meant.

"Don't worry about her, Slate. I'm going to be right here with her the whole time, making sure she's safe and doesn't get frightened in the dark. Once the others give me the all clear, I'll be in touch with you letting you know where you can find her, got it?"

"Let me talk to her first."

I heard some muffled conversation, then Sammie's voice on the other end.

"Slate - did you find it?"

"I sure did, baby. You did great. I'm going to do everything he wants so that you're safe. Do you trust me?"

"You know I do."

"That's my girl. Just hang tight and don't do anything to piss them off, okay?"

"Yep," she said with a tired sigh.

"I love you, Sammie."

"I know you do, Slate."

Slash got back on the phone, giving me instructions on where to drop the envelope with the key inside. It was about sixty minutes from Indianapolis. I told him I was leaving now. He said he'd check my progress in an hour.

Chapter 54

~ SLATE ~

I was on schedule for the drop off. I was about fifteen miles from the designated location. My cell phone rang. It was Taz.

"Everything's in place in Fort Wayne," he confirmed. "We have plain clothes local officers and U.S. Marshalls. The owner of the storage facility has opened up the empty storage locker next to the one Susan rented. They're stationed inside, ready and waiting."

"Great job," I said. I never had to worry about Taz fucking up. He always came through. "What about Garnet?"

"She's in the car sitting next to me. A bit reluctant, but I used my powers of persuasion to get her on board."

If I hadn't been so concerned about Sammie, I'd have found a bit of humor in that. Taz had, evidently, let her blow him.

"Does she have any idea where they might be holed up?"

"Given the location of the drop-off point and its proximity to Fort Wayne, she's pretty sure it's an old deserted farm that the bikers used to rent in the fall for their annual 'bike-in.' It's near Kokomo."

"My drop off point is just south of Marian," I said. "I'm ten minutes away. Where are you?"

"We're on Route 31. She thinks she might be able to remember the location once we get near Kokomo. It's all we've got, bro."

"Keep with it, Taz. I'll be back in touch as soon as I complete the drop."

My cell phone rang about thirty seconds later. It was Slash, asking my current location. I told him. He then gave me turn by turn locations to the exact point of drop off. I followed his directions, reporting various landmarks and intersections back to him so that he knew I was following his instructions. He must know this area fairly well.

I finally reached a residential neighborhood, as guided by him. There was an elementary school on the right. I was to drop the envelope off outside of camera range at the edge of the parking lot. There was a brick near the sidewalk. I was to put it underneath the brick and drive away. He informed me that he had people watching.

I located the brick and deposited the envelope underneath. I hustled back into my truck and took off, heading back the way that I'd come.

He told me once everything went as planned and his associates returned to pick him up, he'd call me with her whereabouts in a couple of hours to ensure they had a head start towards their ultimate destination.

If his associates failed to return or respond to his attempts to contact them within a reasonable amount of time, he'd assume the worst and slit her throat. My blood ran cold. Taz and I had to fucking get to her - and fast.

I called Taz immediately to get his location. They were on Fletcher Road off of Route 31. The fact that it was now getting dark was hindering Garnet's ability to identify a deserted farm that would have no lights on anywhere to help with recognition. I relayed Slash's latest conversation.

"Don't worry Slate, we'll find her."

Chapter 55

It was getting dark outside. Very little light was filtering in now between the rotted out wooden planks of the barn.

Slash had dozed off. I'd taken advantage of his eyes being closed by looking around trying to figure out some way I could feel less helpless. Slate always said that people are almost never helpless.

I'd spotted my cell phone over on top of the wooden crate. Once I'd sent the text message to Slate, they'd pulled the battery from my phone so it couldn't be tracked. Somehow, the battery had ended up on the pile of straw next to me. It must have fallen out of Darrell's pocket when he'd bent down earlier to re-tie my hands.

If I could somehow get my hands untied so that I could pick up the battery and get it back into my cell phone, I could maybe sneak a text to Slate. Having both my hands and feet tied made that impossible. I was going to have to enlist Slash's help.

"Slash" I called out. "Hey Slash!"

He stirred and his eyes flew open.

"I hate to wake you, but I really, really need to pee. I mean could you at least let me pee and then maybe let me have a drink of water? I'm pregnant for Chrissake. How much of a flight risk could I possibly be?"

"Alright, alright - stop your yammering."

He got to his feet, stretching. I twisted my position so that he could unbind my ankles without glimpsing the cell phone battery on the ground next to me.

Once my feet were unbound, he pulled me up by my arm to a standing position. It took a couple of moments for my circulation to regulate in my feet. The heat and humidity had made my ankles swell up.

He led me over to a far corner of the barn, behind a stack of baled straw.

"You can cop a squat over there, milady. I'll even give you some privacy."

"What about my hands?"

"What about 'em? It ain't like I got toilet paper to offer you. Drip-dry like a normal chick."

"This normal chick wears underpants, Slash. How am I supposed to get them down?"

"I can help with that," he snickered, coming closer.

I froze in fear, poised to run from him if I had to, knowing I would never be able to get away from him.

"Relax," he sneered, grabbing my wrists and yanking the ropes off. "Pregnant chicks don't do it for me. I guess that's lucky for you, huh?"

I scrambled behind the bales of straw and relieved myself, not caring that he was standing two feet away and could hear my stream. No bashful kidneys here. I allowed myself to 'drip dry' as he'd so eloquently put it, because I had no other option.

Once I'd recomposed myself, I went back around to where he waited. I walked back over to my pile of straw and he bent down to grab the ropes to bind my hands and feet again.

"Wait," I said, sounding pitiful. "You can see how swollen my feet and ankles have become because of the circulation and heat. Can I please have a few minutes without being tied up so they can get some relief? I just need a little bit of water to cool down, and then you can tie me back up. Where would I go anyway? I don't even know where we are, for Chrissake."

"God damn, you're a whiner," he griped. "How in the hell does Slate put up with your shit?"

He walked over to the blanket on the floor where he'd been dozing and picked up a water bottle. It was nearly empty. He tossed it back to the ground.

"Shit, alright. I'm going out to my bike to get another bottle of water. You sit tight. I'm closing and locking the barn door behind me, so it ain't like you have any other way out. I'll be back in sixty seconds. I repeat - stay fucking put."

I nodded my head up and down. He sauntered out through the door and as promised, I heard him throw the latch down on the other side.

I scrambled quickly to my feet, grabbing the battery from the floor, and crossing the twenty feet between me and my cell phone. I slid the battery in, and hit the power button.

"C'mon, c'mon," I repeated in my mind. My hands were shaking. It powered up. I quickly located 'G-Man' and typed a quick text.

'Phone on - Slash doesn't know. Track location - in a barn somewhere.'

I hit 'send' and then made sure that the phone's sound settings were all on mute.

I hurried back to my pile of straw. Slash was none the wiser when he came through the barn door ten seconds later with a bottle of cold water for me.

I thanked him, taking a long drink of the water. I poured some in my hands and splashed it against my face. I poured a little of it on my head, immediately feeling myself cool down.

The barn was nearly pitch-black now. Slash had left the barn door open, so a bit of a breeze trickled in. The stars and moon offered a bit of light from the pitch blackness of the countryside. He'd brought a flashlight in with him, leaving it turned on to provide a bit of light. He pulled his track phone out and checked to see if he had any text messages. Apparently, he didn't.

"Well, we should be hearing from Darrell in another twenty minutes or so. At least you better hope we do," he said with his evil smirk. "So, break's over. Time to get you trussed back up again."

He bound my hands and feet once again. At least now that darkness had enveloped this godforsaken place, the heat had dissipated somewhat. I sat back once again in the scratchy straw and tried to relax. I had to believe that everything would be alright. It was all I had.

Chapter 56

~ SLATE ~

My heart stopped when my phone beeped that I had a text message. I nearly swerved off of the road when I saw it was from Sammie.

Good girl - she'd somehow gotten her cell phone back on. I'd been trying like hell to track her location from that all afternoon. I figured the sons of bitches had taken the battery out of her phone so it couldn't be tracked.

I pulled the application of GPS tracking up on my cell. Sammie's number had already been synchronized with mine. I'd done that the same day I'd programmed my contact info into her phone. I didn't think she would mind.

I hit the button again for 'search' and waited. Bingo! There it was. The location of the farm Garnet had mentioned.

The GPS screen said I was a little more than five miles away. I tapped the screen for audio directions. I was going in the wrong direction so I screeched to a halt and did a three point turn. I called Taz while listening to the GPS directions.

"Taz, the address is 11455 Millerstown Road. I'm about five miles from there. Plug it in to your GPS and haul ass. She's in a barn. That's all I know."

"Got it," he said, ending the call.

I wasn't sure if he was any closer than I was, but I needed him with me. I didn't need to instruct Taz to park away from the site and make his arrival on foot. He knew all of that. That's the reason I knew he wouldn't fuck up.

Damn, this place was fucking remote. These narrow, country roads had cornfields on each side that looked ready for harvest. It sure as hell was making it difficult for me to see a damn thing. Each mile seemed to take forever. My adrenaline was pumping at full throttle.

Finally, the computer voice on GPS indicated my destination was five hundred feet ahead on the right. I pulled my truck over so that it was in the ditch.

I had my gun in my leg holster; another was tucked into the waistband of my black flak pants. I placed my night vision glasses on. I'd worn hiking boots that made it easier to move through these fucking cornfields.

I'd traveled about a hundred yards when I hit a clearing. It was a narrow gravel driveway that must lead up to the farm. I crept as quietly as possible, staying in the weeds along the drive, so as not to make noise in the gravel. Up ahead I could see what was left of the old farmhouse. It was just the shell; no windows, no roof left to speak of.

I spotted the barn about fifty yards behind the house. Slash's bike was parked up by the side of it. I didn't see any other bikes or vehicles around.

Certainly, he wasn't pulling this off by himself. Shit - maybe there was only one another person involved. Maybe two others at the most, I figured.

I spotted a large double barn door that looked to be padlocked. At the other end of the barn, there was a single entry door. I needed to scope out each side of the barn, along with the rear to see if more vehicles were parked.

Piece of cake.

Chapter 57

The twenty minutes must be up, I thought as I watched Slash periodically check his phone while he paced. He'd left his flashlight on so there was some light inside now.

I wondered if Slate had even received my text message. If so, how long would it take for someone to get here? Slash was making me nervous because I could tell that he was nervous.

"What time is it?" I asked.

"What fucking difference does it make to you what time it is?" he spat angrily. "All you need to know is that if I don't get a call here within the next five minutes, your fucking time is up and I'm splitting."

"Geez," I said, acting insulted. "You know, maybe he ran into traffic or something."

"Yeah - it's the 'or something' that you better hope isn't the reason. Shut up. I don't like bitches talking when they don't have nothin' to say."

"Excuse the hell out of me."

He shot me a dirty look and took a couple of steps towards me. I guess he didn't like sassy bitches either.

"Listen bitch, I'm going to step outside to see if the reception's bad in here. You keep your mouth shut and say your prayers."

I looked away from his evil face, vowing not to let him see that I was scared.

He traipsed out of the barn, shutting the door behind him. I lowered my head against my knees, softly sobbing into them.

I felt something fall into my hair. There it was again. Oh God! What if it was some deadly spider lowering itself down from its web? Spiders were nocturnal, right? I shivered.

Then I saw what it was. From above, bits and pieces of straw were floating down from the loft above me. I heard the soft creaking of the floor above me.

Someone dropped down behind me. I felt his warm breath on my neck as his hands worked to free mine.

"Be still, baby. I'm here. Everything's going to be alright."

I nodded.

My heartbeat quickened as he freed my hands then crept around to get my feet untied. He was in my line of vision then.

I saw him all in black, moving swiftly and precisely getting the rope untied so that I could finally stand when directed. My ninja-Slate was here.

"He's coming right back," I whispered.

"How many?"

"Just Slash here. Darrell took a truck to Fort Wayne."

"Yeah, he won't be back," Slate whispered with a grin. He pulled the small handgun from behind him and pressed it into my hands.

"Hang on to this. Be ready to use it if you have to, Sammie. Stay put for the moment."

Then he was gone. He moved quietly and lithely over to the door that Slash was due to walk through any moment.

I clutched the gun behind me so it still looked as if my hands were tied behind my back. I heard Slash's footsteps outside of the barn. The latch to the door slid back and he opened it, crossing the threshold into the barn.

In a nanosecond, Slate was on him, kicking him to the ground with one swift movement. Slash was caught off-guard, but not for long. He leapt to his feet and pulled a chain from his back pocket. He wound part of it around his hand then snapped his arm and I saw the ball at the end of it land against Slate's neck.

Oh my God, whatever was on the end of that ball had cut into his neck. I saw Slate put his hand up to the wound to stop the flow.

Oh God! I have to do something!

Slash was using Slate's momentary pause to his advantage. He was winding the chain back around his hand, preparing to deliver another blow.

Slate was creeping towards him, but I wasn't sure how dazed he might be from the shock of that blow. It looked like it had landed damn close to his jugular. I didn't have time to debate it. I needed to do something.

I brought my arms around from my back. The revolver was clutched in both hands. My fingers and wrist were still numb. I didn't trust my aim to shoot. The two men were too close, circling one another, ready to strike. I aimed for the window and pulled the trigger. The shot rang out. Glass shattered, giving Slate the split second he needed to bring Slash down.

He was on top of him, pulling the chain from his hand and slamming the ball at the end of it against Slash's face and head. I crept closer to him and the look on Slate's face was one that I'd never seen. It was pure rage. He wasn't going to stop until Slash was dead. I couldn't let that happen.

Slash wasn't fighting back any longer. He was out cold.

"Slate - he's out," I said loudly. "You need to stop and take care of your neck. You're bleeding badly!"

He didn't stop. He continued to pummel Slash with his fists, over and over again. Slash's face was a bloody pulp. I was going to be sick.

"Eric!" I shrieked. "For the love of God, please stop. For me please. I love you. Please, stop!"

He froze and looked up at me slowly, his eyes meeting mine. I needed to see the sanity return to them. It hadn't yet.

"Don't you see, Eric, if you kill him, he'll never have to face what he's done? You'll be giving him the easy way out."

"He killed Laney. He was prepared to kill you. I can't let him kill the people that I love."

"But you saved me, baby," I said, putting my hand out to him. "Now let me save you, okay? I need you and Landon needs you."

He took my hand and stood up, stepping over the motionless body of Slash, pulling me to him. Blood was still trickling from the gash. I needed to get something clean wrapped around it.

"Don't move," I instructed him.

I ran over to where they'd pulled my car into the barn and popped the trunk open. My wardrobe bag with my dancing outfits was still in the trunk. I pulled a clean spandex monokini with long sleeves from the plastic garment bag. I grabbed the flashlight from the wooden bench and headed back over to Slate.

"Hold this," I instructed handing him the flashlight so that the beam illuminated his face and neck. I wrapped the clean spandex material around his neck, securing it by tying the sleeves together.

"There," I said, relieved that the bleeding had stopped. "You're going to need some stitches. You're lucky that didn't hit a quarter of an inch over."

"Sammie," he said quietly, "who the hell's Landon?"

I patted my rounded belly. "Your son, silly."

He shook his head, pulling me close so that he could kiss me.

"I love you, Samantha."

"I love you, Eric."

Our lips met in a tender kiss just as Taz barged through the barn door, his weapon drawn. The multi-colored lights of multiple law enforcement vehicles were flashing on the horizon.

"He needs to get to the hospital now, Taz."

"Got it," he said, motioning for the others to come in.

Chapter 58

It was September 3rd, Slate's birthday.

I'd invited my parents over for dinner. It was about time they met the soon-to-be father of my baby. Lindsey was coming, too. She was bringing Adam. I'd asked her to arrive prior to my parents. I needed to let her know what was going on. She was heading back to Cornell the day after tomorrow.

Slate was healing up. His neck had been stitched up and the doctor agreed that he'd been lucky. Katy was coming for dinner, too. I was nervous making the preparations for this 'family' get together that wasn't really a family yet.

All of the arrest warrants had now been served. Everyone that needed to be arrested had been, with the exception of Jack and Susan. Slate said it was just a matter of time for them.

I'd put my house on the market. I didn't need to be rambling around in this huge house and worrying about upkeep. My life had changed and I truly felt it had changed for the good. I'd no need for 'trappings.' The equity would finish paying for Lindsey's college tuition.

I'd learned some extremely important life lessons this past year. I'd learned about love, about trust, and about taking control of one's own life. I wasn't sure how things would end up with Slate and me. What I was sure of was that I loved him and that he loved me. For now, that was enough.

I knew that we would welcome this baby boy together. I just needed to know that Lindsey would be okay with that.

I was on the phone with Becky, explaining what had happened after the incident in that barn less than two weeks ago. I'd come as close to death then as Slate had. I truly believed that Slash would've killed me. I didn't even know, at the time, that Slate suspected him of killing his younger sister, Laney.

Slate told me that when Slash told him on the phone that he'd 'slit' my throat, he knew with all certainty that he was Laney's murderer. He said that was Slash's signature preference when killing.

Becky listened quietly as I revealed everything that had been discovered when they made the bust in Fort Wayne when Darrell had shown up at the storage unit. Come to find out, the 'goods' that Jack had sold them happened to be a shitload of teddy bears for the launching of the 'Toys for Tots' run in November.

OMC, along with Ohio Iron bikers, were meeting in Fort Wayne to start the run that would have taken these stuffed bears, along with legitimate toys to Charlotte, North Carolina. Slate said that the stuffed bears had been torn open. A sealed container holding a kilo each of cocaine had been discovered. There were a total of thirty kilos.

"How did that benefit Jack?" Becky asked.

"Well, Slate explained that Jack had been the connection for the cocaine. He'd negotiated a fairly good price from his connection in Chicago: around $12,000 per kilo. Jack had purchased twenty kilos. He then commissioned the chemists at Banion to cut it with some sort of baking soda and magnesium/silicon mixture. After that, the twenty kilos became thirty kilos."

"Oh my God," Becky replied. "He pulled a 'bait and switch' on the bikers?"

"Apparently so, he figured they'd never find out because they were moving it to the Charlotte area where a kilo of cocaine sells for around $27,000. So Jack invested $240,000 for twenty kilos, and then he sold thirty kilos to the OMC for a total of $441,000. He netted a $200,000 profit; no one was any the wiser."

"So, that means that Jack and Susan fled the country with about a million dollars in total?"

"At least," I said. "Slate says they were pretty good at laundering the money, so it could be more. He says, eventually, they'll surface. It could be years, though."

"Wow," she sighed. "How's Lindsey with all of this?"

"She's come to terms with the harsh reality of the man her father is, I guess. Her relationship with Adam couldn't have come at a better time. Did I tell you she received a letter from Jack?"

"No shit?"

"He must've paid someone to mail it from El Paso a couple of weeks after he crossed the border. It was brief and to the point: he told her he was sorry; that he loved her and always would, and to make better choices than he did."

"Oh, wow. Small consolation for the pain and misery he's caused everyone," she replied. "So, what now?"

"I'm having my family meet Slate this evening. I'm going to let Lindsey know about us. I really think she'll be okay with it."

"Well good luck with that. Call me tomorrow and let me know, okay?"

"I sure will."

I was in the kitchen, marinating the chicken breasts when Slate got home. He came over and gave me a warm kiss, hugging me as he always did when he got home.

"Sammie, we need to talk," he said.

That's never a good thing to hear from someone you love.

He took my hand and led me to the living room, pulling me down on the couch next to him.

"My job here in Indianapolis is over. I've got to wrap things up and report back to D.C. next week."

My heart thudded. I'd known this day would come eventually, but I still wasn't prepared for it.

"What does that mean for us?" I asked softly.

"I guess that depends on you. I love you. I want to marry you. I want you with me in D.C."

"You know that I love you, Slate."

"Call me Eric, please? When we're having talks of this nature, it just helps if you call me Eric."

I smiled at him. "I love you Eric, but there are some major obstacles with all of this. You have to know that."

"Like what?"

"Like our age difference, for instance. You may think you want this right now, but marrying a cougar might not be so appealing a few years from now."

He broke into a wide grin, his dimple appearing.

"Sammie," he said, "my age was part of my cover for this investigation, just like my 'biker' persona. I'm not turning twenty-seven today."

"You're not?"

He shook his head, grinning like a fool.

"You mean I'm not a cougar?"

He laughed his beautiful, sexy laugh and pulled me to him, kissing my face.

"Technically, I think you're a puma," he said. "I turned thirty-two today. So, you see? You're just a smidgeon over four years older. No biggie, right?"

"Why the hell didn't you tell me this sooner?"

"I meant to, babe. I'm sorry. Forgive me?"

"I suppose," I replied. "But there are other issues besides that."

"What else?"

"What you do for a living. I've seen first-hand how dangerous it is. I don't know if I could handle always being worried about you, or the things you have to do as part of your cover."

"Like what?"

"You know what I'm talking about," I said, my cheeks turning rosy.

"You mean the thing with Garnet?"

"Yes."

"Well babe, it's not like that's in my job description you know? I basically let that happen because I was pissed off at you."

"Oh really? I thought it was a way to get inside info?"

"There are other ways. I wouldn't do anything to lose your trust," he stated. "As far as being in a dangerous line of work - it comes with the job, at times. I can't promise you that I'll never be in danger again. It's what I do, Sammie."

I knew that I loved Eric no matter what. I loved him for everything that he was. I wouldn't change a thing about him.

"What would I do in D.C?" I asked.

"Be my wife and my son's mother," he said with a grin.

"What if I want to be more than that? I mean, that's what I was to Jack, and you can see how well that worked out."

"Babe, if you want a career, you're free to have one with the obvious exception: no dancing."

"I can handle that restriction," I said, "as long as I can still dance privately for you."

"That's a must," he said softly, leaning in and covering my lips with his, kissing me gently.

"I'm not even divorced yet," I said, pulling away. "How do I go about doing that when I don't know where to find Jack?"

"I already checked into it. You can file for a divorce on the grounds of desertion and abandonment. Notices of the filing have to appear in the hometown paper four times within a period of a year. If Jack files no answer or counterclaim to the suit, your divorce is granted at the end of the one year period."

"I guess we're going to have an appropriate engagement period then, Eric."

"Then you will come with me?" he asked, his eyes warm with love and happiness.

"I always do," I replied softly, circling my arms around him and pulling him to me for a kiss.

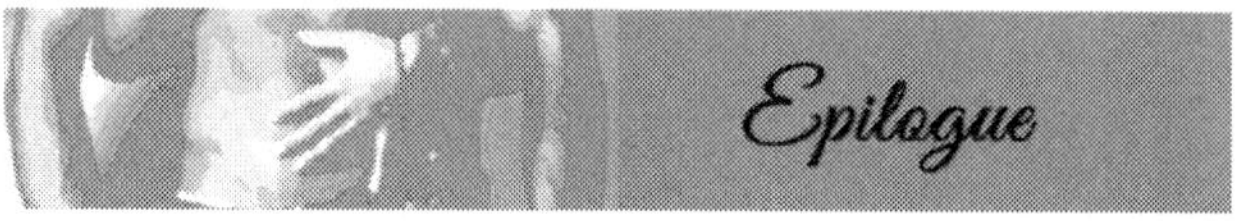

Epilogue

Falls Church, Virginia

November 5th (The following year)

I was putting the finishing touches on my make-up. Lindsey was fussing with my hair. She was trying to weave the tiny white flower and beaded garland through the hair piled up on top of my head.

"You're a beautiful bride, Mom. I'm so happy for you."

"I'm so lucky to have you, Eric and Bryce," I replied, smiling at her reflection in the mirror.

I thought back to a little more than a year ago on Eric's birthday when we had sat Lindsey down and filled her in on everything. She'd been fine with it. She understood that we would be married soon after the divorce was final.

She had looked at Eric and me; our happiness was evident.

"There's just one thing," she retorted. "Don't expect me to call you 'Daddy, got it?"

Eric and I'd looked at her glimpsing the slow grin that graced her face. She was more than okay with it.

Lindsey had switched schools so that she could be closer to us. She was now attending University of Virginia in Charlottesville. It was about two hours away.

Her relationship with Adam, unfortunately, had fizzled. She didn't share the details with us, but she was adamant she was cursed. I knew it was simply a matter of time. Look how long it had taken me to find love. She was going to be taking a position with Banion Pharmaceuticals after graduation. For now, she remained focused on finishing up with her degree and starting a career.

My home had recently sold, along with Jack's car, providing a sufficient nest egg for Lindsey's tuition, along with a nice down payment on a house for Eric and me in Falls Church. We had agreed his bachelor pad wasn't an appropriate place to raise our baby.

Bryce Eric Slater had been born on December 2nd of last year in Falls Church, Virginia. Eric had been right there with me during his birth, which had gone well. He'd been a week early, but weighed 7 lbs. Eric said he was destined to be a football player. He also said he wanted one more baby, insisting it be a girl next time. I'd told him I would do my best.

There had been no further word about Jack or Susan. The warrants were still out for them. Everyone else that had been involved in the criminal activities now spent their days and nights behind bars in various prisons. Most of them wouldn't see life on the outside for many, many years, if at all.

Becky came bustling into the dressing room in the church basement with the bouquets for Lindsey and me. She'd arranged them herself in radiant fall colors. They were gorgeous.

"You both look ravishing," she said with a sigh. "I've got to get back upstairs. Your mother and your soon-to-be mother in-law are about ready to come to blows over whose turn it is to hold Bryce. Eric has assigned me to referee. Here's something borrowed for you Sammie," she said, pressing a small velvet box into my hand.

I opened it. It was a beautiful diamond pendant...very delicately encrusted in a gold, filigree setting.

"Oh, Becky," I breathed, "It's exquisite."

"It was my grandmother's," she said, fastening it around my neck. "I wore it when I married George, and look how well that has turned out. I wish the same for you and Eric."

She leaned over, kissing my cheek. Her eyes had tears in them.

"Don't start crying, Bec. If you do, I will, and then my make-up will have to be totally re-done," I said, waving my hand in front of my face to dry any tears that were trying to surface.

"I love you like a sister, Sam."

"I love you too, Becky. Make my mother share, okay?"

She gave me a wink and quickly departed. I fingered the beautiful pendant gently.

"Are you ready, Mom?" Lindsey asked, handing me my bouquet.

"I am," I breathed happily.

The sound of organ music floated downstairs. It signaled it was time for Lindsey and me to make our way upstairs to the vestibule where we would wait for the wedding march to begin. Lindsey was my maid of honor. Taz was Eric's best man.

Lindsey gathered up the train to my gown, throwing it over her arm until we got upstairs.

"Come on Mom, they're playing your song."

I stood at the front of the church facing Slate. I called him Eric now, because that's what he wanted, but he was still 'Slate' in my heart.

He was the one who had taught me about love and passion. He was the one who fought against intimacy because he didn't trust it. We had both learned to trust it just as we trusted one another. He was my lover, my protector, my very best friend.

I gazed up into those incredibly blue eyes that were watching me with love and passion. Behind us, we could hear Bryce's little voice getting fussy in his Grandma Katy's arms. My parents were sitting next to her, helping her to entertain him as the ceremony was beginning.

Eric and I both glanced over at them and smiled as the baby quieted and the minister began the traditional recitation of vows. He took my hands in his and squeezed gently. I raised my eyes to his once again as he quietly whispered, "I love you, Diamond Girl."

Andrea Smith is a *USA Today* and *Amazon* best-selling author. She is native of Springfield, Ohio, currently residing in southern Ohio. Having previously been employed as an executive for a global corporation, Ms. Smith decided to leave the corporate world and pursue her life-long dream of writing fiction.

Indie Authors appreciate readers taking the time to leave reviews on the sites where purchased and on Goodreads.

Other Books

Ms. Smith's Books Include:

The G-Man Series

Diamond Girl (Book #1)

Love Plus One (Book #2)

Night Moves (Book #3)

G-Men Holiday Wrap (Book #3.5)

These Men (Spin-off)

Taz   (Book #5)

Baby Series - Need to be read in Order:

Maybe Baby, Baby Love, Be My Baby, Baby Come Back

Limbo Series

Silent Whisper (Book #1)

Clouds in my Coffee   (Book #2)

September Series - New Adult Romance

Until September   (Book #1)

When September Ends   (Book #2)

Made in the USA
San Bernardino, CA
13 April 2016